**R. Barri Flowers** is a̶ ̶ ̶ ̶ ̶
crime, thriller, mystery a̶ ̶ ̶ ̶ ̶ ̶ ̶ ̶ ̶
three-dimensional protagonists, riveting plots, unexpected
twists and turns, and heart-pounding climaxes. With an
expertise in true crime, serial killers and characterising
dangerous offenders, he is perfectly suited for the Heroes
line. Chemistry and conflict between the hero and heroine,
attention to detail and incorporating the very latest
advances in criminal investigations are the cornerstones
of his romantic suspense fiction. Discover more on popular
social networks and Wikipedia.

**Addison Fox** is a lifelong romance reader, addicted to
happily-ever-afters. After discovering she found as much
joy writing about romance as she did reading it, she's
never looked back. Addison lives in New York with an
apartment full of books, a laptop that's rarely out of sight
and a wily beagle who keeps her running. You can find her
at her home on the web at addisonfox.com or on Facebook
(Facebook.com/addisonfoxauthor) and X (@addisonfox).

# CAMPUS KILLER

## R. BARRI FLOWERS

# THREATS IN
# THE DEEP

## ADDISON FOX

MILLS & BOON

First Published in Great Britain 2024
by Mills & Boon, an imprint of HarperCollins*Publishers* Ltd
1 London Bridge Street, London, SE1 9GF

www.harpercollins.co.uk

HarperCollins*Publishers*
Macken House, 39/40 Mayor Street Upper,
Dublin 1, D01 C9W8, Ireland

ISBN: 978-0-263-32239-2

0724

This book contains FSC™ certified paper and other controlled sources to ensure responsible forest management.

For more information visit: www.harpercollins.co.uk/green

Printed and Bound in the UK using 100% Renewable Electricity at CPI Group (UK) Ltd, Croydon, CR0 4YY

# CAMPUS KILLER

R. BARRI FLOWERS

In memory of my beloved mother, Marjah Aljean, a devoted lifelong fan of Mills & Boon romance novels, who inspired me to excel in my personal and professional lives. To H. Loraine, the true love of my life and best friend, whose support has been unwavering through the many terrific years together; and Carole Ann Jones, who left an impact on me with her amazing talents on the screen; as well as the loyal fans of my romance, mystery, suspense and thriller fiction published over the years. Lastly, a nod goes out to my great editors, Allison Lyons and Denise Zaza, for the wonderful opportunity to lend my literary voice and creative spirit to the Mills & Boon Heroes line.

*Prologue*

Debra Newton loved being a journalism associate professor in the College of Communication Arts and Sciences at Addison University in the bustling college town of Rendall Cove, Michigan. In many ways, it was truly a dream come true for her, having graduated from the very school a decade earlier. Now she got to teach others, inspiring young minds for the formidable challenges of tomorrow. And with the summer session well underway, she was doing just that, putting her journalistic skills to the test with each and every passing day.

She only wished her love life could be nearly as thought-provoking and satisfying. Bradford Newton, her college sweetheart turned husband, had turned out to be a total jerk, with a roving eye that went after anyone wearing a skirt at his law office. After one time too many of being played for a fool, she finally kicked him to the curb five years ago, and Debra only wished she had done it sooner. Since her divorce, she had just dated occasionally, with most men seemingly less interested in her brain and sense of humor than her flaming long, wavy red hair, good looks and shapely physique. While these various sides to her were important in and of themselves, she wanted to be seen as the total package and wanted the same in a partner.

Which was why she had turned down a date with a handsome and persistent colleague who, though also single, was a little—make that a lot—too full of himself and a bit scary at times in his demeanor. Similarly, a former administrator, who on paper checked a lot of the boxes for what she was looking for in a potential mate, did not measure up in practice and real time, forcing her to reject his half-hearted advances.

As if that wasn't almost enough to turn her off of romance for good, there was the fact that one of Debra's students had become fixated on her to the point of stalking. Though she had made it abundantly clear that she would never even consider dating a student—not even one who was nearly her own age, having been a late bloomer as an undergrad—this one didn't seem to take no for an answer. She had decided that enough was enough. She would bring it up to the director of the School of Journalism, as well as report it to the campus police, for the record.

After classes were over, Debra hopped into her black Audi S3 sedan and headed home. Peeking into the rearview mirror, she could have sworn that she was being followed by a dark SUV. Was her imagination playing tricks on her? Maybe she was getting paranoid for no reason, brought on by her musings.

This apparently was the case, as the vehicle in question veered off onto another street, the driver seemingly oblivious to her imaginative thoughts. Much less, out to get her. Relaxing, Debra drove to her apartment complex just outside the college campus on Frandor Lane, parked in her assigned spot and headed across the attractively landscaped grounds. She climbed the stairs to her building's second-floor two-bedroom, two-bath unit. Inside, she put down her mini hobo bag with papers to grade, kicked off mule loafers and strode barefoot across the maple hardwood flooring to the galley kitchen. She took a bottle of red wine from the refrigerator, poured herself a glass and considered if she should eat in or go out for dinner.

While still contemplating, Debra bypassed the contemporary furnishings and took the wineglass with her to the main bedroom. *Maybe I'll just have a pizza delivered*, she told herself, while removing the hairpin holding her bun in place, allowing her locks to fall free across her shoulders.

Then she heard the sound of a familiar voice say almost comically, "I was beginning to think you'd never get here, Deb."

The unexpected visitor's words gave Debra a start, causing her to drop the glass of wine, its contents spilling onto the brown carpeted floor. He was standing in her bedroom as if he owned the place. How did he get inside her apartment? What did he want?

"When I sensed that you might be on to me as I followed your car, I took a shortcut to beat you here, while giving you a false sense of security."

She recalled the SUV that had been following her and then seemingly wasn't. Why hadn't she remembered the type of vehicle he drove?

"Sorry about the wine," he said tonelessly, glancing at it and the glass on the floor. "At least you managed to have a sip or two. As for what's probably foremost on your mind, honestly, it wasn't all that difficult to break into your apartment. It has a relatively cheap lock that's easy to pick for someone who knows what he's doing."

Debra froze like an ice sculpture while weighing her options, then asked him tentatively, "What do you want?" Was he actually going to rape her to get what he wanted? Then what? Leave her alone to forever remember what he did? Or report it to the police and have him arrested and charged with a sex crime?

Why couldn't he have simply put the moves on someone else who may have been interested in his advances? Or did he get his kicks from power tripping by forcing the action? No matter how she sliced it, Debra didn't like the outcome. Maybe she could outrun him and escape the apartment, wherein she could whip the cell phone out of the back pocket of her chino pants and call for help. Except for the fact that he was now standing between her and the exit from the room.

"It's not good for you, I'm afraid." His voice burst into her thoughts, while taking on an ominous octave. "You need to die, and I'm here to make sure it happens."

As her heart skipped a few beats in digesting his harrowing words, this was when Debra knew she had to make her move before it was too late. What move should that be? The answer was obvious. Anything that could get her out of this alive. And, hopefully, not too badly injured.

HE ANTICIPATED THAT she would try to hit him where it hurt, easily blocking her futile efforts. He was also way ahead of her next instinct to try to somehow worm her way around his sturdy frame and escape what was to be a veritable death trap. He caught her narrow shoulders and tossed her toward the platform bed, expecting her to fall onto the comforter. But she somehow managed to stay on her feet and was about to scream her pretty head off, alerting neighbors. He couldn't let that happen.

It only took one well-placed hard blow to her jaw to send Professor Debra Newton reeling backward and flat onto the bed, where she went out like a light. Now it was time for him to finish what he started. She had no one to blame but herself for the unfortunate predicament she was now in. They were all alike when it came right down to it. Believing they could screw guys like him over and not be held accountable. Wrong.

Dead wrong.

He lifted the decorative throw pillow off the bed and, just as she began to stir, placed it over her face, pressing down firmly. Though she struggled mightily to break free, he was stronger, far more determined and, as such, took away her means to breathe air before she lost her will to resist altogether and became deathly still. When he finally removed the pillow, he saw that her blue eyes were wide open, but any life in them had gone away for good.

He sucked in a deep breath and tossed the pillow back on the bed beside her corpse, pleased with what he had done to the professor and already looking ahead for an encore. After all, she wasn't the only one who needed to be taught a lesson that only female educators could truly appreciate. He laughed at his own sick sense of humor before vacating the premises and making sure he was successful in avoiding detection while engineering his masterful escape.

IT WASN'T LONG before he picked up right where he'd left off. Again and again. Now yet another one bit the dust. Or, if not quite ashes to ashes, dust to dust, the good-looking professor was very much dead. He had seen to that, watching as the life drained out of her like soapy water in a tub. She had been expecting someone else, apparently. But got him instead. Her loss. His gain.

Like the ones that came before her, he did what he needed to do. What they forced him to do, more or less. Suffocation was such a tough way to die. Fighting for air and finding it in short supply when being cut off from the brain was challenging, to say the least. But that was their tough luck. He made no apologies for playing the villain, falling prey to his inner demons. The ones that drove him to kill and get a charge out of it when the deed was done.

He took one final look at the dead professor and imagined her looking back at him, had her eyes not been shut for good. Maybe she would meet up in the afterlife with the others and form a dead professors' society or something to that effect. He nearly burst into laughter at the devious thought but suppressed this, so as not to alert anyone of his presence.

Leaving the scene of the crime, he made his way down the back stairs, and like a thief—make that murderer—in the night, he moved briskly away from the building without looking back. Only when he was in the safety of his car and on the road did he allow himself to suck in a deep and glorious breath, knowing that he had escaped successfully and could go on with his life as though he hadn't just committed another cold-blooded murder that, like those before her, she never saw coming.

Not till it was much, much too late.

# Chapter One

"Looks like the Campus Killer has taken another professor's life." The words lodged deep in Detective Sergeant Paula Lynley's throat like a jagged chicken bone stuck there, as she relayed this depressing information over speakerphone to Captain Shailene McNamara, her immediate superior in the Investigative Division of the Department of Police and Public Safety at Addison University. Paula was behind the wheel in her duty vehicle, a white Ford Mustang Mach-E, en route to the crime scene, the office of Honors College Associate Professor Odette Furillo.

Shailene made a grunting sound. "That's not what I wanted to hear to start my day."

*You and me both*, Paula told herself, in total agreement on a Wednesday at 9:00 a.m. Unfortunately, there was no getting around this, painful as it was for both of them to digest. "Ms. Furillo was apparently working late. Her body was discovered by a student this morning," Paula informed the captain, implying that it didn't appear to be an active crime situation to prompt a shelter-in-place order. "All signs seem to indicate that the victim was suffocated to death."

At least this was what Paula was led to believe by the first responder to the scene, Detective Michael Davenport, one of the investigators under her command in the AU DPPS. If true, this would mark the fourth suffocation-style murder of an Addison University female professor on or close to the campus in Rendall Cove over the past few months. The first came during the early part of the summer session, when a thirty-three-year-old associate professor in the School of Journalism, Debra Newton, was found asphyxiated to death in her apartment. And a month later, thirty-four-year-old Department of Horticulture Assistant Professor Harmeet Fernández was discovered dead in the Horticulture Gardens.

Near the end of the summer session, thirty-six-year-old Kathy Payne, a professor in the College of Veterinary Medicine, was fatally suffocated in her residence. Now, just a couple of weeks into the fall session, Paula had to consider the very distinct possibility that a fourth professor had been murdered in a similar manner by the so-called "Campus Killer," the moniker the unsub was given by the press. If so, that would leave little doubt that they were dealing with a bona fide and devious serial killer on and around the campus, where there had been an increase in patrols after the first professor was murdered near the university. Apart from a general belief that they were likely dealing with a male perpetrator—based on the nature of the crimes and circumstantial evidence—as of now, there had been no identifiable DNA or fingerprints to point the blame at anyone in particular. And no reliable surveillance video that could give them a clue about the unsub. Nor had any of the suspects panned out thus far. Would it be any different this time around?

The ongoing case was being jointly investigated by the Rendall Cove Police Department, considering that the first and third murders linked to the killer had occurred off campus, within the Rendall Cove city limits. Paula hoped that they would be able to soon crack the case with the latest purported homicide at the hands of the unsub. "Of course, we won't know anything for certain on this front till the autopsy is completed," she told her, as if Shailene wasn't aware of this.

The captain responded tersely, "I get that. Keep me posted on the developments in this disturbing investigation."

"I will," Paula promised as always, before disconnecting. She sighed, feeling just as disturbed that they were involved with this type of crisis in what was normally a peaceful, beautifully landscaped campus environment, split by the Cedar River, with countless imposing trees, lush green spaces, winding paths and newly renovated buildings. But someone had chosen to threaten that tranquility in the worst way possible.

While keeping her bold brown eyes on the lookout for bicyclers, who at times recklessly believed they owned the roads, Paula's thoughts slipped to her personal trials and tribulations over the past eighteen months. At thirty-five, she was a year removed from her divorce from Scott Lynley. The veteran FBI special agent had once been the love of her life. It was a love that seemed destined to last forever. But somewhere along the way, things fizzled between them and, once it became apparent that no magical elixir would fix them, they decided it would be best to go their separate ways. For Paula, an African American, an interracial marriage was never a problem to her. A clash of strong wills between her and Scott, however, proved to be a major issue.

Deciding she needed a clean break, she relocated from Kentucky to Central Michigan, where in a lateral transfer, Paula landed an opening with the Addison University PD.

Equipped with a Bachelor of Science in Criminal Justice and a minor in Law, Justice and Public Policy from the University of Louisville, where she excelled and was a member of a sorority, she welcomed the opportunity to return to a campus atmosphere for police work. But now it was being put to a major test, and it was one she fully intended to pass at the end of the day.

Same was true for her love life that had been nonexistent since her divorce. Though her past failure in a relationship had made Paula extra cautious and extremely picky, she believed there was still someone out there for her. Just as she was available for the right man. For whatever reason, the new criminology professor at the university, Neil Ramirez, came to mind. Aside from being a drop-dead gorgeous Hispanic, the ATF special agent and renowned criminal profiler seemed to know his stuff in the classroom as a visiting professor, and had proven to be popular among criminology students, from what she understood. Out of curiosity, she had sat in on his lecture a couple of times, only speaking briefly to him afterward, but leaving with a favorable impression nonetheless as someone she could imagine building a rapport with.

She knew little of his backstory, other than that he had recently lost someone close to him, a fellow ATF agent, who was killed in the line of duty. As would be expected, apparently Neil Ramirez took it pretty hard, just as Paula knew would be the case were someone in the department dealt a similar fate. The special agent's reputation as a hardworking, honest and dependable agent made him a valued addition to Addison University and the School of Criminal Justice, both of whom apparently welcomed him with open arms.

Paula was indeed a bit curious about his life off the job.

Or if Professor Ramirez even had a life outside of work, which she found herself short on these days. For all she knew, he was happily married and had a few kids to go back to. Paula lamented over never having started a family with her ex and wondered if that might have made a difference in her failed marriage. Or was she grasping at straws for something that had simply run out of steam, no matter how painful it was to have to reconcile herself with that?

She returned to the here and now as she pulled into the parking lot of the Gotley Building on Wakefield Road that housed the Department of Mathematics. After finding a spot, she parked and exited the vehicle. Slender, at five feet nine inches in height, she was wearing a one-button black blazer over a moss-colored satin charmeuse shirt and mid-rise blue ponte knit pants, along with square-toed flats. Tucked inside her jacket in a leather concealment holster was a SIG Sauer P365 semiautomatic pistol. In a force of habit, she tapped it as if to make sure it was still there, and then ran a hand through her brunette layered and medium-length haircut, parted squarely in the middle, before heading into the building.

On the third floor, where Professor Furillo's office was located, Paula found it already cordoned off by barricade tape, and members of the Crime Scene Investigation Unit were busy at work processing the site. Bypassing them, she was greeted by Detective Mike Davenport. The tall, forty-year-old married father of three girls was blue-eyed and had short dark locks in a quiff hairstyle and a chevron mustache.

"Hey," he said tonelessly.

"Hey." She gave him a friendly nod and then got down to business. "What's the latest?"

"It's not good." Davenport frowned. "Appears as though

Professor Furillo was grading papers when someone took her by surprise," he remarked. "From the looks of it, she apparently fought with her attacker but, unfortunately, came up short. The seat cushion beside the body suggests it was the murder weapon used to suffocate the victim."

Paula wrinkled her dainty nose at him. "And a student discovered her?"

"Yeah. Name's Joan McCashin. Says she had a scheduled meeting with Furillo this morning, came upon the body and then immediately called 911. McCashin's prepared to give a formal statement to that effect."

"Good." Paula glanced over his shoulder. "Which office is the professor's?"

"This one," he answered, leading the way as they passed by two closed office doors to an open door.

Stepping into the small and cramped windowless office, Paula glanced at the gangly and bald-headed crime scene photographer who gave her a nod, then resumed his snapping of pictures routinely, before she spied the deceased associate professor on the floor beside an ergonomic computer desk. Odette Furillo was lying flat on her back on the beige carpeted floor. In her thirties, she was slender and about five-six, blond-haired with brown highlights in a stacked pixie, and fully dressed in a button-front light blue blouse, navy straight-leg pants and black loafers. Next to her head was a gray memory foam office chair pillow. The impressions on it seemed to contour with that of a face when pressed against it.

Cringing, Paula could only imagine the horror of knowing you were about to die and not being able to do a thing to prevent it. Still, she noted what appeared to be blood on one of the hands of the professor, suggesting that she might have scratched her attacker, collecting valuable DNA in the process. "Maybe Professor Furillo got the unsub's DNA to help us ID the killer," Paula pointed out optimistically.

"I was thinking the same thing," Davenport said, knitting his thick brows. "Hopefully the medical examiner and forensics will make that happen and we'll go from there."

"We need to find out who else may have been working in the building last night. That includes students and custodial workers. Let's see what surveillance cameras can tell us." In Paula's way of thinking, no one could be excluded as a suspect, given that more than a few people had access to the Gotley Building.

"Yeah." Davenport scratched his jutting chin. "And then cross-check it with anyone who might have been in the vicinity of the second victim of the alleged Campus Killer on school grounds."

Paula eyed the professor's laptop and wondered if her computer and online activities before, during and after the attack might provide clues about the unsub. "Let's get the Digital Forensics and Cyber Crime Unit over here pronto and see what they can find from the laptop, if anything. Along with Odette Furillo's cell phone," Paula added, noting it on the desktop.

He gave a nod. "Will do."

They heard some chatter and left the office, careful not to taint potential evidence. In the hallway, approaching them was Detective Gayle Yamasaki of the Rendall Cove PD's Detective Bureau. In her midthirties, single and slim with small brown eyes and long, curly black hair tied in a low bun, the pretty Indigenous Hawaiian was heading the investigation into the murder of Professor Debra Newton, who was strangled to death in her apartment in June.

"Came as soon as I got the word," Gayle said, wringing her thin hands. "So, what are we looking at here?"

Paula furrowed her brow. "You can see for yourself, but by all indications, including the appearance of the victim and the killer's MO, we're looking at another homicide courtesy of the Campus Killer."

Gayle sighed and took a peek at the deceased before muttering an expletive. "Four and counting," she groaned.

"Tell me about it." Paula made a face. "We need to find out if the victims were connected in any way." *And if so, how exactly*, she thought.

"Assuming these aren't just random killings," Gayle countered.

"There is that." Paula understood that if they were in fact chasing a single killer, the unsub could just as easily be someone the victims knew as a total stranger. Whatever the case, as they were all professors, that in and of itself indicated some relationship to this institution of higher education.

"The bottom line," Davenport told them, "is that someone is on a killing rampage on this campus and in our town, and it's up to us to stop him."

"There's no other option," Paula agreed, knowing that to think otherwise would be playing right into the unsub's deadly hands. "We have to figure this out, sooner than later."

Shays County Chief Medical Examiner Eddie Saldana arrived, and they parted the way to let him through. In his early fifties, short and of medium build, he had red hair blended with gray in a side-swept style to partially cover his pate and wore square glasses over sharp gray eyes.

"This is getting to be a bad habit," he grumbled, frowning.

"One we're all hoping to kick," Paula said humorlessly.

"Whatever you can give us on the deceased would be helpful in that regard, Dr. Saldana."

"I'll see what I can do." He stepped into Odette Furillo's office and, after squeezing into nitrile gloves, methodically did a quick examination of the victim, before saying glumly, "All things considered, my initial assessment is that the professor likely died as a result of violent asphyxia. I'll be more definitive once the autopsy is completed, including an estimation of the time of death."

Even the preliminary conclusion was more than enough to convince Paula that this was not only a homicide, but one that mirrored the three other deaths attributed to a single killer with a singular modus operandi. "We'll look forward to reading the autopsy report when it's ready," she told him, which Paula assumed would be the next day. Until then, they needed to do whatever was necessary to try to gather evidence and build a case toward eventually pinning the crime on the one responsible.

THE CAMPUS KILLER relished this opportunity to catch the action, hidden very much in plain view. Endless chatter about the death of Professor Odette Furillo seemed to grip those around him, as though it was the worst possible thing that could happen. Actually, even worse for those standing around would be if they themselves suffered the same fate as the attractive Honors College associate professor. He laughed inside. As it was, they were not the targets of his murderous ways. Unfortunately, the same could not be said of the other three pretty professors who managed to find their way into his crosshairs and were given a one-way ticket to an early death.

He mused about the campus and city police trying to stop

him in his deadly tracks. They were undoubtedly freaking out about his uncanny ability to run rings around them while handpicking his victims right under the authorities' collective noses. Another laugh rang in his head as he wound his way through the bystanders, speaking only when spoken to. And even then, limiting what he said and how he said it, so as not to tip his hand in the slightest as to his guilt. For all they could see, he was merely one of them, content with complaining and speculating about the homicides, but otherwise keeping the worst of it at a safe distance so as not to be contaminated like spoiled food.

He watched as the good-looking female university detective left the building, seemingly in a huff, while giving only a cursory glance his way, as one of many. Not having the slightest clue that she was looking at the Campus Killer and was within her power to take him into custody. Except that she never really saw him for who he was. Just as he anticipated when making himself visible as part of the thrill from the kill.

As Detective Paula Lynley headed down the sidewalk, he resisted the desire to follow her, deciding it was more of a risk than he was willing to take at this time. Something, though, told him that an opportunity would likely present itself for them to meet face-to-face. At which time, she would very likely regret having ever laid eyes on him in ways she would never see coming.

Till it was much too late.

OUTSIDE THE BUILDING, some professors and students milled about aimlessly, probably in somewhat of a state of shock, while likely wondering when and if they would be let back inside. Or perhaps, Paula considered, if and when it would be safe to do so. She wondered the same thing herself. Or, for that matter, when the entire campus could go back to normal, without the looming threat of a serial killer hanging in the air like an unsettling dark rain cloud.

Short of solving this case overnight, Paula suspected that her boss would soon be sending out a request to the FBI to join in on the investigation. A routine thing when it came to creating serial killer task forces and utilizing the far reach of federal law enforcement and seemingly unlimited resources of the federal government. She had seen this all too often when married to an FBI agent, who also had a brother working in the Bureau. At the very least, Paula believed that a behavioral profiler was needed to help them better size up who and what they were after in the dangerous and lethal unsub.

This brought Neil Ramirez back to the forefront of her thoughts. As a criminal profiler, who also happened to be an expert on violent serial offenders from what she learned during one of his lectures, the professor was just the person they needed to utilize his expertise in their current investigation. Would he be up to the task? Or would his professional demons stand in the way? Those notwithstanding, she was sure that Captain McNamara would welcome Neil Ramirez into the fold as a paid consultant. As would Gayle Yamasaki and her boss with the Rendall Cove PD's Detective Bureau, Criminal Investigations Sergeant Anderson Klimack.

Paula walked to Horton Hall, three buildings over on Creighten Road, where Professor Ramirez was currently giving a lecture. She was eager to speak with him and a bit nervous at the same time, though unsure if that was due to her impending request. Or the sheer presence of the good-looking man himself.

The latter was on full display as she slipped in the back of the packed room, but had no trouble sizing up the ATF special agent, filling in the blanks of her memory. Standing in front of the class, Neil Ramirez was a good six feet, three inches tall at least, and rock solid in a way that could only come from regular workouts and a healthy diet. His thick brown hair was cut in a high razor fade. He had a diamond-shaped, square-jawed face, gray-brown eyes that shone in their intensity, and sported a heavy stubble beard that looked really good on him. Wearing a red Henley shirt, black jeans and tennis shoes, he seemed to fit right in as a college professor.

When he seemed to home in on her, Paula's heart did a little leap and check. But just as quickly, as if she had suddenly become invisible to him, Professor Ramirez turned in a different direction as he talked about profiling a criminal, giving Paula time to catch her breath and put together enough of a sell to bring him on board.

VISITING CRIMINOLOGY PROFESSOR NEIL RAMIREZ would've had to be foolish not to notice the stunning African American detective sergeant with the Department of Police and Public Safety at the college, Paula Lynley. As it was, his sight was better than twenty-twenty the last time he had his eyes examined, and he had no trouble seeing what was staring him right in the face, more or less. In fact, he'd been checking her out each time she decided to pay his lecture a visit. And even once or twice when he happened to notice her elsewhere on campus from afar. Tall and well put together on a slim frame, she thoroughly captivated the detective with her caramel complexion, heart-shaped face, big and pretty brown eyes, delicate nose, wide mouth and most generous smile. She had a stylish look to the chestnut brown hair grazing her shoulders.

Though they had exchanged a few words now and then, Neil had resisted going beyond the surface in getting to know the detective better. Still dealing with some personal and professional issues, he had chosen for the time being to focus on just trying to fit in to his temporary new world of teaching college students about criminology, criminal justice and criminal profiling.

As a thirty-six-year-old Mexican American special agent with the Bureau of Alcohol, Tobacco, Firearms and Explosives, Neil had gone through the ATF National Academy, located at the Federal Law Enforcement Training Center in Glynco, Georgia, and been assigned to the Federal Bureau of Investigation's Behavioral Analysis Unit to earn his stripes. Before that, he had graduated from the University of Arizona in Tucson with a Bachelor of Science in Criminal Justice Studies and a focus on Social and Behavioral Sciences. Now, thirteen years into his career, he was primarily working out of the ATF's field office in Grand Rapids, Michigan, as a behavioral profiler and providing technical support in ATF, FBI or task force investigations.

Neil lamented as he pondered the death of his colleague, Ramone Munoz, who died during a shoot-out last year with drug traffickers as a member of the ATF Special Response Team. Between that and Neil's breakup with his girlfriend, Constance Chen, who went looking for another man and found him in a musician, Neil had decided to take a step back from his full-time duties as a special agent, giving him some time to clear his head.

With a bestselling book on criminal profiling to his credit, he accepted a position as a visiting professor with

Addison University's School of Criminal Justice this past summer. The short-term contract left the door open for a longer commitment both ways, if all went well. But Neil wasn't looking beyond the current fall semester at this point. Especially since he had also been tasked by the ATF with gathering intel on a suspected arms trafficking operation in Rendall Cove that had been uncovered through chatter on the dark web. With an undercover agent on the inside working with the Rendall Cove Police Department's Firearms Investigation Unit and the Shays County Sheriff's Department, Neil was confident they would be successful in putting the brakes on this purported online trafficking in contraband firearms and ammunition operation, as well as unlawful possession of arms and ammunition.

Neil forced himself to take his eyes off the detective just long enough to snap out of the trance. He gazed at Paula Lynley again, curious as to why she was there. *Maybe she'll decide to fill me in*, he thought. It wasn't lost on him that an investigation was underway between the school's DPPS and the city's police department involving the murders of three female professors. Were they actually connected? Was there a single perp involved? It admittedly piqued the interest of the profiler in him. Up to a point.

He turned back to his students, remembering how difficult it was when he was in college to hold his attention. So far, so good. They seemed to be buying what he was selling in offering them a well-rounded look at criminality and the devious minds of hard-core criminals. But for how long?

When the class ended, Neil finished routinely with, "We'll pick it up the next time. But don't let that stop you from heading over to the library, where I've got some books on reserve, for further insight into the subject matter."

After the students, about half male and half female, began filing out of the classroom, Neil watched Paula Lynley come forward in measured steps as he was placing some papers into his faux-leather briefcase. He grinned at her and said curiously, "Detective Lynley. Nice to see you again." He met her eyes for a long moment, trying to read into them but having little luck. "So, what brings you to my class this morning?"

She held his gaze and, without preface, responded straightforwardly, "Professor Ramirez, I need your help."

# Chapter Two

Paula was momentarily at a loss for follow-up words as she took in the very good-looking visiting professor. It somehow seemed easier to approach him when it was just a hello in passing than when she had to seek his assistance in an important criminal investigation. But rather than chicken out like a schoolgirl with a crush on the star quarterback, she managed to gather herself and say coolly, "I'm sure you're aware that three female professors at the university have been murdered over the past three months."

Neil nodded to that effect. "Yeah, I know about it," he said cautiously. "Sad thing."

"That's putting it mildly." Paula took a breath. "This morning, a fourth professor was found murdered in her office."

"What?" He cocked a slightly crooked brow. "I hadn't heard about that one," he confessed.

"We're just getting the word out, while trying to wrap our minds around the fact that this is happening at all."

"Has anyone been arrested?" Neil seemed to rethink the question. "I assume that would be a no?"

"Correct assumption." She lifted her chin. "Unfortunately, the unsub is still on the loose and obviously has to

be considered as possibly armed and definitely dangerous,"
she pointed out. "But as of now, we don't believe there is an
immediate threat to students and staff, per se. That could
change, of course, as more info comes in on the homicide."

He regarded her with interest, then asked with a catch in
his voice, "So, what exactly did you need from me?"

Paula pushed a strand of hair away from her forehead
and responded frankly, "Your expertise as a profiler, Professor Ramirez. Or should I say Special Agent Ramirez?"

"Neil will be fine, Detective Lynley," he told her evenly.

"Okay, Neil. And please call me Paula," she said, feeling as though they had already broken the ice in getting
what she needed from him. "Anyway, it appears as if we're
dealing with a serial killer here that the press has already
dubbed the Campus Killer. The Department of Police and
Public Safety is working with the Rendall Cove PD to bring
the perp to justice and solve the case. In the meantime, we
can use all the help we can get in developing a profile on
the unsub to aid in the investigation. As a visiting professor who also happens to be a criminal profiler, I thought
I'd reach out to see if you'd be interested in working with
us as a paid consultant on the case?"

Neil rubbed his prominent jawline. "I kind of have my
hands full at the moment," he said ambivalently. "Teaching
these kids can be exhausting."

Though in complete agreement from her own college
years and dealing with some of the misbehaving students
today, Paula locked eyes with him and responded sharply,
"So can murder. I understand that you're here to teach. But
keeping them safe is even more important, don't you think?
I could reach out to the FBI, as long as it isn't to my ex-husband," she found herself saying candidly. "However, since

you're on campus, I wanted to give it a go first." She realized she was putting him on the spot unfairly, but desperation at times called for dirty tactics.

Neil gave her an amused grin. "Since you put it that way, ex-husband and all, I'll be happy to come aboard as a profiler in your investigation."

"Thanks." Paula blushed. "I'm sure that tapping into your expertise will give us some valuable insight into the unsub, before and after apprehension."

"Why don't you email me what you have on the unsub and case," Neil said, "and I'll take a look for a preliminary assessment."

"I'll do that," she promised, excited at the prospect of getting to know him. At least on a professional basis.

He nodded and grabbed his briefcase. "I'll walk you out."

Paula smiled, leading the way into the hall. "So, how's it been teaching, compared to working out in the field as an ATF agent?" She immediately saw the question as too trivial.

Neil laughed. "Well, for one, the teaching is mostly inside and investigations for the ATF are often outside. But apart from that difference, I have to say, I love trying to influence young minds, even if only for a short while, whereas I'm not as keen on having to take down the bad guys these days. But that's a story for another time…" He frowned thoughtfully. "Anyway, it's a good living, so I suppose I shouldn't complain."

Paula considered the tragedy he'd experienced with the death of a fellow agent. She wondered if there was more that soured him on working for the ATF. Maybe there would be another time to get the scoop. "Believe me," she told him, "we all have professional complaints from time to time.

Comes with the territory." Not that she had issues with her current employer, but she knew that there were always good and bad days for every job. Hers was no exception. Such as now, when she was dealing with a serial perp and needed it solved sooner than later.

"You're right, of course," he said. "Life is always about what you make of it, for better or worse."

"True." Neil brushed shoulders with her and Paula immediately felt an electrical spark surge through her. Had he experienced this as well? At the door to the outside, he flashed a sideways grin and said, "My office is on the third floor."

She smiled, understanding that he was headed there and, as such, this was where they parted. "Thanks for agreeing to work with us," she expressed.

"I'm happy to do what I can to help out." He opened the door for her and said, "By the way, no pay is necessary to consult on the case as a profiler. Consider it an extension of my work as a visiting professor that maybe my students can learn a thing or two from."

"If you say so." Paula welcomed his involvement, whatever the terms. And she did believe that his criminal justice students stood to benefit from whatever he chose to bring to the table. As she would herself, she believed.

Out of Horton Hall, Paula headed for her car, equipped with a new weapon in the ongoing investigation.

Neil Ramirez.

NEIL WATCHED FOR a moment as Paula Lynley walked away from the building. He found himself undressing her in his mind, sure he would like every bit of what he saw. How could he not? Coming back down to earth, he knew that he needed to stay on another track where it concerned the police detective sergeant. At least till he had a chance to get a read on the so-called Campus Killer. Then maybe the vibes he'd picked up when they touched shoulders—or even met each other's eyes—might be something to explore further. Or was the sour taste in his mouth from his last failed relationship still bitter enough not to want to jump back in the ring with another woman?

Inside his temporary office, Neil sat at the L-shaped computer desk in a well-worn brown faux-leather chair and mused about the lovely detective he would be working with. So, she'd been married to an FBI agent. Any children in the marriage before they parted ways? How did Paula's ex ever let her get away? Or was it a mutual thing of simply growing apart and wanting something different in their lives?

Neil wondered if she was seeing anyone right now. Or was Paula cautious about opening her heart to another man any time soon? If so, could he really blame her? Was he any less guilty of preferring not to rush into anything these days? Then again, would it be foolish not to keep an open mind for the right person, whenever she entered his orbit?

His thoughts moved back to the consulting as a profiler job he'd just agreed to. He questioned just how advisable it was to take on another assignment with his plate already full. Since when had that ever stopped him? He always tried to do what was best in any given situation. In this instance, how could he not agree to assist in the case, with what sure looked like a serial killer lurking on and around the campus? One who threatened the lives of female professors. And could easily target female students as well, if the unsub was not stopped.

*Paula drew a hard bargain*, Neil told himself, sitting back. He looked forward to reviewing the particulars of the case and lending his knowledge in the hunt for the killer. Beyond that, Neil still had to deal with the fact that a suspected arms trafficker was also in their midst and needed to be brought under control before unleashing more gun violence in Rendall Cove and abroad.

PAULA PARKED IN the employee parking lot of the Addison University Police Department on Cedar Lane. She went inside the building and headed straight for the office of Captain Shailene McNamara. After being waved in, Paula stepped through the door. Shailene was at her standing desk on the phone. She studied the captain, who was fifty years old, on the slender side and had strawberry blond hair styled in a choppy bob. Her blues eyes looked bigger behind prescription eyeglasses. Shailene was on her second marriage and the mother of four children.

She ended the call and, gazing at Paula, said, "So, where are we on the case?"

Reiterating what had already been reported, Paula filled her in with more details on Associate Professor Odette Furillo's murder, which fell short of naming a suspect. Or having the official cause of her death, pending release of the autopsy report. Then, as Paula watched the captain's expression meander between frustration and resignation, she told her, "I've asked Visiting Professor Neil Ramirez to join the investigation as a criminal profiler."

Shailene perked up upon hearing this. "Really?"

"Yes. Given his expertise on killers, including serial killers, it seemed like a good idea to take advantage of the ATF special agent's presence at Addison University. To pick his brain, if you will," Paula stressed.

"A very good idea." Shailene nodded in agreement. "With

the murder of four of our professors, at this point, getting Agent Ramirez on board is a smart move." She touched her glasses. "I take it he accepted the offer?"

"Yes," Paula was happy to announce. "Moreover, Neil doesn't want any compensation, believing that it's his duty as a visiting professor and profiler to lend a hand to the investigation."

Shailene's face lit with approval. "Actually, I read Agent Ramirez's book on profiling. Good stuff. You should check it out, when you get a chance."

"I will." Paula exchanged a few more thoughts while glancing about the spacious office with its contemporary furnishings and plaques on the wall. When Shailene's cell phone rang, it was Paula's excuse to leave.

En route to her own office, she ran into Detective Mike Davenport. "Hey," she said to him.

"Hey." His broad shoulders squared. "Got some info for you."

"Okay." She met his eyes with curiosity. "Why don't we step into my office?"

"All right."

He followed her into the corner office, which Davenport had once thought would be his, until Paula got it instead, after being promoted to detective sergeant. Though things had been a little tense between them for a while, he had seemingly gotten past the disappointment and they were in a good place right now, as far as Paula was concerned. She believed Davenport was a good detective and valued having him on her squad.

Rather than essentially pulling rank by taking a seat at her three-drawer desk and inviting him to sit on one of the two vinyl black stacking chairs on the other side, Paula remained standing. Eyeing the detective, she asked, "So, what do you have?"

Davenport ran a hand through his hair and replied matter-of-factly, "Well, I was able to pull up security camera footage from inside and outside the Gotley Building, where Professor Odette Furillo was killed. Seems as though a number of people, mostly students by the look of it, were out and about, along with vehicles, between last night and this morning. Once we get the official time of death, we can better sort through them and see if we can narrow down potential suspects."

"Good." Paula nodded, expecting to get this information from the autopsy report in the morning. "Anything else?"

"Yeah," he said. "As expected, we'll be checking out any cell phones that pinged around the time Furillo was murdered. And, of course, we're waiting to see if there's DNA to work with in unmasking the unsub."

Paula smiled thinly, knowing they were going about this the right way. "I have some news too," she told him.

"What's that?"

She told him about Neil Ramirez agreeing to work with them. "As a criminal profiler, Professor Ramirez should give us some crucial insight into the killer," she finished.

"I agree." Davenport bobbed his head. "Heard about Ramirez's successes in helping to nab some perps. If he's willing to step away from teaching long enough to profile our unsub, more power to him. It's all about solving the case and making the campus and surroundings a safe environment again, right?"

"Absolutely." Paula showed her teeth, glad to see that he didn't believe Neil was somehow using his fed credentials as an ATF special agent to take over the case. On the contrary, she believed that the visiting professor was an asset, lending his skills in teaming up with the DPPS's Investigative Division and the Rendall Cove PD's Detective Bureau in their pursuit of justice.

After Davenport left the office, Paula sat in her ergonomic mid-back leather desk chair and phoned Gayle Yamasaki to let her know that Neil Ramirez would be assisting them.

"That's wonderful," Gayle expressed. "Seems that Agent Ramirez's reputation as a profiler precedes him."

Paula chuckled. "Appears that way."

"What have you gotten out of him so far?"

"Not much. I'm sending him the info we have on the unsub shortly."

"Can't wait to get his take on the perp," Gayle said.

"Same here," Paula had to admit, as if Neil's assessment alone could nab the unsub. If only it were that simple. As it was, cracking this case had been anything but simple, thus far. Only diligence in their collective efforts would lead to favorable results.

Later, Paula copied some digital files, emailed them to Neil and did some paperwork. Her thoughts drifted here and there between her former married life and the present, where she was divorced but still wanting to be in a stable relationship with respect that was mutual and not one-sided. She couldn't help but wonder if this was something that Neil was looking for too in a partner. Had he left someone behind during his current stint on campus? Or was he seeing someone locally these days?

*Better not allow my imagination to run wild*, Paula scolded herself, no matter how tempting to do so.

After work, she headed over to the campus bookstore

on Blaire Street and picked up a copy of Neil's book, entitled appropriately, *Profiling the Killers*. From there, Paula stopped off at Burger King and ordered a fish sandwich and onion rings for takeout, not in the mood for making dinner.

She drove home, which was an upscale penthouse condominium in Northwest Rendall Cove on Sadler Lane, a block from Rendall Creek Park. Exiting her car in covered parking, Paula bypassed the elevator and scaled the flights of stairs to her two-bedroom, two-bath fourth-story unit. The two-level unit had an open concept, with a nice great room and engineered eucalyptus hardwood flooring. Floor-to-ceiling windows and a covered deck overlooked a creek, where Canada geese loved to hang out, and pawpaw trees. She had picked out some great rustic furnishings and accent pieces for downstairs. The gourmet kitchen came with granite countertops and stainless steel appliances.

Sitting in a corner of the kitchen, as though waiting for Paula to come home, was her cat. She'd had the female Devon rex for a year now, named it Chloe, and thought she was adorable. Setting her Burger King bag on the counter, Paula scooped up the medium-sized cat and said, "Bet you're hungry too, huh?"

Chloe purred lovingly. Paula set her down on the floor, put some shredded chicken cat food in a bowl and watched as Chloe went for it hungrily. After heading up the quarter-turn staircase to the second floor, Paula stepped into the spacious bedroom with its large windows and farmhouse-style furniture, where she removed her sidearm and holster, before freshening up in the en suite.

Back downstairs, she poured herself a glass of white wine and ate her meal standing up, while watching Chloe scamper off as if having something better to do than hang out with her, now that she had been fed. Paula finished eating and took the wineglass with her to the great room, where she sat on a barrel club chair and started to read Neil's book with interest.

NEIL HAD RENTED the custom and newly built, two-story home in a subdivision on Leary Way in Rendall Cove at the start of the summer session. It was right across the street from Rendall Creek Park. He still maintained his colonial-style house on a few acres of land in Grand Rapids. But for the time being, he was living in this college town and making the most of his surroundings, which included a woodland behind the house with a running trail. Inside, it had crown molding and a symmetrical layout with wide open spaces and interesting angles, a high ceiling, large windows, vinyl plank flooring, a traditional kitchen with an island and an informal dining room. It came fully furnished with modern chairs and tables.

Basically, the place had everything he needed and more, Neil believed. If he didn't count living there alone when, deep down inside, he would have preferred sharing his space with someone who actually wanted to be there. Maybe that day would come again. Or maybe he was asking for too much, after what turned out to be a debacle in his last relationship.

With a bottle of beer in hand, Neil sat on a solid wood leisure chair in the living room and opened up his laptop. He accessed the files Paula had sent him on the Campus Killer case. Since June, there had been one, two, three and now four murders to occur on and off the college grounds, with all the victims female professors. Each victim had been suffocated by the unsub, who somehow managed to get away, with little to tie the perp to the murders.

"Hmm," Neil muttered out loud. He was sensing a distinct pattern among the homicides. One that was hard to ignore for a profiler. The actions by what appeared to be a serial killer were deliberate and methodical. In Neil's mind, the perp—most likely a male by serial murder standards—had to have been stalking the victims, targeting them one by one.

Tasting the beer, Neil took a sharp breath, knowing that the unsub would almost certainly not call it quits. Being successful in the killings thus far was only inviting the perpetrator to strike again when the opportunity presented itself.

That thought was perhaps scariest of all.

## Chapter Three

The following afternoon, the Campus Killer Task Force assembled in a Department of Police and Public Safety conference room at the university for the latest information on the investigation. Paula, who got little sleep last night after reading Neil Ramirez's entire book on profiling, was happy that he showed up today with her invitation. She was mindful that even with his participation in the case, he still had his duties as a visiting professor that had to be respected.

*As much as I might like to, I can't hog up all of the special agent's time*, Paula thought, as she gave him a friendly nod before she took to the podium. She glanced at Mike Davenport and Gayle Yamasaki, both of whom would have something to say in the scheme of things, and then Paula got down to business. Grabbing a stylus pen, she turned to the large touch-screen monitor and brought up an image of the first victim.

"In June, Debra Newton, a thirty-three-year-old associate professor in the School of Journalism, was smothered to death in her apartment on Frandor Lane in Rendall Cove." Paula was glad that, for the purpose of identifying them today, they had photos of the victims when they were alive and healthy, rather than their melancholy images after death.

She regarded the attractive, white, blue-eyed professor with long wavy crimson locks and feathered bangs. "Professor Newton was divorced and had no known enemies, but obviously ended up with a real target on her back."

Paula switched to another image of a striking Latina, with pretty brown eyes and long, straight brunette hair, and said, "In July, thirty-four-year-old Harmeet Fernández, an assistant professor in the Department of Horticulture, was found dead in the Horticulture Gardens on Moxlyn Place, due to suffocation. She had just broken off what was described as a contentious relationship with a fellow professor, Clayton Ricamara. His alibi of being at an economics conference in London when she was killed held up."

After taking a breath, Paula brought up on the screen a picture of an attractive African American woman with blondish boho braids and big sable eyes, before saying, "In August, Kathy Payne, a thirty-six-year-old professor in the College of Veterinary Medicine, was murdered in the same fashion in her Rendall Cove residence on Belle Street. Dr. Payne was a widow and not known to be seeing anyone at the time of her death."

The last image Paula put on the monitor was of a gorgeous white woman with long blond hair with brown highlights in a stacked pixie and green eyes. "In September, just yesterday morning, Odette Furillo, a thirty-four-year-old recently separated associate professor in the Department of Mathematics, was discovered on the floor of her office in the Gotley Building on Wakefield Road. According to the autopsy report from the county chief medical examiner, Professor Furillo's death was ruled a homicide, with the cause being asphyxia. Estimated time of death was somewhere between eight p.m. and eleven p.m."

Paula sighed and furrowed her brow. "All four homicide victims were suffocated to death by whom we believe to be the same unknown assailant. There is no evidence that any of the women were victims of a sexual assault. While we are still gathering and processing information, as of now, this unsub remains at large and can be considered extremely dangerous for female professors specifically, and all women who spend time on campus or who reside in the local community—so long as the perp is able to dodge being identified and taken into custody." Paula gazed at Neil, who seemed attentive in gazing back at her. "To that end, we've brought on board ATF Special Agent and criminal profiler, Neil Ramirez, who's currently doing double duty as a visiting professor of criminal justice. Agent Ramirez will give us his take on our unsub. But first, Detectives Mike Davenport and Gayle Yamasaki will provide updates on the investigation."

Paula gave both a brief smile and waited for them to come up and take her place. Davenport put a friendly hand on her shoulder and said in earnest, "This isn't easy for any of us, but we'll get through it and solve the case, one way or the other."

Paula nodded. "I know," she agreed, while feeling that day couldn't come soon enough for all concerned.

Gayle said to her, "You nailed it in setting things up, Paula, especially for our newcomer, Neil Ramirez. Hope I can add a bit more clarity on my end of the investigation."

"I'm sure you will," she told her with confidence, as Paula squeezed her hand and walked off to the side. She glanced at Neil, eager to hear what he had to say, especially after reading his excellent book last night.

Gayle went through the backstories on Debra Newton and

Kathy Payne, the two professors killed off campus. Gayle was operating as the lead investigator with the Rendall Cove PD in trying to piece together some of the similarities in the homicides beyond the surface, which included relatively easy points of entry into the residences and lack of security systems. In an annoyed tone of voice, she concluded, "It's pretty clear that our unsub is deliberately choosing to rotate the kills off and on campus, perhaps to throw us off the trail, or otherwise play a deadly game of cat and mouse. We have to find a way to turn the tables and stop this before it gets much worse for both our police departments."

She stepped away from the podium and Davenport took her place. He wasted little time in getting to the heart of the evidence in the latest murder at Addison University, as Davenport said evenly, "As you all know, we have surveillance cameras covering most locations on campus. Kind of makes it tough to do something bad and slip away quietly, even in the dark of night. At least not so we can't eventually track you down. I've had a chance to take a look at video recorded on campus the night that Professor Odette Furillo was murdered."

Lifting the stylus pen, he brought security camera footage to the large screen. "What you see is surveillance video taken outside the Gotley Building, where Furillo's office is located, around the estimated time of her death. Here, on the south side of the building, you can see what appears to be a white man moving away quickly on foot, as if he'd just seen a ghost. But more likely, it was because he had just committed a heinous crime and was making his getaway."

Paula homed in on the monitor. Though the video was grainy, it was clear enough to see that the unsub did seem to be an adult male who was tall, solid in build and wearing dark clothing and a hoodie, obviously intended as a deliberate means to camouflage his appearance. He was certainly making haste in vacating the building and surroundings. Was this their Campus Killer?

*The man's making a good case for being guilty of something*, Paula told herself.

"We're still studying other surveillance camera video, with different angles and distance from the Gotley Building, to see if the unsub got into a vehicle and where else he might have gone," Davenport pointed out. "As well as to see if any other serious suspects might emerge, given the timeline. But as of now, I'd have to say that the man you see is definitely a person of interest we need to track down."

Paula couldn't agree more, and she glanced at Neil to see him nod his head in concurrence. She turned back to Davenport, who was saying, "DNA was collected from beneath the fingernails of Furillo. As this doesn't belong to the professor, the forensic unknown profile was sent to CODIS, in hopes of getting a hit in the database of convicted offender or arrestee DNA profiles, or forensic indexes from crime scenes." He frowned. "Unfortunately, there was no match. Looks like the unsub isn't in the system. But we have this DNA sample and we have a person of interest on our radar. We just need to find him, interrogate him, compare his DNA with the unidentified DNA profile and see what happens."

*With any luck, we'll be able to do just that*, Paula mused, optimistic that they could and would track down the suspect.

When Davenport was through, she reintroduced Neil to those in attendance as he stood and approached her.

NEIL TOOK IN everything that was said as he shook the hands of Paula, noting how soft her skin was, Gayle Yamasaki and lastly Mike Davenport, who said to him, "Great to have you as part of the team, Agent Ramirez."

"Thanks." Neil noted that he had a firm grip in the hand-shake, matching his own. "Happy to help in any way I can." As the detectives walked away, he regarded the members of the task force, having already been acquainted with some from the Rendall Cove PD, doing double duty, like him, with the Firearms Investigation Unit. "First, let me say thanks to everyone here for bringing me up to speed on what I didn't know when looking at it from a small distance as a visiting professor. Hopefully, the surveillance video and DNA evidence will lead to an arrest soon. As a criminal profiler and ATF special agent, I doubt that it would surprise many of you in my belief that, based on the modus operandi in the murders, it's a safe bet that we are looking at a serial killer in our midst." In his mind, Neil considered that these days the FBI defined even two such homicides fitting the criteria as serial murders. Double that number and it left little doubt that they were dealing with a serial killer.

"On the other hand, you may or may not know that serial killers operating on university campuses and in college towns is far from unusual," Neil had to say. "Quite the contrary, with the warm and fuzzy welcoming environment and relatively easy and multiple escape routes. In many ways, this is the perfect setting for serial killers to prey upon victims. Think of Ted Bundy, John Norman Collins and Donald Miller, to name a few, all of whom went after female college students—any of which among the predators could just as easily have turned their deadly attention to female professors."

Neil allowed that to sink in for a moment and then continued, "As for this so-called Campus Killer, my early read is that the unsub is obviously someone who has knowledge of the campus and its surroundings—such as a professor, student or university employee—and uses it to his advantage to target those whom he has likely stalked surreptitiously and gone after when most advantageous to him. I see the unsub as a narcissistic, opportunistic vulture, who likely has a giant chip on his shoulder and has chosen to use this to go after the women whom he may deem as beneath him or think they are better than him. He could have been rejected by one or more of the victims," Neil reasoned. "Or simply used rejection of his advances or desires in general to target these victims who, through one means or another, came into his crosshairs."

Davenport, who was standing off to the side, asked him curiously, "What are your thoughts on the racial and ethnic mixture of the victims? Is this the unsub's way of saying he hates all women? Or at least those who are involved in higher education as educators?"

"Good question," Neil acknowledged. As it was, the differences between the four victims in terms of being white, African American and Hispanic were not lost on him. He contemplated this for a moment or two, then responded coolly, "I don't see this as hating all women, per se. Or racist. Or even the unsub fancying himself as an equal opportunity serial killer. More likely, it's a ruse or smoke screen, meant more to throw the investigation off by questioning the nature of the attacks, rather than the real reason behind them. My guess is that the perp may have homed in on one victim, in particular—whether acquainted with or a complete stranger, and not necessarily the first—then cleverly mixed up the other murders, by race or ethnicity, to make it more difficult to identify the culprit and bring him to justice."

"So, Agent Ramirez, is there any chance the unsub will save us the trouble of capturing him by turning himself in, with the guilt eating away at him like an insidious cancer inside his body?" Gayle threw out seriously.

"Afraid there's little chance of that," he responded honestly. "In my experience of profiling serial killers, in particular, and observations of the lot, in general, very few have a case of conscience where it concerns owning up to what they have done. Certainly not where it concerns walking into a police station and giving up. Unfortunately, most such killers have no wish to be captured and held accountable for their crimes. And few will actually stop killing, as long as the fever for continuing to victimize persists and the risk for detection remains low, in their minds."

"Figured as much." She made a face. "Had to ask."

"Of course." Neil flashed a small smile. "That's why we're here."

Paula, who had taken a seat, leaned forward and asked directly, "What else can you tell us about the unsub's psyche that might be helpful in understanding who we're up against, in terms of what to look for in our pursuit? As well as when we have him in custody...or have eliminated the threat."

Neil knew that in that last point, she was referring to the reality that the unsub might choose not to surrender when given the opportunity, leaving them no choice but to take him out. As far as he was concerned, Neil preferred that the Campus Killer, if convicted, spent the rest of his life behind bars. But that would be up to him, by and large. Gazing at Paula, Neil responded to her question. "With respect to the psyche of the killer, we're definitely talking about ASPD here—antisocial personality disorder," he stressed, lifting his shoulders. "The unsub's not delusional, based on his actions and skillful ability to have avoided capture thus far. But his penchant for such antisocial behavior with little regard for the human lives he's taking makes him a serious threat to the public, for as long as he's on the loose. I see the unsub as both control-driven and hedonistic in his killings," Neil told her. "That is to say, he gets off on having the power to decide when they live and die."

Paula wrinkled her nose. "What a creep."

"And some other choice words might apply too," Neil said thoughtfully.

"How about the off campus, then on it again killing pattern of the unsub?" she wondered. "Is there some method to this? Or is he merely toying with us in this regard?"

Taking a moment to consider what was an inevitable question, Neil answered evenly, "My guess is that it's largely an attempt by the unsub to keep us guessing by targeting professors on campus and off. But he could also be more haphazard and opportunistic in his MO, whereby he picks his prey and location to murder based upon whatever he deems the most effective and least vulnerable to himself for exposure."

"Hmm…" Paula smoothed an eyebrow. "What about some of the other dynamics, like character traits and background of the unsub, that may be a factor in his homicidal behavior?"

"In this regard, the unsub is just as likely to have come from a stable family as to have been a victim of child abuse and/or broken home," Neil made clear. "And be in a current relationship as much as a loner, and vice versa. He probably supplements his murderous appetite by using alcohol, illegal drugs or both, as an added means to drive him to kill. Whether or not the unsub has been motivated by other serial killers who have made news over the years, such as Bundy, Jeffrey Dahmer, John Wayne Gacy or even Jack the Ripper—or, for that matter, the plethora of true crime documentaries on cable and streaming television or the internet—could go either way."

"Got it," Paula told him, with an amused catch to her voice.

She offered him a weak smile to imply TMI, but Neil took it as more of an indication of satisfaction that he had laid out a solid foundation about the unsub to work with. He suspected that she may have wanted him to go even further in profiling the perpetrator. He was happy to oblige, but didn't want to overdo it by getting too academic or technical in advancing his remarks, at the risk of losing his audience and, in the process, any usefulness in applying this to the investigation.

If the case went on much longer, Neil could see himself adjusting his characterization of the unsub accordingly. But for now, he needed to see how this played out and hope they could get the bead on the Campus Killer sooner than later.

AFTER THE TASK force meeting ended, Paula approached Neil, who was chatting with Davenport, and invited them both to join her and some others for a drink at Blanes Tavern, a local hangout for cops. It had been Gayle who prodded her to ask him. Not that she needed much prodding concerning Neil, as Paula welcomed being able to spend more time with him. Between reading his book and listening to his characterization of the Campus Killer unsub, she was even more fascinated with the man, professionally and personally.

Davenport responded first, saying, "Wish I could. Unfortunately, I have to get home to the missus, who keeps me on a short leash, and my girls, adorable as they are."

"I understand." Paula smiled, envious of him as a family man. She turned her attention to Neil, wondering if this was a path he too was interested in going down, if given the chance. "What about you?"

His jaw clenched as Neil responded musingly, "Sorry, I'll have to pass too. Already have plans."

"I see. No problem," she assured him, even while wondering just what those plans might be. Perhaps to get together with someone he was dating? Would it be so surprising that he had a love life, even if she didn't at the moment?

"Rain check?" he threw out, as if a lifeline.

"Yes, that works for me," she told him, not wanting to put either of them on the spot for making any plans beyond that.

"Great." He favored her with a sideways grin.

Paula smiled back and walked away from the two men, while wondering if they were comparing notes on the investigation. Or her.

"Will they be joining us?" Gayle asked, approaching her.

"Afraid not," Paula almost hated to say. "Both have other things on their plates this evening."

"Too bad." Gayle frowned. "Oh, well. I think we can survive with whomever shows up."

"Agreed." Paula glanced over her shoulder and caught Neil spying on her, alone, as Davenport had already left the room. This eye contact seemed to be the trigger for Neil to follow suit, while avoiding her.

# Chapter Four

*Damn*, Neil muttered to himself as he left the Department of Police and Public Safety. He regretted missing out on the opportunity to hang with Paula in a more relaxed setting than a task force meeting. Or even a classroom, for that matter. He expected other opportunities would present themselves, as he definitely wanted the chance to get to know the detective sergeant better.

Unfortunately, in this instance, duty called. He had a pre-scheduled meeting with the ATF undercover surveillance agent, Vinny Ortiz, working on the inside in their arms trafficking investigation. Neil couldn't afford to jeopardize the mission, even if Paula Lynley had managed to occupy a portion of his thoughts.

He climbed into his dark gray Chevrolet Suburban High Country and texted Ortiz to say he would be there in ten minutes. Neil drove off while running through his mind the ultimate goal of getting illegal weapons off the streets, both at home and in other countries when coming from the United States.

Turning onto Prairie Street, his thoughts switched to the Campus Killer investigation. The task force seemed well suited to solve the case. Even if he could feel the frustrations from the meeting that were so thick you could almost cut through them with a knife, Neil was sure that the unsub would not get away with this. Most serial killers either got sloppy, unlucky, ran out of steam or were upended through strong police work. He was always betting on the latter when push came to shove, as there was no stronger motivation for those in law enforcement than putting an end to a serial killer or mass crimes of violence. Whatever it took. There would be no difference here.

The fact that Paula was spearheading the investigation, along with Gayle, gave Neil the confidence that, with his help, and the advances in forensics and digital technology, it was only a matter of time before the unsub was apprehended.

And it couldn't come soon enough for female professors.

On Tenth Street in a low-income part of town, Neil pulled his car up behind a red Jeep Wagoneer. He could see a man behind the wheel but couldn't identify him. Reaching for the ATF-issued Glock 47 Gen5 MOS 9x19mm pistol in his duty holster, Neil wondered if he would need to use it. Those tensions lessened when he watched a husky man with messy brown shoulder-length hair, parted on the left side, and a beardstache, emerge from the Jeep, and Neil recognized him as Agent Vinny Ortiz. The thirty-five-year-old Hispanic divorced dad had worked in undercover assignments for the past four years, successfully meandering between risky operations involving arson, explosives and illegal firearms. It had played havoc with his love life, though Neil knew that Ortiz was currently romantically involved with an international flight attendant.

Putting his gun away, Neil waited for Ortiz to get into

the passenger seat. Once he did, Neil said cautiously, "Hey. Everything okay?"

"Yeah, I'm fine," Ortiz said, running a hand across his mouth. "Took me a minute to get away without being noticed, if you know what I mean."

"I do." Neil understood fully just how risky the covert work was, having gone undercover himself a time or two during his career with the ATF. He certainly didn't want to jeopardize the operation. But Ortiz's safety was even more important. "What do you have for me?" Neil asked him.

"The arms trafficking operation is on," Ortiz replied in no uncertain terms. "The gunrunner, Craig Eckart, is setting up shop in Rendall Cove, using the dark web as a back door to collect and traffic in contraband firearms and ammunition, as well as gun trafficking in our own neck of the woods. Berettas, Glocks, Hi-Point, Uzis, Walthers, you name it."

"Yeah, I gathered as much." Neil considered the intel he had picked up on Craig Eckart, a forty-five-year-old who'd presented himself as a legal gun dealer and internet businessman, while operating on the fringes in his criminal enterprises. Though his legitimate interests had proven to be a good cover, selling guns and ammo on the black market had proven to be far more profitable. But if this didn't go south, they would soon be putting Eckart out of business, once and for all.

"I've set myself up as a buyer," Ortiz said, "promising to bring in loads of cash and a distribution system to kill for, figuratively speaking, both domestically and abroad."

"Good." Neil grinned at his ability to remain poised and use humor in the face of danger. He knew that the ATF was willing to front the money needed with a bigger payout in return, in breaking up the arms-dealing network. "When is this going to go down?"

"Soon," the agent promised. "I need a bit more time to ingratiate myself with Eckart, ever wary, and his goons, then we should be all set to blow this thing wide open."

"Okay." Neil regarded him. "If you ever get the sense that they're on to you, get out of there in a hurry and we'll do what we need to."

"I will." Ortiz jutted his chin. "You know me. I try to stay two steps ahead, at least, while watching my back at every turn."

"I get that." Neil nodded. "I also believe you can never be too careful. If you're ever in trouble, you know where to reach me."

"Back at you," Ortiz said, meeting his gaze. "Heard from one of the guys in the FIU with the Rendall Cove PD that you were getting involved in the Campus Killer investigation."

"I was asked to come on as a profiler," Neil acknowledged, "in hopes of nailing the unsub before anyone else gets killed."

"Good luck with that. A serial killer on the loose is bad for everyone, including Craig Eckart, who's been living with a professor, Laurelyn Wong, when he's not dirty dealing."

"Hmm… Interesting." Neil reacted to the irony. "Does she know about him as a gunrunner?"

"I don't think so," Ortiz indicated. "Eckart seems to have her totally fooled as Mr. Nice Guy."

"Could Eckart be responsible for the serial killings?" Neil wondered seriously. "Perhaps as a deadly diversion to his arms trafficking?"

"I doubt it. In my opinion, we're talking about two lanes

here. I've been watching Eckart like a hawk for weeks now and, though he's deadly in his own right in pushing contraband small arms and ammo, leading to gun deaths around the world, I don't see him masquerading on the side as a serial killer. Wouldn't be very good for business with law enforcement on the case stepping into his space, with Eckart's full knowledge that he's in the hot seat. As opposed to what he's not privy to," Ortiz added in reference to his undercover assignment.

"Maybe you're right." Neil gave the gunrunner the benefit of the doubt, knowing that they were angling at the moment for the unsub picked up on surveillance video that likely wasn't Craig Eckart. Particularly with Ortiz shadowing his every move.

"Anyway, hope you nail the son of a bitch," the undercover agent said. "Soon."

"Yeah," Neil muttered. "Back at you."

"That's the plan, right?" Ortiz ran a hand through his hair. "I better go."

"Okay." Neil certainly didn't want his cover to be blown. Or his life endangered any more than it already was. "Talk to you soon."

Ortiz nodded and left the car. Neil watched as he got back in the Jeep and drove off. He followed suit, detouring in a different direction as Neil headed home, his mind on the dual investigations he was now part of.

BLANES TAVERN WAS on Mack Road and already pretty busy by the time Paula arrived with Gayle in separate cars. They sat together, separate from colleagues, and ordered organic beer. For her part, Paula wished Neil could have joined them. But he was otherwise engaged. Maybe next time. She wasn't about to allow herself to get too attached to the visiting professor—who may or may not have been single—even if she felt comfortable conversing with him.

Gayle broke into her thoughts by asking, while holding a mug, "So, what do you make of Professor Ramirez's observations about our Campus Killer unsub?"

"He nailed it," Paula decided, based on what she already knew about serial killers, thanks in part to her former husband and his siblings in law enforcement. "Or at least he certainly seems to know what he's talking about in characterizing the unsub and what we need to look for in our search."

"I agree. His perspective can certainly aide the cause in knowing what we're likely up against."

"Yes, it can." Paula tasted the beer.

"Doesn't hurt matters any that the man's hot," Gayle remarked.

"True." It was something Paula could not deny one bit. She regarded the detective, who had recently ended a long relationship and almost immediately jumped back in the ring. Was she angling for Neil?

"Unfortunately, he's not my type," Gayle said, as if reading her mind. "Seems more like yours."

"You think?" Paula blushed.

"Based on what you've told me you look for in a man, definitely." Gayle sipped her beer. "Whether or not he's available is another matter. If you're interested, maybe you should find out."

"We'll see." Paula was noncommittal as to whether or not to go down that road. "My divorce is still relatively recent, so I have to tread carefully in putting myself out there again."

"I understand. But a year is an awfully long time to do without. I'm just saying, if you know what I mean," Gayle said with an amused grin.

"I think I do." Paula laughed at her brazen nature. "Still, I can wait till the right guy comes along, whoever that might be."

"Okay." Gayle tasted more beer. "Speaking of Agent Ramirez, I learned from the guys in the department's Firearms Investigation Unit that he and the ATF are working on a major illegal weapons probe."

Paula cocked a brow. "Really?"

"Yep. From what I understand, it's international in scope." She grabbed a handful of peanuts from a bowl on the table. "Not too surprising that the visiting professor can walk and chew gum at the same time, to coin a phrase."

"That he can, and then some," Paula concurred, while curious about the arms investigation and even more so about other aspects of his life. "We'll take whatever Agent Ramirez can send our way in the Campus Killer investigation."

"Amen to that." Gayle laughed and popped a couple of peanuts in her mouth. "So, how's your friend doing on her vacation on Maui?"

"Having a ball." Paula was mindful that Gayle grew up on the Hawaiian island and lived on Oahu as well, in Honolulu, before she relocated to the mainland and Michigan a decade ago. "She can't seem to get enough of working on her tan and sipping piña coladas."

Gayle gave a chuckle. "Sounds like she has the Hawaii fever."

"I think so." Paula grinned and grabbed some peanuts,

while wondering when a fever for stepping out of her comfort zone would overtake her.

When she got home an hour later, Paula watched as Chloe jumped off a chair and rubbed against her leg. She giggled. "Show the love," she teased her.

After feeding the cat, Paula phoned her sorority sister and former college roommate, Josie Woods, knowing that while on vacation with her latest boyfriend, Rob, Josie was on Hawaii time, which was six hours behind Michigan time.

Josie accepted the video chat request, appearing on the small cell phone screen as Paula stood by the window in the great room. The thirty-five-year-old senior analyst for a Wall Street firm was attractive and green-eyed, with long, straight brown hair and curtain bangs. She broke into a big smile. "Aloha!"

"Aloha." Paula grinned. "Hope I didn't catch you at a bad time?"

"You didn't. Rob's out for a game of golf on a Ka'anapali course, leaving me all by my lonesome to soak up the afternoon sun."

Paula laughed. "I can see that." She could tell that Josie was lounging on a beach chair beneath an umbrella on the West Maui coastline, while wearing a red tankini.

"Wish you were here," Josie told her.

"Me too." Paula was envious, having never been to Hawaii. Between Josie and Gayle singing its praises, this was something she hoped to rectify. "Maybe someday I'll hop on a plane and check out Maui and the other Hawaiian Islands for myself."

"You should. It's like no other place on Earth."

"Hmm…" Paula didn't doubt that. But visiting it alone might not be half as enjoyable as being in the company of a romantic partner. She wondered if Neil had ever been to Hawaii. The thought that he might well have taken another woman to paradise somehow ruined the fantasy, which Paula felt she had no right to have at this stage, if ever.

"Imagine what trouble we could get into if we went together." Josie broke into her reverie.

"That's what I'm afraid of." Paula giggled and watched as Chloe came over to her, as if jealous that she was being ignored.

"I'm sure you'd keep us on the straight and narrow at the end of the day, Detective Lynley," Josie quipped.

"Absolutely," Paula concurred, as her mind turned to the current serial killer case and where it might be headed with Neil on board as part of the task force.

WITH HER LEGS folded beneath her, Gayle Yamasaki sat on a faux-leather love seat in the living room of her Pine Street town house, watching cable television. Or trying to anyway. Her mind was elsewhere. Weighing heavily on it was her latest case. Having a serial killer in their midst, terrorizing females who happened to be teaching at Addison University, wasn't exactly what she'd signed up for when joining the Rendall Cove Police Department ten years ago. Or even, for that matter, when she'd been promoted to the Detective Bureau six years later. Both had followed her time as a detective with the Honolulu Police Department, once she'd graduated from the University of Hawai'i Maui College with an Associate in Applied Sciences Degree in Administration of Justice.

But, then again, no one she currently worked with wanted to be going after the so-called Campus Killer. Not that they had much choice. The unsub was still at large and needed to be stopped. As the lead detective in the investigation—at least for the two murders that occurred within the city limits outside the college—she felt the pressure to solve this case. With time being of the essence.

Gayle knew that the same was true for Paula Lynley, her detective sergeant friend who headed the university's Department of Police and Public Safety probe into the murders, with two occurring on campus. Together, along with their task force, Gayle hoped one thing led to another in putting the brakes on the unsub's homicidal tendencies before they got totally out of hand.

Having Professor Neil Ramirez on board as a criminal profiler might be just what they needed to unmask the perpetrator. The handsome ATF special agent was equally important to the Rendall Cove PD's Firearms Investigation Unit for his role in the joint investigation into the sale and distribution of illegal arms. Based on what she'd heard about him, she felt that Agent Ramirez was up to the challenge of juggling his multiple assignments without missing a beat.

Gayle's thoughts shifted back to the Campus Killer investigation. Or more specifically, one of the detectives working the case for the DPPS, Michael Davenport. Honestly, she had the biggest crush on him. Definitely her type. Too bad he was a happily married family man. Or was that only a facade?

Not that she wanted to test the waters, even if tempting. Yes, she was single again after her last serious relationship fell apart. And she'd started dating again. But she knew where to draw the line. Davenport was nice to be around, but that was it. She would turn her attention elsewhere as it related to romance.

Gayle grabbed the remote to turn off the big-screen television. She unfolded her legs and stood up, her bare feet feeling the cold of the hardwood flooring, and headed up-stairs for bed.

ON FRIDAY MORNING, Paula tied her hair in a short ponytail and threw on a black tank top, pink high-rise leggings and black-and-white running sneakers for a quick jog in Rendall Creek Park before work. Though Paula had found it to be a safe place to run, or otherwise spend time in the forested setting with plenty of trails and great scenery, mindful of the serial killer at large, she had begun bringing along her SIG Sauer pistol. She kept it in an ankle holster, but she'd have no trouble grabbing it quickly, if needed, to defend herself. Beyond that, she had taken some classes in Krav Maga, a method of self-defense comprising a combo of such tech-niques as boxing, karate, judo and even wrestling.

*I've never had to put it in practice, knock on wood*, Paula told herself, as she started her jaunt though the eastern white pines and maple trees and thick shrubbery in the park. She spotted a squirrel or two, along with some robins and spar-rows, none of which seemed to pay her much mind.

She had just begun to get into a comfortable groove when Paula heard footsteps behind her. They seemed to be grow-ing closer, even as she sought to put some distance between her and the runner. With her heart pounding, as much due to the rise in her heart rate from jogging as an overac-tive imagination in being brazenly attacked by the Campus Killer, Paula was determined not to go down without a fight. Instincts kicked in, and she mentally prepared to grab her firearm and whip around to face her assailant, even while continuing to move forward. Though she had no reason to believe that she had suddenly gone from a detective hunting the unsub to becoming a target of the killer, Paula was taking no chances in having her life cut short.

Just as she slowed her movement, bent down and removed the SIG Sauer pistol, Paula heard a familiar voice say in an ill at ease tone, "Paula…?"

Having already been in the process of turning and pointing the barrel of her gun at him, she gazed into the intense gray-brown eyes of Neil Ramirez. He came to a screeching halt, close enough to kiss her, before taking an involuntary step backward, with the SIG Sauer separating them.

Raising his hands in mock surrender, Neil said, wide-eyed, "Whoa! Don't shoot. You've got me, Detective Lynley."

*I do, at that*, Paula mused, still gripping the pistol firmly, but lowering it ever so cautiously. "Neil. You startled me!"

"My apologies," he asserted. "Didn't mean to come up on you like that. Guess I was caught up in my own thoughts."

*Or was that a convenient excuse?* Paula asked herself. She held his gaze. "Are you following me?" Her first thought was that perhaps he was doing so as another secret assignment, in protecting her from a serial killer, while part of the joint task force. But, if so, wouldn't her boss, Shailene McNamara, have told her?

"Wish I could say that were true, in the nicest way, of course," he answered, an amused grin playing on his lips. "As it is, I just happened to be out for a run, like you. Believe me, I'm just as surprised to see you as you clearly are to see me. I assure you that our nearly running into one another was purely happenstance. Nothing more."

"Oh, really?" Paula was still a little suspicious but knew it was totally unwarranted. Even if unexpected. She gave him a once-over and could see that, like her, he was dressed for a run, wearing a black workout jersey, gray jogger pants and black running sneakers. His muscular long arms had her imagining being wrapped in them. "So, you live around here?" she asked curiously.

"Right across the street from the park," he explained. "I'm renting a nice little house while I'm in town." He paused. "Where are you?"

"I live a block away," she told him, knowing he could easily have found out for himself, had he been interested.

"I see. So we're neighbors?"

"I suppose." The idea of having him so proximate did admittedly have its appeal.

He brought his arms down and peered at her gun, still halfway raised. "You want to put that thing away?"

"Yes, sorry." Embarrassed that she had held on to it as long as she had, Paula stuffed the pistol back into its holster. "Guess I'm just a bit spooked these days, with a serial killer on the loose."

"Perfectly understandable." Neil's voice was soothing. "Better safe than sorry, right?"

"Right." She flashed her teeth and said, "Better get back to it."

"Care for some company?"

"Yes, I'm up for a running partner who can keep up with me," Paula expressed boldly.

"Sounds like a challenge." Neil laughed. "I'll try my best not to disappoint."

Something told her there was little chance of that. She put him to the test anyway, breaking away speedily, only to see him catch up with little to no effort at all. "Do you run at the park often?" she wondered, while acknowledging that it was entirely possible that they had simply missed each other previously.

"Not so often," he told her. "I usually try to get in a short run on campus between classes, given all the inviting paths with lots of scenery for distractions. How about you?"

"I run in the park maybe three times a week and go to the gym once a week," Paula added, as if she needed to prove her fitness.

"Good for you. Haven't gotten to the gym yet since I've been in town, but I try to work out whenever I can."

"Could've fooled me," Paula teased him, needing only to get one look at the man as a physical specimen to know that he was in tip-top shape. "I'm sure that comes often enough."

Neil chuckled. "Ditto. You obviously know what it takes to maintain an amazing physique, from what I can see."

She blushed. "Back at you."

He grinned. "So, how was the outing after the task force meeting?"

"Good," she said. "Just drinks and conversation, before everyone went home for the night." Paula eyed him. "How did you make out with your plans for the evening?" Did she truly want to know if he was with another woman?

"Good," he answered vaguely. "Just had something I needed to tend to."

*So, he doesn't want to elaborate*, she thought. Maybe that was a good thing. "I bought a copy of your book."

"Really?" He lifted a brow.

"Yes, and read the entire thing in one sitting," Paula admitted, at the risk of giving him a big head. "It was quite interesting in giving a deeper perspective on criminal profiling."

"Glad you were able to pick up something from it," Neil

said, wiping perspiration from his brow with the back of his hand. "You never know how much will register and how much won't."

"It registered," she assured him. "As did what you had to say during the task force meeting."

"Good." He grinned sideways. "I really do want to help in any way I can to bring this unsub to justice. Or at least give you more to work with in delving into his psyche as a serial killer."

She nodded. "You're succeeding on both fronts."

Abruptly, Paula raced him to the clearing, beating him by a fraction, though suspecting he had let her win this time. As they caught their breaths, laughing like being in on a good joke, she suddenly decided to kiss him. Cupping Neil's chiseled cheeks, she just laid a big one on his mouth, which he returned in kind till Paula unlocked their lips, feeling embarrassed at her unusual boldness. Yet she wasn't at all sorry she did it.

"Sorry about that," she apologized nevertheless. "It was just something I wanted to do and went for it."

"Nothing to be sorry about." Neil grinned out of one corner of his mouth. "Happens to the best of us. And it was a nice kiss at that."

Though she didn't disagree in the slightest, Paula felt this probably wasn't the best moment to go down this road. So, she told him awkwardly, "Uh, this is where I head home. I have to go get ready for work."

"Okay." He met her eyes, but his own were unreadable. Was that good or bad?

"I'll see you later." She turned away and started to jog

down the sidewalk, almost expecting Neil to follow, as if he had nothing better to do.

It never happened, leaving Paula to ponder the kiss and the man himself alone.

# Chapter Five

Neil welcomed a hot shower after his run, but felt his temperature rise while thinking about the unanticipated kiss from Paula. Her full lips were as soft as cotton and contoured perfectly with his own. He'd be lying if he said the thought of kissing her hadn't crossed his mind once or twice. Hell, even more than that. But she had beaten him to the punch, indicating they were on the same wavelength.

Then Paula had hastily left him hanging, even if understandable that she, like him, still had another workday to prepare for. Neil could only wonder where they went from here. Or had her divorce made Paula more squeamish when it came to anything more than a quick kiss before a goodbye?

After dressing and having a quick bowl of cereal to go with a strong cup of coffee, Neil dropped by his office at the college, picked up the exams for his first class and went to it. Waiting for him there, before the undergraduate students began to pour in, was Desmond Isaac, a twenty-five-year-old graduate teaching assistant.

Working on a Master of Arts in Criminal Justice, Desmond was about his height and more on the slender side, with dark blond hair in a layered men's bob and a chin puff goatee. Behind retro glasses were blue eyes. "Hey," he said casually.

"Hey." Neil sat his briefcase on the desk and opened it. "Brought something for you." He handed him the exams, which Desmond would soon be handing out and collecting from the students.

"Think they're up to the challenge?" Desmond joked.

"If not, then I haven't been doing my job very well."

"We both know that's not true. Seems like you have them eating out of your hands."

Neil laughed. "Don't know if I'd go quite that far. But I am here to teach what I can."

"Speaking of which, I heard that you're working with the Department of Police and Public Safety in trying to identify and flush out the Campus Killer."

"Word travels fast," Neil quipped, though not at all surprised, as the school newspaper had picked it up. "I'm offering my thoughts on what—and whom—the authorities investigating the case are up against," he said, downplaying his credentials as a criminal profiler.

"Well, it's smart of them to take advantage of your presence on campus," Desmond told him. "We'll all be a lot better off when this serial killer nightmare is over."

"I hear you." Neil spotted students beginning to file in. "Right now, let's see if we can get the next generation of law enforcement personnel to pass my class and graduate."

"Yeah. There is that hurdle they need to climb." Desmond dangled the multiple-choice tests in his hand.

Neil greeted students, while also collecting their cell phones to be returned after the exam. "Good morning," he said routinely, often getting in return, "Morning, Professor Ramirez." He was still trying to get used to being seen as a visiting professor instead of an ATF special agent. Could the former replace the latter as a more permanent thing?

He honed in on one student, in particular, named Roger Woodward. The twenty-two-year-old senior and honors student stood out because of his rainbow-colored gelled Mohawk hairstyle, lanky frame and dark eyes. Neil saw him as one of his smartest students, who had indicated a strong interest in working for the Bureau of Alcohol, Tobacco, Firearms and Explosives. He grinned at Roger and said, "Good luck with the exam."

"Thanks," Roger said, a crooked smile on his lips.

Not that Neil thought he needed any luck acing the test. This common, but useful for some, phrase was passed along to other students that Neil engaged, with Desmond following suit.

THE KISS THAT landed on Neil Ramirez's firm lips was admittedly still on Paula's mind as she pulled up to the two-story Tudor home on Winsome Road in Rendall Cove that Odette Furillo had owned with her estranged husband, Allen Furillo. Paula had been trying to speak with him since his wife was murdered, but the man had seemingly kept them running around in circles. Till now. Furillo had requested the meeting, while making it clear that he didn't need to have a lawyer present. That by no means made Paula believe he had nothing to do with the murder, but at the very least suggested that he wanted to give that appearance.

Exiting her car, she noted the blue Dodge Charger parked in the driveway. Paula knew that a white Honda Insight belonging to Odette Furillo that she'd driven to the campus was still being processed for possible evidence in a homicide. Paula's sidearm was tucked away in her gun holster but could be quickly accessed, if needed. The thought of pointing it at Neil this morning crossed her mind, causing her to blush as the potential threat had turned out to be the ATF agent turned visiting professor, whom she wound up kissing instead of killing.

*I need to not be so jumpy in the future*, Paula mused. At least where it pertained to Neil. But when it came to the Campus Killer, all bets were off.

Before she could ring the doorbell, the door swung open. Standing there was a medium-sized, short man in his midthirties with dark hair in an undercut fade and blue eyes. Paula showed her badge and said, "Detective Lynley. Are you Allen Furillo?"

"Yeah, that's me," he muttered. "Come in."

She followed him inside and took a sweeping glance around at the traditional furnishings and gray carpeting.

"Would you like something to drink?" Furillo asked her.

Glancing at some empty beer cans on the kitchen counter, Paula wasn't sure if he was referring to alcoholic beverages or not. Either way, she passed. But she did agree to sit on an accent chair, while he sat across from her on a sofa, so she could keep her eye on him. "We've been wanting to talk to you about your wife's death…"

"I know. I just needed some time to clear my head before speaking with anyone," he said, lowering his eyes. "The way Odette died really shook me."

"I understand that you and your wife were separated," Paula pointed out, not yet willing to give him the benefit of any doubt. "What was that all about?"

"That was her choice, not mine." Furillo pursed his lips. "I wanted to try and make the marriage work, even if we had trouble seeing eye to eye of late. But she wasn't interested in that and asked me to leave. I did, but still hoped she might come to her senses, before it was too late."

Paula peered at him and asked bluntly, "Did you kill your wife, Mr. Furillo?"

"No, I could never have done such a horrible thing," he asserted. "I loved Odette."

*Isn't that what most say before and after killing their spouses?* Paula thought. "I need to know where you were the night your wife was murdered," she demanded, supplying him with the estimated time frame.

Squaring his shoulders, Furillo responded straightforwardly, "I was at work as a warehouse picker on the afternoon shift at a distribution center on Hackett Road. Didn't leave till after midnight. Plenty of other workers saw me. You can check."

If true, Paula knew this would mean he couldn't have been at his wife's office on campus during the time of her death. "I'll do that," she promised. She regarded him directly. "Do you know of anyone who may have wanted to harm your wife?" Paula didn't discount that the unsub could have targeted a specific victim and added the others for effect, and to throw them off his trail.

Furillo's brow furrowed. "Maybe the man Odette decided to give her affections to."

Paula narrowed her eyes. "Are you saying your wife was having an affair?"

"Yeah, she was." His voice thickened. "Hard as it is for me to come to terms with, even if she believed our marriage was over."

"Do you know the name of this other man?" Paula asked interestedly.

"Yeah. His name is Joseph Upton. He worked with her as

a professor in the mathematics department at the university," Furillo muttered glumly. "He could've killed her if Odette had a change of heart and wanted to come back to me."

"I'll have a chat with Professor Upton," Paula promised, while wondering if Odette Furillo might have done a reverse course. Or had her relationship with her husband been doomed either way? Paula understood all too well that was inevitable in some marriages.

She asked Furillo a few questions about the other victims attributed to the Campus Killer and decided that it was unlikely that he had anything to do with their deaths.

"HE CAME IN VOLUNTARILY," Mike Davenport told Paula an hour later, as they looked at the video monitor of Professor of Mathematics Joseph Upton sitting in an interview room in the Department of Police and Public Safety.

"Smart move on his part," she uttered, after an attempt to reach Upton had come up short. Paula studied the professor, who was white, blue-eyed, fit and in his late thirties, with jet-black hair worn in a short pompadour cut.

"There's more," Davenport indicated. "Upton says he's the man in the surveillance video from outside the Gotley Building that we released to the media."

"Really?" Paula eyed the professor again and wondered if he was there to confess to killing his lover. "I'd better get in there and see what he has to say."

"Let me know if you need backup on this one."

"Okay." She headed into the room, where the suspect sat in a metal chair at a square wooden table. "Joseph Upton, I'm Detective Lynley. Mind telling me what you're doing here?" She decided to be coy about it.

Fidgeting, he responded, "To talk about Odette Furillo."

Paula sat across from him and advised that the conversation was being video recorded, having hit the switch to activate it on the way in. "What about her?"

"Odette and I were having an affair," he said thoughtfully.

"For how long?" Paula wondered.

"A few months." He paused. "But it wasn't just about sex. We were in love, and she was preparing to file for divorce."

Paula peered across the table. "But that never happened…"

Upton lowered his head. "I know she was murdered… and that security video showed someone fleeing the building where Odette and I had our offices." He drew a breath. "That was me," he repeated what had already been told to Davenport.

"Are you saying you murdered Professor Furillo?" Paula asked point-blank.

He lifted his eyes and met hers unblinkingly and said firmly, "No, I didn't kill her. But I saw Odette in her office, where we were supposed to meet." He sighed. "She was dead. Someone had killed her."

"Did you call 911?" Paula asked skeptically.

"No."

"Why not?"

"I don't know," he claimed. "Guess I panicked, not knowing if the killer was still on the floor. Or if I would be blamed for what happened. Not thinking clearly, I just took off, knowing there was nothing I could do to save Odette. It was too late for that."

Paula didn't disagree, per se, based on the autopsy report. But who knew for certain, had he acted promptly? "Did you see anyone else coming or leaving the building?" she pressed him.

"No." Upton's brows knitted. "There were other people outside, going about their business and whatnot, but I was in too much of a hurry to get away, so I never really focused on anyone else. Sorry."

"How did you get to the Gotley Building in the first place?" Paula asked, knowing it was centrally located on campus, but not usually walkable.

"I drove," he admitted. "But I didn't want to go to my car, fearing it would be seen on surveillance video, so I ran off and came back for it in the morning. As I said, I panicked. I know it was an unwise thing to do. When I saw the video footage on my tablet, I recognized myself and knew it was only a matter of time before someone else did. So... here I am—"

She glanced at the camera and wondered what Davenport thought. For her part, Paula felt the professor's story was credible, if not suspicious and sad at the same time. "Would you be willing to submit a DNA sample?" she asked him.

Upton hedged, but then responded as if having an epiphany, "Yes, since I have nothing to hide insofar as what happened to Odette."

*That remains to be seen*, Paula thought, but welcomed the opportunity to collect his DNA to see if there was a match with the unidentified DNA profile scraped from underneath Odette Furillo's fingernails. There would be more questions for Joseph Upton down the line, but this was certainly a good step forward in seeing whether he was a killer. Or a misguided former lover to a dead woman.

Twenty minutes later in her office, Paula made the same observation to Davenport, while they awaited the DNA results. "My gut tells me that Upton did not kill Professor Furillo. Much less the other professors."

"You're probably right," the detective concurred, frowning. "The unsub likely wouldn't have been as sloppy in his comings and goings, based on the trajectory of the other killings attributed to the Campus Killer."

"Upton almost certainly contaminated the crime scene," she complained.

"As did Joan McCashin, the student and presumably first to arrive at the scene that morning," he observed. "That notwithstanding, and even if it turns out that Upton isn't our unsub, we still have enough to work with in moving ahead."

Paula did not disagree. "If Upton's on the level, his own life might have been spared," she contended, "had the unsub stuck around long enough to make sure there were no living witnesses to the perp's criminality."

"You're right." Davenport twisted his lips. "In this case, timing does seem to be everything. The killer is using it to his advantage. But that won't last forever."

"It had better not." She frowned at the thought, with a serial monster undoubtedly still hungry for more victims.

As THE NOON hour approached and turned into 1:00 p.m., Neil wondered if Paula was free for lunch. If she was like him, she probably passed this up often when in the heat of an investigation. On the other hand, a person had to eat sometime. He hoped this would be a chance to get to know one another better.

He was in his office when he phoned her. "Hey," he said when she answered, the thought of that kiss immediately entering his head.

"Hey." She left it at that.

"If you're not busy and haven't eaten yet, I was wondering if you'd like to join me for lunch?" Neil didn't want to spook her by calling it a date, in case that wasn't something she was open to right now. "We can talk shop and—"

"Yes, I'd be happy to meet you for lunch," Paula broke in enthusiastically. "Where?"

"I thought we could eat at the Union Building food court," he suggested, as a neutral spot.

"Sounds perfect. I can be there in five minutes."

"See you then." Neil disconnected and found himself excited at the prospect of seeing the lovely detective in mere minutes. He conferred briefly with his TA, Desmond Isaac, who would be grading the exams and either putting smiles or frowns on the faces of students, before heading out of the building.

In his Chevy Suburban SUV, Neil drove across campus to the Union Building on Bogle Lane. He parked in the lot and went inside to the food court, where he was surprised to see that Paula was already there.

He grinned. "Hope I didn't keep you waiting too long," he kidded.

"Maybe just a bit," she tossed back at him lightheartedly. "But I'll live."

Neil laughed. "That's good to know."

They found a table, and he went with the mac and cheese, while Paula settled for street-style nachos. Both had coffee.

Rather than get back to the kiss and what it could potentially mean, Neil asked casually, "Any news on the investigation?"

Paula, who had been deep in thought while eating, looked at him and said, "As a matter of fact, there has been some…"

"Oh?" He met her eyes curiously.

"The man seen in the surveillance video at the Gotley Building has been identified as Joseph Upton, a mathematics professor," she informed him. "Who also happened to be the lover of Odette Furillo."

"Really?" Neil knew she was estranged from her husband. But still.

"Yep. Upton came in voluntarily and admitted to coming upon Professor Furillo's body, after making plans to meet in her office." Paula dabbed a napkin to her mouth. "He says he panicked and fled the scene without calling 911."

"Did you believe him?" Neil asked.

"Honestly, I was on the fence there, but he agreed to supply a sample of his DNA."

"And...?"

"Upton's DNA didn't match the unidentified sample collected from beneath Odette's nails." Paula furrowed her brow. "Apart from leaving the scene of a crime, there was no reason to believe he's the unsub."

"Makes sense." Neil scooped up some macaroni and cheese on a fork. "What about the husband?"

She poked at her nachos. "Allen Furillo has a solid alibi for the time frame in which his wife was murdered. He couldn't have done it."

"Can't say I'm too surprised in either instance," Neil remarked thoughtfully. "As victim number four of the so-called Campus Killer, Odette Furillo most likely wasn't intimately connected to her murderer as much as the unsub could have been to the first or second victim—then moved beyond that, were it the case, in the subsequent killings."

"Sounds logical, coming from a profiler," Paula agreed. "Of course, as a crime investigator, we can't afford to leave any stones unturned."

"Wouldn't expect you to." Neil sat back in the chair and

lifted his coffee cup. "Until you get the guy, no one's above suspicion. Nor should anyone be."

She smiled. "I figured we'd see eye to eye on this."

*And even more*, he thought, tasting the coffee and grinning at her. "Absolutely."

Paula lifted her own cup in thought. "As for going after bad elements, I hear that you're working with the Rendall Cove PD on an arms investigation."

Neil wasn't at all surprised that information flowed back and forth between the DPPS's Investigative Division and the city police department's Firearms Investigation Unit, given that they typically worked hand in hand on cases with common ground. Consequently, he didn't try to dance his way around this. Even if, technically speaking, he needed to keep a low profile on the case while it was at a near tipping point.

"Yes," he confessed without elaborating.

"I see." She met his eyes musingly. "Is that the real reason you're in Rendall Cove?"

Neil thought about his friend and late fellow ATF agent, Ramone Munoz. And then his ex-girlfriend, Constance Chen, who turned Neil's life upside down. Locking his eyes with Paula's steady gaze, he told her straightforwardly, "Not exactly."

## Chapter Six

It occurred to Paula that perhaps Neil was on a mission that she was not supposed to pry about. Even if they were on the same team in her serial killer investigation. Or was there something more to his taking a position at the university as a visiting professor?

"Sorry if I've overstepped," she put out, after nibbling on more of her nachos.

"You didn't," he insisted, flashing her a small grin. "You're entitled." He paused. "I can't really talk about the ongoing arms investigation, other than to say it's what the ATF does, and sometimes with help from its partners in law enforcement."

*So, there's obviously a big operation going down*, Paula told herself. One she was not entitled to be privy to, in spite of working with him as a profiler in a separate case. "I understand," she said tactfully.

Neil rubbed his jawline. "Apart from that, I took the position as a visiting professor as a needed getaway from the life I had…" He pressed his hands together. "Last year, a good friend of mine, ATF Special Agent Ramone Munoz, was ambushed during an ATF Special Response Team raid on a drug trafficking compound. He was killed in the process, leaving behind a wife and two little girls. The entire thing shook me up like I'd never been before."

Paula was almost speechless in hearing the shocking details of Agent Munoz's death and its aftermath, having already learned the basics about the mission gone awry. "I'm so sorry," she managed.

"Me too." Neil stared at the remnants of his macaroni and cheese. "Ramone deserved a hell of a lot better than he got as a dedicated ATF agent. But it is what it is and I have to accept that, no matter how difficult."

"These things can take time…" Paula resisted the desire to reach across the table and touch his hand. "And there's no hurry." She sensed there was more to his story.

He nodded and met her eyes musingly. "A few months back, I was in a relationship with an anthropologist named Constance Chen. She dumped me for another guy, without giving me a good reason, and I needed to come to terms with this as well. Putting some distance between me and Constance seemed like a good idea. Along with taking a break when it came to romance."

"I'm sorry that happened to you." Paula meant every word of it. Even if in the process, it told her that he was, apparently, not seeing anyone. She felt like jumping for joy that he was available, but wondered if this was true. Perhaps in guarding his heart, he wasn't looking to jump back into a relationship any time soon.

"It was probably a good thing," Neil told her in earnest. "If I'm honest about it, things had been treading in the wrong direction between us for a while. But I chose not to see it for what it was."

"I know what you mean," Paula couldn't help but say.

"What happened with your marriage?" He regarded her intently, taking the opening she had given him.

Holding his gaze, she admitted straightforwardly, "We simply ran out of steam." She tasted her coffee, which had started to get cold, knowing he wanted more from her than that. "Scott was a good man. His parents and siblings were either in law or law enforcement. In some ways, this seemed to put extra pressure on our relationship, in addition to us both being in law enforcement ourselves. Eventually, it, along with personality clashes, took its toll on the marriage and we decided to end things."

Neil tilted his head. "Any regrets?"

"There are always regrets whenever a relationship fails and you play the blame game and wonder what you might have done differently," she answered, "which I'm sure you would attest to. But if you're asking me if I still love Scott and want to get back together with him, the answer is no on both fronts. He'll always be a part of my history," Paula did not deny. "Not my future." She looked at Neil. "Does that answer your question?"

"Yes, it does." He grinned sheepishly. "And you're absolutely right. We all have regrets on past failures. But they can—and should be—a bridge to getting things right the next time. Or the time after that."

"Agreed." She smiled back at him, believing they had climbed one hurdle in getting to know one another better. Would there be more to follow?

"Do you have family?" Neil asked, sitting back while taking a sip of water.

Paula bobbed her head. "My mom lives in Georgetown, Kentucky. I lost my dad to a heart attack when I was a teenager."

"Sorry to hear that."

"It came without warning, but was quick," she told him sentimentally. "I have no siblings. What about you?"

"Just an older sister," Neil said, resting an arm on the table. "Yancy works these days as a freelance translator in Brazil. I lost my parents in different years to cancer and an accidental fall."

It was Paula's turn to tell him she was sorry, knowing how devastating it could be without one's parents. She recalled that Scott and his siblings lost their parents in a car accident and, fortunately, had each other to lean on. "Are you and your sister close?" she asked Neil.

"Yes," he replied with a smile. "Yancy's four years older, but the difference never seemed that great when we were kids. In any event, we've always had each other's back."

"That's nice to hear." Paula wished she'd had siblings to always be able to lean on. She would have to settle for her best friend, Josie, along with her ex-sister-in-law, Madison, whom Paula had remained close with since her divorce. Even better was the notion of forming a bond with someone she could share her life with.

After they left the Union Building, Neil walked Paula to her car. "Thanks for lunch," she told him, after he'd insisted on paying for it.

He nodded, grinning. "Anytime."

She waited a beat then, looking into his eyes, said, "Guess I'll catch you later."

"All right." Neil flashed her a serious look. "About that kiss…"

"What about it?" She was almost afraid to ask, her heart pounding.

He suddenly cupped her cheeks and kissed Paula on the mouth. The kiss was powerful enough to make her go weak in the knees. Something told Paula that Neil would catch her were her legs to go out from under her.

After his lips parted from hers, his voice dropped an octave when Neil uttered soulfully, "I just wanted to let you know that the feeling of something between us is mutual."

As she caught her breath, Paula realized that he had just given them permission to try and unwrap those feelings over the course of time.

BACK AT HIS office that afternoon, Neil reflected on what he saw as a breakthrough on the connection he was starting to feel with Paula. He had no idea if it would go anywhere. Or if both of them were merely spinning their wheels in seeking to get beyond broken relationships. He, for one, was willing to put one foot in front of the other and see what happened. From the way Paula's lips contoured perfectly with his, it indicated to Neil that she was up for meeting him halfway. That was all he could ask for at this point, given that they both were in the midst of criminal investigations, occupying their time.

On his laptop, Neil contacted his sister for a video chat. He noted the minor time difference between Rendall Cove and São Paulo, Brazil, where Yancy lived with her bank manager boyfriend, Griffin Oliviera. She accepted the call and Neil watched his sister's face light up. At forty, she looked ten years younger, with dark blond hair in a medium-length A-line cut. Like him, Yancy had their father's deep gray-brown eyes.

"Hey," he said.

"Hey back, Neil."

"You busy?" Like him, he knew she worked long hours,

often at the expense of quality time, in spite of being in a long-term relationship with Griffin.

"I think I can spare a few minutes for my brother," she teased him.

"Okay. Just wanted to check in with you."

"And I thank you for that." Yancy went on to bring him up to date on her current comings and goings, before he talked a bit about himself.

"So, being a professor agrees with you these days?" she asked curiously.

"Yeah, you could say that," he told her. "Still keeping my day job, though, just in case teaching blows up in my face."

"I doubt that will happen." Yancy laughed. "But at least you'll have two directions you can go in."

"That's true." *Make it three directions*, Neil considered, when it came to Paula.

As if on the same wavelength, Yancy eyed him carefully and asked, "So, how's your love life these days? Or shouldn't I ask?"

"You can ask." He grinned wryly.

"Then I'm asking. And please don't tell me you're still pining for the one who let you get away?"

"I'm not," Neil made clear. Not by a long shot. "There is someone in the picture," he told her.

"Really?" Yancy's eyes brightened. "Tell me more…"

He did, while being clear that things were still in the early stages with Paula, with neither of them knowing if, like birds, they had the wings to make this fly. But at least she was giving him something to shoot for, and vice versa.

His sister concurred and wished them both luck, while even being presumptuous in inviting them to come for a visit to Brazil. Neil laughed, while taking that under advisement as something he could imagine happening down the line, should things progress accordingly with the nice-looking detective.

When Neil noticed that his TA had poked his head in the office, the call to Yancy was ended, with the promise to speak again soon.

"Sorry, didn't mean to interrupt," Desmond said.

"It's all right." Neil looked at him. "What's up?"

"Finished grading the exams." He stepped inside the office.

"How did they do?" Neil wondered.

"Better than expected," Desmond said. "At least for some, who aced it. Others still need to study harder to get up to snuff."

Neil nodded. "I'll have to do better to motivate them in that regard."

"You're doing a great job," the TA contended. "The onus is on them to get with the program, if they hope to graduate and move on to bigger and better things."

"Can't argue with that." Neil smiled. He was glad to see that Desmond was able and willing to keep the pressure on students to try and be the best they could be, instead of being handed life on a silver platter. Just how many students would buy into this argument remained to be seen.

"I'll send out the exam scores and wait to see how they respond," Desmond said.

"Good. I'll go over the results and see where to put greater focus," he told the TA and watched him leave. Neil then got on the phone with Doris Frankenberg, the resident agent in charge of the ATF's Grand Rapids field office, to update her on the illegal arms joint operation.

ON MONDAY MORNING, Paula was at her desk, comparing information on the four homicides credited to the Campus Killer. There appeared to be little commonality among the murder victims, per se, apart from being victimized female professors. Though this, in and of itself, showed an undeniable pattern of targeting that needed to be taken into account, there was no indication that the victims were connected otherwise in a meaningful way. This lent credence, to some degree, to the random or opportunistic theory on the crimes. But what were they missing in this equation?

There must be something, she told herself, sipping coffee, while poring over the individual case files. Her mind wandered briefly to the passionate kiss she shared with Neil the other day. The man could kiss, she established. Made her believe he could be just as great a lover. If not better. As a flicker of desire coursed through her, Paula allowed it to dissipate, filing it away for another time and place, as she put her eye back on the ball.

She went back through the cases and searched for anything that could link them together insofar as a pattern that might lead to a serial killer. Something suddenly caught her eye—or someone—as Paula honed in on the name Roger Woodward. The twenty-two-year-old senior had been questioned this summer about the murder of Debra Newton, because the associate professor had mentioned to at least one other professor that a student in her journalism class had been stalking her.

That student was identified as Roger Woodward. He had produced an alibi and been let off the hook as a suspect in her death. Now Paula saw that Woodward, an honors student who had a dual major in journalism and criminology, had been taking a class in mathematics as an elective this semester, with Professor Odette Furillo. *Hmm, coincidence?* Paula had to ask herself. Or not?

She looked up his current class schedule and saw that Roger Woodward also happened to be taking a criminology course with Visiting Professor Neil Ramirez. One that was in session right now.

*Think I'd better have a little chat with Woodward,* Paula told herself. If he had something to hide, such as a pattern of serial homicides, perhaps with Neil on hand they could flush it out of the honors student together.

AFTER GOING OVER Friday's exam results without mentioning any names or grades specifically, Neil put on a good face and tried to make all the students feel as if they could talk to him if they had any trouble grasping the lectures and reading assignments. In the meantime, he would continue to do his job in the classroom as a visiting professor of criminology and hope that it was resonating to the point of motivating those in attendance to do their best in getting a good education and doing something with it.

It was about five minutes before class ended when Neil got a text message from Paula. He glanced at his cell phone, reading with interest.

One of your students, Roger Woodward, is a suspect in the Campus Killer investigation. On my way. Keep him there till I arrive.

Neil couldn't help but cock a brow with shock that someone in his class was considered a possible serial killer. He gazed at Roger Woodward, who was sandwiched in the middle row between Adriana Tilly and Fiona Liebert. Roger, not too surprisingly, had aced the exam. *He clearly got it*, Neil thought. And seemed to enjoy playing the role of amateur sleuth. Could this have evolved into becoming a real-life serial killer? He didn't seem to fit the profile. But then, profiles didn't always tell the tale where it concerned the capabilities and modus operandi of killers.

Neil turned away from him, not wanting to tip his hand that something was up. But he couldn't allow Roger to leave either. Not till Paula had questioned him and determined he was not the unsub.

Dismissing the class a little early, Neil gave them a new assignment, then casually asked Roger Woodward if he could stick around for a moment to talk about his test results.

"Yeah, sure," he responded, wide-eyed at being singled out.

After the others had left, Neil eyed him intently and said, "You did great on the exam, Roger."

"Thanks."

Neil paused. "I was asked to hold you over."

Roger looked at him warily. "By who?"

"A police detective who would like to ask you a few questions pertaining to a homicide investigation…" Neil gauged his reaction, while trying to picture one of his prized students doubling as a serial killer. Before he could respond to the question, Paula walked into the room.

"Professor Ramirez," she spoke formally. "I can take it from here…"

"Okay." Neil ceded to her authority in the matter as the lead investigator on the case, but was more than an interested observer.

Paula walked up to the student and said equably, "Roger

Woodward, I'm Detective Lynley. We spoke before, during the investigation into the death of Professor Debra Newton."

"Yeah, I remember." He ran a hand nervously through his hair. "I had an alibi," he reminded her.

"You did," she conceded, "which checked out. Now I'd like to ask you about another one of your professors, Odette Furillo, who was found murdered in her office last Wednesday."

"I heard about that. Like everyone else on campus." Roger put his weight awkwardly on one foot. "What does that have to do with me?"

Paula glanced at Neil and back. "Maybe nothing. Or maybe everything."

"I don't follow," Roger said, furrowing his brow. "Are you accusing me of something?"

"Not yet." Her tone deepened. "I do find it odd though that you happened to be taking classes with two dead professors—at least one of whom you had a fixation on."

"I admit that I was attracted to Professor Newton, okay? I thought the feeling was mutual. Guess I was mistaken. But I didn't kill her and I didn't kill Professor Furillo." His nostrils flared. "Or, for that matter, the other murdered professors. I'm not this Campus Killer."

Though Neil wanted to give him the benefit of the doubt, that didn't work on the face of it when on the hunt for a serial killer. He gazed at the student and decided to get in on the questioning. "Relax, Roger. Detective Lynley is simply doing her job," Neil told him, playing the good cop, bad cop game as he regarded Paula and got her approval through an expression. "I assume you have an alibi for when Professor Furillo was murdered?" He gave him the date and time of death.

"Yeah, I do." Roger set his jaw. "I was with my girlfriend. Spent the night in her dorm room."

Paula peered at him. "Does this girlfriend have a name?"

"Last I checked," he quipped. Then Neil flashed him a stern look and Roger said, "Her name's Adriana... Adriana Tilly—"

"Adriana?" Neil said, reacting to the name of another student in his class. Like Roger, she tended to stand out with her mermaid hairstyle, featuring a blend of orange, green and red long locks with a round face. "I didn't realize you two were an item, and not just classmates."

"Yeah, we've been hanging out for a few weeks now," Roger stated coolly. "Been pretty much inseparable of late at night, if you know what I mean."

Neil took him at his word. "What you do and who you choose to do it with outside the classroom is your business." *So long as it doesn't involve criminal behavior*, he thought.

"I'll need to talk with Adriana," Paula made clear.

"Be my guest." He shifted his weight to the other foot. "She just left. If you hurry, you can probably catch her..."

Before Paula could respond, all three of them received a text message on their cell phones. Neil regarded his and frowned as he favored Paula with a look of concern.

A bomb threat had been made at Addison University. More specifically, someone had claimed that pipe bombs had been planted at Horton Hall, the building they were currently standing in, set to detonate at any moment.

# Chapter Seven

With an active bomb threat at Addison University's Horton Hall, the building was ordered evacuated immediately. A lockdown went into effect at other buildings across campus as a safety measure. Paula had been through this before. More than once. Most times, it turned out to be a false alarm. A prank that was anything but funny. This did little to quell the tension in the air, thick as fog. In the post-9/11 era, nothing could ever be taken for granted when it came to potential terroristic activities.

Not knowing if a hidden bomb could explode at any time, Paula was admittedly on pins and needles as she, along with Neil and Roger Woodward, headed hastily toward the nearest exit, followed by others. A Regional Special Response Team, which included highly trained members from the DPPS, Rendall Cove PD, Shays County Sheriff's Department, and the Bureau of Alcohol, Tobacco, Firearms and Explosives, stormed past them and entered Horton Hall tactically. They were prepared for anything they might find in trying to defuse the situation.

"Let them do their job," Neil told her firmly, as Paula had fought her instincts to want to go back inside to be in on the action in confronting the threat on campus. She knew he was right in leaving this to the RSRT.

"I will," she promised smartly, as they moved away from the building and behind barricades that had been set up. Paula took note that Roger Woodward and other students were being escorted by law enforcement to a location that had been cleared. "So, what's your take on Woodward?" she asked Neil, though having already sensed that he believed she was barking up the wrong tree with him as a suspect.

"Well, he's one of my best students. But that doesn't make him incapable of being a serial killer." Neil brushed up against her and Paula felt it down to her toes. "I don't see that here, honestly. Especially if his alibi for the first suffocation murder held up."

She considered this. "Woodward said he was at the school library at the time. A number of other students who were there verified this, more or less, though surveillance video from the library was unable to substantiate this conclusively," Paula pointed out.

"I don't see other students covering for him intentionally," Neil said doubtfully. "That includes his alibi for the latest campus killing, Adriana Tilly."

"The girlfriend student of yours," she stated knowingly.

"Afraid so." He gave her a plain look.

"I'll see if she will corroborate his story."

"If not, we'll go from there…"

Paula nodded. She liked the *we* in his words, knowing that beyond being a visiting professor, his loyalties lay with helping them get to the bottom of their serial killer investigation. Wherever it took them, on campus or off.

She lifted her eyes to his face. "Do you think this bomb threat could have anything to do with the Campus Killer case?"

Neil turned to her. "Doesn't seem likely. What would the unsub gain by diverting attention from the serial killer probe only temporarily, especially since this would be under a different set of investigators. Unless the connections put us all under the same tent in terms of a serial killer bomber."

"I was thinking the same thing," Paula told him. "We certainly wouldn't be scared off in pursuing our mission till completed, even if there were a bomber on campus. Still, it's odd that the latest threat should manifest itself at this moment in time."

"Can't argue with you there," Neil said. "But it happens. Let's just see what the RSRT comes up with, if anything."

As the situation remained tense for the next hour, they were approached by RSRT Lieutenant Corey Chamberlain. In full uniform, the tall, brawny, fortysomething man had gray hair in a military undercut. His blue eyes were narrowed as he uttered, "We located two crude homemade pipe bombs hidden on the lower level. Both have been successfully deactivated and removed from the building."

"Wow." Paula's mouth hung open for a moment at the thought of someone being killed had the bombs exploded in their presence. Herself and Neil included. "Could there be more bombs inside?"

"I don't think so," Chamberlain said. "We've done a sweep twice and come up empty, insofar as any more pipe bombs."

"What do you know, if anything, about the bomber?" Neil asked him, brows knitted.

"Still working on that. The threat was posted online to two social media sites—as if to ensure we didn't miss it." Chamberlain jutted his chin. "These were traced back to a computer in the university's main library. We have investigators and technicians at the scene examining surveillance video and collecting forensic evidence, even as we speak."

"That's good," Paula commended him. "The unsub or unsubs cannot be allowed to get away with this."

"They won't," the lieutenant assured her. "Not on my watch."

"Be sure to keep us in the loop," Neil advised Chamberlain.

"Will do." He eyed them and said thoughtfully, "If you need to go back into Horton Hall, the evacuation order has been lifted."

Paula felt relieved to know that. She imagined this was even more true for Neil, given that it housed his classroom and office. As she watched Lieutenant Chamberlain move away from them to confer with his colleagues, Neil got on his cell phone, explaining, "I need to check in with the field office on this bomb incident."

"I understand," she told him, offering a tiny smile as he put a little distance between them. She wondered just how long it would be before he had vacated the visiting professorship and moved on to other ATF duties. The idea that whatever this was between them would be short-lived disturbed her. But she had no right to expect anything lasting. Did she?

When Paula's cell phone rang, she pulled it from the back pocket of her pants and saw that the caller was Mike Davenport. "Hey," she answered.

"Are you okay?"

"I'm fine. The situation has been neutralized."

"Glad to see that the all clear has been issued on campus," he remarked tentatively.

"Me too." Even so, Paula still felt unsettled for some reason, as if the proverbial shoe had yet to drop. "And no one got hurt, thankfully."

"Yeah. Unfortunately, we have another problem to deal with…" Davenport sighed. "Another female professor has been found dead—"

Paula's heart skipped a beat. "On campus?"

"Off," he replied tersely. "According to an officer on the scene, it looks like the same MO as the other victims of the Campus Killer."

She winced and got more info before disconnecting, only to find Neil standing right beside her. "What is it?" he asked perceptively.

Swallowing thickly, Paula told him soberly, "We have a new murder on our hands that is believed to be the work of the unsub serial killer."

THE CAMPUS KILLER celebrated his latest kill, while knowing full well that others would find it unsettling, if not downright horrific. He laughed to himself as he drove down the street, making sure he didn't go over the speed limit, drive erratically or otherwise give the cops a reason to pull him over. Were that the case, they just might be suspicious enough that he could be brought in and his carefully constructed life and living could well come tumbling down like dominoes.

Never mind the fact that he'd suffocated the good-looking professor hours ago. More than enough time to have put some distance between himself and the scene of the crime.

She had been taken by surprise. Or he made it seem that way when accosting her and allowing a very false sense of security. Could he help it if she should have known not to trust anyone? Especially right now with a serial killer on the prowl.

But, like the others, she had played right into his hands like putty. And he had been more than willing to act accordingly in seeing it through. Right up until her breathing had ceased entirely and her days of teaching pesky students had come to an end. Then, like clockwork, he had left his magnificent handiwork behind for others to discover.

The Campus Killer turned left at the light, heading back onto the campus grounds—where he felt just as much at home as off campus. It made for an interesting mix while he plied his murderous trade and got away with it like this had been his destiny all along. Made him almost drool for more pretty professors to come into his grasp, before discovering there was no escape but death itself. And who knew who else might capture his fancy while he was in the mood for killing?

DETECTIVE GAYLE YAMASAKI drove her blue Ford Escape down the tree-lined Pickford Road, fretting over both the pipe bomb incident on campus and the more disturbing news that a woman had been found dead. All initial signs pointed toward this being a homicide—with the indicators sounding the Campus Killer alarm, as the victim was identified as another Addison University professor.

*This can't be happening*, Gayle told herself, even in the face of knowing otherwise. She had contacted Paula and Mike Davenport to this effect, warning them of the situation and agreeing to meet at the scene. Gayle pulled into the strip mall on the corner of Fulmore Street. It included a convenience store, dentist's office, shoe store and hair salon. She spotted two patrol cars, lights flashing, parked haphazardly. A male and female officer were talking to a young woman. Eyeing a corner of the small parking lot, Gayle saw that beneath an oak tree was a red Nissan Altima. A lone occupant was inside, behind the steering wheel.

After parking, Gayle checked the Smith and Wesson M&P 5.7 pistol in her custom Kydex holster and got out, approaching the officers. She flashed her identification and said, "Detective Yamasaki. What do we have?"

The twentysomething biracial female officer, who was around Gayle's height of five-five, with a black Afro puff hairstyle and brown eyes, responded glumly, "A female is deceased inside a vehicle. It appears as if she was the victim of foul play."

Gayle nodded perceptively. "We have a name?"

The male officer, who towered over them both, was in his thirties and had raven hair in a crew cut fade style and blue eyes. He answered, "Ran a make on the license plate of the Nissan Altima. It's registered to a Laurelyn Wong."

Gayle nodded and walked over to the car. The driver's side door was open. Sitting there, with the seat belt strapped across her body and wearing a floral-print midi dress, was a slender and attractive Asian female with highlighted brunette hair in a digital perm. She looked to be in her early thirties. Her head was tilted slightly to the right, eyes closed in death. A trickle of blood came down from one nostril onto her face. There was a white cotton towel with bloodstains on it, lying messily atop presumably the victim's satchel bag on the passenger seat, to suggest it was the weapon used to suffocate the victim.

A chill ran through Gayle in that moment as she stared at the woman who could very well have been an Indigenous Polynesian person like herself—telling Gayle that her own number could have come up, under other dire circumstances. She turned bleakly toward the male officer, who glanced at the other woman standing by the female officer, and said, "According to the one who discovered the body, Ms. Wong is a music professor at the university."

Gayle approached the woman, who was older than she had first thought—perhaps midthirties—and petite, with long and multilayered ombré hair, and again identified herself, "Detective Yamasaki. And you are?"

"Jeanne Roth," she told her. "I own the Roth Salon—" she pointed toward the strip mall "—over there. Professor Wong had her hair done yesterday."

"At what time?" Gayle wondered.

"Around seven p.m." Jeanne's voice shook. "She left the salon just before we closed at eight."

"Did you see Professor Wong go to her car?" Gayle cast her eyes back at the vehicle. "And was she accompanied or followed by anyone?"

"She came and left the salon alone," Jeanne responded. "I never saw anyone following her..." She took a breath. "I closed up shop and didn't notice her car till I came in this afternoon. That's when I saw Professor Wong inside, not moving, and called 911."

Gayle looked up at a nearby surveillance camera, believing it could be key to ID'ing a suspect. But the female officer threw cold water on that when she told her, "Apparently, for whatever reason, that camera isn't operational right now."

"Figures." Gayle wrinkled her nose. She could only hope that there were security cameras in the shops on the streets that might provide useful information. As she pondered this, Gayle watched Mike Davenport drive up in his white Mustang Mach-E duty vehicle. He had arrived before Paula. "Hey," Gayle said calmly as she met him halfway, while ignoring the charge she got out of being in his presence.

"Hey." He met her eyes, then glanced at the victim's vehicle. "Where are we on this?" he asked tonelessly.

As she told him and got his initial thoughts, Gayle saw that Paula, accompanied by Neil, who was driving, had pulled up. Both were undoubtedly as disturbed as she was at this latest turn of events, coming after the pipe bomb scare at the college. Though she didn't believe the two were in any way connected, Gayle kept all possibilities on the table, so long as no one had been taken into custody for either criminal act.

THE VICTIM'S NAME, Laurelyn Wong, rang a bell in Neil's head. He'd heard it before. It took a moment or two before suddenly registering. According to ATF undercover agent Vinny Ortiz, the gunrunner they were investigating, Craig Eckart, had been living with Professor Laurelyn Wong. Now she was dead—in what was all but certain a homicide and fitting the MO of the Campus Killer—and Eckart had to be considered a suspect, all things being equal involving victims acquainted with their offenders. This definitely complicated the arms trafficking case being built against the suspect.

Neil didn't shy away from that when coming clean with Paula—once he had pulled her off to the side and away from the other detectives, crime scene technicians and the chief medical examiner, all who had a part to play in the investigation. "Professor Wong may have been killed by the gun trafficker who's currently under investigation by the ATF," he told her candidly.

"Seriously?" Paula frowned. "What am I missing?"

"Just that the suspect in our arms case, Craig Eckart, was romantically involved with the professor, which was told to me recently by an undercover agent." Neil dipped his chin. "Laurelyn Wong's name stuck in my memory."

"You think she may have been involved in gun trafficking?"

"I doubt it," he contended. "The romance was likely unassociated with the illegal weapons network. But with this latest twist, Eckart could also be moonlighting as a serial killer." Though Neil had strong doubts about that, especially since Ortiz was tracking the gunrunner's movements, they had to consider all possibilities in the serial killer probe. That included those closest to the victim being involved in her death.

Paula regarded him dubiously. "Please don't tell me you want us to look the other way, with your federal case taking priority over our local investigation?"

"Actually, it's just the opposite." Neil held her gaze without blinking. "I'd like you to stay the course in your investigation, while determining one way or the other, sooner than later, if Eckart is in fact the unsub. If not, you need to take him off the suspect list, so as not to impede our ongoing arms trafficking case."

She nodded. "Understood."

"In the meantime, the fewer people who know about Craig Eckart being the subject of a federal probe, the better," Neil thought to warn her. Not that he believed for one instant that Paula would do anything reckless to jeopardize their investigation. But the same might not be true for everyone working the Campus Killer case.

"I get it." Paula touched his arm and Neil felt the warmth radiate through the sleeve of his shirt. "I, for one, will do my best not to step on your toes, Agent Ramirez, where it concerns questioning Craig Eckart about the murder of his girlfriend."

"Okay." He flashed her a grin and got one back in return, giving Neil a good feeling inside and confidence that there was something between them that needed to be explored more thoroughly.

THE VISUAL OF the latest presumed victim of an unsub serial slayer gnawed at Paula like a hideous replay of a movie she wished would just go away, as she went with Gayle to the address on Vernon Drive, where Laurelyn Wong reportedly lived with her boyfriend, Craig Eckart. In respecting Neil's wishes that Eckart be treated as only a suspect in the Campus Killer case, while not revealing that he was also the primary person of interest under federal investigation for trafficking in contraband arms and ammunition, along with other firearms-related offenses, she kept this information to herself. Once the story broke, Gayle would learn about it from her department's Firearms Investigation Unit.

*If Eckart did murder Professor Wong and the other women, he would be held fully accountable, irrespective of the federal case against him*, Paula told herself determinedly, as they left the car. Passing by a silver Lincoln Navigator Reserve parked in the driveway, they headed up the walkway to the two-story American foursquare home to notify the next of kin or significant other about the professor's death.

"I hate these moments," Gayle remarked softly.

"Don't we all," Paula said, knowing that it came with the territory, no matter how painful it was having to upend the lives of the dead's loved ones. Only, in this instance, the victim's boyfriend could have more than one thing to hide in his grieving.

Gayle rang the bell, and there was the instant sound of a large dog barking inside, before it was told in a commanding voice to be quiet. A moment later, the door opened. Standing there was a tall and muscular man in his mid to late forties, with dark hair in a disheveled cut and a salt-and-pepper corporate beard.

He trained gray eyes on Paula and asked cautiously, "How can I help you?"

She showed him her ID while saying, "Detective Lynley, Investigative Division of the Department of Police and Public Safety at Addison University."

Gayle flashed her badge and said, "Detective Yamasaki, Rendall Cove PD. And you are…?"

He hesitated, then answered, "Craig Eckart. You want to tell me what this is about?"

"Maybe we should go inside," Paula suggested, while wondering if this was where he was storing the illegal weapons. As he contemplated this, she added, "It's about Laurelyn Wong… She does live here?"

"Yeah." His mouth pursed, ill at ease.

"And what is your relationship with Ms. Wong?" Paula asked for the record.

"I'm her partner," he said matter-of-factly.

Gayle peered at him. "Can we come in?"

He nodded. The moment they stepped through the door, Paula picked up the pungent odor of marijuana. She also noted the Staffordshire bull terrier, growling threateningly, standing on all fours on bamboo flooring beside a leather sectional in the great room. Before she or Gayle needed to react, both armed, Eckart claimed, "She's harmless."

"All the same, would you mind putting your dog in another room while we talk?" Paula demanded.

"If you say so." He snickered. "C'mon, girl."

As he led the dog away, Paula glanced around at the contemporary furnishings, which may have been a facade for a criminal enterprise being investigated by the ATF. Then there was the question of multiple murders that could lead right to Craig Eckart.

When he came back into the room, Eckart eyed them back and forth and spoke bluntly, "Laurelyn's dead, isn't she?"

Gayle glanced at Paula and responded straightforwardly, "Yes. She was found in her car in a strip mall parking lot early this afternoon." Gayle paused. "She was murdered..."

Eckart's broad shoulders slumped and an expletive escaped his lips. "By that Campus Killer?"

"The investigation into Ms. Wong's death is still ongoing," Paula responded simply. After a beat, she asked directly, "When did you last see her?"

He ran a hand roughly across his mouth. "Yesterday, around noon."

"That's more than twenty-four hours ago," Gayle pointed out. "Why didn't you report her missing?"

Paula knew that one could file a missing person report at any time, even if the authorities might take longer to act upon it, depending on the circumstances.

"Didn't think she was," he replied matter-of-factly. "We both have busy schedules and came and went as we pleased.

It wasn't unusual for us to miss one another during the course of our days—or nights."

Paula regarded him skeptically. "Do you mind telling us where you were last night between eight and nine?" she asked, knowing that Laurelyn was likely killed shortly after leaving the hair salon.

Eckart looked Paula directly in the eye while answering without preface, "I was at Rennie's Bar on Twenty-Second Street, having drinks with my buddy J. H. Santoro. We met there at seven and didn't leave till after midnight."

"Where can we reach this J. H. Santoro?" Gayle asked him.

"He's staying at an apartment complex on Yackley Road past Diamond Street. I have his number."

As Gayle added it to her cell phone, Paula considered digging deeper but, mindful of the arms case against him, thought better. Instead, she said evenly, "While we check out your alibi, we'll need you to come to the morgue to identify the body of Laurelyn Wong."

# Chapter Eight

"J. H. Santoro is the moniker of ATF undercover agent Vinny Ortiz," Neil informed Paula after he'd invited her over to his rented house for a nightcap and she'd brazenly accepted.

"Really?" She eyed Neil as they stood in the kitchen, both holding wineglasses half-filled with red wine. Its open concept provided a nice view of the downstairs and, from the pristine looks of it, it was clear that he spent little time there socializing. She wondered if the same were true in his permanent residence. Or was it more a matter of merely having the right reason to socialize—and the right person to do so with?

"Yeah," Neil told her. "And Ortiz confirmed that he did drink the night away with Craig Eckart at Rennie's Bar—pumping the arms trafficker for information to use to take him down."

"Well, apart from that, it looks like Eckart's off the hook, insofar as the murder of Laurelyn Wong," Paula said, tasting her drink. "And ostensibly this would extend as well to all the murders perpetrated by the unsub we're referring to as the Campus Killer."

"That's a solid deduction. It feeds into the theory that,

though the victims are likely being targeted by the unsub, the targeting, per se, may be more opportunity driven in a random way than the work of someone intimately acquainted with the victims." Neil sipped the wine. "This, in and of itself, would've put Eckart lower on the totem pole as the serial killer, with his girlfriend apparently the fifth victim of the unsub."

"I suppose, when you put it that way." Paula gave a little smile as Neil seemed totally in his element as an ATF special agent profiler. It made her wonder if he could ever give it up. Perhaps to become a full-time professor?

Neil grinned and said, "And what if I were to put it this way…" He lifted her chin and then kissed her solidly on the mouth. After she felt like she was floating on air, he pulled away. "What do you think?"

Paula touched her inflamed mouth and knew precisely what she was thinking. No reason to deny what she sensed they both wanted, over and beyond solving their criminal investigations. Gazing into his eyes, she responded honestly, "I'm thinking that I'd love to pick this up somewhere more comfortable."

"Such as?" he challenged her.

"Such as your bedroom." She took the bait. Why not?

"I was thinking the same thing," he uttered desirously. "Shall I lead the way?"

She took another sip of the wine, set it on the quartz island countertop and said bluntly, "Yes, please."

Neil smiled and kissed her again. "It would be my pleasure." He set down his drink and took her hand.

They headed up a central staircase to the second floor, passing by a couple of rooms down the hallway, before arriving at the primary suite. Stepping inside the spacious bedroom, they engaged in some more passionate kissing that left Paula breathless and wanting so much more. She backed away from Neil and scanned the room, taking in the mid-century modern furnishings and sash windows with Roman blinds. Her gaze landed squarely on the king-size platform bed with its fluffy pillows and navy patchwork quilt.

The thought of making love to Neil excited Paula beyond words, if the hot kisses between them were any indication. But that moment was also a realistic reawakening. Always responsible in her sexual practices, there was no reason to turn away from that now, no matter how strong the desire to have him. "Do you have protection?" she asked equably.

"Absolutely," Neil responded, as if anticipating the question. "I believe in better safe than sorry with sex too," he assured her with a straight face.

"Cool." She offered him a smile and watched as he disappeared into the bathroom and returned with the condom packet.

"Do I do this now?" Neil held it up. "Or later?"

Paula chuckled. "Uh, I think you can take your clothes off first."

He laughed. "Yeah, there is that."

She watched him set the packet atop a walnut nightstand and start to disrobe, as she did the same, feeling slightly self-conscious in the process. That went away for the most part as Paula reveled in checking out Neil's six-pack abs and the rest of his taut frame.

She hardly realized he was just as riveted on her till Neil commented, while giving Paula the once-over, "Has anyone ever told you just how gorgeous you are?"

Blushing, Paula admitted, "Not lately."

"Then I'm saying it," he declared. "You are stunning... and perfect, all of you."

"Back at you," she assured him, gazing at him from head to toe and in between.

They bridged the gap and resumed kissing, before making their way to the bed, where more intimacy followed with sizzling foreplay. When she could stand it no more, Paula cooed, "Make love to me, Neil..."

"Are you sure you're ready?"

"Oh, yes, I'm definitely ready for you," she declared.

"Then why wait a second longer," he uttered in a raspy voice, kissing her passionately again.

After Neil put on the condom, Paula waited with bated breath as he made his way between her legs, and she took him in whole, meeting him two-thirds of the way with each deep thrust into her. Their bodies pressed together and heartbeats were in sync as Paula felt the orgasm course through her in rapid fashion, moaning as she quivered with delight. She clung to Neil while he followed suit shortly thereafter, his body quaking as his own powerful release manifested itself wildly.

When it was over, their sexual appetites satiated through their actions and the invigorating scent of intimacy left behind, Paula rested her head on Neil's chest. She gushed, "Wow. That was amazing!"

He laughed. "It was, wasn't it?"

She blushed. "Yeah, truly."

"Some things in life have a predictable outcome," he suggested. "This was definitely one of them."

Paula giggled at his confidence. "Oh, you think so, do you?"

"I saw the sparks between us early on," Neil maintained.

"It was just a matter of letting the flames erupt, sizzle, or whatever."

"How poetic," she said with a chuckle but couldn't disagree, having felt the connection too practically from the moment they first laid eyes on one another. But now that the spell had been broken, where did they go from here? If anywhere?

He laughed. "You bring the poet out in me, Paula, what can I say?"

She could think of a few things, but perhaps it was best not to delve too deeply in what this could mean potentially. Realizing the time, she separated from him and said, "I have to go."

"So soon?" Neil frowned. "I was hoping we might make a night of it—continuing this carnal exploration."

"Hmm... I'd love to," she admitted, climbing off the bed, "but I need to go feed my cat."

Neil sat up. "You have a cat?"

"Yep, her name's Chloe. She gets pretty ornery when she's hungry."

"I know the feeling. Need some help?" He eyed her body devilishly.

Paula got past the self-consciousness, knowing full well he liked what he saw, and then some. "Feeding the cat?"

"Sure." He grinned sideways. "I'm pretty good with my hands."

"That you are." She laughed thoughtfully. "You're welcome to come and help feed Chloe. Or whatever," she added, leaving the door open for whatever might come next.

NEIL FOLLOWED PAULA to her penthouse condo, eager to check out her place and extend the time they got to spend together. He was admittedly still caught up in the after-glow of the mind-blowing sex they had earlier. Though confident they would click in that department, the proof was very much in the pudding, as both had measured up beyond his expectations. It made him wonder where this thing was headed. Could she see a future with him? Could he see one with her?

What Neil knew for certain was that he wanted more than one quick romp where Paula was concerned. Beyond that, he was certainly willing to keep a very open mind as to what may lay in store for them once his time as a visiting professor had run its course.

Once they reached the condominium and went inside, Paula said, waving her arms around, "Well, here we are."

"I love it," Neil told her, sizing up the condo and the furnishings that seemed a perfect fit.

"Thanks." She smiled. "Make yourself at home while I give Chloe something to eat."

"Allow me," he insisted, figuring this was a good way to score points with Paula by warming up to her cat. He spotted Chloe wandering along the baseboard as though lost. Neil enticed the cat to come his way and scooped her into his arms. He gently rubbed her head and ears. "I'm Neil," he said lightheartedly. "Let's get you fed and content for the night."

"Looks like she's warming up to you in a hurry," Paula said with amusement.

Neil grinned. "I have that effect on—" he was about to say people, or her, in particular, but changed course mid-sentence "—cute, furry felines."

She laughed. "I can see that."

After feeding the cat, Neil turned his attention to Paula,

and vice versa, as they made their way upstairs to her bedroom and upholstered farmhouse bed for another round of sexual relations. Only this time, without the sense of urgency, Neil was able to more slowly explore Paula's beautiful face and every inch of her body, giving her the same courtesy with him, as they made love into the wee hours of the night, before sleep and sheer exhaustion overtook them.

In the morning, Neil awakened from a bad dream about a killer running amok using illegal firearms. He didn't get a look at the unsub's face, but he was certain that the nightmare was a confluence of the Campus Killer meets the gunrunner, Craig Eckart. Only the two weren't one and the same in real life, Neil knew. Meaning that both cases were still open and needed to be successfully brought to a close, with the perps taken into custody.

When turning over and expecting to find Paula, naked, hot and still bothered, instead Neil saw that her spot beneath the covers was empty. He got up, slipping on his pants that had made their way onto the wood flooring, and looked for her.

He found her downstairs in the kitchen, where his nostrils picked up the scent of cooked sausage, before Neil saw Paula fully dressed and making breakfast.

"Hey," she said, offering a smile. "Hope you like blueberry pancakes and sausage, to go with coffee?"

"Absolutely to all." He smiled back, walked up to her in his bare feet and kissed her. "But most of all, I like you." He made no bones about it.

"I like you too." She beamed. "So, let's eat and we can talk about our plans for today."

"Okay. Let me go put on the rest of my clothes and I'm all yours."

Her lashes fluttered while standing over the griddle. "We'll see about that."

Though his words may have been a metaphor, Neil felt they had a good ring to them nevertheless and he was beginning to take them quite literally. In spite of not knowing if they both had what it took to see it through, for better or worse.

IN HER OFFICE, Paula pushed past thoughts of last night's red-hot sex with Neil or whether or not she was falling in love with the ATF special agent—and instead focused on the autopsy report on her laptop on Laurelyn Wong's death. As expected, the Shays County Chief Medical Examiner Eddie Saldana ruled this as a homicide. Similar to the other homicides thought to be perpetrated by the Campus Killer, the cause of the associate professor of music education's death was asphyxia. The time of death was believed to be between 8:00 p.m. and 10:00 p.m. A towel left at the crime scene was thought to be the murder weapon.

*I'm sorry you had to die this way,* Paula thought, knowing that Laurelyn Wong, like the other victims, had plans for her life. Now these had been squelched permanently by a cold-blooded killer who decided their lives were not worth living.

But who was the unsub? With Laurelyn's lover, Craig Eckart, ruled out, it brought Paula back to Neil's student, Roger Woodward. He had alibis for the murders of two of his professors, Debra Newton and Odette Furillo. But Paula had yet to check out his alibi for Professor Wong's murder. Was he enrolled in Laurelyn Wong's music class?

Pulling up Woodward's class schedule, Paula did not see him as a student of Laurelyn's. She checked the last semester and got the same result. Similarly, there was no information that directly linked the honors student to professors Harmeet Fernández or Kathy Payne. But did that mean he was innocent? Or a clever serial killer, above and beyond an obviously bright senior?

AT THE SCHOOL OF CRIMINAL JUSTICE, Neil sat in the conference room with the other faculty and two teaching assistants, Desmond Isaac and Rachelle Kenui. Director Stafford Geeson, the former police chief of Mackinac Island, Michigan, had convened the hastily arranged meeting to talk about the pipe bombs discovered in the building yesterday.

Geeson, who was fifty-five and thickly built, with slicked-back gray hair and a receding hairline, stood in front of the room and shifted his blue eyes as he said earnestly, "I'm sure everyone here knows about the bomb incident that took place on the ground floor of Horton Hall. Though the Regional Special Response Team was able to locate the pipe bombs and deactivate them before they could explode, it's still troubling that this happened on campus—and in this building, in particular." His chin sagged. "As of now, the perpetrator or perpetrators remain at large. Till apprehended, I'm asking everyone who works for the School of Criminal Justice to be extra diligent in looking out for anyone acting suspicious. The directors of the other departments in this building are telling staff the same thing. And if you know anyone who might have a beef against someone in Horton Hall or the university itself, don't hesitate to bring this to my attention or the authorities."

Geeson took a breath and, eyeing Neil, said, "As our resident criminal profiler, Professor Ramirez, I'm hoping you can maybe shed some light on the pipe bomber and what's behind this terroristic attack on the campus."

Neil said evenly, "Sure, I can shed a bit of light on the subject." He had anticipated he might be called upon in this manner. Standing, he walked to the front of the room, got a pat on the shoulder from the director, and then Neil got right to it, saying thoughtfully, "Well, without being privy to the specifics about the current case, my general view on bomber unsubs is that they tend to be narcissists who choose to use fear tactics such as a bomb threat to get attention and/or cause death and destruction as a matter of retaliation for perceived wrongs against them. Or to make a statement of one type or another.

"Though they are often loners," he explained, "and obviously antisocial, some are paranoid schizophrenics, while others are mentally sound but still willing to involve themselves in abnormal behavior for reasons aforementioned. We'll have to see which way the pendulum swings in this instance."

Desmond asked, "So, are we talking about a student or ex-student bomber with a grudge against the school or a professor?"

Neil peered at him. "Is there something you want to confess to us, Isaac?" he asked the TA lightheartedly.

"Not that I can think of," Desmond said with a chuckle.

"Just checking." Neil flashed a crooked grin. "As for whether or not the unsub is a current or former student, that's a distinct possibility. But—" he felt it needed to be emphasized "—the perp could also be an employee or ex-worker at the university. As well as someone who has no connection at all, but found the campus location attractive and had the means to both use the library to announce the bomb threat and deliver the pipe bombs, while managing to get away."

"Sounds very much like the Campus Killer," Rachelle Kenui remarked. The twentysomething TA was thin, green-eyed and had short wheat-blond hair in a mullet cut. "Could they be one and the same?"

"Anything's possible," Neil stated. "Generally speaking, though, unless we're talking about a serial bomber, heaven forbid, the profiles of a single incident bomber and serial killer do not usually measure up. As for the school bomber, hopefully we'll get a better idea of who—and what—we're looking for once forensics has examined the pipe bombs for DNA, prints, etc."

After a little more insight into the bombing incident, the meeting broke up and Neil headed to his office to prepare for his next class. Even with the current uneasiness on campus, given the unusual criminal activity of late, he wanted to keep the classes as normal as possible for his students, in spite of Neil knowing that this would be next to impossible. As long as a serial killer and pipe bomber remained on the loose.

## Chapter Nine

Paula walked down the fifth-floor corridor in the Acklin Residence Hall on Wells Lane. Along the way, she passed a group of giggling female students, before reaching Room 557. The door was open, and Paula could see a slender young woman with multicolored long hair, standing while looking at her cell phone. A knock got her attention. "Are you Adriana Tilly?"

"Yes, I'm Adriana." She put the phone in the back pocket of her jeans.

Paula stepped inside the cluttered two-person room and showed her identification. "Detective Lynley. I'm investigating the murder of Honors College Associate Professor Odette Furillo. Mind if I ask you a few questions…?"

Adriana arched a thin brow worriedly. "You think I had something to do with that?"

"I'm sure you didn't," Paula responded, giving her the benefit of the doubt. "A name that's come up in the investigation is of one of Professor Furillo's students—Roger Woodward. Do you know him?" she asked for effect.

Her blue eyes grew wide. "Yes. Roger's my boyfriend."

"He says that he was with you the night Professor Furillo

was killed," Paula said, giving her the date and time frame. "I need you to verify his alibi."

Adriana wasted little time doing just that. "Yes, Roger was with me the entire night," she confirmed unabashedly.

Paula gave her a direct look. "You're sure about that?"

"Yes." She paused before adding, "Roger would never kill anyone. Certainly not one of his professors."

*Maybe you don't know your boyfriend as well as you think*, Paula thought, aware that denial was often the order of the day when someone you were close to was suspected of murder. "Had to ask as part of my job," she told her. While at it, for the record, Paula thought to ask if Woodward was with her when Professor Laurelyn Wong was killed. Adriana claimed calmly that he was.

With no real reason to dispute this, Paula went with that and saw herself out. It appeared as if Neil's student, Roger Woodward, was not their Campus Killer. Which meant that the hunt to unmask and apprehend the unsub was still on.

At 4:00 p.m., Neil pulled his car up behind Agent Vinny Ortiz's Jeep Wagoneer on Quail Lane in Rendall Creek Park. Ortiz, aka J. H. Santoro as his undercover handle, had requested the meeting to discuss the latest developments in the arms trafficking investigation. For his part, Neil was curious as to whether the murder of suspected gunrunner Craig Eckart's girlfriend, Laurelyn Wong, had changed the dynamics of the case any.

Ortiz exited the Jeep and made his way to the passenger side of Neil's Chevy Suburban, where Ortiz muttered, "Thanks for meeting with me on short notice."

Neil regarded him. "What's up?"

"Not sure," the undercover agent said flatly. "With the

death of Eckart's girlfriend, Laurelyn, at the hands purport-edly of a serial killer, it's kind of freaking the man out."

"How so?" Neil hesitated to ask.

"Well, apparently Eckart feels it's bad karma that some-one he had a thing for has been murdered. He's wondering if it's trying to tell him something."

"Such as?"

"If he has an X on his own back," Ortiz said bluntly. "Though Eckart was glad we happened to be hanging out at a bar together the night she was killed, he believes Laure-lyn's death is a sign that he needs to put his plans for arms trafficking into a higher gear—so that he can get rich and maybe get out of the business."

"That so?" Neil didn't see that happening of his own free will, karma or not. For most traders of contraband small arms and ammo—especially when operating on the dark web—the money they could make and perceived lower risk of detection made the illicit activities almost addictive. He doubted it was something Craig Eckart could easily walk away from, even though someone had murdered his girl-friend. Neil gazed at the ATF agent. "What do you think?"

Ortiz shrugged. "I don't see him calling it quits. He's got too nice of an operation going. Or so he thinks. But I do believe that Eckart is even more suspicious that he's being set up. Meaning, I have to go even deeper undercover to protect myself, without stepping over the line."

"Do what you need to do," Neil advised him. "Be smart about it. We can get you help whenever you need it."

"I'll keep that in mind." Ortiz scratched his beardstache. "I think things are about to go down. When it happens, I'll be sure to get the word out so we can nail this bastard. Hopefully, before any more illegal weapons can change hands, in this country or abroad."

"The team will be ready to pounce," Neil assured, wanting this to be over almost as much as Ortiz did.

Ortiz tilted his face with curiosity. "So, with Laurelyn yet another victim, are you any closer to getting the jump on the Campus Killer?"

Neil furrowed his forehead. "I'd like to think we're closing in on the unsub with each and every hour," he responded, his voice steady and thoughtful. "But that's not exactly the same as knowing who we're dealing with and having him locked up behind bars, is it?"

"No, it isn't." Ortiz sighed. "You'll get the perp. He can't go on killing professors forever and not have to face the music for his crimes."

"I'm thinking the same thing." Neil squirmed. "Not much consolation, though, for those who fall prey to the unsub." This told him that the task force needed to step up even more than they already were, if this meant sparing the lives of other professors that could come within the unsub's viewfinder.

"Talk to you soon," Ortiz said succinctly.

Neil nodded. "Yeah."

After Ortiz drove off, Neil followed suit and once again found himself weighing his options on what to do with the rest of his life beyond his current caseload. Was he truly cut out for being a full-time educator? Or was being an ATF special agent and behavioral profiler too much in his blood to ever truly want to walk away from?

Then there was Paula. She had come into his life practically out of the blue. And just at a time when he wasn't sure he would ever again click with a woman who could

earn his trust. She had already passed both tests with fly-
ing colors. But would he be enough to check all the boxes
she had for a workable relationship, after falling short in
her marriage to another man who made his living in federal law enforcement?

Neil knew that whatever decisions he made could well
rest on how he fared on Paula's litmus test or desire to carry
on with what they had started.

ON WEDNESDAY AFTERNOON, the latest task force briefing
took place at the Rendall Cove Police Department. Gayle
stood alongside Paula at the podium in the conference room,
knowing that all eyes were on them as they had to give the
highlights and lowlights of the investigation now that yet another victim had been added to the list of those targeted by
the Campus Killer. This was starting to get old in a hurry,
Gayle felt, sure that Paula concurred. But this was where
they were and they had to put on their best faces in meeting the challenge head-on.

Holding the stylus pen, Gayle turned to the large monitor and brought up the image of the latest victim to die at
the hands of an unsub. "Two nights ago, Laurelyn Wong, a
thirty-two-year-old music professor, was murdered in her
vehicle, after having her hair done at a salon on Fulmore
Street," Gayle reported. "According to the autopsy report,
Professor Wong's death was due to asphyxia, with the murder weapon being a cotton towel. It was the same cause of
death attributed to four other female professors at Addison
University. Though the investigation is well underway and
we're looking at each and every angle here, as of now, the
killer remains at large…"

Gayle swallowed as she looked at the man in charge of

the Detective Bureau, Criminal Investigations Sergeant Anderson Klimack. At fifty-five and solid in build beneath his uniform, with short, tapered brown-gray hair parted to the side and blue eyes, he was bucking to become lieutenant. She was sure that putting this case behind the bureau would help him make his case for the promotion.

Averting his stare, while feeling the pressure, Gayle made a few more comments, before turning it over to Paula, who gave her a supportive little smile and then said in a serious tone, "Losing another professor to a senseless murder is something none of us wanted to hear. Much less have to investigate. But a cold and calculating serial killer has reared his ugly head again in targeting the popular music professor Laurelyn Wong. In the process, the unsub has put us on notice that he has no intention of ending the killing of professors off and on campus—not till we stop him."

After going over the victims again, locations of the murders and efforts to gather forensic evidence and surveillance video on the latest homicide as with the earlier deaths, Gayle and Paula took turns laying out the investigative efforts. Neither sought to sugarcoat the frustrations within the task force in its inability to solve the case as yet. But both insisted that this made them even more determined to do just that—whatever it took.

Davenport and another investigator from the Detective Bureau, Larry Coolidge, a tall and bald-headed five-year veteran of the PD, provided additional updates; then Neil pitched in with observations, while doing his best to try and put the Campus Killer case into proper perspective by stating coolly, "Undoubtedly, losing five women in the prime of their lives to a serial killer is almost too much to bear for all of us. But, just to be clear, the number of victims thus far pales to those killed by such serial monsters as Samuel Little, who murdered at least sixty women over several decades, Gary Ridgway, convicted of forty-nine murders, Juan Corona, found guilty of killing twenty-five. Even the infamous female serial killer, Belle Gunness, claimed at least fourteen victims. Or, in other words, we have time to stop the perp long before he can reach these goals as a serial killer."

To Gayle—and she read as much in Paula's expression—this was something to keep in mind as further motivation to prevent the unsub from joining the ranks of these killers in their bloodthirsty appetite for murder.

THAT NIGHT, Paula slept in Neil's bed, where the two recreated the first time they made love. Only this occasion was more thorough, demanding, fervent and, yes, all-consuming. Neither seemed to want it to end. At least this was how Paula read the passion. Could she have mistaken Neil's body language for anything other than being just as intoxicated by the experience?

When they were totally spent and gratified, she laid in his arms, with neither saying a word. For her part, Paula hesitated sharing her thoughts for fear of having her heart broken. Telling someone you were starting to fall in love with them could backfire, she believed. Especially if it was not reciprocated by a person who likely wouldn't be around much longer. She wondered if there was any wiggle room in the special agent's future plans. Or were they set in stone, and he had no desire to start a relationship he couldn't finish?

IN THE MORNING, they got up early for a run in the park. Had it been up to Neil, he would have let Paula get more sleep and gone it alone. Between the passionate lovemaking and restlessness from the stresses associated with tracking a serial killer, neither had gotten much shut-eye. But she had been insistent upon joining him, having kept jogging clothes in her car for that purpose.

If the truth be told, Neil welcomed her company, as Paula was growing on him in ways that he could never have anticipated fully upon coming to Rendall Cove. Last night only reinforced that. Having someone to open his heart to again excited him. He could tell that the feeling was mutual. But there was still the matter of what it all meant for the future. And if their relationship had what it took to survive the criminal investigations that brought them together.

The run was mostly silent, aside from the chirping sounds of black-capped chickadees in the woods. After taking turns racing ahead of the other, Neil broke the ice by asking perceptively, "What's on your mind?"

Paula faced him and said point-blank, "You...and wondering where this—" she pointed her finger at him and then herself "—is going. Or do you even know?"

He took a breath. "I'm wondering the same thing," he admitted, following with, "Honestly, I haven't a clue."

"That's helpful," she said sarcastically.

"Not sure what you expect me to say." He stiffened. "I care for you, Paula. I'm sure you know that. I think that we have something here." Another pause came. "I'm just not sure how things will play out once my time at the university is up. Are you?" If she had a concrete plan for them, he was certainly ready to listen.

Paula sucked in a deep breath. "No, not really," she confessed.

"So why don't we just go with the flow and see how

things turn out?" Neil put forth. He hoped he wasn't backing her into a corner so she wanted to end things between them prematurely.

"All right." She favored him with a convivial smile. "We'll do that."

"Good." *That tells me she wants this to work as much as I do*, he told himself. This gave Neil hope that they were truly on the same wavelength. Even if the future was still very much up in the air. But at least it had given them a sense of direction that neither could turn away from.

WHEN THEY ARRIVED back at his house, Paula was still pondering the prospects for making a life with Neil. Or not. With much dependent upon who would be willing to sacrifice the most in making this work between them. Selfishly, she would love to see him stay in Rendall Cove as a professor. But was that even feasible? Could she handle giving up her job, if it came right down to it, in the name of love? Or would she be falling into an old pattern with predictable results?

Her reverie was broken while they were in the kitchen making breakfast—French toast, orange juice and coffee— when both their cell phones rang at the same time. Paula grabbed hers first and saw that the caller was Mike Davenport. "Hey," she answered.

"If you're by the television, you might want to put on the news to see what's about to break."

As she was hanging up with Davenport, she saw that Neil had been told the same thing, as he had already stepped inside the living room and was holding the TV remote, turning the set on. Joining him, Paula watched the flat-screen LCD television as an attractive red-haired female news anchor was saying animatedly, "An arrest has been made in connection with the pipe bombs found two days ago at Horton Hall on the campus of Addison University." An image of a dark-haired, grim-faced young man appeared on the screen. "According to sources, taken into custody was Harold Fujisawa—a twenty-two-year-old former student at the university. The global history major, who was reportedly expelled from school last year because of unspecified threats made, was arrested without incident outside a café on Long Street in Shays County."

Neil cut the TV off and, with his brow furrowed, uttered, "Looks like we've nipped one headache in the bud."

"Hope so." Paula wrinkled her nose thoughtfully. The arrest of the pipe bomb suspect was certainly a relief. "The university doesn't need a disgruntled ex-student resorting to terrorism to settle a score."

"Tell me about it." Neil met her eyes. "Nor does it need a serial killer run amok. But that will be dealt with too."

She nodded agreeably. "Not soon enough."

"I'm with you." He put his hands on her shoulders, pulling them closer. "In more ways than one."

"Same here," she promised him, resolving not to look too far ahead while still trying to sort out feelings and happenings between them in present terms.

When Neil dipped his head and kissed her, Paula returned the kiss in full, enjoying the firmness of his mouth upon hers and the overall way it made her feel.

Minutes later, they returned to the kitchen and the French toast, ate the breakfast and talked about the crimes being investigated, while avoiding discussing things best left off the table for the time being.

## Chapter Ten

That morning, Neil attended a Regional Special Response Team briefing in a Shays County Sheriff's Department conference room. The subject matter was the pipe bomb terrorist attack on the Addison University campus. Neil was all ears in wanting to know just how they identified and took down the suspect. Just as important was whether or not the perp could have been involved in the suffocation murders of female professors.

RSRT Lieutenant Corey Chamberlain was at the podium, giving the update. "As you know by now, at approximately seven twenty-nine a.m. today, we made an arrest in relation to the pipe bombs planted at the university. The suspect is Harold Fujisawa, who was kicked out of the school at the junior level last fall, due to making threats against faculty in the College of Social Science, where he was enrolled, after he was caught cheating on exams. Though there were no formal charges filed, Fujisawa, twenty-two, had been on our radar ever since.

"We were able to link him to the computer used at the school library to post bomb threats on social media through forensic analysis and surveillance video," Chamberlain said. "Once identified, we located the suspect—who was apparently living on the streets these days—at the Creekside Café. We waited for him to emerge before placing Harold Fujisawa under arrest. He made a full confession, blaming his actions on an addiction to the so-called zombie drug, Xylazine. Mr. Fujisawa is being charged with a number of federal offenses related to the manufacturing and possession of an explosive device, planting two pipe bombs on university property and more…" The lieutenant took a breath. "As of now, we believe the suspect acted alone."

Neil was confident that Harold Fujisawa would no longer pose a threat to Addison University or the city at large. But it still begged another important question that needed to be answered. "What can you tell us about the suspect's DNA and prints in relation to any other crimes?" Neil asked interestedly.

Chamberlain ran a hand across his face and responded, "We collected a sample of Fujisawa's DNA, along with fingerprinting him. The DNA was put into CODIS to check for a match. Unfortunately, it came back negative."

*Or, in other words, Fujisawa's DNA was not a match for the unknown DNA profile taken from beneath the nails of a victim of the Campus Killer,* Neil told himself, which corresponded with his feelings that the serial killer and pipe bomber were likely two different perpetrators. "And the prints?"

Chamberlain frowned perceptively. "The suspect doesn't have a criminal history to work with. So, no fingerprints on file and verified as such through the Michigan Automated Fingerprint Identification System."

Which, Neil knew, corresponded with the FBI and Homeland Security AFIS. Meaning that Harold Fujisawa almost certainly wasn't at the crime scenes of the murdered professors, with no match to any of the finger and palm prints collected and entered into the databases.

As such, his attention as a profiler had to be refocused on an unsub in the search for the Campus Killer. Neil thought about Paula, who had left his rented house shortly after breakfast. He believed they had turned the corner somewhat in their relationship, even if neither of them knew precisely what road they were headed down. Or how long it might take to get there. But at this point, he would take any positive development in terms of building something together, which he felt ready for at this point. He could only hope she would not let her own past romance drama stand in the way of what they could potentially have.

PAULA STOOD ON the deck, observing Canada geese huddled together by the creek, as she called her former sister-in-law, Madison. They had stayed in touch as real friends, in spite of Paula's divorce from her brother, Scott.

When Madison came onto the small screen, her bold turquoise eyes lit up, surrounded by an attractive face and long blond hair worn in a shaggy wolf cut with curly bangs. "Hey, there," she said sweetly.

"Hey." Paula grinned, noting that Madison was in uniform as a full-time law enforcement ranger in the Blue Ridge Mountains of North Carolina. She had recently gotten married to a National Park Service Investigative Services Branch special agent. "How's life treating you these days in the ranger's world?"

"Good. Rarely a dull moment on and off the Blue Ridge Parkway," Madison told her, referencing the 469-mile National Scenic Byway that meandered through North Carolina and Virginia. "Keeps me on my toes. What's up with you?"

"Well, besides investigating a serial killer on campus and surviving a bomb threat in one piece—" Paula pretended like they were merely run-of-the-mill occurrences "—I've met someone," she ventured forth. She felt comfortable sharing this with her, knowing Madison had encouraged her to move on past Scott.

"As if a serial killer and bomber aren't enough to deal with, right?" Madison made a face. "We'll get back to that. So, who have you met and it's about time…?"

"His name is Neil Ramirez," Paula told her. "Neil's an ATF special agent who's currently a visiting professor at the university."

"Hmm…" Madison widened her eyes with curiosity. "Interesting. Tell me more."

Paula did just that, while not getting carried away in her fondness for the man. Or what may or may not be in store for them. Only that they got along well and liked one another. "We'll see how it goes," she finished with, resisting the urge to admit she hoped it could go as far as possible between two people attracted to one another.

"I'm definitely pulling for you," Madison promised. "You deserve to be happy. We all do."

"Thanks, Madison." Paula knew she was referring to her ex as well and had no problem with that, wishing him the happiness that had eluded them over the long term. She told Madison a bit more about her current investigation before hanging up.

After setting out food for Chloe, Paula headed off to work.

IN THE AFTERNOON, Neil had the pleasure of having not one, but two teaching assistants in Desmond Isaac and Rachelle Kenui on hand to pass out the essay exams in the Auditorium on Slane Drive, where Neil taught a class in criminology to a captive audience of students. He was optimistic that they would be able to keep their eyes on the ball, as it were, even in the midst of some of the unsettling events happening on campus of late.

Handing Desmond and Rachelle a batch of the exams, Neil joked, "Think you two can handle this very tough assignment and earn your stripes?"

Rachelle giggled. "Can't speak for Desmond here, but I believe I'm more than up to the task."

Desmond gave a little laugh. "It's going to be challenging, I admit," he quipped, "but I'll just have to push myself harder and not quit before I get started."

Neil chuckled. "Figured I could count on you both." He grabbed more of the exams from his briefcase. "So, let's do this before my class thinks they'll get lucky and get a free pass here, or a delayed exam. Not happening."

"Not on our watch," Rachelle agreed, flashing her teeth.

Desmond looked at her and said, "As Prof Ramirez said, let's get this over with, and we can have fun watching them sweat it out while seeing if they've learned anything."

"They better have," she voiced in earnest.

Neil eyed the two TAs as they headed toward the students seated throughout the lecture hall. He suspected that Rachelle and Desmond may have started dating. Whether this meant they had a future together was anyone's guess. Neil was more concerned about his own relationship with Paula and if the love he was feeling for her was the real deal. If so, he didn't want to blow it with her. But he did have his career to think about too. As did she as a campus detective sergeant. Was there enough room in their lives for each other when all was said and done?

PAULA WAS IN her office going over notes on the Campus Killer case when the Addison University alert came in, reporting a suspected armed robbery near the Communication Arts and Sciences Building on Rafton Street. The suspect was described by the female victim as a tall, slender and blue-eyed female in her early twenties, wearing dark clothes and a hoodie that was still able to expose curly crimson hair beneath. Patrol officers had been dispatched to the location, with the unsub having fled the scene and still at large.

*Hmm, that's not too far from here*, Paula thought, getting up from her chair. Maybe she could help nail the culprit, even if it was a distraction from her current investigation. She checked the SIG Sauer P365 semiautomatic pistol tucked in her concealment holster and then was out the door.

No sooner had she left the building and was about to hop into her car, when Paula spotted someone who resembled the unsub running north down the sidewalk. Trailing her, Paula narrowed the distance, while noting that the suspect appeared to be holding a pocketknife. *No match for a loaded gun*, Paula told herself.

Removing the semiautomatic pistol, she wasted no time barking orders to the suspect. "Stop! Drop the weapon!"

The young woman stopped on a dime and rounded on her. "This isn't what you think," she expressed, with the hood still covering her head.

"I've heard that line too many times," Paula said sardonically. "I'm Detective Lynley, campus police department. Drop the weapon—please—so I don't have to shoot you."

"Okay, I give up." She placed the knife on the sidewalk and pulled the hood down, revealing a cropped red pixie around a pretty heart-shaped face, and then raised her hands.

"Keep them raised!" While keeping the gun aimed, Paula

approached her carefully and ordered, "Turn around." The suspect obeyed and Paula removed chained handcuffs from a nylon handcuff holster attached to her waistband on the back side and, twisting the suspect's arms around, quickly cuffed her. "So, what's your name?"

"Nikki Simone."

Paula faced her. "Are you a student here?"

"Yeah. I'm a senior."

*And you want to destroy your life this close to graduating*, Paula mused sadly. "Nikki, you're under arrest for a suspected armed robbery," she told her flatly.

"I never robbed her," Nikki snapped. "I only took what was rightly mine—the engagement ring she got from my ex-boyfriend, Lester Siegel. He gave it to me, then stole it from me, once I ended things after I caught him cheating on me with her."

Paula lifted a brow to the tale that seemed too incredible to be untrue. "You have the ring on you?"

"Yeah, in my pocket." Her eyes watered. "I just wanted it to remember him from when things were good, you know?"

"I sympathize with you," Paula had to admit. "Unfortunately, you went about getting back your property the wrong way and will now need to sort it out through the criminal justice system. If you're lucky, your ex won't press charges and you can chalk this—and him—up to a bad experience."

As a squad car approached, Paula reluctantly turned the suspect over to the two fresh-faced officers, while explaining the situation as the suspect told it to her, leaving it for them to decide if they wanted to let her go.

She texted Neil to see if he wanted to grab a coffee. He quickly responded, asking her to meet him at the Auditorium, where he had a class. Agreeing, Paula headed for her car, still wondering how they might make things work once Neil's stint as a visiting professor was over. Did any long-distance, relatively speaking, relationships ever work over the long term? Or might they find an acceptable way to bridge the gap?

After parking, Paula went inside the Auditorium and had just arrived at the lecture hall as the students were filing out. She went inside and saw Neil conversing near the front with a twentysomething male and female.

Neil looked up and grinned when he saw Paula and said, "Hey."

"Hi," she responded.

"These are my teaching assistants, Desmond Isaac and Rachelle Kenui." Neil introduced them. "Detective Paula Lynley."

"Hey," the two TAs said in unison, smiling.

"Hey." Paula smiled back at them.

"They make my job a whole lot easier," Neil claimed.

"I'm sure they do." Paula went along with this.

"I think it's more the other way around," Desmond said. "Prof Ramirez is easy to work with."

"True." Rachelle beamed and regarded Desmond. "We should go."

"Yeah." He placed a hand on the small of her back. "Let's get out of here." He eyed Neil. "We'll have the graded essays to you tomorrow afternoon."

Neil nodded. "Good."

"Later," he told Neil and glanced smilingly at Paula and back to Rachelle.

After they left, Paula asked Neil, "Are you ready?"

"Yeah. Let me just get my briefcase."

They walked in silence the short distance to the Union Building food court, where both ordered lattes and took a seat.

"Got a briefing on the bombing at Horton Hall," Neil remarked, sipping the coffee. "Looks as though the suspect, Harold Fujisawa, had a beef against the College of Social Science faculty after being expelled. This was his misguided attempt at payback, using the excuse of being high on Xylazine to justify his actions."

"Excuses, excuses." Paula rolled her eyes and shook her head. "When will they ever learn?"

"Not soon enough for too many." Neil sat back. "Though Fujisawa's going down for various terrorism charges, he's not the Campus Killer unsub. His DNA and prints didn't match those found at any of the crime scenes of the serial murders."

Paula tasted the latte and said, "Not too surprised to hear that." She noted that Neil had already, more or less, believed that the unsub bomber didn't fit the profile of the Campus Killer and vice versa. "Would've been nice though if the two perps were one and the same and we could have wrapped up our case in one fell swoop." She shrugged. "Oh, well…"

"That's the way it goes," Neil said, taking it in stride. "There are many dangerous individuals out there waiting to do bad things that we have to clean up, one way or the other."

"You're right. Can't exactly read their minds ahead of time, can we?"

He tilted his head to the left side. "If only."

Paula thought about her latest crime incident. "I just caught an armed robbery suspect," she told him.

"Really?" Neil gazed at her. "I saw the campus alert through the emergency notification system on my cell phone."

"Yeah. Only it wasn't exactly what I expected." She drank the coffee, then recounted the unbelievable circumstances that apparently led up to the armed robbery.

Neil laughed. "Talk about getting on one's bad side, not once, but twice…"

Paula thought of the irony, knowing that Neil had been the victim of a cheating girlfriend. Only he had handled it much differently—thank goodness. "I guess when it comes to having one's heart broken, and having the audacity to take back the ring for good measure, people can lose their minds."

"Unfortunately, that's true," he concurred thoughtfully. "For some of us, we simply move on from infidelity and try not to look back."

She favored him with a thin, pensive smile. "I think that's the best way to go."

"Me too." He grinned at her, and Paula felt a tingle from its effect on her and the firm belief that he was better off having gotten past a failed relationship. As had she. While positioning themselves to learn from it in forging new paths toward happiness.

When her cell phone rang, Paula paused those thoughts and lifted it off the table. She saw that the caller was Davenport and answered, "Hey." She listened to the detective and said tersely in response, "All right."

Neil fixed her intuitively. "What?"

Paula's chin jutted as she responded bleakly, "A female professor has been reported missing."

## Chapter Eleven

Charlotte Guthrie, a forty-one-year-old associate professor of fisheries management in the Department of Fisheries and Wildlife at the College of Agriculture and Natural Resources, was last seen late yesterday afternoon. The avid runner and widow loved to jog on campus and had apparently gone for a run after finishing her last class of the day at 4:00 p.m. With her blue Tesla Model 3 located in the employee parking lot, and no signs of a break-in or other criminal activity, a search for the missing professor had begun on the campus grounds.

"I don't like the looks of this," Paula voiced as a gut feeling told her that the professor's disappearance would not end well. From all accounts, Charlotte Guthrie was a responsible and careful person and not prone to disappearing like a magician in a staged performance without explanation. No, Paula sensed that her mysterious absence was far more sinister in light of the murdered female professors at the university, two of which occurred on campus. Charlotte's faculty photograph—she was white, attractive and hazel-eyed with shoulder-length blond hair, parted to the side—had been posted on the school newspaper site and popular social media sites for Addison University students online.

"Neither do I," Neil said, as they joined in the search, walking through dense shrubbery near the Pencock Building, where the college was located and the professor had completed her last class. "There is the possibility that she was kidnapped by someone and could still be alive."

"Yes, that's a possibility," Paula allowed. Realistically, she wasn't very enthusiastic that this was an abduction that Professor Guthrie would be able to walk away from. The more likely scenario was that she had run into harm's way from which there would be no escape for her. Still, why put the cart ahead of the horse? Stranger things had happened. Maybe, just maybe, the professor hadn't been targeted by the Campus Killer. Or even someone else.

As a runner herself, who had occasionally run off course and could have potentially gotten hurt with a stumble here or there, Paula didn't discount altogether the possibility that Charlotte had injured herself during the run and, against the odds, been unable to call for help. Or hadn't been discovered by someone.

*If that's the case, hopefully, we can find you in time*, Paula told herself, as she moved alongside Neil, with Davenport, Gayle and others ahead and behind them, in what had quickly become a desperate search for the missing associate professor—with her very life possibly hanging in the balance. If she was alive at all.

As they moved along the banks of the Cedar River, Paula heard Davenport yell, with a disturbing catch to his voice, "I think we may have found her—"

Paula raced ahead with Neil, until they came upon an area with a large group of mallard ducks congregating by the river. Thick fauna lined the winding riverbank. In it, Paula spotted what was undeniably a thin and pale arm.

She cringed when, upon closer inspection, it became clear that it was the arm of an adult female, who lay face down in the dirt.

"IT'S PROFESSOR GUTHRIE!" A petite female student, with a face-framing layered brunette bob and wearing pink square glasses, shrieked from outside the perimeter of the cordoned-off crime scene as the Shays County Chief Medical Examiner Eddie Saldana turned the decedent's body over.

Neil had already reached that conclusion, along with Paula, Gayle and Davenport, based on the physical description of the missing professor, along with her attire of an orange striped V-neck T-shirt, black track pants and white running sneakers. Beyond that, he could see that her blond hair was matted around a dirt-smudged face. Though there was no murder weapon or signs of trauma, with the generally good shape that the professor appeared to be in as a runner, there was little doubt in Neil's mind that she was the victim of foul play. He guessed that, based upon the initial positioning of the body, she had likely been caught from behind and forced down to the dirt before being able to adequately react.

Saldana was of the same mind and said, his brow furrowed, "The decedent appears to have been suffocated by someone pressing her face down into the soft dirt till she could breathe no more. I would estimate the time of death to be somewhere between four p.m. and six p.m. the prior day."

"So, we're looking at a homicide, to be sure?" Paula threw out, her expression exaggerated.

"That would be my preliminary conclusion," the chief medical examiner responded levelly, flexing the nitrile gloves he wore.

Gayle pursed her lips. "She was obviously targeted by our serial killer—"

Saldana's chin sagged. "I would assume this to be the work of the so-called Campus Killer, based on the similarities to the recent murders of Addison University female professors. But that will need further investigation from us all, I think."

"It's pretty clear to me that this is the work of our serial killer," Davenport said bluntly. "The MO is there, along with the calling card, if you will. In this case, it's the victim herself, whose death was by asphyxia, I'm sure you'll confirm, Dr. Saldana."

"Can't argue with you there, Detective," he concurred. Then, almost as an afterthought, Saldana lifted one of Charlotte Guthrie's discolored hands, studying it like an archeologist might a rare artifact. "Looks like there might be blood beneath at least two of the fingernails."

"Which likely belongs to her attacker," Neil ascertained.

"Seems a reasonable conclusion, unless proven otherwise," Saldana said, standing and removing his gloves. "We'll get her to the morgue and have the autopsy completed by ten a.m. tomorrow."

Paula angled her face and said with a sigh, "I look forward to your report, even if the results are predictable, more or less."

Davenport added humorlessly, "Hate to say it, Doc, but she's right. The autopsy reports are beginning to sound all too familiar these days—not too surprisingly."

Saldana refused to take the bait. "Let's just wait and see," he said in a toneless voice.

Neil considered the probability that the DNA would be a match for the forensic unknown profile collected from beneath the nails of Professor Odette Furillo. Which would therefore tie the two homicides to one unsub, plausibly connecting them to the other murders attributed to a single killer.

After the victim's body was removed, crime scene technicians went about their duties searching for evidence, and investigators were dispatched to interview witnesses and persons who knew Charlotte Guthrie, as well as access surveillance videos on campus that might reveal the unsub's identity or other useful information. Neil watched as Paula directed things like a maestro. He knew that she was in her element as a university detective sergeant and seemed as though her feet were planted firmly on the ground insofar as having made a solid career on the college campus.

Unlike him, who was there on a short-term contract. Would she ever be comfortable relocating to Grand Rapids—hours away—where they could be closer? Or would it be unfair to ask her to upend her life again, after having moved from Kentucky to Rendall Cove? Could they give it a go even if they were living their lives hundreds of miles apart?

Or would one or the other need to be totally unselfish in breaking from comfort level and any necessary sacrifices in the name of finding love and all the happiness that came with it?

THE CAMPUS KILLER watched gleefully as bystanders and law enforcement wandered around in seemingly a state of shock near the banks of the Cedar River, where the latest body had been found as intended. Professor Charlotte Guthrie had made it painfully easy for him to pick up her

*Campus Killer*

routine, play nice and then, once she let her guard down, strike with total efficiency and satisfaction.

As she staggered from the blow he'd landed to her head from behind, it didn't take much to assist her into falling flat on her face onto the dirt. He pounced upon her like a leopard and held her head down, ignoring the indecipherable sounds that somehow managed to escape her mouth. They didn't last long before there was total silence, save for the quacking mallards hanging out lazily along the river's outer banks and a flock of cedar waxwings occupying sprawling eastern red cedar trees that bordered it.

His work was done, as he'd added the good-looking associate professor to his list of killings and had once again gotten away with it. But even he didn't believe that would be a given every time. The authorities weren't that naive. Sooner or later, they might figure things out. Or maybe they never would and this might never end. Either way, he needed to hedge his bets, so he didn't wind up going down—and never getting up again.

He regarded Detectives Paula Lynley and Gayle Yamasaki. They were conversing almost conspiratorially. He could only imagine what they were talking about. Most likely him. Wouldn't they love to get their hands on him. If the detectives played their cards right, he just might give them their wish.

Only it would be on his terms. Not theirs. And with him having the advantage of being invisible in clear view, he was totally in the driver's seat and would have no problem running them down, metaphorically speaking. In reality, should this come to pass, he'd rather they met the same fate as the other victims of the Campus Killer.

Only time would tell.

He looked grim-faced while playing his part to mourn the loss of the professor as another educator fell victim to a murderer on the loose who no one could seem to lay a finger on.

AFTER WORK, Paula met up with Gayle at the Rendall Cove Gym on Newberry Drive. Paula loved going to the gym as a way to decompress and stay fit at the same time. She had a like mind in her fellow police detective and wasn't afraid to take advantage of that. They both had on their workout clothes as they moved their arms and legs on the side-by-side elliptical exercise machines.

"It's so annoying," Gayle complained, "having this jerk picking off professors like flies and right under our noses."

"I know, right?" Paula didn't disagree with her in the slightest. How could she when they were singing out of the same book of hymns. Only there was nothing lyrical about a serial killer targeting women working in higher education. Nor was there any reason to believe he planned to stop the killing any time soon. Not as long as he stayed seemingly a few steps ahead of their efforts to capture him. "The fact that the unsub appears to have no qualms about going after professors in broad daylight—on a campus filled with students coming and going—tells me that the perp is either extremely confident that he's untouchable or is overconfident and getting reckless. Which is it?"

"That's the million-dollar question," Gayle said, taking a swig from her water bottle. "I wish I had the answer, believe me. If so, maybe I could use that info to help nail him to the wall. As it is, we're still trying to play catch-up with him. We're not exactly losing the battle, but we're not winning it either. At least not soon enough to have prevented yet another poor professor from losing her life at the hands of this monster."

"That's not our fault," Paula defended their actions. "We're police detectives, not magicians or mind readers. Like you, I feel absolutely terrible at the precious loss of life here. Just as everyone working in our departments does, I'm sure. But we can only work our butts off in investigating the murders and seeing where it takes us. I'm confident this will not turn into a cold case that is never solved. We won't let that happen, right?"

"Right." Gayle grinned. "Okay, so you've convinced me to not let it become too personal. The fact that we're both under pressure to crack the case doesn't mean it has to crack us. Not if we don't allow that to happen."

"We won't." Paula lifted her hand and they did a high five. "We're two strong women and more than capable of leading this investigation," she stressed. "I'm more determined than ever to finish what we've started, even if there are a few road bumps along the way that we just need to deal with."

"Me too." Gayle picked up the pace. "So, does that mean finishing whatever you've started with Neil Ramirez?"

Paula blushed. Was it that obvious? "Of course," she admitted freely. "Wherever things are meant to go between us, they will."

Gayle took a breath and, gazing at her, asked thoughtfully, "Does that include going down the aisle again, should it ever come to that?"

Paula laughed. "We're nowhere near that point in our relationship," she had to say. At least she didn't think so. "But, generally speaking, yes, I think I would be willing to marry again, if the right person came along."

"Maybe that right person already has," she said brashly.

*Or not*, Paula told herself as she grabbed her water bottle. Far be it for her to try and read Neil's mind as to how far he wanted to take things. Maybe he didn't consider marriage in the cards for him. She would just have to wait and see which way the arrow pointed as they both weighed the future.

Paula imagined the same was true for Gayle. She knew the detective had a crush on Mike Davenport. Wisely, she didn't go after the happily married man. No reason to rock the boat and risk it sinking for all parties concerned. Besides, she was sure that Gayle would have no trouble attracting someone who was single and available. As long as it wasn't Neil, whom she had already said wasn't her type, but was very much Paula's.

THAT EVENING, Neil watched through his rearview mirror as Vinny Ortiz's Jeep Wagoneer came up behind him. The undercover agent emerged from the vehicle and headed toward Neil's Suburban. He glanced around to make sure neither had been followed—or was otherwise in danger of being exposed as they rendezvoused.

When Ortiz climbed into the passenger seat, he said with an edge to his tone of voice, "Heard that another professor has been murdered on campus."

"Yeah." Neil took a ragged breath. "Wish it weren't true. Unfortunately, the Campus Killer seems to have struck again—seemingly becoming more and more emboldened to take down his prey."

"Too bad. This dude's definitely creating a stir around town, even in the gunrunning business. Craig Eckart is still lamenting over the murder of his girlfriend, Laurelyn Wong, by this serial killer."

"Nice to know that a man who sells and distributes illegal guns and ammo that kill people would be torn up when someone he's close to becomes a victim of violence." Neil made a sardonic face. "Cry me a river."

"I get where you're coming from, trust me," Ortiz said and ran a hand through his hair. "Eckart's definitely not one of the good guys. But you and I don't have the luxury of picking and choosing between creeps."

"Very true." Neil leaned back musingly. He needed Eckart to go down as much as the serial killer unsub. With Ortiz's work, they were about to make that happen. One victory at a time. "So, where do things stand?" he asked him anxiously.

"Everything's falling into place," Ortiz responded intently. "Eckart's got his dark web operation in full gear, with a variety of guns and ammo he's ready to make available to anyone who wants them. At the same time, he's built up a stash of firearms locally that he's prepared to distribute across the country to gang members, drug traffickers and others who want to purchase guns on the black market."

"Sounds like Eckart is ripe for the taking," Neil remarked knowingly.

"Yeah. It's definitely going to blow up in his face."

"What do you need from me?" Neil fixed his eyes on the undercover agent, aware that he had the most at stake in the dangerous operation.

"You need to let all the relevant parties know that it's crunch time," Ortiz told him tensely. "I'll text you just before, so everyone's in place to do what's needed to put the gunrunner out of commission."

"I'll take care of it," Neil promised, more than ready to do his part in harnessing the combined power of the ATF,

Rendall Cove PD's Firearms Investigation Unit, with assistance from the Shays County Sheriff's Department, to put an end to this major arms trafficking enterprise.

"Okay." Ortiz gave him a solid nod and exited the vehicle.

As Neil started the ignition and then drove off, he only hoped this thing went down without a hitch. Beyond that, there was still the issue of trying to help Paula and company to put a perilous serial killer behind bars before the unsub could add to the string of victims he'd left behind.

Half an hour later, Neil showed up at Paula's front door. When she opened it, he said sheepishly, "Thought you could use some company."

Her lashes fluttered interestedly. "Oh, did you?"

He grinned, raising an arm to show what he was holding. "I brought white wine."

"Hmm..." She licked her lips and took the bottle. "Come in."

The moment Neil did, her cat, Chloe, pedaled across the floor and affectionately rubbed herself on the leg of his pants. He laughed. "Looks like someone missed me."

Paula smiled nicely. "Guess you're starting to grow on her."

"Must be catching," Neil tossed back at her, feeling that she was growing on him in ways that cut deep into his heart and soul.

"Must be," she agreed without hesitation.

## Chapter Twelve

On Friday morning, Paula was at her desk, going over the autopsy report on Charlotte Guthrie. As expected, the chief medical examiner determined that the associate professor of fisheries management's death was due to forceful asphyxia and ruled a homicide. Paula winced at the thought, hating the notion that doing something Charlotte obviously loved—running for fitness—should end this way.

*Under other circumstances, I could have run into harm's way myself*, Paula considered, while reading more of the mundane details of Eddie Saldana's official report on the decedent. The DNA removed from beneath Charlotte's fingernails was sent to the forensic lab for analysis, while the unsub remained at large.

Paula pulled up the surveillance video on her laptop of that section of campus, near the Cedar River. A male was seen running away from the area. Though the image was less than sharp, she could see that he was white, with short dark hair, tall and of average build, wearing a red jersey, blue jeans and black tennis shoes. It was enough to shake her foundation as a potential breakthrough.

*Who are you?* Paula asked suspiciously, believing

his identification could be crucial as a viable suspect in the investigation.

She headed over to the Department of Police and Public Safety's Forensic Science Lab, where Paula met with Forensic Scientist Irene Atai, who was in her thirties and petite, with brown hair in a braided bun and sable eyes behind oval glasses.

"Hey," Irene said from her workstation. "I think I know why you're here, Detective Lynley."

Paula gave a little smile. "So, what do you have for me on the DNA removed from beneath the nails of our latest homicide victim, Charlotte Guthrie?"

"Well, when the DNA sample was compared with the forensic unknown profile analyzed from below the nails of Professor Odette Furillo, it was a match." Irene's face lit up. "The two DNA samples belong to the same unsub," she asserted.

"Meaning the professors managed to scratch a single assailant who was present at both murders," Paula uttered, having anticipated this finding.

"Exactly," Irene said succinctly. "Though the unsub was able to avoid being clawed by the other victims, this certainly links two of the murders in building your case against the Campus Killer."

"You're right, it does." Paula knew they still needed more to really put the squeeze on the culprit. A confession would be nice. But since she doubted that would come voluntarily, the next best thing was to stitch together the hard evidence to make the unsub's guilt all but certain. "Did you come up with anything from the Crime Scene Investigation Unit's work at the site of Charlotte Guthrie's murder?"

"Yes," Irene responded with a lilt to her voice. "There

was a partial footprint discovered in the dirt near the body that did not match the shoes worn by Professor Guthrie. Our analysis indicated that the print came from a male tennis shoe that was likely a size eleven. It may or may not have come from the killer," she cautioned, "given that, from what I understand, it's a popular area for runners on campus."

"That's true," Paula allowed. "But where there's even a little smoke, there could be fire ready to light up." She thought about the suspect on the surveillance footage who was wearing tennis shoes. Coincidence? Or a further indication of guilt?

IN HIS OFFICE, Neil touched base by video chat with the Grand Rapids field office's resident agent in charge, Doris Frankenberg, wanting to keep her up to speed on the arms trafficking investigation. In her early forties, with blond hair and highlights worn in a shaggy lob and green eyes behind contacts, she had made no secret of her desire to be promoted to the International Affairs Division. For his part, Neil was pulling for her to succeed. Even as he was thinking more and more about his own future with the organization, and whether or not it was truly where he belonged when looking down the line. Still pained by the death of his friend, Agent Ramone Munoz, Neil was well aware of how one's entire life could change in a flash. He didn't want to shortchange himself when it came to prioritizing the things he felt were most important in life. Such as finding love with someone he could grow old and have a family of his own with.

"Busting this international arms ring wide open would be another coup for the ATF," Doris voiced with eagerness.

"Yeah, it would be great for the organization." Neil offered her a smile. "Even better would be to take the guns and ammo out of the hands of human traffickers, gang members, domestic assaulters, unstable lone shooters, etc."

"That too," she concurred. "Whenever Agent Ortiz gives the signal, we'll be ready to go in with everything we've got to take down Craig Eckart and his associates."

Neil nodded to that and talked a bit about the recent bomb threat at the university and the ongoing Campus Killer investigation.

Doris shot him a supportive look. "It's how we roll, Agent Ramirez," she said matter-of-factly. "Whatever the bad guys do, we—along with our law enforcement partners—are even better at stopping them. Even if the path can be downright bumpy at times."

"That's a good way to look at it," Neil told her, knowing that winning the war was what it was all about in the final analysis, in spite of losing a few battles along the way sometimes.

"It's the only way," she told him keenly. "Agent Munoz lost his life with that very philosophy in mind."

"I know." Neil thought about Ramone making the ultimate sacrifice, with his wife, Jillian, being left to raise his two girls alone. "I have to go," he told the resident agent in charge.

"All right." She flashed him a smile. "I'll see you soon back in the office."

"Yeah." He grinned weakly at her and ended the chat, while again contemplating his life as he looked ahead and behind at the same time. In each instance, what stood out was meeting Paula and not wanting to lose her, whichever direction he chose to take in his life.

PAULA WAS STANDING in Captain Shailene McNamara's office, briefing her on the latest in the investigation, when Mike Davenport interrupted. His expression was indecipherable before he said intently, "We just received a tip that the unidentified male in the surveillance video is Connor Vanasse, an undergrad at the university. I looked him up and saw that he's twenty-two years old and a junior, majoring in biochemistry and molecular biology in the College of Natural Science."

"Does he live on campus?" Paula asked curiously.

"Actually, he's living off campus in a nearby apartment building," Davenport said. "But he should be at school right now. I have his class schedule."

Shailene leaned forward from her wooden desk, practically rising out of her high-backed leather chair. "Find him," she ordered, moving her gaze between them. "If this Connor Vanasse is our Campus Killer, we don't want him to target any more professors before we can get him off the streets."

"I couldn't agree more," Paula said, peering at Davenport. "Do we know who the caller is?"

"No, it was anonymous," he replied.

She didn't put too much stock in that at the moment, as Paula understood that people knowledgeable about persons suspected of crimes were often reluctant to identify themselves for fear of reprisal from the suspect. Not wanting to get involved officially. Or, in some instances, preferring to keep a low profile from the often intrusive media that lived for stories on real-life serial killers.

"Let's go bring Connor Vanasse in," Paula told Davenport, adding, "I'll give Gayle and the Rendall Cove PD a heads-up on the suspect as a serious person of interest in our investigation." And Paula intended to do the same in keeping Neil in the loop on what seemed to be a major breakthrough in the case.

WHEN GAYLE RECEIVED the news alert that a credible suspect named Connor Vanasse was wanted for questioning, she wasted little time in heading for the Moonclear Apartments on Drake Drive where he lived. Was this actually their killer? A student? How had he managed to stay one step ahead of them—till now?

She pulled up to the complex and drove around the parking lot, looking for the white Toyota Camry registered to Vanasse. It was nowhere in sight. As Gayle had been told that the suspect was likely on campus at this hour, she assumed he wasn't in his apartment. But she was not taking any chances that Vanasse could somehow slip through the cracks.

With Paula and Davenport searching for the suspect at the university, Gayle left her car and rendezvoused with other detectives and officers from the Rendall Cove PD. A knock and then another on Vanasse's second-floor door produced no response. There were no sounds coming from within and no reason to believe he had been tipped off that they were looking for him, as Gayle preferred the element of surprise.

She left the officers there, in case Vanasse showed up, and to secure the scene, should they need to go in with a search warrant later. In the meantime, Gayle hopped back in her vehicle and headed to Addison University, eager to be in on a takedown of the suspect who was now at the top of the list as the possible Campus Killer terrorizing professors since June.

NEIL JUST HAPPENED to be in Horton Hall for a lecture, when he was informed by Paula via text that they had identified a suspect in the serial killer investigation, a third-year student named Connor Vanasse, who was thought to be in a different class in Horton Hall presently. Having been sent a student ID photograph of the suspect—he was white and square jawed with blue eyes and black hair in an Edgar haircut—and given a general description of being around six feet, two inches in height and of medium build, Neil sprang into action. Wanting to do his part to assist in detaining the person of interest till the school authorities could bring him in, he headed straight for the second-floor classroom where a lecture on the pharmacology of drug addiction was underway.

Entering the room up front, Neil gazed at the forty or so students seated, looking for anyone who resembled Connor Vanasse. No one stood out at first glance. He caught the attention of the slender, white-haired male professor in his sixties, who stopped lecturing on a dime as Neil approached him.

"Can I help you?" the professor asked curiously.

Flashing his ATF special agent ID away from the view of students, Neil whispered, "As part of an investigation, I'm looking for Connor Vanasse. I understand that he's one of your students, taking this class—"

The professor cocked a thickish white brow. "That's correct. Only I don't believe that Mr. Vanasse is attending class today, for whatever reason. You're free to check for yourself, though," he offered.

Though he had no reason to doubt the professor, Neil knew that, as a visiting professor, he was able to establish in his smaller classes who was in attendance and who was not. Still, given the stakes, he had to be on the safe side, so he peered again into the classroom, looking more carefully at each face. Finally, convinced that the person of in-terest was not present, Neil said levelly to the students, "I'm looking for Connor Vanasse. Does anyone know where I can find him?"

"Yeah, I think so," said a husky male student with dark hair in a two block cut and a Balbo beard. "At least later. Connor can be found most Friday nights hanging out at the Dillingers Club on Young Street."

"Thanks." Neil made a note.

"What's he done this time?" the student asked humor-ously, getting a laugh from other students. "Or should I ask?"

"Probably better that you don't," Neil said expressionless, believing it was best not to tip his hand. "Just need some information from him regarding a class I'm teaching." He wasn't sure they were buying that, but hoped it was enough to keep them from giving Connor Vanasse a warning that someone was looking for him.

Neil left the classroom just as Paula was walking toward him, along with Mike Davenport. He caught up to them and said, "Hey."

"Hey." Paula met his eyes. "Is Connor Vanasse in there?"

"Afraid not," Neil replied. "But short of finding him in his next class for today, I have a lead on where we can find Vanasse tonight."

"Where's that?" Davenport asked with interest.

"According to a student, Vanasse spends his Friday nights at Dillingers, a nightclub on Young Street."

"I know the place," Davenport said. "It's known for being pretty rowdy."

"Not too surprised to hear that," Neil said, knowing that the college town had a reputation for partying, drinking and recreational marijuana usage.

Paula sighed and said, "It could also be the location where a serial killer has chosen to hide out."

Neil nodded and responded accordingly, "If so, we'll be there to flush him out."

AT 9:00 P.M., Paula showed her badge to the burly and bald-headed man at the door to the Dillingers Club to be let through without explanation. Neil, Gayle and Davenport followed suit and all went inside. As expected on a Friday night, it was packed with students and twentysomethings, milling about or standing in place with drinks in hand, chattering as loud music was piped through loudspeakers overhead.

"Why don't we fan out," Paula suggested to the others, knowing they were all carrying concealed weapons, with armed officers and sheriff's deputies waiting outside the club as backup. "If anyone spots Connor Vanasse, keep an eye on him and text the location."

"Will do," Gayle said tensely.

"If he's here, he might make a run for it if we're made," Davenport told them.

"We have to consider that he's armed and dangerous, assuming Vanasse is our killer," Neil pointed out.

Paula didn't discount that in the slightest and responded, "True, which is why we can't spook him. But we also can't allow him to leave this building and endanger others."

Neil met her eyes. "If it's all the same to you, I think I'll just tag along—as an added measure of precaution."

Holding his gaze, she understood that this was his way of wanting to protect her as someone he cared about beyond their jobs in law enforcement. As she felt the same way toward him, Paula nodded with approval, wanting them both to get through this in one piece. "Let's head out," she ordered and started moving through the crowd.

"Maybe we should have waited till Vanasse came out," Neil said, trailing her close enough that Paula could feel his warm breath on the back of her neck. "He'd be easier to spot."

Though he made a good argument, she countered with, "Given the situation we're facing with six victims, there's nothing easy about this. We need to catch the perp wherever he happens to be—before someone else gets hurt."

"Point taken. I'll follow your lead, Detective."

"Good." A tiny smile of satisfaction that they understood each other played on Paula's lips. As they moved about, she peered through the throng of bar goers, looking for the suspect. She wondered if the intel on him was faulty. Perhaps Vanasse had never shown up at the club. Had yet to arrive. Or had already given them the slip. Then Paula homed in on a man who was putting the moves on an apparently interested attractive, curvaceous blonde female. "That's him," Paula told Neil as she recognized the suspect from his picture.

"Yeah, I can see that," he agreed. Neil moved alongside her. "Why don't we see if Vanasse will come in peacefully…?"

Just as she agreed, Paula got an answer from the suspect, who spotted them and intuitively saw them as cops and abruptly shoved the young blonde woman at them and took off running.

Instinctively, Paula took off after him, with Neil hot on her heels. Along the way, they had to dodge others, clueless as to what was going on, as Paula felt her heart pounding rapidly. She saw that Gayle and Davenport were now also in pursuit of the suspect.

When Vanasse appeared to be reaching for something in the pocket of his jeans, Paula was about to remove her SIG Sauer pistol from its holster, when Neil stepped in front of her and leaped onto the suspect. Both fell to the ground, with Neil on top. In the blink of an eye, he had twisted Vanasse's arms behind his back and was joined by Davenport, who handcuffed him and declared toughly, "Connor Vanasse, we're taking you in on suspicion of murder—"

Paula reminded the suspect of his rights as he was lifted to his feet and the four of them led him off as quite possibly the Campus Killer.

## Chapter Thirteen

Early Saturday morning, Paula sat beside Gayle in the interrogation room at the Department of Police and Public Safety. On the opposite side of the table, Connor Vanasse was seated, with a dour expression on his face. His hair was a bit longer than on the student ID but was still in the same style. She noted a small cut on his neck and wondered if that had come from Charlotte Guthrie, before he killed her. If so, the DNA sample collected upon his arrest last night would link him to both her death and that of Odette Furillo.

Admittedly, chomping at the bit to get the suspect to confess, Paula got right to the questioning, having already made it clear that he could stop this and request legal representation at any time. "Mr. Vanasse, as was indicated, we brought you here to see what you know about a murder that occurred on the Addison University campus on Wednesday—the victim being Associate Professor of Fisheries Management Charlotte Guthrie."

Vanasse's nostrils flared and he snorted, "I had nothing to do with what happened to that professor!"

"Is that so?" Gayle's tone was cynical. She narrowed her eyes at the suspect. "We have you on surveillance video near the scene of the crime. You care to explain that...?"

Vanasse flinched. "There's nothing to explain," he argued. "Yeah, I hung out a bit by the river like I always do. But I never saw Professor Guthrie. And I sure as hell didn't kill her."

"Why don't I believe you?" Gayle rolled her eyes. "I think you took note of her jogging pattern, and when an opportunity came, you attacked her."

"That's not true!" His voice snapped, and he gazed at Paula as if to help him out.

She wasn't inclined to do so, but did want to keep him talking. "Would you mind telling me how you got that cut on your neck?"

He shrugged. "Cut myself shaving."

"Is that so?" Her eyes narrowed with skepticism. "Does that happen often?" She thought again about the unidentified DNA found beneath the fingernails of not one, but two victims of the Campus Killer.

The suspect rubbed his nose. "Not so much," he claimed.

"What size shoe do you wear, Mr. Vanasse?" she asked politely.

"Eleven." His response was without hesitation, and he eyed her with misgiving. "Why do you need to know that?"

Paula gave him a direct gaze and answered bluntly, "A size eleven tennis shoe footprint was found near Professor Guthrie's body—" she glanced under the table at his tennis shoes "—much like the ones you're wearing."

Vanasse's expression grew ill at ease. "Hey, you can't plant this on me! I was never near her body, I swear."

Paula wasn't necessarily buying this. Far from it. "So, if you're innocent, why did you run when you saw us at the nightclub?" she challenged him.

He hesitated, running a hand nervously across his mouth

and glancing from one detective to the other. Then, in a shaky voice, he said, "I panicked, okay. I've been dealing drugs on campus. Mostly prescription pills, weed and ketamine. I thought that's what this was all about and freaked."

As Paula weighed his response, Gayle dismissed it. She scowled and said to Vanasse, "That's not very convincing, in light of the circumstances. Why don't we go over this again. Why did you run away from the crime scene, in effect, if you had nothing to hide as it related to murdering a professor…?"

Vanasse stiffened but maintained his story. "I never knew it was a crime scene. All I did was walk alongside the river, smoking a joint, and left. That's it."

Glancing at Gayle and aware that Neil and Davenport were watching this in another room on a video monitor, Paula chewed on the suspect's claims and decided to shift gears a bit. "Let's talk about Mathematics Professor Odette Furillo—"

Vanasse lowered his brows. "What about her?"

"Did you know the professor?" Paula had gone over his classes for the entire school year and gotten no indication that he had taken classes with Professor Furillo. Or, for that matter, any of the deceased professors. But this didn't mean he hadn't become fixated from afar, or had otherwise targeted them.

"Not personally," he said wryly.

"You think this is amusing?" Gayle snapped at him.

"Of course not." Vanasse wiped the grin off his face. "No, I didn't know the professor—personally or otherwise—and I didn't kill her. If that's what you're thinking."

*The thought has crossed my mind, and with good reason*, Paula told herself, but said to him, "We're only here investigating a series of homicides, on and off campus, including the aforementioned professors. Getting back to Professor Furillo, do you have an alibi for the time of her death?"

Paula provided this information. The suspect was unable to account surely for his whereabouts, claiming that he had probably been on a drug high somewhere. The same pathetic story was used when asked where he was when professors Debra Newton, Harmeet Fernández, Kathy Payne and Laurelyn Wong were murdered by suffocation.

When Paula received a text message on her cell phone, she looked at it and whispered to Gayle, "We have the results of the DNA testing." As she reacted to this, Paula stood and, fixing her eyes on Vanasse, told him comically, "Don't go anywhere."

Outside the room, Paula called Irene Atai in the Forensic Science Lab for a video chat. "Hey, what did you find out?" Paula asked her attentively when she appeared on the screen.

Irene flashed her a look of excitement. "The DNA sample collected from the suspect, Connor Vanasse, was a direct match with the two DNA unknown profiles obtained from beneath the nails of professors Odette Furillo and Charlotte Guthrie."

"You're sure?" Paula asked this more out of habit than questioning the validity of the DNA testing by the forensic analyst.

"Absolutely." Irene's voice lifted an octave. "Vanasse's DNA was definitely taken off him somewhere by both decedents. He's your unsub—"

"Thanks, Irene." Paula gave her a smile. "Good work."

After ending the chat, Paula considered this for a moment, before heading back inside the interrogation room, where she conveyed the information in Gayle's ear, who said gleefully, "We needed that."

It proved to be more than enough solid evidence to make their case for the suspect being the Campus Killer. Paula cast her eyes upon him and said doggedly, "Your DNA was found below the fingernails of Charlotte Guthrie and Odette Furillo, leading me to believe that you murdered the professors."

"No way!" Vanasse yelled an expletive, then said in fear, "I think this is where I ask for a lawyer—"

"I understand," she told him, knowing this was a wise move on his part. "You probably should lawyer up, at this point."

Upon ordering him to stand, Gayle cuffed him and said inflexibly, "Connor Vanasse, you're under arrest for the murders of Charlotte Guthrie and Odette Furillo, with other charges sure to follow."

NEIL WATCHED THE whole thing unfold in the monitoring room, along with Davenport, who remarked with confidence in his tone, "Looks like we've got him!"

"Seems that way." Neil couldn't knock the unmistakable DNA evidence that linked Vanasse to two of the serial murders. The MO of the killer and similarities of the homicides made it all but a certainty that they were perpetrated by the same person.

Connor Vanasse.

"Let's see if forensics can match the pattern from Vanasse's tennis shoe with the print found at the crime scene of Guthrie's murder," Davenport said.

"That would help," Neil admitted, in making the case for Vanasse as the Campus Killer.

"Yeah, definitely." The detective sighed. "This college town was certainly under siege as long as he remained on the loose," he uttered.

"I couldn't agree more." Having worked there these past few months, Rendall Cove had almost begun to seem like home to Neil. That was made more so by the presence of Paula in his life. The thought of ever losing that was something he suddenly found hard to even comprehend. Much less see put into practice.

When she and Gayle joined them in the hall, Neil could see the relief in Paula's face as she said with a catch to her voice, "Making an arrest in this case was imperative on so many levels."

"You're telling me," Gayle said and gave her a friendly little hug. "It was obvious that, when faced with the hard evidence of his guilt, Vanasse was completely tongue-tied."

Neil agreed somewhat, telling them, "Deny, deny, deny— or unwillingness to face up to one's own actions, even when they hardly have a leg to stand on to the contrary—is usually the case whenever a suspect is cornered like a rat and doesn't have anywhere else to turn, short of fessing up. Clearly, this was where Connor Vanasse found himself."

"Up a creek without a paddle," Davenport quipped, grinning.

Gayle laughed. "Hope the man's a good swimmer."

"Before we get too comfortable about Vanasse being put away for good," Paula stressed, "let's make sure that the Shays County prosecutor, Natalie Eleniak, plays ball in throwing the book at Vanasse."

"Give it time," Neil said prudently. "If Vanasse is the Campus Killer, he's not about to be let off the hook by the prosecutor or anyone else with a vested interest in seeing that justice is served."

"You're right." Paula showed her white teeth, which he loved seeing. "That process has only just begun, and I'll be around to see it through as long as it takes."

"Same here," Gayle pitched in. She eyed Neil curiously. "How about you, Agent Ramirez? Or will you have moved on to bigger and better things?"

He met Paula's gaze uncomfortably, knowing she was even more keen to hear his response. Though he didn't particularly like being put on the spot—with Gayle obviously knowledgeable about his romantic involvement with Paula— Neil didn't shrink away from the question. He couldn't do that. "You can be sure that whenever a verdict is reached in this case, I'll be on hand to watch the guilty party hauled off to prison." He knew that this wasn't necessarily what Paula wanted to hear but, for now, it was the most he could commit to while putting a few more important things in order in his life.

Neil sensed that Paula was all right with that for the time being.

WITH MORE THAN enough probable cause to believe that Connor Vanasse was responsible for multiple murders, a judge signed off on search warrants of the suspect's Toyota Camry and apartment—looking for any physical, forensic, demonstrative, digital and other evidence against Vanasse as it pertained to the Campus Killer investigation.

Paula and Gayle, along with other armed detectives and crime scene investigators, entered the suspect's apartment. It was only sparsely furnished and included two bedrooms and an open concept, stained brown carpeting and evidence throughout of illicit drugs and drug paraphernalia.

"A dealer and a druggie by his own admission," Gayle pointed out straightforwardly.

Paula concurred, but had to say, "That's the least of Vanasse's problems."

"True, even if they're all likely linked to one degree or another."

"Let's see if he can use the substance abuse and drug trafficking defense for murdering six professors," Paula said humorlessly. Once the all-clear signal was made, she put her gun back in its holster and continued surveying the premises.

By the time the team was through, having confiscated Vanasse's laptop, along with other potential evidence, taken photographs and headed out, Paula was satisfied that they had done their job as part of the overall investigation that figured to ultimately put Connor Vanasse away for the rest of his life.

ON SUNDAY, Paula went jogging with Neil at Rendall Creek Park. Though they spent the night together, with neither seeming to be able to get quite enough of the other, there was little talk about building bridges and crossing over them together, which she had agreed to. Instead, both settled into enjoying what they had and neither made any waves. That didn't prevent Paula from hoping there was a serious path forward that could give her the type of lasting love and committed relationship that had evaded her with Scott.

Neil, who had worked up a good sweat, broke her reverie when he said contemplatively, "I was thinking... What if Connor Vanasse didn't kill those professors?"

Paula arched a brow. "The evidence suggests otherwise."

"Evidence can sometimes be misleading. Distorted. Or even planted."

"What are you saying?" All she could think of was that he was implying that the police had set up Vanasse. Did Neil truly believe them capable of this?

"Whoa…" Neil made an expression as if reading her mind, as they continued to meander side by side through the groves of maple and eastern white pine trees. "I wasn't suggesting that the case against Vanasse was manufactured by the DPPS or PD," he made clear. "Nothing of the sort. I was only putting out there the notion that this all somehow seems just a little too cut-and-dried for me."

She narrowed her eyes at him. "We have Vanasse's DNA on two of the victims, a matching shoe print at one crime scene, security camera footage showing him fleeing the area and circumstantial evidence tying him to the murders. What more do you need, short of an outright confession?"

Neil sucked in a deep breath. "So, maybe I'm way off base here." He paused. "There's still the motive to nail down. It's just something to think about."

*Seriously*, Paula mused. What was there to think about? Did he know something she didn't? "If Vanasse is innocent, who do you think is the Campus Killer?"

Neil took a long moment before favoring her with a determined look and replying candidly, "I have no idea. Just call it a gut instinct by a criminal profiler."

Though she respected his expertise, Paula wondered if he was searching for something that wasn't there. Or were his instincts spot on? Was it possible that Connor Vanasse, against all odds, was being railroaded? With the guilty party still on the loose? If so, why? And by whom?

## Chapter Fourteen

On Monday morning, Neil followed his instincts that told him something felt off about the case against Connor Vanasse. The last thing he wanted to do was poke holes into the investigation and presumed guilt of the suspect. Or overstep his bounds as a criminal profiler and not one of the actual investigators, such as Paula—certainly not wanting to get on her bad side—who did all the dirty work in reaching the consensus on Vanasse.

But Neil went with his gut on this one. No harm. No foul. Right? Simply having a little chat with Vanasse would in no way hinder the progress of the case, which the Shays County prosecutor had yet to sign off on. *If Vanasse, who has maintained his innocence thus far, tries to play me, it won't work*, Neil told himself, from a metal chair as he watched the serial killer suspect enter the interview room at the Rendall Cove City Jail on Flagstone Avenue.

Wearing a horizontal black-and-white-striped jumpsuit while handcuffed, Connor Vanasse peered at him curiously and barked, "Who the hell are you?"

"Special Agent Ramirez," Neil told him. "Have a seat." He proffered his long arm toward the metal chair across the square wooden table.

Vanasse did as told, while Neil asked the tough-looking, bald headed, husky guard who accompanied him into the room to leave them alone. Though seemingly reluctant to do so, the guard left.

Vanasse cocked a brow. "So, why am I here?" he asked tentatively.

"I'd like to discuss the case against you." Neil got right to the point.

The suspect stared for a long moment and shrugged. "What's there to discuss?"

"Why did you do it?" Neil asked straightforwardly, peering across the table.

"I didn't do anything!" Vanasse stuck to his story. "Like I told the other detectives, and my lawyer, I had nothing to do with those murders."

Neil snickered. "If I had a dollar for every time a suspect claimed innocence when the evidence clearly suggested otherwise, I'd be a very rich man and probably living the good life in the Caribbean or Hawaii."

"It's the truth!" Vanasse snapped. "Whether you choose to believe it or not."

*Not—at least not necessarily*, Neil told himself. He asked point-blank, "Mind telling me how your DNA ended up beneath the fingernails of two professors who were suffocated to death?"

"I have no idea." Vanasse pursed his lips thoughtfully. "Must have been a mistake or something."

"Highly unlikely." Neil knew that while cross contamination was always possible with people coming and going across crime scenes, any notion that the DNA was not his would not fly. "Forensic testing puts you at the crime scenes and, by extension, that makes you the prime suspect in several other homicides. Do you have any thoughts of how it might have gotten there, since you allege you weren't there?"

Vanasse's shoulders slumped. "Maybe it was planted."

"Try again." Neil dismissed this at a glance. He regarded the small cut on the suspect's neck. "You said you cut yourself shaving. Is that true? And, if so, who had access to the blood other than yourself?"

Vanasse leaned back contemplatively and, after a moment or two, responded evenly, "Someone else cut me."

"Who?"

"Just a friend who was goofing around while we were getting high. It was no big deal."

"What's the friend's name?" Neil asked.

"Desmond Isaac," Vanasse answered matter-of-factly.

Neil's eyes widened at the name of his teaching assistant. "Desmond Isaac?" He repeated this as though having misunderstood.

"Yeah," Vanasse confirmed. "We were smoking weed and whatever...and when he was playing around with a switchblade, it accidentally nicked me."

*How the hell did my TA wind up in the middle of this?* Neil wondered, disturbed at the thought. "Where did this take place—and when...?"

"At my apartment—the same day that Professor Guthrie was killed."

"Who cleaned up the cut?" Neil asked curiously, in wanting to give Desmond the benefit of the doubt that his role was purely innocuous.

"We both did," Vanasse claimed. Then he changed this to say, "Actually, Desmond had a handkerchief that he used to wipe away the blood, then I grabbed a paper towel to finish it up." He frowned. "Wait a sec... You're not suggesting that Desmond—a friend—would use my blood...my DNA to set me up, are you?"

"I'm not suggesting anything of the sort," Neil argued, even if the possibility suddenly was weighing heavily on his mind. "Just looking for other ways that your DNA might have been beneath the nails of two victims, if you weren't scratched by them."

"I wasn't." Vanasse hunched his shoulders. "As I said, it must have been some kind of mix-up in the lab or something."

The *something* was what intrigued Neil more. "It's not possible that this would be the case in two different homicides that occurred days apart. Let's talk about Professor Odette Furillo," he said. "Since your DNA was also found underneath her nails, did you or someone else happen to cut you that day too?" He provided the day and time of death for Vanasse to ponder, aware that he had no solid alibi for any of the Campus Killer murders.

"Truthfully, I can't remember," he claimed. "I think I may've had a nosebleed that day."

"Did your buddy Desmond Isaac happen to be around at the time?" Neil asked intently.

"Yeah, probably. We've been hanging out a lot lately—doing drugs...and just kicking back between classes." Vanasse furrowed his brow. "Me and Desmond are cool. He wouldn't betray me like that. Or, for that matter, kill professors. To believe otherwise is just plain ridiculous!"

Neil's jaw clenched. "Would it be any more ridiculous to think that your good friend Desmond could plant your DNA at crime scenes rather than be arrested and charged with multiple murders that you claim you didn't commit?"

Vanasse snorted on a breath. "No, I guess not."

Admittedly, Neil still had his own doubts about pointing the finger at his TA as the Campus Killer. But as an ATF criminal profiler and visiting professor who needed to have an open mind, even when he was looking at the presumed serial killer, Neil was not about to give Desmond Isaac a free pass as a possible killer.

"What do you have to say about the fact that your size eleven tennis shoe, including dirt on the bottom, was a match for a print left at the crime scene of Charlotte Guthrie's murder?" Neil asked pointedly, narrowing his eyes at Vanasse.

"Can't explain it," he argued, "other than to say that half the dudes I know on campus are size eleven and wear the same brand of tennis shoes. Some of them even like to hang out on the banks of the Cedar River, like me. Does that make them guilty?"

"Does that include Desmond Isaac?" Neil couldn't help but wonder, even as he pictured the TA routinely wearing black tennis shoes that could have been a size eleven.

Vanasse wrinkled his nose. "You'll have to ask him that."

"Okay." Neil sighed thoughtfully and stood. "I'll be in touch."

"Does that mean you believe me?" Vanasse made a face. "That I'm being railroaded?"

"Let's just say I'm not as convinced as some that you killed those professors," Neil told him honestly. "Of course, if the evidence continues to prove me wrong, then you'll have your day in court."

Neil called the guard to come in and left the detainee there to ponder this.

"So, YOU'RE BACK!" Paula smiled while sitting at her desk as she took the video call from her friend, Josie Woods, recognizing the floor-to-ceiling windows overlooking New York City in Josie's Wall Street office.

"Wish it weren't true but, unfortunately, all good things must eventually come to an end." Josie pouted. "It was fun while it lasted though."

"I'll bet." Paula still dreamed of going to Hawaii herself someday—perhaps with Neil, if things worked out between them as she hoped would be the case. "So, what's happening in the Big Apple?"

She listened for a few minutes as Josie droned on about business meetings and her millionaire boyfriend Rob's latest obsession with rare collectibles. Paula had just skimmed the surface on her latest investigation and begun to touch on her relationship with Neil, when her cell phone buzzed and she saw that he was the caller. "I need to take this," she told Josie, who smiled with understanding before they disconnected.

Paula hoped to get out to New York to visit soon as she answered the phone. "Hey, there. What's up?"

"As out there as this sounds, I think my teaching assistant Desmond Isaac may have set up Connor Vanasse to take the rap as the Campus Killer," Neil said tonelessly.

"What?" Paula's lower lip hung down as she pressed the phone to her ear with disbelief.

"I went to see Vanasse," he confessed.

"You did?"

"Yes. I wanted to clear up some things that, as a profiler, rubbed me the wrong way during his interrogation." Neil breathed into the phone. "According to Vanasse, he and Desmond did drugs together."

Paula jutted her chin. "And that proves what?"

"Vanasse says that on the same day that Charlotte Guthrie

was killed, Desmond accidentally cut Vanasse's neck with a switchblade when toying around—and used a handkerchief to wipe the blood. Desmond could have technically rubbed Vanasse's DNA beneath Guthrie's nails after he suffocated her to death," Neil argued.

"You really believe that's possible?" Paula asked doubtfully.

"It's not impossible to think that someone clever enough—a criminology student, for example, with knowledge of crime scene techniques, DNA evidence, planting evidence and such—could have found an unsuspecting scapegoat to take the fall for a string of murders and allow the true culprit to go unpunished."

"But what about the DNA found beneath Odette Furillo's nails?" Paula questioned. "Are you saying this was a setup as well?"

"Why not?" Neil answered tersely. "Vanasse claims that he can't remember for certain if he had a nosebleed or how he ended up losing blood the day Furillo was murdered. But he does think that he may have been hanging out with Desmond at the time. This might all be nothing more than happenstance," Neil indicated, "but my instincts are telling me otherwise."

"Meaning what exactly?" she asked him keenly, knowing that reopening the investigation—and coming away with a different conclusion—would still need more than just a hunch and questionable circumstances.

"For starters, I think you need to go through the surveillance videos—before and after the murders," he told her. "Some serial killers like to come back to the scene of their crimes. If that's true here, we might expect to see Desmond lurking about here or there, knowing he wasn't on our radar.

Basically, revisiting everything you have in the case against Connor Vanasse that may open up the possibility that he's not the Campus Killer. If there are no loose ends or discrepancies to that effect, then Vanasse is your killer."

*And if he's not, I can't let an innocent man go down*, she told herself, wanting to keep an open mind against the present trajectory of the investigation. "All right," Paula agreed. "And what will you do next to check out your TA?"

"Whatever is necessary to see if he's been playing us all and is truly a stone-cold killer," Neil said with an edge to his voice.

WHEN TEACHING ASSISTANT Rachelle Kenui walked into his office, Neil was sure she believed this was a routine visit pertaining to her duties for one of his classes. He only wished it was that simple. As was the case, this was anything but simple, if his fears about Desmond held water.

"Have a seat," Neil offered, as he leaned against a corner of his desk. Once she was on the black accent chair, he asked her knowingly, "I'm sure you heard that there has been an arrest made in the Campus Killer investigation?"

"Yes. The news spread like wildfire across campus." Rachelle pushed up her gold retro horn-rimmed glasses. "It was a real relief to know that the killer's behind bars."

Neil regarded her. "Do you know Connor Vanasse?"

"Not directly," she replied. "I've seen him around campus, but that's as far as it went."

"Do you know if Desmond knows him?"

"I couldn't say." Rachelle shrugged. "If so, he never shared it with me."

Neil paused musingly. "I need to know the nature of

your relationship with Desmond. Are you two just colleagues or…?"

"We're friends," she responded quickly. "We've been
spending time together lately, but it's nothing serious." She
hesitated. "Why are you asking about this? Did you hear
something…?"

"To be clear, what you and Desmond do outside the department is your business," Neil needed to say. "This has
nothing to do with that, per se… As part of the Campus
Killer Task Force, I have some concerns involving Desmond."

Rachelle's lashes fluttered. "What type of concerns?"

Gazing at her, Neil said sharply, "I have reason to believe
that Desmond not only hung out with Connor Vanasse, but
may have set him up for the murders…"

"Seriously?" She pushed her glasses up again. "How's
that even possible?"

"You'd be surprised," he told her forthrightly. "People
can be capable of almost anything, if given the right tools,
cunning and motivation." Neil gazed at her. "Did Desmond
ever talk to you about the Campus Killer murders or any of
the professors as victims?"

Rachelle thought about it and said, "Well, yeah, he—or
we—talked about the murders as they happened. I figured
his interest was that of a criminology grad student, wanting to pick my brain and vice versa on the dynamics of the
murders. I don't know if I can say he had a particular fixation on the Campus Killer's crimes."

"Did Desmond ever ask you to be his alibi?" Neil wondered.

"No, not that I can recall."

*That doesn't mean he wouldn't have, were such an alibi*

*needed*, Neil thought. He angled his face and asked if she was with Desmond at the times the victims were believed to have been killed—giving these to her one by one. In each case, Rachelle asserted that they were not together, taking away any potential line of defense for the TA, which now had Neil believing there could be a far darker side to him than ever imagined.

"Do you really think that Desmond could be capable of such heinous actions—including pinning this on someone else?" she questioned with incredulity.

"That's what we need to find out," he replied, a catch to his tone. "Was there anything at all that stood out to you with Desmond where it concerned the Campus Killer investigation?"

She sucked in a deep breath, and her voice shook while saying, "Actually, there was one thing I found kind of weird… After we were introduced to Detective Lynley, Desmond did comment that he had the hots for her—saying that she reminded him of someone he once dated and wished he could have another shot at. I had the strange feeling that he would have welcomed the opportunity to go out with the detective, if he had the chance."

Neil cringed at the thought of someone like Desmond trying to put the moves on Paula. Had he tried to romance any of the Campus Killer victims? Was he the guilty party? Instead of the one languishing in jail?

*I have a bad feeling that Desmond is guilty as hell*, Neil told himself. And just might decide to go after Paula to fulfill some dark and deadly fantasies. He wasn't about to let that happen.

After Rachelle left the office, Neil called Mike Davenport and said gravely, "Hey, I need you to get me everything you have on the anonymous tip that pointed the finger at Connor Vanasse as the purported killer of Charlotte Guthrie and, by virtue, the Campus Killer."

"Uh, okay," Davenport hummed. "You wanna clue me in on what this is all about...?"

"I'd be happy to. I have strong reason to believe that one of my teaching assistants may have set up Vanasse to take the rap," Neil told him sadly. "Now I just need to prove it..."

And make sure that justice didn't take the wrong turn in bringing the hammer down on the Campus Killer.

## Chapter Fifteen

Paula studied the surveillance video taken outside the Gotley Building the morning after Odette Furillo was murdered. She zoomed in on one of the bystanders. *It's him*, she told herself, recognizing the face.

Desmond Isaac.

He appeared calm and collected, while fitting in, almost unnoticeable. His gaze was constantly shifting—as though on guard, even as he presented himself as an innocent onlooker in the wake of a homicide.

Was this a serial killer returning to the scene of one of his crimes?

Paula considered that, according to Neil, this was part of the MO of some killers, who liked hiding in plain view at crime scenes as part of some vicarious thrill of pulling one over on their pursuers. *Is that the sick game you're playing here, Desmond?* she mused absorbedly. Was Connor Vanasse the perfect mark for him to set up?

Going through more security camera footage, Paula saw in at least two other instances at or near crime scenes of other victims of the Campus Killer, Desmond Isaac's face showed up. How had they missed this? Was he merely a true crime addict?

Or a lethal killer, who got his kicks out of pushing the limits of exposure and apprehension?

As she contemplated this, Davenport came into her office, his expression unreadable. "What is it?" Paula asked perceptively.

"Looks like we have a problem…"

"Would that problem have anything to do with Desmond Isaac?"

Davenport nodded, his brow creased. "Neil phoned me an hour ago, asking for info about the anonymous call we received that identified Connor Vanasse as the unsub on video seen running from the area where Charlotte Guthrie was killed."

Paula shifted in her chair. "What did you learn?"

"Well, for starters, the caller used a burner phone," Davenport told her. "Given the obvious implications pertaining to our case against Vanasse, I obtained a search warrant to track the location of the phone. It pinged from inside the Quinten Graduate Center. According to Neil, his graduate student TA Desmond Isaac lives in this dormitory—and was believed to have been there at the time the call was placed."

Though this wasn't necessarily an indictment of guilt in being a serial killer in and of itself, Paula felt that this only added to the case that was quickly starting to build against the teaching assistant. And move away from Connor Vanasse.

"Ramirez made a compelling case for Isaac setting up his drug buddy, Vanasse, by planting his DNA to take the fall as the Campus Killer," Davenport remarked, leaning against the wall. "Seems like Rachelle Kenui, his other TA, has some interesting things to say about Isaac that lends credence to him being our killer."

"There's more," Paula told him. "Come take a look at the surveillance videos I pulled up that show Desmond lurking about at more than one of the murdered professors' crime scenes."

After digesting this, Davenport muttered strongly, "We need to bring Desmond Isaac in for questioning."

"I agree. The sooner, the better." The last thing Paula wanted was to let the latest—and perhaps most cunning— person of interest somehow worm his way out of the weeds as a killer, without being held accountable for his crimes. If, as she was beginning to believe, Desmond Isaac proved to be the Campus Killer. Still very much at large. And perilous.

Once they took this to the captain, she didn't hesitate to come on board in the fight for justice. And against an injustice. In Paula's mind, these were one and the same. Desmond had a lot to answer for. But would he play ball? Or try to climb out of a hole that seemed to be getting deeper and deeper for the TA?

WHEN NEIL GOT the word that the anonymous tip came from the Quinten Graduate Center on campus, his focus on Desmond Isaac grew more intense. As it was, the timing of the call, using a burner phone, corresponded within minutes to a call Neil made to his TA's cell phone number. He recalled Desmond telling him that he was at the dorm when the call was made. Coincidence?

*I don't think so*, Neil told himself, as he left his office. Not when combined with other damning evidence against his TA.

He headed to Jamison Hall where, according to Associate Professor George Tyler, Desmond was currently in Tyler's Criminal Justice Behavior and Ethics class. Given his strong suspicions toward him, Neil found it almost laughable in a humorless way that Desmond would be enrolled in the class, contrary to his own suspected behavior as a purported serial killer.

After driving to the building, Neil went inside and, though armed, hoped Desmond would allow himself to be taken into custody peacefully. But he had to be prepared that the killer suspect could resist. And even potentially use the professor or other students as shields to hide behind.

All of that proved to be a moot point when Professor Tyler sent Neil a text, just before he entered the classroom, to report that Desmond Isaac had abruptly left the class moments earlier. After verifying this, Neil searched for his TA, believing that he must have used the back stairwell to escape. Had he been tipped off? Or had the alleged Campus Killer developed a sixth sense as part of his cold and calculating psyche, warning him of danger?

While heading back to his office, Neil notified Paula and other members of the team that Desmond had managed to evade him.

WITH NEWS THAT Desmond Isaac was still on the loose, Paula drove with Davenport to the Quinten Graduate Center, equipped with arrest and search warrants for the individual now suspected of being a suffocation-style serial killer.

"This case keeps getting weirder and weirder," Davenport commented from behind the wheel with a frown on his face.

"I know." Paula pursed her lips. "The pieces did seem to fit where it concerned Connor Vanasse," she noted. "Which made him the perfect patsy for the criminology graduate student, Desmond Isaac."

"Yeah," the detective concurred. "Except his master plan has started to unravel."

"Which makes him all the more dangerous, with his back suddenly against the wall," Paula said thoughtfully, as they drove into the Quinten Graduate Center parking lot.

After checking the lobby and cafeteria for any signs of the suspect and finding none, they headed for his fifth-floor room in the east wing and knocked, to no avail.

Davenport sighed with annoyance. "Doesn't look like he's come back here."

"Unless he wants us to believe that's the case," Paula said suspiciously. "Why don't you stand guard here and keep an eye out for him. I'll go get someone to let us in…"

"All right."

Down at the front desk of the dorm, Paula flashed her identification at the hazel-eyed slender young female attendant, with thick hair in a platinum blonde balayage style, and told her, "I'm Detective Lynley. I have a search warrant to get inside the room of Desmond Isaac."

The young woman glanced at the search warrant and sighed with indifference. "What's he done?"

"Maybe nothing," Paula answered dispassionately, though strongly suspecting it was just the opposite.

She rolled her eyes. "Whatever," she said dryly, phoning someone from management to meet Paula at the room.

Moments later, they were inside the single occupant room and found it empty. Judging by the untidiness, it appeared as though Desmond had come and gone in a hurry. Missing was his laptop and any cell phones. Donning a pair of nitrile gloves, Paula searched the suspect's desk and chest of drawers for anything that might be visibly incriminating in the case. All she found was drug paraphernalia, a bag of marijuana and a small amount of illicit opioids.

"You may want to take a look at what's in the closet." Davenport got her attention.

When Paula walked to the closet, the sliding door was open all the way and hanging clothes were pushed to one side. On the back wall were photographs of all the victims of the Campus Killer, printed out from a computer. It gave her a chill. "Who keeps pictures of a serial killer's victims hidden inside the closet?"

"Someone who gets his kicks out of collecting and looking at them whenever the mood suits him," Davenport answered matter-of-factly, wearing gloves. "Such as the Campus Killer."

She wrinkled her brow. "I was afraid you'd say that," she moaned.

"There's something else." His voice dipped uneasily.

Her eyes turned to his. "What…?"

"This." Davenport moved the clothes to the other side of the closet to reveal a school newspaper clipping on the wall of Paula and Gayle during the investigation. "Looks like the creep has a fascination for female detectives too…"

Paula gulped as another chill ran through her at the thought of her or Gayle being suffocated to death by Desmond. She voiced firmly what surely went without saying, "We have to find him—"

"I know." Davenport favored her with a supportive look.

A BOLO was put out for Desmond Isaac and the black Mazda CX-30 the murder suspect was believed to be driving.

GAYLE WAS IN disbelief that they apparently had the wrong person in jail in Connor Vanasse. The persuasive evidence—

if you could call it that—while compelling, to say the least, had been an attempt by the real Campus Killer to point them in the wrong direction. Hard as it was to believe that Desmond Isaac had nearly pulled this off, she trusted Paula, Mike and Neil in the investigating they'd done that led them to conclude Neil's teaching assistant was actually the true culprit. He'd used his grad student studies in criminology and evidence manipulation to make Vanasse the fall guy.

Equally disturbing to Gayle, as she drove on Ellington Street at Addison University in search of the suspect's vehicle, was the thought that Isaac had evidently had her and Paula on his target list, along with the professors. Would the so-called Campus Killer have really come after them, while trying to finger Vanasse as the serial killer? Or had Isaac fully intended to kill her and Paula beforehand, but never had the right opportunity to do so?

Whatever the case, Gayle was on guard for as long as the suspect was on the loose. She had no wish to die before her time and by his hand, any more than Paula, as both had too much to live for. In Paula's case, she needed the longevity to move things along with Neil in the proper direction. And for herself, Gayle was sure there was someone out there for her. She only needed to stay alive to find him.

Her reverie ended when she spotted the black Mazda CX-30 parked crookedly across the street, next to the Intramural Sports Building. Knowing it matched the description of the suspect's vehicle, Gayle did a U-turn and pulled her Ford Escape up behind the Mazda. It appeared to be empty. She ran the license plate and saw that the car was indeed registered to a Desmond K. Isaac.

Gayle called it in and requested backup. She got out of her car and drew her weapon, in case the suspect was hiding inside the Mazda. Approaching carefully, she determined that there was no one inside. Scanning the area, she decided that Isaac had ditched the vehicle and was on the run. But where to, as a desperate man who may be even more dangerous if he believed he had nothing to lose?

NEIL LEARNED THAT Rachelle Kenui had texted Desmond Isaac, asking that he turn himself in. Rachelle believed she was helping facilitate a peaceful surrender of her fellow teaching assistant. For that, Neil did not fault her. Unfortunately, giving Desmond a heads-up seemed to have backfired as, by all accounts, he was making a conscious effort to avoid capture.

Of even more concern to Neil was the clear indication that Paula, along with Gayle, was in the serial killer suspect's crosshairs. When combining Rachelle's intuition about Desmond with the proof Paula and Davenport had found in Desmond's dorm room of his fixation on Paula—in spite of the attempt to lay blame for the Campus Killer murders on Connor Vanasse—Neil was even more fearful that Desmond might go after Paula.

*I can't allow him to hurt her*, Neil told himself, as he headed out of Horton Hall, having just received word that the suspect's vehicle had been found abandoned nearby. Paula was on her way over to his office, where Neil had hoped to strategize more with her in putting the finishing touches on this case, once and for all. With Desmond on the loose and in the area, Neil didn't want to take any chances that he might actually show up at the building, for whatever reason.

Desperate people could do desperate things, Neil knew. Desmond Isaac certainly fit into that category. Along with being a cold and calculating serial killer, as it now appeared was all but certain.

All Neil could think of at the moment was that he loved Paula too much to let Desmond take what they could have away from them. But when Paula was not responding to calls or texts on her cell phone, Neil feared that he may already be too late to stop his soon-to-be former TA.

# Chapter Sixteen

Paula wondered how Desmond Isaac had managed to slip through the cracks earlier in their investigation, as she headed over to see Neil to compare their notes and coordinate their efforts toward bringing his teaching assistant in for questioning. With the signs all pointing toward his guilt and Connor Vanasse being set up to take the fall as the Campus Killer, it was imperative that they put an end to this. Before Desmond Isaac could do more damage.

In Paula's mind, that included going after her or Gayle, as the hidden newspaper clipping inside his closet seemed to imply. The fact that Desmond had ditched his car on campus meant that he was likely on foot. Though she couldn't rule out that he had grabbed a bicycle or moped in a desperate means to evade capture. With the BOLO alert, there were few places he could hide on campus, or in Rendall Cove, for that matter. This meant that his arrest was imminent.

But until such time, Paula knew neither she nor Gayle could or should rest easy. *I'm sure Neil feels the same way*, Paula told herself, pulling into the parking lot of Horton Hall. With the connection between Desmond as his TA and the School of Criminal Justice, Neil had added incentive to want him off the streets and the investigation into the Campus Killer finally brought to a close the correct way.

Beyond that, Paula found herself wondering where that would leave her and Neil on a personal level. She wanted so much more with and from him—the man she had fallen hopelessly in love with—and couldn't imagine their momentum hitting a brick wall once his work as a visiting professor had come to an end. But that would have to wait, with other matters more pressing at the moment.

When she emerged from her car, Paula realized that her cell phone was buzzing. She pulled it from the pocket of her high-rise flare pants and saw that it was Neil, bringing a smile to her face. *Can't wait to see you, too*, she thought.

Only before she could answer the call, Paula heard a low but steady male's voice say intently, "I wouldn't answer that if I were you, Detective Lynley."

Paula looked into the icy eyes of Desmond Isaac and then down at the Beretta 3032 Tomcat Kale Slushy pistol in his hand, pointed at her, recognizing the .32 ACP gun from a previous case she had worked on. She resisted the urge to respond to the call and tell Neil she was in danger, and instead furrowed her brow at the suspected serial killer and said sharply, "Just what do you think you're doing, Desmond?"

"I'm sure you're well aware what's going on, Detective Lynley." His brows twitched. "You and your colleagues, thanks to Prof Ramirez, are looking for me... Well, it's my lucky day—you've found me. I'll take that phone from you now."

How had he managed to remain on the loose? Paula peered at him. "You're making a big mistake, Desmond."

"You'll be making a bigger one, if you don't do as I asked!" he countered menacingly. "The phone, please..."

She did as he requested, handing it over, then watched as Desmond tossed it into a clump of common witch hazel shrubs. "Now I need your gun, Detective!"

As Paula weighed whether or not she should comply, or even attempt to take out the firearm and use it in self-defense, Desmond had taken it upon himself to remove the SIG Sauer P365 semiautomatic pistol from the holster that was tucked just inside her beige one-button blazer. He placed it in the pocket of his black fleece shirt jacket and said, "Next, I need you to help me get off this campus—in your car," he snorted.

"If you want the car, take it," she spat, ready to hand him the key fob.

"I don't think so." His expression hardened. "You're driving."

Paula hesitated, knowing that getting into any car with him—even her duty vehicle—was not in her best interests. She wrinkled her nose defiantly at Desmond. "Seriously? Are you really going to add to your troubles by kidnapping a police detective?" Even in asking this, Paula knew that it was not likely going to move the needle in her favor for someone who had nothing to lose at this point of desperation. She was even more concerned about what he might have in mind for her, given what she had seen in the closet of his dormitory room.

Desmond gave a derisive chuckle. "I'm way past wondering if it's a smart move or not, don't you think? As it is, Detective Lynley, you've really left me with no other choice, given the rather precarious predicament you and the other cops hunting me have put me in." He aimed the gun at her face and said forcefully, "Let's go…"

Knowing he had her at a disadvantage, Paula didn't make

any waves just yet, if only to buy time without being shot. She began heading toward her Mustang Mach-E, hoping that someone—if not Neil—would spot Desmond as a passenger in her car and prevent them from getting too far. Short of that, she needed to be prepared to do anything necessary to come out of this alive.

Or die trying.

NEIL HAD JUST come out of the building when he spotted Paula's white Mustang leaving the parking lot, with her in it. At first glance, he found this odd. Where was she going? Why hadn't she responded to his calls or texts?

Then he saw that she wasn't alone in the car. As it turned onto Creighten Road, it became apparent to Neil that the occupant in the passenger seat was Desmond Isaac.

His heart skipping a beat, Neil knew instinctively that his former teaching assistant had taken Paula against her will. Most likely at gunpoint. Desmond was hoping to dodge the dragnet for his capture by using her as an escape mechanism.

Then what?

Neil had good reason to fear that Desmond would like to add Paula to his victim count before this was through, given his track record and knowledge that they were on to him. *Not if I have any say in it*, he told himself determinedly, as Neil raced toward his own car. He was well aware that allowing them to leave the campus would place Paula in even greater danger. The alternative of stopping this from happening at risk to her life would undoubtedly get under Desmond's skin too, should he fail. It was a chance Neil was willing to take, with stakes that couldn't be higher for the woman he loved.

Along with everything they dreamed of that was within their grasp. So long as a serial killer didn't destroy it, as he had so many other dreams.

Getting on his cell phone, Neil told Davenport, "Desmond Isaac's got Paula."

"What?"

"He abducted her in broad daylight from outside Horton Hall and forced her to drive him in her vehicle." Neil was certain. "They're headed down Creighten Road."

Davenport muttered an expletive, then said solidly, "I'll notify patrols to set up roadblocks at Grand Avenue, Rockfield Road, and Notter Street. They won't get very far."

*I'll believe it when I see it*, Neil thought, not taking anything for granted where it concerned the cunning killer grad student. He got into the car, started the ignition and said, "We need to bring in a SWAT team, K-9 unit—and even a hostage negotiator in case that's necessary."

"I'll get right on it," Davenport promised, seemingly masking his own concern for Paula's safety. "I'll let Gayle and the Rendall Cove PD know what's going on," he added, and Neil was certain this was for his benefit, so as to present a united front in tackling this latest turn in the investigation.

"Yeah," he told the detective simply and drove onto the street. "I'm going after them."

"You really think that's a good idea?" Davenport questioned. "If you're made by Isaac, there's no telling how he might react..."

Though this consideration was surely on his mind, Neil responded straightforwardly, "And if I do nothing and something bad happens to Paula, apart from being nabbed by a man we think has already murdered six females, I'd never be able to live with myself."

As if he understood that Neil was speaking from the heart in his words, Davenport told him, "Do what you need to." He paused. "We'll get through this."

Neil disconnected. He sure as hell was not leaving that to chance. Something told him that Paula felt exactly the same way, as he sped down the street until he caught sight of her vehicle.

PAULA SPOTTED IN the rearview mirror a car that had seemed to be moving fast, but then slowed down. As if to give them some room.

Neil.

How did he know? Did he somehow find her phone?

It meant Neil had notified others and, as such, help was on the way. But not necessarily soon enough to keep her gun-toting passenger from becoming suicidal and taking her with him.

*I have to distract him*, Paula thought as she glanced at Desmond. He was holding the gun on her and definitely jittery, as she rounded the traffic circle and headed onto Aspen Lane. She sucked in a deep breath and said, "So, what was this all about, Desmond? Why did you kill those professors? What did they ever do to you?"

He gave an amused chuckle, glancing out the side window and back. "What did they do to me?" he asked mockingly. "Well, other than Debra Newton—who decided I wasn't good enough for her, too young, too weird or whatever, and had to pay the ultimate price—the other professors had to die because they thought the world revolved around them. At least that was how I took it while observing them from afar. Someone needed to knock them off their pedestals. I volunteered for the job," Desmond boasted and laughed.

*So full of yourself,* Paula thought as she drove. "Why kill them off and on campus?" she asked curiously. "Or was this all just a big game to you, sadistic as it was?"

He jutted his chin. "Yeah, I suppose you could say it was a game of sorts," he admitted. "I definitely got my kicks out of suffocating some of them to death on campus and others elsewhere. But, truthfully, I also wanted to keep you guys off balance by mixing things up a bit. Beyond that, the laws of average told me that killing them all on campus, which was my natural inclination, was only asking for trouble, with surveillance cameras, too many people out and about, and so forth."

Paula shook her head in disgust. "Did you really think you would get away with this," she decided to challenge him, "by setting up Connor Vanasse to take the fall for what you did?"

"Uh, yeah, I thought it was a good possibility," he admitted. "I laid out my game plan to near perfection. Taking out one victim after another, using what I'd learned as an Addison U criminology graduate student and basic common sense to put this into motion." Desmond laughed with satisfaction. "It was also admittedly good research for my thesis on homicides in society and its impact on local communities." He chuckled again. "As for poor Connor, it wasn't all that difficult to take advantage of his distractions with taking and dealing drugs to collect his DNA and plant it on a couple of the victims. The nosebleed Connor had gave me the perfect excuse to relieve him of some of the blood to smear beneath the nails of Professor Odette Furillo. Later, I pretended to cut Connor accidentally and insisted upon cleaning up the blood. Unbeknownst to him, I kept enough to rub below the nails of Professor Charlotte Guthrie."

"That's sick," Paula hissed at him, trying to fathom the lengths he was willing to go to as a serial killer. "Too bad it's all fallen apart now."

Desmond sneered. "Honestly, I wondered how long it would take you and the others to figure out who was truly behind the killings—if ever. Then Prof Ramirez had to interject himself into the case, thanks to you, and used his skill set as a profiler to piece everything together."

Paula glanced at the rearview mirror and saw that Neil was still lying back, undoubtedly not wanting to rock the boat prematurely. "Don't blame him for what you did," she said snippily. "That's all on you—"

"And I own up to it." He chuckled nastily. "At least now I do. With the cat out of the bag, I might as well enjoy the glory of being the Campus Killer—who's not quite through yet…"

He kept the gun on her, as if to prove his point. This told Paula what she already sensed. She would not come out of this alive. Not if Desmond had his way. She prayed that wouldn't be the case.

NEIL WATCHED AS Paula approached the roadblock on Grand Avenue, then took a sharp turn onto Beasley Road, headed toward Rockfield Road. It too would be cut off, preventing Desmond Isaac's escape with his captive. With nowhere to go, what might the suspected serial killer do next?

The thought made Neil cringe as he continued to trail them from a safe distance, though he seriously doubted that anyone with Desmond's cunning and awareness would be kept from knowing they were being followed for long. When backed into a corner, he might go on the attack at any time. With Paula being left to fend for herself.

*I trust that she's capable of doing whatever it takes to survive*, Neil told himself. He just wasn't nearly as certain it would be enough against the likes of a heartless serial killer, seemingly wanting to win at any and all costs.

Putting on his criminal profiler hat, Neil found himself sizing up more of the negative character traits of his ex-teaching assistant. He saw Desmond as the classic narcissist, somehow believing himself to be smarter than everyone else—and certainly more bloodthirsty in his thought patterns. From what he knew about him, as seen in a new light, Neil was sure that Desmond also suffered from borderline personality disorder and antisocial personality disorder.

It went without saying that his former TA had proven himself to be a sadist, Neil concluded. Meaning that Desmond would have no sympathy for Paula, no matter how Neil sliced it. He had to find a way to save her, as well as put a stop to Desmond's unnatural thirst for murder.

"Looks like we've got company," Desmond said with a sneer as he looked behind them. "Professor Neil Ramirez. Or should I say ATF Special Agent Ramirez? Why am I not surprised? He seems to have a real knack for continuing to stick his nose in my business."

Paula saw no reason to deny the obvious. "All of the law enforcement personnel involved in this case are on to you, Desmond," she pointed out matter-of-factly. "Why do you think the roads leading off campus are being blocked?"

Desmond grumbled as he looked ahead and saw patrol cars forming a barrier in front of Rockfield Road. He muttered an expletive, then barked defiantly, "If you want me— come and get me!"

"It's over, Desmond." Paula hoped to convince him to

quit while he was ahead. And while both of them were still alive. "There's no way out of this for you. Why don't you let me pull over. Just give yourself up and no one else has to get hurt."

"By *no one*, you mean yourself?" he snickered.

She eyed him keenly. "I mean either one of us," she offered succinctly. "Killing me means killing yourself. You don't want that. Think of all you could offer from your experiences. Let's end this now!"

He cackled, the gun still firmly aimed in her direction. "I don't think so. I have a better idea. Why don't we bypass the patrol cars up there and take a little drive around the circle to the Campus Arboretum…and wait for Prof Ramirez to join us."

Paula recoiled at the thought of leading Neil into a deadly trap. But given that Desmond was unstable enough to shoot her right then and there, she didn't see where she had much choice. Other than to go along with the Campus Killer, knowing that Neil and the rest of the team were converging on them to end the threat.

One way or the other.

NEIL WAS SURPRISED to see that Paula had circumvented the roadblock by turning onto Leland Road, the last street before Rockfield Road. They were headed toward the Campus Arboretum. He notified Gayle and Davenport of this development, and the SWAT unit was already getting into place for a shot at the kidnapper and alleged serial killer.

*What is Desmond up to?* Neil asked himself. He had to put himself in the shoes of his former teaching assistant turned villain. All things considered, Desmond had probably come to realize that this was likely the end of the line.

But it was unlikely that he intended to go down without a fight. Or at least without ending things on his own terms.

To Neil, this meant positioning himself away from easy targeting by SWAT members or other authorities. Desmond most likely wanted him as payback for ruining his best-laid plans with Connor Vanasse. And taking Paula's life too would give Desmond the ultimate satisfaction to take with him to the grave.

Neil sucked in a deep breath as he headed for the Campus Arboretum, while hoping to avert a catastrophe that could cost him and Paula their lives.

Not to mention a future together.

PAULA PARKED IN an area that was off Mumbly Drive, the main road to the Campus Arboretum. She was quickly forced out of the car by Desmond at gunpoint and made to move through the woodlands—featuring a plethora of silver maple, black ash and beech trees, various herbaceous plants and a migrant bird sanctuary.

"This is pointless, Desmond," she protested, trying to buy more time. "Give it up. I can protect you from harm, if you hand me your gun and mine. You'll get a fair trial—"

"Yeah, right." He gave a sardonic chuckle. "There's not much defense for suffocating six pretty professors. And, very soon, you can add to that killing a visiting professor with ATF credentials. Oh, and did I forget—a good-looking campus police detective too. Thanks, but I think I'll see what awaits me on the other side after a bit of unfinished business…"

They heard the rustling of trees and crunching of dirt, causing Desmond to instinctively grab Paula from behind and place the gun to her temple. "Come out," he demanded.

"Or I'll put a bullet in Detective Lynley's pretty head before you can even think about dropping me."

"All right, all right," said the deep and most familiar voice. Out of the trees came Neil, who had his Glock 47 pistol out and aimed directly at Desmond. "I'm out. You've got me, Desmond. I assume this is what you wanted…?"

"Yeah, sure." Desmond laughed. "I have to admit, Professor Ramirez, you gave me a bit of a start. Thought I had more time to work with in getting my captive here to a more secluded location, while waiting for you."

"You thought wrong." Neil's voice raised an octave. "I'm a profiler, remember? I was able to anticipate your latest moves before you could make them. Now let her go and we can settle this man to man."

Desmond growled like an animal. "You'd like that, wouldn't you?" He tightened his grip on Paula. "She stays right where she is. I suggest you drop your gun, Special Agent Ramirez. Or I'll simply blow the detective's brains out, right here and now. Then you can shoot me to death before the cavalry arrives and take all the credit for downing the Campus Killer. Your call."

It was clear to Paula that Neil had no intention of giving in to Desmond's demands, no matter how tempting, knowing full well that to do so would be signing both their death warrants. On the other hand, she could feel the tension in the killer's body, pressed up against hers. He was a powder keg that was ready to explode at any time. She couldn't let that happen. She wouldn't allow Desmond to call the shots any longer. Not when it literally meant the difference between life and death for all three of them.

For two, at least, she had a better plan of action and survival. Paula lulled Desmond into a false sense of security by saying meekly, "You win, Desmond. I'm done with this. Go ahead and get it over with and I'll die knowing that Neil took a serial monster off the streets of Rendall Cove…"

As the Campus Killer seemed momentarily confused, using her skills in Krav Maga, Paula caught him off guard by swiftly slamming the back of her head into his face as hard as she could. At the same time that she heard his facial bones fracturing, she pushed the gun away from her head as it fired off one round up into the trees.

Desmond howled like a seriously wounded animal, and his firearm fell harmlessly onto the ground while he put both hands to his face. Whipping around, Paula was taking no chances for a quick recovery by the serial killer—using a self-defense technique to knee him hard in the groin.

While he bowled over in pain, her adrenaline rush was still high, but Paula felt herself being pushed aside. She watched as Neil took over, landing two solid blows to Desmond's head, before the kidnapper and killer fell flat on his bloodied face, knocked out cold. Neil quickly put Desmond's arms behind his back and Paula cuffed him.

"Are you all right?" Neil asked her gingerly, taking her into his protective arms.

She nodded, glancing at Desmond. "I'm a lot better than him," she answered unsympathetically.

"Did he hurt you?"

"Not really." She made a silly face. "Only the pain of knowing he'd managed to get away with it for so long."

"Well, that's over now. Thanks to you." Neil pulled back, so she could see the little grin playing on his mouth as he looked at the still unconscious serial killer. "I didn't realize you had that fighting combo in you. Wow!"

She laughed. "Guess there are still things you need to learn about me."

"I suppose. Where did that come from?"

"A very wise self-defense instructor in Krav Maga," she told him, separating from him as she went over to the fallen foe and reclaimed her SIG Sauer pistol. She put it back into its holster. "Figured the martial arts would come in handy someday. Guess today is that day."

"And very timely, if I say so myself," he said with a laugh.

Paula met his eyes. "Can't argue with you there." She paused. "Desmond fessed up about everything, including setting up Connor and hoping to get away with it."

"I expected as much." Neil gave a knowing nod. "Guess Desmond was glad, in his own way, to get this off his chest."

She tilted her face and glanced at his former TA. "That he did, though you'd know better than I would about how the psyche of a serial killer works."

Neil regarded her in earnest, and his voice cracked when he uttered, "If I had lost you—"

Paula put a finger to his lips, knowing she felt the same way about losing him. "You didn't," she told him. "And I didn't lose you either, thank goodness."

"True." He took a breath. "But with the thought of that, and before the team comes and takes over, I don't want to wait a moment longer to tell you just how much I love you, Paula."

"Then don't," she teased him.

Neil laughed. "Yeah, I love you, Detective Lynley."

"That works both ways, Agent Ramirez. Very much so." She cupped his cheeks and laid a hearty kiss on Neil's lips, so as to leave no doubt.

Paula only wished that the same could be true for where

things went from here, as the criminal investigation that brought them together wound down with the capture of the real Campus Killer, at last.

# Epilogue

Members of the Bureau of Alcohol, Tobacco, Firearms and Explosives, Rendall Cove Police Department's Firearms Investigation Unit and the Shays County Sheriff's Department converged on the American foursquare home on Vernon Drive. Parked in the driveway was the silver Lincoln Navigator Reserve registered to alleged gunrunner Craig Eckart, and a blue BMW 228i Gran Coupe registered to known Eckart associate Salvador Alonso, and a red Jeep Wagoneer belonging to ATF agent Vinny Ortiz. The undercover operative had just sent out a text, signaling that the time had come to break up the firearms trafficking network, once and for all. They hoped the raid would send a message that would resonate globally.

Wearing a ballistic vest and armed with his Glock 47 Gen5 MOS 9x19mm pistol, Neil joined his heavily armed law enforcement partners, equipped with arrest and search warrants for the takedown. That included bringing in an officer from Animal Control to handle the potentially aggressive Staffordshire bull terrier that Eckart was known to own. Waiting in the backdrop were crime scene investigators and an ambulance, if needed.

Using fierce determination, overwhelming power and a

battering ram, the front door was forced open and the house inundated with the team, able and ready to handle any resistance. The dog was quickly subdued and removed from the premises. Fanning out to each and every room, arrests were made of three men and two women. The former included Craig Eckart and J. H. Santoro—Ortiz's alias. Ortiz, who put up a good act of appropriate belligerence and outrage over the arrest, was handcuffed along with the other suspects.

"Tell it to the judge," Neil snapped at him believably, while handing him over to an FIU detective.

"I will," Ortiz muttered convincingly, as he was led away without further incident.

Neil watched as Craig Eckart looked shell-shocked at the prospect of his gunrunning business going up in smoke, while facing potentially decades behind bars for his trouble.

When the dust finally settled, along with a treasure trove of detailed information on contraband firearms and ammunition seized with five cell phones and three laptops, the raid uncovered a cache of unlicensed firearms and rounds of ammunition, huge quantities of fentanyl and quantities of methamphetamine and further evidence of criminal activity that Eckhart and his colleagues were engaged in.

FRESH OFF THE successful raid of Craig Eckart's illegal weapons enterprise, Neil was back at Horton Hall, having already mapped out his future where it concerned Paula and a life together, when he was summoned to the office of School of Criminal Justice Director Stafford Geeson.

He walked in to find Geeson standing by a picture window, seemingly deep in thought. Neil imagined that he was wondering how he could have missed the signs of the evil that lurked within his teaching assistant, Desmond Isaac.

*Believe me, I'm asking myself the same thing*, Neil thought, but he took solace in knowing that he had figured out Desmond's true character before he was able to successfully pin the murder rap on Connor Vanasse. Not to mention add Paula as another notch on his belt of victims.

"Stafford—" Neil got his attention.

Geeson faced him and forced a grin. "Neil—thanks for coming."

"No problem." He met the director's eyes curiously. "Everything okay?"

"Yeah, I'm fine. The School of Criminal Justice will continue to do its thing in educating and preparing the next generation of people in law enforcement to fight the good fight, in spite of our one giant setback and disappointment in Desmond Isaac."

Neil frowned. "We're all disappointed in him and the horrible choices he made."

"He'll have a lot of time to digest it behind bars," Geeson pointed out with satisfaction in his voice. "Anyway, I didn't ask you to drop by to talk about him." He paused. "Have a seat."

"All right." Neil sat on a blue task chair by the window and watched as Geeson sat nearby. *So, is this where he cans me with my contract nearing an end?* Neil mused. Or the opposite?

After a moment or two, Geeson eyed him squarely and said, "I'm not sure what your plans are, insofar as returning to full-time work as an ATF special agent or another avenue, but during your short tenure here at Addison University, you've become one of the most liked and respected professors in the School of Criminal Justice. Using your expertise to help flush out the Campus Killer—especially when it was one of our own—only enhanced your stature around here." He paused. "What I'm trying to say is that I'd like to offer you a full-time position as an associate professor of criminology—if you're interested…?"

"I'm definitely interested." Neil didn't have to think very long about the offer. Particularly since it was an avenue he would have pursued, had the director not beaten him to it.

"I'm happy to hear that." Geeson's face lit up. "So, are you in…?"

"Yeah." Neil grinned. "I'm in."

"Welcome aboard for the long term, Professor Ramirez." They stood up and shook hands firmly.

Back in his own office, Neil rang his boss at the Grand Rapids ATF field office, Doris Frankenberg, and said in earnest, "We need to talk."

A few minutes later, he was in his car, where Neil got Paula on speakerphone and asked coolly, "Where are you?"

"On my way home," she told him, and he could hear some background noise. "Where are you?"

"Headed to your house," he responded simply. "See you shortly."

"I'll be waiting…"

After disconnecting, Neil couldn't wait to be face-to-face with her. But first, he had a stop to make.

PAULA WAS HAPPY to chill at home, following a workday that included clearing up a few loose ends in the Campus Killer case. There would still be more to come, even with Desmond Isaac's capture and confession. Such as piecing together how he had been able to succeed in his depravity for as long as he had and what could be learned from this for future serial killer investigations by the Department of Police and Public Safety.

But at the moment, Paula admitted that she had butterflies in her stomach knowing Neil was on his way over. She suspected he wanted to talk about their future. Or perhaps his waning time as a visiting professor. For her part, she had decided that as much as she loved her job, it paled in comparison to the love she felt for Neil. She would gladly relocate to his work place if that was what it took for them to be together.

When he knocked on the door, Chloe meowed, as if she'd been anticipating his arrival and welcomed his presence as much as Paula. The cat ran to the door, and Paula followed the Devon rex in her bare feet and opened it, only to see a grinning Neil standing there, holding a dozen long-stemmed red roses.

"What's this?" She batted her eyes demurely.

"For you," he said with a lilt in his voice. "Just a little something I picked up along the way."

Neil handed them to her, and Paula put the roses up to her nose and took in the delightful floral scent. She flashed her teeth at him. "They're lovely," she gushed as they made their way into the great room.

"Not half as lovely as you," he asserted while allowing Chloe to rub against one of his brown Chelsea boots.

"Thank you." She blushed and went into the kitchen to put the roses in water.

When Paula returned to the great room, she could tell that something was on Neil's mind. *Me, I hope*, she told herself, but asked evenly, "So, what's up?" She'd heard that the ATF-led operation against suspected arms trafficker Craig Eckart had been successful. It was a big win for the task

force and city of Rendall Cove in curbing the proliferation
of illegal weapons across the globe.

After he commented keenly on this, Neil took her hands
and looked Paula directly in the eyes and asked casually,
"Feel like getting married again?"

Her eyes ballooned at his face. "Is that a proposal?"

"Yeah, it is," he made clear. "I'm in love with you,
Paula. You already know how I feel. I think the same is
true from your end. So, why not make it official? Be my
wife and we can have a great marriage and all that comes
with it."

Paula felt the beat of her heart, erratic as it was. This was
something she had dreamed of—a second opportunity to
find true love. Neil checked every box in that department
and then some. There was one other thing to address though,
even if it had no bearing on her decision, per se, but was
important nevertheless.

"What did you have in mind for us once your visiting
professorship stint ends?" She angled her eyes at his curiously. "To be sure, I'm more than ready and willing to relocate to Grand Rapids—or elsewhere, if necessary, to be
with you…"

A smile played on Neil's lips as he said nonchalantly,
"Actually, about that… I was just offered a full-time position by the director of the SCJ, which I happily accepted.
So, I'm not going anywhere. Not unless you want to leave
Rendall Cove. If that's the case, count me in on wherever
you want to set up shop. It doesn't matter, as long as we're
together."

Paula beamed. "Congrats on the wonderful news in becoming a faculty member and no longer just a visiting professor. I'd love to stay put in this college town in my current

position with the Investigative Division of the DPPS—and build a family with you, Neil."

"Are you saying what I think you're saying?" His voice cracked.

Her teeth shone. "Yes, I'm madly in love with you, Professor Neil Ramirez, and would be delighted to become your bride and mother to any children you'd like to have."

"As many kids as we're comfortable with, while being able to balance that with our work lives and quality time as a couple," he told her, his tone genuine.

"Well, all right, then." She chuckled, excited at what was to come for them. "It looks like we're now engaged to be married." Paula knew the engagement ring would come soon enough. Right now, she was more than content simply to have his heart.

"I couldn't be happier," Neil promised, wrapping his arms around her protectively. "But I think it's imperative that we seal the deal with a…"

He pulled them apart just enough for Neil to give her a hearty kiss that left Paula light on her feet and feeling that, in this instance, a single action truly did speak louder than hearing the word.

EIGHT MONTHS LATER on their honeymoon, Neil and Paula Ramirez lounged on beach chairs at the Ka'anapali Beach Resort on the island of Maui, Hawaii. Wearing sunglasses and floral-print swim trunks while sipping on a lava flow, Neil checked out his wife as she talked on her cell phone with her friend, Josie, the two comparing notes on their Hawaiian experiences.

Paula had on a hot red halter bikini top and matching bottoms, showing off her shapely legs. *She's so hot*, Neil told himself admiringly, as Paula took a sip of her blue curaçao before resuming the conversation. She was even more beautiful as the blushing bride when they tied the knot a month ago, showing off her princess-cut diamond wedding band to everyone she saw. Attendees included Paula's mother, Francine, and Neil's sister, Yancy, along with Gayle Yamasaki, Mike Davenport and Vinny Ortiz, among others.

Neil shifted his gaze to the seemingly endless Pacific Ocean. There were a few gentle waves brushing against the shore and a couple of boats out for some leisure time. Neil thought about the happenings since he and Paula took Desmond Isaac out of commission. They had located Desmond's laptop and cell phone, each of which contained important evidence attesting to his guilt as the Campus Killer.

His full, official confession to six murders, one attempted murder and kidnapping and a few other charges thrown in for good measure landed Desmond Isaac in the Ionia Correctional Facility, or I-Max, in Ionia County, Michigan. There, the maximum-security state prisoner would spend the rest of his life. Thanks in part to Connor Vanasse, whose cooperation in the case against Desmond allowed Vanasse to cop a plea for drug-related offenses, rather than multiple murders, resulting in a few years behind bars.

With Desmond's reign of terror at Addison University over, the campus had returned to being a great place to study. Not to mention a perfect setting for Neil to teach criminology full-time as an associate professor. He had been retained by the Bureau of Alcohol, Tobacco, Firearms and Explosives as a consultant on high-profile cases. Such as the one that brought down arms trafficker Craig Eckart, who, it turned out in an ironic twist, had sold Desmond the

Beretta 3032 Tomcat Kale Slushy pistol he used to abduct and try to kill Paula.

Eckart had been convicted on a slew of federal charges and would be spending decades rotting away in the Federal Correctional Institution, Milan, in York Township in Washtenaw County, Michigan. Joining him in FCI Milan was pipe bomber Harold Fujisawa, who would also be incarcerated for a very long time as a convicted domestic terrorist.

But, most of all, Neil was delighted to be a husband to Paula, the gorgeous detective sergeant who continued to make her mark in the school's Investigative Division, in helping to keep it a safe environment for professors and students alike. He was just about to have another sip of his cocktail, when instead Neil felt the softness of Paula's lips on his.

"Just wanted to make sure you were awake," she teased him after the long kiss had ended.

"I am now," he joked, tasting her blue curaçao on his lips.

She laughed. "What do you say we jump into the water for a swim?"

Tempting as that sounded, Neil responded desirously, "I have a much better idea. How about we head back to our room and flex our limbs in a different way?"

"Hmm…" Paula pretended to think about it while flashing her teeth. "Why, that sounds like a fabulous idea, Mr. Ramirez. Works for me."

"I was hoping you'd say that, Mrs. Ramirez." His eyes lit up lovingly as Neil got to his feet, bringing Paula up with him. He kissed her again, allowing it to linger a bit, enjoying this. Then a bit more and a little more after that, before he stopped for now and said definitively, "Let's go."

\* \* \* \* \*

# THREATS IN
# THE DEEP

ADDISON FOX

For everyone who believes their past dictates their future. There's more joy and wonder and beauty awaiting you than you can ever know.
Reach for it—always!

# Chapter One

*Special task force.*

Those words swirled through Gavin Hayes's mind as he prepared himself for a morning in the waters around New York City.

He stared up at the beautiful stretch of the majestic Verrazzano-Narrows Bridge as his police boat moved through the tidal strait that separated Brooklyn and Staten Island on their way toward the Statue of Liberty. The bridge's arches speared toward the bright blue early spring sky, a testament to man's ingenuity and sheer prowess at building over, around and *through* nature.

He was on a patrol shift, and while they had no overt mission at the moment, he had no doubt something would come in before the day was out. He'd worked two recovery jobs yesterday and had done structural checks the day before that. So it was a nice change of pace to just be out on the water, focused on the city that rose up as majestically as the bridge.

The quiet moments were also just low-key enough that he had plenty of time to think through Captain Reed's invitation to join a special task force in collaboration with the Feds, the Coast Guard and the DA's office.

It was a welcome change from the endlessly roiling thoughts that hadn't left him since welcoming in the new year with a gorgeous redhead who'd fled on New Year's Day never to be seen or heard from again.

*Put it in the past, Hayes. Firmly in the past.*

There were bigger challenges ahead. Ones that he had some control over. Unlike the reality of being left all alone around three in the afternoon after the most incredible sex of his life.

Which was only a small portion of the problem. The bigger issue was that the sex—amazing as it was—had only been the physical outcome of the most extraordinary eighteen hours he'd ever spent with another person.

*Sera.*

He could still feel her name on his lips and could still picture the way a lock of her deep auburn hair lay over her cheek as she slept.

Damn, he needed to let this go.

Because all he had were the memories of those eighteen hours and her first name.

He caught the light spray of water as it foamed up from the boat's wake and imagined it as a cool slap in the face.

*Let.*

*It.*

*Go.*

It was time. He had an exciting new opportunity in front of him and recognized it would be a challenge. A task force full of large governmental entities was a big deal. But the moment you mixed local and federal jurisdictions, things could get sticky quickly.

As much as that was true, he also recognized that New York was different. And while everyone liked returning to their own corners at the end of the day, everyone also understood that governance and security in the largest city in America was unique.

Which only added to his excitement. He'd worked his tail off to make the Harbor team, and he loved what he did in the water, but he also saw it as a path toward his future. The men and women who worked the Harbor team might have expertise in diving, but they were NYPD cops, and as such, he wanted to make detective and continue his progression up the ranks.

The task force would go a long way toward supporting those ambitions.

It was also an opportunity to show what Harbor could do. While he'd felt respected from day one, the uniqueness of his job and the work they did wasn't as well understood by outsiders. Joining a team with federal as well as local government resources would give him an opportunity to raise the profile of their diving work, too.

While there was a lot of overlap between the Coast Guard's responsibilities and the Harbor team's, there were significant differences, as well. The Coast Guard's remit was far broader, including search and rescue, marine safety and fisheries law enforcement. Gavin and his team supported search and rescue in extreme circumstances, but their work was far more narrowly defined in the realm of public safety and police work, and specific to the waters surrounding the city.

As such, there was clear sharing of jurisdiction in a way that provided minimal friction and maximum benefit to the city of New York.

Especially because once a problem hit Atlantic waters, the Coast Guard took over.

He understood it, Gavin thought as he looked out over the harbor, the Statue of Liberty growing larger as they narrowed the distance. The work. The jurisdictions. Even the politics.

And when you understood something, you could influence the good and help support change of the not-so-good.

"Gav!"

He turned to find their dive lead for the day, Detective Wyatt Trumball. Wyatt had been a force for change on the Harbor team, leading several cases over the past few years that had been both high-profile and well-executed to ultimately help reduce crime in the city.

It had also led him to his new wife, Marlowe McCoy. Granddaughter of one of the 86th Precinct's most respected detectives, Anderson McCoy, Marlowe was practically a legend in her own right in their Sunset Bay neighborhood. She was the precinct's favorite lock-and-vault technician and was frequently pulled in on jobs to help open recovered items in the course of casework.

A series of safes, strapped to bodies, that Gavin and Wyatt had pulled up early last fall had been a huge case for the Harbor team.

One that had also created the unexpected proximity for Marlowe and Wyatt to fall in love. Sadly, the case also brought the disturbing news that her grandfather had used his well-respected position of authority in the precinct to hide Marlowe's father's misdeeds decades ago.

They'd all reeled from that unsettling revelation, and the lingering fallout hadn't fully subsided, but Wyatt had held up well under it and so had his new wife. Anderson had come clean and, while not fully exonerated, had been able to avoid jail time due to his overarchingly positive contribution to the NYPD. Now working off his remaining debt in volunteer service, the man was doing some great things with an at-risk youth program several days a week.

Was it justice?

Gavin knew there were several around the 86th who didn't think so. But others who had already seen some improvements in those at-risk youth thought the tradeoffs were more than fair.

"Hey." They shook hands in greeting.

Wyatt had already been in the wheelhouse when Gavin boarded, so they'd missed initial hellos as they'd started their shift. Wyatt settled in against the rail as the boat steadily navigated through the harbor.

"Heard the good news about the task force."

"Word travels fast."

Wyatt smiled before shrugging. "When the captain asked for recommendations, there was no one else who came to my mind. I couldn't put you forward fast enough."

Although they'd always had a good relationship, the endorsement went a long way.

"Thank you."

"You're going to knock this one out of the park."

"It'll reduce my time on Harbor for the next few months."

It was the only fly in the ointment of the opportunity, and Gavin had weighed that aspect when Captain Reed first approached him.

"Which will be a loss for us," Wyatt acknowledged, "— but you have to do this. The opportunity's too big, and frankly, it's time to spread your wings a bit. Good things happen here, but the only way we keep getting better is to expand perspective and grow our talent."

This mindset was a key element of Wyatt's management.

Even bigger than that, it was the ethos of the entire 86th Precinct they were part of in Brooklyn. Under Captain Dwayne Reed's leadership, those who showed promise were given opportunity.

And, in a virtuous cycle, because people knew there was opportunity, they worked harder and smarter and more collaboratively for it.

"I do think I can make a difference." Gavin said it because he believed it. Way down deep.

"I know you can."

"Speaking of different, how's married life treating you?"

Wyatt had only returned from his honeymoon a few weeks before. "Married life is amazing. Marlowe is incredible. And she proved just how awesome she is by indulging me in a honeymoon full of diving in Grand Cayman."

It was good to see his friend so happy. More, Gavin admitted, it was encouraging to see him come out the other side. The case that had pulled him and Marlowe together had been difficult, for the work itself, the impact on the precinct and the fact that Marlowe's father was murdered in the process.

He was well aware that sort of grief didn't just vanish, but it was good to see people he cared about showing signs of moving past it with the right partner to make it through.

Sometimes the right people did find each other.

It was a sobering thought, especially when all it did was bring to his own mind images of deep blue eyes and lush auburn hair.

Shaking it off, Gavin gave Wyatt a hearty slap on the back. "So you spent two weeks with an amazing woman and crystal-blue water, and now you're back here."

He and Wyatt turned to look over the other side of the

railing. Although the Hudson had improved considerably over the past decade, the river still surrounded a major city, in a shade of blue that bordered on gray. Along with the less-than-appealing color, they regularly dived through all manner of undesirable things.

Wyatt nodded, his grin broad and most definitely sincere. "A dream all its own."

Gavin recognized those words for truth just as a shout went out from the wheelhouse. They were heading up toward the George Washington Bridge for evidence recovery after an accident.

And as he slipped into the cold, late March water under the bridge ten minutes later, clad head-to-toe in his gear, Gavin couldn't help but grin. He really was living the dream. Wide awake, full of the sweetest adrenaline, every damn day.

Now if he could only get a certain redhead out of his nighttime ones.

SERAFINA FORTE REACHED for the clean tissue she'd had the foresight to stuff into her suit jacket pocket and wiped her mouth as she got up from the floor beside the toilet. She'd gotten lucky this afternoon. The ladies' room at the courthouse was empty, and she hadn't had to worry about being overheard.

A fate she had failed to escape several times over the past few months. A woman could only claim a winter stomach bug or a "touch of food poisoning" so many times.

The only upside to her daily visit to the ladies' room— and really, what idiot called it *morning* sickness when her visits could happen at any time?—was that she hadn't put on much weight. Her body was still changing, though, and she could see that in the fit of her work suits.

A fate that was going to catch up with her before she knew it.

With a sigh, she laid her head against the cool tiles of the wall, grateful she'd chosen the last stall so she could give the misery in her stomach time to settle a bit.

What was she going to do?

The question had been her constant companion for the past two months since she'd discovered her pregnancy and, as of yet, she hadn't come up with much beyond *take it one day at a time*.

Perhaps the advice she should have taken was *don't have amazing sex with a man you've known five hours as a way to ring in the new year*.

It seemed sound and eminently smart now, but was nowhere near as loud as the clanging voice in her head—one that had echoed through her body—on New Year's Eve. That night, all she wanted to do was get as close to Gavin as possible.

*Gavin.*

That was all she knew. His name was Gavin, and he was a cop. They'd met at a local bar in Brooklyn and had struck up a conversation so engrossing it had taken a while for them to realize their friends had moved on to another party down the street.

Neither one of them had cared.

They'd agreed to only discuss who they were in broad strokes, which is why she'd only told him she was a lawyer, not an ADA with the city. And all she knew was that he was a cop. Since the NYPD employed roughly 36,000 people, it was a bit of a needle in a haystack.

Even if he'd wanted to get a hold of her, she hadn't made

that easy, fleeing his apartment after a bout of lovemaking that had left her breathless.

And scared.

Because people didn't feel this way about each other—or have this sort of reaction to one another—that quickly after meeting.

Hadn't she learned that young?

And hadn't she been paying the price ever since?

Since that thought only produced profound misery, pregnant or not, Sera shook it off and pondered, yet again, how she could have played this differently.

They'd gone to his apartment, and it had been full of boxes. When she'd teased him on his decorating skills, he'd confirmed that he was moving in a few weeks. It was the perfect segue into a congenial conversation about why he was moving and did he like his building and where was he going?

Only their need for each other had taken over and they'd ended up kissing against said boxes, evaporating any questions she might have asked about where he was moving *to*.

Which now only left her with one dead end and absolutely zero lines to tug.

She had no last name. No cell phone. No known address.

And she was pregnant with his child.

On a sigh, she pushed off the wall and fixed her skirt. She slipped a breath mint out of the package she'd taken to carrying in her other jacket pocket and smoothed her hair.

Between her crushing workload, her random acts of morning sickness and her endless mooning over Gavin, she'd sort of drifted through her days—and nights. She needed to get her head back in the game.

Today's case was big, and it meant they could get a solid

handful of thugs out of the local drug trade. She'd prepped well, and she had a strong case. It was time to put her focus back on that and *off* her memories.

Off her worries.

Off her stupidity.

After all, crime in the city didn't stop. And she'd be damned if she was going to let her current lapse in judgment stop her from her work.

She would figure this out. And while it wasn't what she'd planned, in a relatively few short months, she'd have a child. One she was already beyond excited to meet. That was her reality, and her child needed to be her full focus.

Not the child's father.

And not the way she'd become pregnant.

Even if she did look for him every time she walked the neighborhood. She'd even tried going back to their bar a few times, although once she'd realized she was pregnant, she'd switched to club soda instead of her usual wine spritzer as she'd sat alone in the bar, her breath catching in her throat each time the door opened.

But to no avail.

Gavin was a memory, and whether she liked it or not, he was going to stay there.

Their child was her future.

Gathering her things along with her renewed focus, Sera headed for the door and the waiting courtroom. Which made the presence of her boss in the hallway something of a surprise.

"Sera?"

"David. Hello."

David Esposito was a formidable presence in the Brooklyn courts, their district attorney as adept at his job as he was at working the media. Tall and dashing, he had just the right amount of gray in his dark hair to make people feel he had the necessary gravitas to prosecute the criminals of the city and his broad shoulders filled out his suits to perfection. The media loved him, and lucky for her, his ADAs loved him, too.

He had an agile, exemplary legal mind, *and* he was a champion of his people. She loved working for him.

"Do you have a minute?"

"Of course." She moved to take a seat on one of the benches that lined the hallway, but he gestured toward a small meeting room.

"Let's go in there. I want to discuss something with you."

"About the Landers case?"

He smiled as he waited for her to enter the room before him. "I read your brief. You've got it more than well in hand."

Although she appreciated the compliment, it only added to her confusion. But he was the boss, which gave him the right to be a bit mysterious. Resolved to let him tell her in his own time, she took a seat at the small table that filled most of the room.

"I know how hard you've been working, Sera."

"It's the job." She gave a light shrug, knowing that for the truth. "And I love the work."

"Which is what I want to talk to you about."

Although all lawyers were subject to scrutiny and the highest of expectations as to their behavior, the bar was set infinitely higher for the district attorney's office. They were scrutinized, evaluated and, ultimately, held to a standard that was beyond the beyond. She'd always believed herself up to the task, but she knew there would be raised eyebrows as her pregnancy became widely known. She wouldn't be fired for it—she had full confidence on that front—but she would get knowing glances. A fact that would only be further exacerbated by the reality that she wasn't dating anyone.

Was that why David had pulled her into this discussion? Had her bathroom retch sessions somehow tipped someone off?

Her mind raced, and she nearly missed his words until she finally keyed back into what he was saying.

"I'm proud of all my ADAs, but you have to know, Sera, just how much your work stands out. Your dedication and your passion for the law is something to see. Our city is better for it, and my office is better for it."

"Thank you."

"It's why I'm willing to give you time away to take advantage of this opportunity."

"Away?"

He smiled at that, his expression lighting his normally serious face. "I've put you in for a borough-wide task force. It'll be members from my office, the NYPD, the Coast Guard and several federal agencies."

"A task force on what?"

"The drug trade is out of control. The governor and the mayor have been in talks with the Feds, and we want to put a team together to evaluate what can be done with the situation."

"But I'm not a cop. I have no real knowledge of how to apprehend or take down criminals."

"That's why your contributions are so valuable. This is a problem we want to attack from every angle. From the jurisdiction to those running the ops to the way we prosecute. We need every mind on this and all the effort we can muster to get ahead of the enterprising criminals who make New York their home."

It was a huge ask, and her pregnancy flashed quickly through her thoughts as a reason to decline. In fact, she nearly came out with it before Sera stopped herself.

Why say no?

What example did that set for her child? More, what did it say to herself? She was pregnant, not dead. And motherhood aside, she fully expected to have a long career in front of her.

Now would be the worst time to say no.

"I feel like I should ask you a few more questions, but you know I'm in, David."

"I hoped so. Which is why you need to be at the 86th bright and early Monday morning." David leaned forward and laid a hand over the back of hers folded on the table. "I'm going to miss having you in the office, but we'll get your caseload redistributed. I want to keep you on the Landers case as well as the discovery on the Nicholson murders, but everything else will be shared out."

Sera mentally calculated the workload. While both of those were huge cases, the reprieve from her other work would be welcome.

"It's an amazing opportunity, David. I won't let you down."

He gave her hand a quick squeeze before he stood up, effectively ending their meeting. "That thought never crossed my mind."

SERA WALKED THE last few blocks from the subway, her umbrella up, albeit ineffectively, against the howling spring rain overhead. April had come in with a vengeance, and the city felt like it was practically underwater as she dodged puddles and what looked like a small lake at the intersection just shy of the 86th Precinct.

She'd opted for one of her pantsuits, but the thick rain boots pulled up over her calves, her slacks firmly tucked inside, were the height of frump. A fact she'd willingly overlooked as she anticipated dry feet for the day. The boots could be stowed in a corner of whatever conference room they'd be stuffed in this morning, so the fashion faux pas wasn't permanent.

She hadn't spent much time at the 86th, but she'd been here before. Captain Dwayne Reed ran an outstanding team, and she always enjoyed working with his officers when it was necessary for a case.

Captain Reed's style of leadership—and his belief in his people—had caught on, and there had been clear winds of change blowing through the other neighborhoods in an effort to emulate the precinct.

*We need every mind on this and all the effort we can muster to get ahead of the enterprising criminals who make New York their home.*

David's pitch for the task force had lingered in her mind all weekend as she prepared for this morning. She wanted to start off strong and make a good impression, meeting the other professionals she'd work with for the next several months.

Could they get ahead of the criminal element?

While she wasn't an inherently negative person, she would admit to moments of frustration and disillusionment with the system. Too many criminals flooding the streets. Too few people to catch them and ultimately prosecute them. And a bad life for the ones who were caught, locked up in a system that, while often full of well-intentioned people, was home to many who weren't.

She'd always understood it, but had also believed the work she did to serve the goal of justice would result in good outcomes. Even if her pregnancy had made her start to question some of those things and the reality of the world she was bringing her child into.

Her parents had never set a very good example, and she'd had to forge a path forward on her own. It was only recently that she'd begun to wonder if her dogged pursuit of justice was more because of them than in spite of them.

"Sera!"

Saved from her own maudlin musings by the loud shout, she glanced up to see a former law school classmate waving to her from down the hall. Picking up her pace, Sera headed his way.

"Sam, how are you?" They quickly exchanged hugs. "It's great to see you, but what are the odds we're here on the same day?"

"Pretty good if we're both on the new task force starting up this morning."

"You're a part of it?"

He smiled before pointing toward the conference room a few feet away. "I am and will confess to getting here early *and* seeing your name badge on the sideboard. I'm glad we're working together again. I'm representing the local FBI office."

"I'd heard the Feds snapped you up. Lucky for them."

"Lucky for me, too. I love the work."

Although she'd always known she wanted the DA's office, Sera was happy for him. His agile mind and love of complex cases likely made him a huge asset to the government.

"I love it, too, but I do have to say I'm disappointed in us."

"Oh?" His blue eyes widened.

"We're both guilty of that dreaded post-law school sin of spending most of our waking hours together for three years and then abandoning one another for the work after getting out."

"Proof they didn't lie about the work."

She shook her head but couldn't hold back the smile. "I wouldn't have it any other way."

"Me, either."

They found seats at the table and, after settling their things, wandered over to the sideboard to pick up their badges and get some breakfast. Sera eyed the pastries with a bit of caution, but was pleased to also see a selection of hard-boiled eggs and some dry toast waiting for toppings.

She hadn't been able to stomach anything that morning, but recognized the breakfast foods as a gift of fate. The protein from the egg and the bland toast with a bit of honey on top would go a long way toward keeping her level throughout the introductory meeting. A bit of tepid tea and she'd have a breakfast trifecta that would hopefully stave off morning sickness.

"You always were a healthy eater," Sam whispered, leaning in conspiratorially.

"Not everyone can eat sugared cereals and donuts for breakfast." She eyed his plate, a match for her own. "What happened?"

Although he'd always been a good-natured person, even in the throes of the most difficult exam periods, Sam lit up in a way she'd never seen before. "I'm a man with a fitness plan. And a wedding in three months."

"Sam! That's wonderful." Sera put her plate down and pulled him in for a hug. "Tell me all about her."

"Her name's Alexandra. Alex." He smiled, his gaze going hazy with love. "We met at the Bureau my second week on the job. She held out for a long time, saying we shouldn't mix personal with work and that it was a bad idea."

Although it wasn't forbidden in the Bureau, Sera could understand the reticence. But she also knew Sam Baxter and figured the woman was a goner when faced with such an earnest and truly wonderful man.

"Is she a lawyer, too?"

"Nope, a field agent. Which puts us in the same office, but not working directly together most of the time."

His happiness was electric, and Sera tried to tamp down the small shot of sadness that filled her as she pictured Gavin's face in her mind's eye.

Would it ever fade?

Even as she considered it, she knew the truth. Did she want it to?

And then she pushed it all away and gave Sam another hug. She could be sad in her own time, but there was no call for anything but joy in the face of such good news for a friend.

Which made the hard cough and rough "excuse me" a bit jarring as she pulled back from Sam's embrace.

And turned to find the one man she hadn't been able to forget standing two feet away.

# Chapter Two

*Sera.*

She was here—actually *here*—with her arms full of another man.

As he tried to maneuver around the hugging couple, Gavin wasn't sure what was more embarrassing. That his heart was exploding in his chest or something worse.

Something that felt a lot like jealousy.

*It's just a hug.*

With some dude who looked like he'd walked out of the pages of a men's magazine in his perfect suit, crisp red tie and artfully sculpted hair.

*Bastard.*

Especially since Gavin had forgotten an umbrella and currently felt like a wet junkyard dog after the run from the subway to the precinct entrance.

The perfect specimen of law and order turned and extended a hand. "Hello. I'm Sam Baxter. Local FBI bureau."

"Gavin Hayes. NYPD." He then turned to Sera, his expression carefully neutral. "I'm Gavin."

"Serafina Forte. Brooklyn DA's office."

Her hand slipped into his, and while it was a cordial handshake, he immediately had the memory of their fingers linking together on New Year's Eve as they walked to his apartment.

Something raw and elemental sparked between them, and Gavin purposely pushed it down. Whatever sparks had flared between them three months ago—and obviously still flashed and burned now based on their touch—had no place here. This was his shot. His appointment to the task force was an essential step in matching his ambitions to the outcomes he wanted at work. And in a span of two minutes, he'd raced through jealousy, envy and embarrassment.

Not the way he'd envisioned his first day on this all-important next step in his career. Yet here they were.

While he'd known she was a lawyer, he hadn't known she was with the district attorney's office. They'd avoided talk of what they did beyond the basics. It had seemed intriguing at the time, the "who do you know" and "what do you do" conversations too mundane for them. Too pedestrian to interfere with the passion that arced between them.

It was only now, face-to-face, that he realized a bit more conversation might have helped in the months that had passed since.

If he'd known she was in the DA's office, he could have…

Could have what?

Gone after her?

Tried to talk to her?

Asked her why she left him?

None of those questions led to good outcomes. Especially because of one, outstanding truth: if she'd wanted to see him again, she'd have found a way.

And she hadn't.

Even with that disappointment, he couldn't fight the bone-deep interest that filled him. That vivid color of her hair was even richer in person than his memories. The sweep of her heavy lower lip still intrigued him, leaving him with the raw, damn near elemental need to draw it between his teeth.

And those eyes.

It was idiotically poetic, but those liquid blue eyes were fathoms deep, full of knowledge and secrets and something that looked a lot like forever.

Which only added to the bad mood that punched holes in his gut.

He'd wondered about her every damn day since the first of the year, and now she showed up on the most important morning of his professional life?

"We were just getting some breakfast." Sera gestured toward the table along the wall lined with breakfast and coffee carafes. "Please, help yourself."

Her voice was low, professional and incredibly polite. Something in it made Gavin wish he could smudge a little bit of that perfection that had gotten under his skin and made him ache.

It was hardly rational. Or fair.

But what about this situation was fair?

Before he had a chance to consider it further, the room was brought to attention, and they were all instructed to get breakfast, pick up their badges and find a spot at the conference room table.

"Looks like the bell for round one," Sam said with a chuckle.

Sera's answering laugh had Gavin crumpling the edge of the notebook he'd grabbed from his locker on the way in, but it *was* enough to pull him out of his thoughts.

Time to get coffee and take a seat as far away from *Serafina Forte* as he could. He had his future to focus on.

And he needed to get his mind the hell off his tempting past.

GAVIN WAS HERE.

In the room. In the building. And *on* her freaking task force.

Gavin *Hayes*.

He was a cop, and in a twist that she should have seen coming, he worked in the precinct that covered her Brooklyn neighborhood.

What were the odds?

Even as that question drifted in and out of her mind, she had to admit, they were pretty darn good. They had met at a local bar, after all. On some level it was a bit of surprise she hadn't seen him sooner.

Only…

He was here. Now. Back in her life as she embarked on one of the most important opportunities of her career. A three-month task force, the lead had told them during introductory remarks, with a possible extension to a fourth month.

And she was pregnant with Gavin's child.

She'd complete the work, of that she had no doubt. But there was no way she'd complete it without everyone knowing she was pregnant.

Which meant Gavin would know.

Hadn't she wanted that?

She'd gone to their bar several times in hopes of seeing him so she could tell him the news. So she could…

Could what?

Apologize for running out? Apologize for getting scared because she didn't do relationships and she wasn't cut out for the emotional commitment required to be with another person? Even as she'd thought, more than a few times, that emotional commitment might be worth the risk with Gavin.

"The purpose of this task force is to ensure cooperation and collaboration." The moderator's voice cut back into her thoughts, and Sera knew she needed to focus.

She could obsess over next steps later. Right now she had to pay attention and find a way forward.

"We're fortunate in a city this size that there's a strong base of support across federal, state and local agencies, but it needs to be stronger. Tighter. It's the only way we'll maximize our strengths. One and one will make three."

Sera nearly choked on the small sip of herbal tea she'd taken as the moderator's words hung over the room. Unbidden, her gaze drifted to Gavin. He'd taken a seat at the opposite end of the room, but since he was on the other side of the table, she could still see him easily enough.

His dark gaze seemed to see through her, and she had the most absurd impulse to laugh.

Because one and one *had* made three.

The moderator pointed toward a screen at the front of the room and a slideshow presentation she'd used to frame the launch meeting. As the woman flipped to a new slide, Sera directed her attention back to her words.

The first week of the task force would focus on getting to know one another and creating an action plan. Every team would build out ideas on how to address crime, expand a plan for social services and address the legal ins and outs of their ideas. One team would be fully local, one fully federal and then two would be a mix, having one federal team member and one local member. It was, their moderator explained, a chance to collectively review how collaborations could grow and how they would look different with varied perspectives.

Sera had already begun to envision the work she could do if she was paired with Sam. They knew each other and had worked well together all the way through law school, and she had every confidence their collaboration would be strong. She was doing this work so she could improve her relationships with federal jurisdictions in the region. Wasn't that the whole point?

"Serafina Forte, DA's office. Gavin Hayes, NYPD Harbor. You're a team."

*Of course we are.*

The urge to drop her head to the table was strong, but she kept her gaze straight ahead and didn't dare glance Gavin's way again. Just like she wouldn't lift a fist to the sky and rant and rail that this was all some cosmic mistake.

She did offer a small smile and nod for the moderator in a show of gratitude for the assignment.

Nothing in her life had been normal or usual for three months now. Why should that change?

She jotted down the conference room where she and Gavin would be paired for the day to begin work on their project before gathering her things from where she'd stowed them beneath the table.

But as she glanced down and saw the thick rain boots still wrapped around her calves and her slacks, Sera was sorely tempted to lift that fist.

Could she look any worse?

Since the room was already in motion, there was no time to slip them off and change into the heels buried at the bottom of her bag, so she picked up her things and proceeded toward the door.

Gavin waited for her just outside, and she lifted a hand in a small waving motion. "Let's go, local team."

"Sure."

*Ooooh-kay.*

What was that joke Sam had made about the bell for round one?

She followed Gavin down the hall and toward an elevator. Several other task force members were with them and their nervous small talk to the others ensured she could avoid talking to Gavin for a few more minutes.

Until they were the only ones left, heading toward the top floor of the precinct.

"Serafina, is it?"

"Sera. I mean, I go by Sera." Damn it, she would *not* stammer before this man. "Serafina is my given name, but I go by Sera." When he only nodded, she pressed for a bit more from him. "And you're on Harbor patrol? Diving?"

The elevator stopped, the doors swishing open on a quiet floor. "That's what I do."

"But you're a cop?"

"Yep."

He was already heading down the hall, and she clomped behind him in the damn boots, each step a sort of squeaky *thwap* on the ground.

Irritation spiked at the quick dismissal and the feeling of following him. They hadn't followed each other three months ago. Instead, there'd been a sort of *entwining*. An equal footing that had engaged them both and pulled them forward with an elemental tug she'd never felt before.

But this?

He had a cold, almost military demeanor. His back was so straight and his gaze deliberately held straight ahead.

Well, fine. She could give as good as she got.

Even as she nearly slipped over her squeaky boots when a terrible, awful thought filled her.

What if he didn't remember her?

Gavin caught her just as she reached out to grip the door frame to their small conference room. She straightened herself, unwilling to read too much into the fire radiating up and down her arm where he'd held her, firm yet gentle, just above the elbow.

"Thank you."

He dropped his hand and just nodded.

God, why did she feel so clumsy? And so off her game?

She hadn't felt this way three months ago. Sure, she'd been a bit nervous, but their time together had seemed to melt away any nerves or concerns. They'd just been Sera and Gavin, and it had been...

Well, it had been wonderful.

And now they were here, and they both had to make the best of it.

But how had she managed to forget just how good he smelled? And exactly how broad his shoulders were? And...

And she needed to get her damn head in the game because there was no way she was going to let a single bit of whatever happened to them three months ago ruin this. She was highly competent, and this task force was a shot at her future.

Mooning over Gavin was *not* the way to start it off right.

So she marched into the room, her head held high, her bearing damn near regal.

She could *do* this, she thought, a fierce sort of righteousness welling up inside of her. She *would* do this.

The conference room might be roughly the size of a broom closet, but she deliberately selected a spot on the

far side, settling her things on the scarred table. Gavin still
stood by the door, his gaze on her when she finally glanced
up after carefully placing each of her personal items.

"Serafina?"

"I told you, I go by Sera."

"Fine. Sera."

"Is this room okay?"

"It'll do just fine."

She stared at him, suddenly realizing her mistake in taking the far corner. The windows might be at her back, but
she suddenly felt her lack of escape. Or, more to the point,
the need to move past him in order to escape.

One more sign she was flustered and off her game. Worse,
that she suddenly felt like his quarry, his deep brown gaze
seeming to size her up.

Where was that man she'd met on New Year's? The one
with the kind eyes and broad smile and caring touch? Had
he been an illusion?

She'd lived with the reality of her momentary lapse in
judgment for three months now, but she'd never felt that
she'd shared herself with a jerk.

A stranger, maybe. But never a jerk.

Resolving to worry about it later, she tapped the folder
she'd settled on the desk, on top of the legal pad she'd used
to make notes during the initial briefing. "Let's get down
to it. We're the local team. Between the police perspective
you bring and the legal perspective I bring, we should be
able to put together a solid plan of local cross-collaboration."

"I'm sure we will."

Heat filled that dark gaze at her reference to collaboration, but Sera ignored it and soldiered on. "We've all seen
the challenges to both our teams with budget allocations,

staffing constraints and the overall volume of what runs the streets of the city." She realized her potential misstep and added, "Or fills the waters around it."

"Day in and day out."

"So where should we start?"

He finally took a seat, but never touched the folder that had been handed to them during the briefing. Instead, his attention was fully focused on her, nearly pinning her to her seat. "I think the first place we start is with the past."

"Oh?" She dimly sensed a trap closing around her, but had no idea why. The city had a legacy of crime—that sort of underbelly was impossible to separate from a place so large—but so much work had been done over the years to make New York not only livable, but a truly thriving, positive place to live for its ever-growing population.

"The city does have a history," she agreed. "But this task force really is about the future."

"The task force is, sure. But I'm talking about you and me. And why you walked out on New Year's Day without so much as a goodbye."

GAVIN TOOK THE slightest measure of satisfaction at the way Sera's throat worked around whatever words she was trying to come up with.

What he couldn't figure out was why the satisfaction was so short-lived. And why this desperate need to question her seemed to live inside of him like some wide-open, gaping maw. They were here—as she'd said—to focus on the future. Why tread through a past that had happened months ago and realistically should mean nothing to him?

He wasn't generally interested in one-night stands, but he could hardly say he'd never had sex with a woman he didn't know well. And since his life up to now had been suspiciously devoid of successful long-term relationships, he couldn't understand the weird, swirling emotions this woman churned up in him.

And yet, she did. From the unceasing thoughts of her these past several months to the spears of jealousy at seeing her hug another man, he clearly hadn't moved on the way he should have.

The way he *needed* to.

So maybe just putting it all out on the table would help him get past it.

"Why I walked out?"

"Yes. We had a pretty amazing night. I don't think I gave any suggestion you needed to leave so quickly, but if I did, I'm sorry."

His apology clearly flustered her, her hand coming up to smooth her blouse.

"We were two consenting adults who welcomed the year in, Gavin. It was great, but all good things have to come to an end, right?"

If he weren't looking so hard, he'd have taken her words at face value. He'd likely have believed her, too.

But the heavy pulse at her throat was evident, as was the barely-there quaver in her voice.

"And now?" he finally asked.

"Now what?"

"Now we're working together. So our good thing hasn't actually come to an end after all."

"Are you suggesting we pick up where we left off?"

She might have been flustered, but he'd give her credit, she could turn on the freeze when she needed to. While something sharp and needy filled him, he was more than aware this task force was a huge opportunity for him. For both of them, no doubt.

Was he even remotely considering muddying the waters with sex?

His body screamed a resounding yes, but the control he was known for somehow managed to prevail at the last minute.

"I'm suggesting we both deserve to go into this partnership fully acknowledging what came before. This is a major step in my career. I have to believe it is for you, too. Not addressing the past is foolish in the extreme." He leaned forward slightly over the table, the incredibly small space ensuring he could see her as clearly as if she were sitting beside him. "Don't you agree?"

That flutter of pulse at her throat never faded, and if he were a fanciful man, he'd say he could practically hear her heartbeat.

But he wasn't given to whimsy. And he had zero illusions about life anymore.

What he didn't expect was her to capitulate so easily. He figured her for a bit more bravado. Maybe even a few excuses. Not the warming of her freeze ray. Or a raw sort of truth that settled hard in his gut.

"We had a lovely night together, Gavin. One I don't regret in any way. But the new day had dawned." She shook her head. "The new *year* had dawned, and it suddenly struck me that sitting around the apartment of my one-night stand wasn't a good look. For either of us, but certainly not for me."

He was tempted to ask again if he'd given her any hint she needed to leave, but opted for a slightly different tack. "Did you want to leave?"

"It was time for me to leave."

It was hardly an answer, but it was the one she was willing to give. He could keep pressing and probing, in hopes he'd get a different reply, but why? Worse, why was he hoping for a different answer?

The knock on the door pulled him out of the question without an actual answer, and he turned to find Wyatt Trumball in the doorway.

"Detective." Gavin nodded as he stood. "How are you?"

"Good. I wanted to talk to you about the dive tomorrow morning. I'm sorry I'm interrupting." Wyatt glanced over at Sera, his smile broad. "The task force started today."

"It did."

Wyatt stepped into the small conference room, extending a hand toward Sera who'd already stood to say hello. "Wyatt Trumball, NYPD."

"Sera Forte. I'm with the DA's office."

"So you two are representing the local team."

Since there was little that got past the seasoned detective, Gavin shouldn't have been surprised by the man's ready knowledge of the work, but it still stunned him how much Wyatt actually *knew.*

"We are. We'll present solutions on how the city's resources can work together," Sera said. "I know everyone thinks the solution to this is working with the Feds, and I don't think that's wrong, but I am excited to show what we can do right here, too."

"Everyone thinks bigger's better. But some of the best work I've ever seen has been local teams who know their neighborhoods, working together to get it done."

"Fewer egos?" Gavin asked, his sole intention to make a joke.

Which made it a surprise when Wyatt's demeanor changed. "The Feds have a lot to offer, but they get in the way, too. They think we're rubes who can't see past the end of the block, or they want to run the show."

Coming from a man who was a quintessential team player, Wyatt's words struck hard. But if he were being fair, Gavin had already seen a bit of that posturing that morning. Hell, they were all posturing, trying to prove their worth to be a part of the team. But that tension was there, all the same.

"We'll be sure to keep our guard up," Sera cut in smoothly. "I happen to like my block quite a bit. I think I've got a rather sophisticated approach to the work, too."

Wyatt's smile returned, his grin broad. "Then I say, go get 'em. I know you two will do great. Let me know if you need anything from me."

Gavin nearly let Wyatt walk away before he remembered. "And tomorrow's dive?"

"I just came to give you the oh-so-happy news that we're diving up at Hell Gate tomorrow."

Gavin sensed Sera's attention to the matter, but didn't want to give Wyatt any indication anything was off. So he went with his usual good-natured humor. "Lucky us. With all this rain, it'll be sure to be churned up and extra gross."

"Which is why the team can't dive it today. Weather's expected to clear up tonight, and we should have a grand time running evidence recovery. Criminals really do love tossing weapons off the city's bridges."

"Only trains run over Hell Gate," Gavin said. "Someone was dumb enough to try to cross electrified train tracks on foot?"

"Not quite that bad, but not much better. Someone ran across the RFK Bridge on foot."

"In the middle of traffic?"

"Yep. Slammed on the brakes when he realized the cops in pursuit were getting close. He jumped out of his car, then raced through traffic to the first break in fencing he could find. Tossed the weapon as hard as he could north." Wyatt smiled, his hands up in the air in a what-can-you-do gesture. "We're the ones who get to go find it."

Wyatt made his goodbyes, and it was only as Gavin took his seat again that he caught Sera's gaze.

"It's really called Hell Gate?" she asked, a small furrow lining her otherwise smooth brow.

"Yep. The upper portion of the East River. We'll be in the area underneath the RFK Bridge and a little farther north probably."

"Wow. I—"

"What?"

"It sounds dangerous, is all."

"It's one of the tougher waterways, but that's why we dive in pairs and have a team working around us, also keeping close watch."

"Sure. Of course. It's just that I…" She stopped again, seeming to gather her thoughts. "I didn't realize just how difficult your job was. Anyone who works in law enforcement has a challenging job with obvious risks. But this sounds like a whole other level."

Although he appreciated the concern and her obvious bother at the work, he wasn't entirely clear where it was coming from. "It's a job I'm trained for. And something I continue to train for regularly. We don't rest on our laurels or ignore our conditioning."

"No, of course not."

"Wow. Be careful there." He gave the warning as he opened his folder, pulling out the briefing sheet they would work against for the next week. He nearly cursed himself for saying anything, but now that it was out, he realized his emotions had about as much finesse as that criminal who'd run out in the middle of traffic.

Emotions he had no business even having.

*Way to be an ass, Hayes. You might as well see it through now.*

"Be careful of what?"

"All that concern. You keep talking like that, and I might start to think you care."

# Chapter Three

*I might start to think you care.*

That rather dismissive brush-off had remained in the back of her mind all day, through her walk home and on through the preparation of dinner.

And damn it—Sera tossed a potholder on the counter after dumping a pot of cooked pasta and boiling water into a waiting colander in her sink—he'd gotten to her. Yes, it was unexpected to walk into the conference room that morning and see him. And yes, she was fully aware that she was nervous and off her game when the two of them had broken off for their committee work.

But that line? Seriously?

*I might start to think you care.*

*Start* to?

What an ass.

Only he wasn't. Despite the tense working conditions and the subtle threads of irritation he wove around her all day, he wasn't a jerk.

She would bet quite a lot on that fact.

The man she'd spent the night with wasn't a jerk. The man the NYPD had selected to represent them on a multijurisdictional task force wasn't a jerk. The man who'd *fa-thered her child* wasn't a jerk.

Unable to pivot well with her reentry into his life? Yeah, she'd give him that one. But he wasn't a bad person. No amount of conference-room bravado was going to change her mind on that point.

Which meant she needed to double down. Leave her ir-ritation at home and focus on the good that would come of working together.

And oh yeah…tell him she was pregnant with his child. But how?

While it was incredibly easy to put their night together firmly in the column of sexual attraction, part of why it had been so incendiary had nothing to do with the sex. It had been the connection between them.

They'd spoken freely and easily after meeting in the bar. It was the only way she'd have actually gone home with him, if she were honest. She needed that connection in order to feel it was worth taking things further.

And oh, they had a connection.

She'd laughed easily, and they'd talked of so many things. Their work in broad strokes, yes, but more *why* they were drawn to what they did. How they'd found their paths in life. And what drove them as people.

It had been wonderful to speak freely about her ambition and not feel it was either being judged as too work-focused or worse, threatening somehow that she had goals for her-self. Instead, he'd asked her questions and seemed genuinely interested in her answers.

And for her, Sera knew, there was no greater aphrodisiac.

She shook the colander of any excess water before scoop-ing out a portion for herself and the waiting sauce she'd made for it. Although she still struggled with food, especially in the morning, by the time dinner rolled around, she was always hungry and had seemingly gotten rid of that day's roiling stomach acid.

Pasta had been one of her steady cravings over the past few weeks, so she'd taken to making extra and preparing a cold salad with it for the next day's lunch. It wasn't perfect, but it seemed to be working, and her doctor hadn't felt the food was problematic, especially when she'd assured her ob-gyn that she was adding vegetables to the mix.

With dinner in hand, she headed for the small kitchen nook to eat just as a heavy knock came on her front door.

Sera set her plate down on the drop-leaf table nestled in the corner of her kitchen and headed for the foyer. Her apartment wasn't huge, but she had some space in her oversize one-bedroom corner unit, courtesy of an uncle who owned the building and had given her a good deal since she'd graduated from college.

*Anyone defending my city deserves to live in a good, safe space while doing it*, Uncle Enzo had intoned as he handed over her rental contract.

She half expected it would be him and Aunt Robin at the door, their occasional drop-ins always welcome.

Only to find Gavin on the other side.

"Hi."

He stood there in her doorway, his shoulders set, and her stomach gave an involuntary flip. Damn, why was he so attractive? Tall, broad and extremely fit from the work he did.

All of which was appealing, but had nothing on the smile that lifted the edges of his lips. A small bouquet filled his hands, and despite his solid bearing, she could see the slightest hint of nerves in the way his foot tapped lightly on the ground.

"Hey." She fought the small smile of her own that threatened to undermine her attempts at being aloof.

"I'm sorry to bother you."

"It's no bother." She stepped back, extending a hand to allow him in. "Though I am curious how you found me. I work for the DA's office. I don't keep my address in public databases."

"I live in the eternally up-to-date database that is Sunset Bay, Brooklyn." When she must have given him a curious look, Gavin added, "Once I knew your last name, I put two and two together. Your uncle, Enzo Forte, is my landlord. I saw him coming into my building this evening with your aunt and some of their friends and mentioned we were working together."

"My uncle gave you my address?"

"I told him I was a pompous jerk during our first meeting, and I owed you an apology. Your aunt couldn't rush fast enough to give me your address." He held out a hand. "She told me you like Gerbera daisies, too."

"I do."

She took the bouquet—a solid peace offering yet not so large as to appear pompous or as if the flowers could solve everything—and gestured toward the kitchen. "I was about to eat some dinner. Would you care to join me?"

"You don't mind?"

Since she'd already invited him, she just shot him a look and headed for the kitchen and the small pitcher she kept on her windowsill. In a matter of minutes, she had the colorful daisies in the pitcher, settled on the edge of the table where they sat across from each other.

He'd taken the portion of pasta she was going to use for tomorrow's lunch, and as she saw him settle his napkin on his lap, Sera had to admit to herself she didn't mind.

She didn't mind at all.

The pasta wasn't much, but Gavin dug into it like a starving man. If she expected him to complain that her vegetable and herb-filled sauce was missing meat, she soon realized she wasn't going to get it.

Instead, she got the opposite.

"This is really good."

"Thanks." She took a sip of her club soda before returning to their earlier topic. "My aunt and uncle really told you where I live?"

"I'll admit to some surprise on that front as well, but I guess I ooze trust." He grinned at her, that bright flash broad and wide. "It also helps I rented right out of the academy in their building over on Eleventh. They have my credit score, my phone number *and* my address. You know, basically it's like they know how to hunt me down."

"I suppose they could."

And while she did get the local connection, it was clear she needed to give her aunt Robin a bit of a drubbing on sharing personal information like that.

"The moment I saw them I made the connection with their last name. And then once I mentioned us working together on the task force, that clinched the deal."

Since Sera could also imagine the twinkle that no doubt had lit up her aunt's eyes, she opted to shift the conversation.

"Is your pasta hot enough?"

Although she'd intended the question as a kindness, all it really served to do was show her extreme nerves at his presence in her kitchen. One that had felt a heck of a lot larger before he arrived than it did now.

"The temperature is fine. It's not really why I'm here, though I'll never turn down dinner with a beautiful woman."

"Flattery?"

"Is it working?"

She didn't want to be flattered by the compliment. Even worse, she didn't want to be caught up in him again or the cute banter that was stamped full of notes of appreciation and...*notice*.

Wasn't that how all this had started? That compelling gaze and ability to make her feel as if she was the only woman in the world?

"I also didn't come here to give you a line," he continued, smoothly shifting gears. "I came to give you the apology you most definitely deserve."

"Oh."

"I wasn't the best version of myself today. I knew it, even as it was happening, but I couldn't seem to see past myself, and I am sorry." He set down his fork. "I'm truly sorry for it."

For all that the apology was a surprise, Sera had to admit it fit the man she remembered. What she'd sensed of his character, even after only spending less than a day together. And with that memory came a resolution of her own.

"If we're being honest—" her gaze drifted to the small bouquet "—I'm not above saying the flowers weren't a smooth touch."

"I'm glad you like them."

"But I wasn't my best self, either. I was surprised to see you this morning. And then we were put together for the duration of the task force and—" She couldn't fully hold back the sigh. "It was like my personal life slammed right into my professional life, and I didn't like it."

"Same."

"This task force is an important step in my career growth. I'm sure it's equally important for you."

"It is," he agreed.

"Then we're going to have to find a way to put what happened between us at the holidays firmly in the past."

"Is it?"

His comment sort of hung there between them, like a pulsing question mark hovering over them in blinking neon.

"Is it what?"

"Is it behind us?"

The irrational urge to laugh hysterically at his question suddenly gripped her and she had one terrifying moment where she thought she actually might break down in laughter. Because that night might be over, but nothing about it was behind them. In fact, in six more months the consequence of their choice would be right there in *front* of them.

She'd had their one night together expressly for the lack of strings. Attachments. Or any consequence other than pure, unadulterated need. She wasn't particularly well-versed in doing that, and it had felt good—better than good, actually—to take something just for herself.

Her life had been about studying and remaining focused and living with a strict, almost rigid, code of behavior. She wasn't going to be her mother. And she had no interest in throwing her life away to listlessness or to excess.

And yet, Gavin had somehow found a way beneath that. In the moment, he'd felt like impulse, but never excess.

So she took a long, deliberate moment to stare at her fork

before lifting it to toy with a few pieces of pasta. "It's all behind us. Of course it is."

"Things ended a bit abruptly."

Whatever distraction her dinner had provided faded as she stared at him head on. "We had a one-night stand, Gavin. By their very definition, they have a short shelf life. A point I've thought was pretty clear based on how neither of us has found the other these past several months."

"Did you try to find me?"

Just like that morning, it was a neat, verbal trap and one she'd walked straight into. Yet even as a part of her wanted to wrap herself up in emotional tinfoil, deflecting the truth with all that she was, she found she couldn't.

"I went to that bar several evenings in hopes I'd see you again. When you never showed, I figured I wasn't meant to see you."

A series of emotions flashed across his face, telling in that he obviously felt *something*, but maddening in that she couldn't actually read a damn thing.

Did he think her needy? Hopeful? Was he glad she'd tried to find him? Or was it more proof what they'd had was only meant to last a few hours?

Which made his quiet, scratchy tone a bit of a surprise when he finally spoke. "If you wanted to see me again, why'd you leave?"

Had she been wrong?

Since there was no way of knowing, she pressed on, willing him to understand her explanation.

"Again, Gavin. New Year's Day. One-night stand. Two strangers. It's sort of the exact definition of awkward."

"It didn't feel awkward."

"No, it didn't."

And when his dark gaze met hers, she had to admit that even now, it still wasn't awkward at all. It was freeing. This strange connection between them that had no reason for existing yet did all the same.

"I wanted to see you again, Sera. I looked for you every time I went out. Each time I walked the neighborhood. Each time I got on the subway."

He'd looked for her? Hoped to see her again?

All those lonely moments, practically willing him to show up at the bar hadn't actually been for naught. Even if they really didn't have a shot at a future, there was a special sort of joy in knowing that he hadn't been unaffected.

And with that knowledge, she couldn't hold back the small smile that she suspected held the slightest notes of sorrow for what could have been. "And here all you really needed to do was call my aunt and uncle. Keep that in mind next time you go hunting for a one-night stand."

"Why would I go hunt for anyone else?"

Whatever humor had pulled at her faded, and something sharp speared through her at the earnest expression that set his face in serious lines.

"This can't go anywhere," Sera finally said, even if she wished she were wrong. "Especially with the task force. It's a conflict now."

"How?"

Whatever outcome he was considering wasn't readily apparent, but the fact he was considering any outcome other than the path they'd been on—going their separate ways—needed to be squelched.

"What do you mean, how? We're partnered on an important work project."

"One that won't last forever. We don't work in the same

department. We don't even work for the same entity. Last time I checked, employees of the City of New York can date each other."

"We're not—" She stopped abruptly, catching herself before trying again. "What we had isn't dating. Let's not pretend there's more between us then there actually is."

Sera wasn't quite sure who she was trying to convince, but knew she needed to hold her ground. Because she *had* wanted to see him again. And once she'd gotten over the shock of seeing him again that morning, it had felt so good to be in his presence once more. To look across the table and see that face that had been emblazoned on her mind as if every feature had been captured in indelible ink.

But she couldn't give in to this.

Nor could she delude herself into thinking somehow this all had a happy ending. They'd come together in a heated rush and had proceeded to go on with their lives. Only now there was a very large secret between them. One that she knew she had to share.

One that he *deserved* to know.

Yet no matter how she spun it in her mind, she couldn't seem to find the words to tell him the truth.

"BUT THERE IS something between us, Sera."

Whatever Gavin might question about his feelings and the odd way they'd come in and out of each other's lives—twice now—there was something there.

Wasn't this very conversation proof of that?

Sure, things had had gotten very personal, very fast. That had been true between them from the start. But at the moment, things had also gotten much too serious. So with his dual police *and* dive training in the forefront of his mind, Gavin did what he knew how to do best.

Pivot and attack the situation from a new angle.

"Let's go get some ice cream."

"Now?"

"You ever heard of dessert, Forte?"

"Well, yeah, but—"

He stared pointedly down at his empty plate before looking back up at her. "Do you have ice cream in your freezer?"

"No."

He shook his head and let out a small *tsk* for good measure. "A crime against nature, but we'll address that later. Let's go get some ice cream."

Based on her initial resistance, Gavin figured she'd put up more of a fight, so it was a welcome surprise to find themselves walking into the Sunset Bay pharmacy and heading for their soda counter twenty minutes later.

"Best ice cream sundaes in Brooklyn." Gavin breathed in deeply of the mixed scents of sugar, cream and chocolate as they took two stools at the counter.

Sera slipped onto the stool next to him, and he took her coat as she shrugged out of it, walking it down to the small coatrack at the end of the bar before returning to her.

"Thanks."

"You're welcome."

As he settled himself on his stool, he couldn't help but notice the two of them reflected in the big mirror that stretched along the back of the soda fountain. Although they didn't touch, they looked like they were on a date, the light tension arcing between them evident even in the old mirror with desilvering in small splotches up and down the length of it.

"This place has seen a lot." He said after a quick glance at his menu.

"It was the heart of Sunset Bay while I was growing up. And even more so for the generation before us. Aunt Robin still talks about how Uncle Enzo brought her here when they were dating."

It was interesting. She'd spoken of her aunt and uncle several times throughout the evening, but still nothing about her parents. Were they absent? Dead? Gavin wondered.

He was about to ask, but a skinny, bored teenager came up to them to take their orders.

"What'll you have?" the kid asked Sera.

"Scoop of chocolate with some peanut butter sauce."

"Banana split for me."

The bored teen trotted off, leaving them to their conversation at the mostly empty counter. It was the distinct lack of people that had him drifting straight back to their unfinished dinner conversation.

"So about this something more between us."

She was in the middle of settling her purse on hooks beneath the counter, her attention focused elsewhere, but Gavin didn't miss the wary lines on her face.

Whatever had gripped her in that moment was gone when she gave him her full focus. Her spine was rail-straight as she sat on the backless stool, and her voice held what he assumed was a match for the formidable tones she'd use in the courtroom.

"There isn't something more."

"Sure there is."

"A single night of passion? And while I won't say it's nothing, it shouldn't stand in the way of what each of us wants to accomplish."

"Why are you so insistent on relating the two things at all?"

"Oh, come on, Gavin. Of course those two things are entwined. They're intimately entwined." She leaned closer before seeming to catch herself. "We've seen each other naked."

While he assumed she'd brought up that enticing fact to make a point, he couldn't help but needle her a bit. "We most certainly did."

"Be serious."

"I'm certainly not laughing. In fact, I'm remembering a few things in rather vivid detail."

"You're impossible."

"And you're combining two things together like they somehow cancel each other out. I'd like to know why."

"My work is important to me."

"As mine is to me."

"We slept together. Do you think anyone on that task force is going to take us seriously if we suddenly start up an affair?"

Although there was a thread of irritation starting to simmer in his blood at her continued pushback, he fought to maintain the steady, easy, nearly carefree notes in his voice. If she didn't want to go out with him, he could live with that. But her arguments centered around what others would think or why they couldn't have a shot at something, *not* basic disinterest.

He just couldn't let it go.

"Two single people having a relationship isn't an affair."

"It is when they're paired up on a work project and keeping it a secret."

"So make it public." As he said the words, Gavin realized

them for solid truth. "To my earlier point, it's not a crime if the city's employees date each other."

"That won't keep people from talking."

"So let them talk."

Their ice cream arrived, cutting into the argument that was steadily building between them. He wasn't going to get anywhere in this conversation behaving like a petulant child. And he certainly wasn't looking to date someone who didn't want to be with him.

So why was he pushing this?

He'd never put that much stock in the romance dance. You saw someone. You liked them. You spent some time with them. Was it simplistic? Sure. But he'd always had far more important priorities in his life, and no one had ever made him see a reason to change them.

Until Sera.

Something in that time they spent with each other—less than twenty-four hours of his life—had wrecked him. He hated the vulnerability, but more, he hated the idea that what they did for a living needed to dictate their private moments.

Sera had already taken a few small bites of her ice cream and he opted to dig into his banana split, hoping the mix of sugar and heavy cream would cool their conversation off a bit.

"Can we maybe chalk it all up to a complicated situation that we don't have to decide right now?" she finally asked.

"Yeah. We can do that."

And he could. While he wasn't ready to fully back off, Gavin could appreciate that a lot had been thrown at both of them and a bit of time to figure it out would go a long way.

"How's your ice cream?" he asked, their heated conversation fading. He'd brought her here to take her out for a treat and it was actually quite nice to sit and enjoy her company.

"Delicious. I haven't been here in a while. Dessert was a good idea."

"Sugar usually solves most problems. Or at least makes them seem less fraught."

"As someone who solves problems for a living, I'd like to say we're more evolved as a species, but—" She stared down at her ice cream, tapping the side of the small metal dish with her spoon. "It's hard to argue with sugar therapy."

Their dessert seemed to diffuse the tension that had spiked when he'd brought up their relationship status, and they sank back into that easy conversation that had been there between them from the first.

It ebbed and flowed, until they both looked down and realized they hadn't just finished their dessert, but their dishes had long been whisked away by the bored server.

With dessert completed, Gavin collected their coats once more, and then they were weaving their way back out into the early spring night.

"Thanks for the ice cream."

"My pleasure."

Gavin fought the suddenly desperate desire to lay a hand low on her back and shoved his hands into his pockets as they headed back in the direction of her apartment. The lights of the pharmacy spilled back onto the sidewalk and illuminated the deep red tones of her hair.

The rain that had dogged them for days had faded, and in its place was a cool breeze that promised spring, even if winter hadn't quite relinquished its cold grip.

"I still think your lack of ice cream in the home is a crime against nature, but I'll do my best to reserve further judgment."

"Maybe I just prefer eating ice cream with others."

That breeze kicked up once more as they passed by the alley between the pharmacy and the old shoe store that was its neighbor. The same kid who'd waited on them had obviously been put on closing duty, and he carried two big black bags in his hand to the curb, the distinct scent of the aging garbage filling the air.

"Maybe we'll—" He broke off as a dire look came over her face, the color instantly draining from her cheeks. "Sera?"

But she'd already bolted, heading straight for a city garbage can at the corner. The distinct sounds of misery rose up into the night air as she lost the remnants of her meal, and he made it just in time to hold her shoulders when a second, wracking jolt ripped through her.

"Oh God!" Her choked sob ripped at his heart, but it was the distinct words that followed that robbed him of breath. "I thought I was past this."

# Chapter Four

Gavin sat on her couch, his gaze unseeing as he stared at the TV she'd flipped on as a matter of habit when they walked in. She'd wanted to say something deeper, or perhaps even an apology, but had opted instead for pointing at the remote control and letting him know he could put on what he wanted and that she'd be right back.

The strong whiff of garbage as they left the restaurant had hit her, its effect swift and immediate. And although she and Gavin needed to talk, her first order of business was to brush her teeth and give herself a moment to freshen up in the bathroom.

But now the time had come to tell him the truth.

She'd spent the past few months since discovering her pregnancy thinking of scenario after scenario of how she'd tell him about the baby.

Now at the moment of truth her mind was a complete blank.

"The Nets have been playing well this year."

"Hmm?" He glanced up from the basketball game playing out on the screen.

"Um, never mind." She snagged the remote, muting the

TV, before taking a seat on the opposite end of the couch. "So I think we need to talk."

His expression suggested an incredulous sort of agreement she imagined along the lines of *you think?* But his words managed a rather different tone.

"How long have you known?"

"About two months."

"All this time…" His voice faded off, his expression oddly blank.

"I wanted to tell you, Gavin. Truly, I did. But I couldn't find you, and then I didn't know how to find you. You'd moved from your apartment, so there was no way of knowing where you'd gone."

"That's an excuse?"

"Well, actually, yes. It's the truth."

"You knew my name."

"Your first name. And that you were a cop. You do realize just how big the NYPD is."

He didn't look convinced. In fact, her argument seemed to ignite something inside of him. "Or maybe you didn't want to find me."

"Excuse me?"

"You walked out in the middle of the afternoon, while I was sleeping. You never had any intention of coming back."

Whatever she'd imagined, no matter how many times she'd played through her mind telling him the news of the baby, this wall of anger wasn't it. "You keep tossing that in my face. What are you really upset about? The fact that I'm pregnant or the fact that your pride is injured because I walked out the door?"

"You're pregnant! I had a right to know."

"I'm not disputing that fact. Our cutesy let's-pretend-we-don't-have-anything-but-this-moment act was heady at the time, but rather inconvenient when I tried to find you after. And you moving only made that worse."

He stood at that, his hands clenched at his sides as he paced back and forth. She wanted to go to him—wanted to comfort him in the same way she'd wanted to be comforted the day she'd discovered the life-altering news—but something kept her rooted to the couch.

His ire? While it was intense, she had zero fear of him.

So what was it? Why was she suddenly itching for a fight? One that would finally—hopefully?—assuage the anger she'd carried for the past three months. "You can stand there and act as self-righteous as you'd like, but it's not like you worked all that hard to come find me, either."

"I had no idea how to find you."

"Neither did I!"

He stilled at that, mid-pace, and stared at her. And in that moment, she saw all the excitement and confusion and raw emotion that she felt herself. "A baby?"

"Yes."

"But we were careful."

"I know. Or I think I know. There might have been that one time. Right around dawn."

His dark gaze clouded with memories, and she knew the moment he took firm hold of that one. "But we—"

"We made a valiant effort, but threw caution to the wind on that one."

And they had. Immense and wonderful, what had been between them had driven both of them nearly mindless. It was wildly out of character for her—she was vigilant about protection—but their conversation earlier in the evening had taken a rather personal turn when both admitted to seeing to their health with regular testing. And she'd believed herself covered with her birth control pills.

Pills she'd forgotten to take with the rush of running around for the holidays and again, after she'd gotten home that day. A lapse that had paid an incredible dividend. One they would now share for the rest of their lives.

"I never wanted to hide this from you, Gavin. Whatever else you might believe, please know that."

"When were you going to tell me? We spent all evening together, and if you hadn't thrown up, I'd still be blithely unaware I was going to be a father."

"Not for long. I was trying to figure out how to tell you and when, but it never crossed my mind not to tell you at all."

He remained where he was but had stopped pacing to stare at her from across the room. That large form she'd so admired, both in and out of clothes, struck her through a new lens as she stared at him.

And in a heartbeat, she *saw* him, their child nestled against his broad chest. She saw him again, hands wrapped firmly around a toddler's as they tried to walk. And even once more, a proud, doting father on one knee adjusting their child's backpack as they headed for the first day of school.

They were bonded by this tiny person who would be here in half a year. A blessing and a gift, one handed to two people who didn't know a thing about each other.

The edge of his lips twitched, a rude awakening in the midst of her thoughts.

"What?"

"Well, come on. You mean you didn't want to share the news in a conference room the size of a cracker box?"

Sera couldn't quite hold back a small smile of her own. "I was actually thinking I'd start our next task force meeting with the entire team. Make the announcement then."

"That certainly gives new meaning to collaborating with your partner."

The humor caught her low and deep in the belly, and she couldn't hold back the peals of laughter that, once started, quickly raged out of control.

Gavin crossed back to the couch, dropping down beside her. His own laughter joined hers, and it was long moments later before they both came up for breath.

But it was that dark brown gaze meeting hers that silenced the lingering humor. "We're actually having a baby?"

"We actually are."

"Garbage scents aside, how are you feeling?"

"I'm fine."

One lone eyebrow shot up. "Try again since I'm finding it hard to believe you. How are you really feeling?"

"I have good days and bad days. It's more the time of the day, to be honest. And I've sort of figured out how to deal with it."

"All by yourself."

"Well, yeah."

"Do your aunt and uncle know?"

It was her turn to shoot him a dark look. "Do you think they'd have been quite so welcoming this evening?"

"Probably not." He waited a few beats before asking, "And your parents?"

"They're not an issue."

He looked about to say something further, but stopped himself. It touched her that he could read her discomfort so easily, even as she felt a strange sort of sadness that she hadn't gotten to share some of that history with him. Some of what had shaped her.

But she stayed quiet and didn't say any of *that*, either.

They might share one explosive night of passion and a child, but there were some boundary lines she still couldn't cross. And there was no way she was ready to talk about *that* aspect of her life.

Which made his next move, so gentle and so innately kind, enough to set her heart to aching.

His hand found hers, his big palm layering over the back of her hand. "Whatever worries either of us will carry for this child, you can remove abandonment from the list." He turned to look at her, his brown eyes searching. "I will be a father for the rest of my life."

HE WAS GOING to be a father.

The thought flowed in and out of his mind along with his breathing.

Inhale: *I'm going to be...*

Exhale: *...a father.*

Over and over as he and his partners worked the churning waters around Hell Gate.

It was an incongruous thought in an even more incongruous place, yet it was his. *All his,* Gavin thought as his heavily gloved hands moved the silt at the bottom of the East River after a hit on his metal detector. When he only came up with what looked like a key ring, he kept going.

His comms kept up a steady flurry of activity in his ear, both from the team up on the surface. Instructions continued coming down to him and Wyatt, along with separate details for the other pair in the water, Kerrigan Doyle and Jayden Houston.

They took no chances when they dived this area. It was always two teams, and they'd be called up when they still had at least ten minutes of air. It was an extra series of precautions Captain Reed had insisted on after a dive on his watch early in his career had nearly resulted in a Harbor team death.

Although Gavin had been fortunate in his years on the team, he appreciated the extra precautions. While today was fairly smooth going, he was well aware things could change in a minute.

The waters here at Hell Gate were actually a tidal strait, with the confluence of the New York Upper Bay, the Long Island Sound and the Harlem River contributing to the unceasing churn of the water. And the reality of the conditions was that high tide was bad, but low tide only reversed all the flow that had built up pressure in the passage, pushing the water right back in the opposite direction.

They'd deliberately selected this early afternoon window for having the least amount of tidal pressure in the day, but they needed to move. And with the rains of the past several days as well as the water's already roiling currents, the evidence they were attempting to recover could be anywhere.

"Needle in a haystack, friends," one of their leads up above in the police boat advised through the comms. "But you've cleared twelve quadrants so far. Hayes and Trumball, move west, and Doyle and Houston, move south. We'll cover one more swath before you ascend. Submersible's capturing the area north of the bridge."

Their briefing before they'd descended matched Wyatt's description the day before in the conference room. Someone had tossed a gun off the RFK Bridge with its estimated landing closer to the waters beneath Hell Gate Bridge. Although they hated to miss any evidence recovery, the perp was already in custody and two cops were eyewitnesses to the gun being tossed off the bridge, with body cam footage to back it up. It wasn't ideal to leave the evidence at the bottom of the river, but the overarching effort had to be weighed against the benefits.

An odd counterpoint to the clanging reality of his life at the moment. Which was also a clear example of effort versus benefit.

Sera had assured him she would have told him about the baby. But would she?

She'd made several quick assurances now that they'd met again, but if they weren't working the task force, how would she ever have found him?

That thought had haunted him all night and into the morning. What would it be like? To have a child of his walking around without him ever knowing?

He needed to keep his head on straight—they *had* met up again, and he *did* know—but the reality of what might have been haunted him.

"Hayes!" Wyatt's voice was garbled around his mouthpiece, but Gavin got the general gist, made even more specific when Wyatt grabbed his calf. They had a variety of physical signals they were all trained on, but this one was pretty straightforward.

He stopped his forward movement, allowing Wyatt to move up beside him. The water was murky, but their headlamps as well as the bright sunshine above gave him a decent view of his dive partner's face.

Gavin pointed toward the floor of the river, turning his hands up in an empty motion.

But it was Wyatt's face, visible through the clear veneer

of his mask, that had Gavin doing a double take. The man held up a gun, the shape more than clear in the murky water, before waving him on.

And although his voice was garbled when he spoke, Wyatt's instructions were clear.

"Wait until you see what I found."

WHAT THEY FOUND was a cache of weapons that they'd be hauling up for hours, Gavin thought as he stared at what they had laid out on the floor of the police boat.

No weapon was designed to shoot flowers and sunshine, he admitted to himself, but these were some of the worst. Retrofitted guns designed to do maximum damage, all with serial numbers removed.

They'd called in a second dive team, who was working the scene now while he, Wyatt, Kerrigan and Jayden took a break.

"What a mess." Wyatt shook his head as he got to his feet. He'd called in for reinforcements, and even now Gavin saw Detective Arlo Prescott, a fellow officer and one of the most decorated detectives at the 86th, stepping onto the police boat after being ferried over.

Arlo and Kerrigan were dating, and Gavin saw them briefly speak, his hand tenderly rubbing her shoulder, before Arlo continued on to the cache spread out on the deck. The man let out a low whistle before crouching down in the same pose Wyatt had just come up out of. "This gives new meaning to evidence recovery."

"You're not kidding." Wyatt pointed toward the three sawed-off shotguns at the edge of the area. "Got a hit on the metal detector, but as soon as I saw the butt of that first one, I realized what we had. And not one damn serial number among them."

Arlo glanced up, frowning. "Kerrigan's talked often enough about hating to dive Hell Gate, but you all are still down there pretty regularly. How long do you think these have been there, unnoticed?"

"Forensics will do some testing," Gavin put in. "But based on some of the decomp on the metal and the state of a few of the barrels we've looked at, I'd say well over six months. Maybe a bit more since much of that would have been winter."

"You think we'll get any prints?"

"We've been careful bringing it all up." Gavin shrugged. "But that's hard to say."

They had been careful, well aware with this much evidence it would be more than possible they'd get a hit on some careless act like fingerprints or a partial serial number.

And still...

Something gnawed at him.

"Something this big?" Gavin finally spoke. "Whoever did it would have to realize they were going to attract attention once everything was found."

Arlo glanced over from staring at the cache of weapons, a faint smile on his lips. "You're assuming this was done by a party of masterminds. Panicked people do stupid things. It's why we get our fair share of cases that wrap up with minimal fuss."

"Maybe—" Gavin let his thought die off. Something about this troubled him, beyond the broader issue of such a large criminal act, but he hadn't quite worked it through in his mind. But there was something.

"Tell me what has you bothered, Gav," Wyatt pressed. "Is it the way we're handling the evidence?"

Despite the display currently on the floor of the police boat, there was a team en route shortly behind Arlo to quickly manage both the chain of evidence as well as the more sensitive aspects of handling the weapons. The Harbor team was well trained in basic recovery to ensure as clean a sample as possible, but they always breathed a bit easier once it had moved on to the folks actually responsible for evidence handling.

"No, not that. We've done this by the book. It's just the volume of it. The location. Whoever did this knew what they were doing." He shot a look at Arlo and offered a grim smile of his own. "These weren't run-of-the-mill criminals or a group of lackeys low on the food chain. Destroying evidence like this? And up at Hell Gate? It feels to me like whoever is responsible has knowledge of our work."

Arlo and Wyatt both stared at him, their gazes focused as they gave consideration to his assessment.

"Knowledge how?" Wyatt asked.

"The tides, for one. Hell Gate doesn't just have a scary name. That channel's always been difficult, and we have protocols specifically for diving there."

Wyatt nodded, his mouth grim. "I can still see you circling. Keep going."

And that was when he hit on it.

"It's the volume, Wyatt. You need time to dump that much, but you also have to know this area's a great place to hide. The tides work in a criminal's favor on that front."

"Tell me more about that," Arlo said. "You know I'm a big fan of what you do, but that's the stuff I'm fuzzy on."

Wyatt brought Arlo toward one of the large maps they had

up in the boathouse, one specifically mapping out the East River. But as one more obvious sign of his leadership, he gestured Gavin toward the wall. "Please, Hayes. Go ahead."

"The tidal patterns are wicked here." He pointed out the various points, the overall geography and the way multiple bodies of water—all with their own tidal push and pull— came together.

It was a credit to Arlo how quickly he picked it all up. "So what you're saying is high tide isn't your friend, but low tide's not much better."

"Exactly." Gavin nodded. "What comes in hard and fast goes right back out the same way. Which means if Wyatt hadn't accidentally discovered that gun there's every chance this dump site would continue to go unnoticed. Over time, especially as things piled up, they'd inevitably get moved with the currents."

"Speaking of which." Wyatt stepped in. "We need to get the team up. Low tide's going to start causing problems next. We'll prep and go back down later."

Wyatt headed out to the dive master manning the comms out on the deck, and Arlo turned away from the map, his gaze veering right back to the cache of weapons already laid out. "We don't have any recent pulses on gun trade activity. With what you found down there, you think there are about fifty weapons?"

Gavin nodded. "Initial estimate, but I think we're going to net out in that range."

"It's a lot in one place, but it's still not huge. Citywide, we take down that amount in an average weekend."

Gavin knew Arlo was right, and in the scheme of overall crime, fifty guns was the tip of the iceberg. And yet...

Was this something for the task force?

The thought popped in with little fanfare, but as Gavin considered it, he realized it could be an interesting approach to the project he and Sera were working on. A real-life case they could present and which then could use the extended brainpower of multiple teams.

He vowed to think on it later as a shout came up from the edge of the police boat. The second dive team had surfaced, more evidence in hand. Arlo and Gavin moved over to help, carefully securing what came up following each of the recovery steps they were all trained in.

Wyatt's focus on planning for a second dive altered Gavin's responsibilities for the rest of his shift. He put together a plan for the next day's dive teams, as well as setting up a pair of uniforms on both ends of the bridge to watch from above and a police boat to keep watch over the cache location still under the water.

It was good work. Solid police work. But as daylight slowly faded, the lights of the bridge coming up over them, he kept circling back around to using the task force and Sera.

Always Sera.

Which was how he found himself knocking on her door after his shift ended, dinner in hand.

SERA GLANCED DOWN once more at her laptop before standing to head to the front door and whoever stood on the other side. Aunt Robin had mentioned stopping by one evening this week with some legal paperwork on one of their rentals, and Sera figured it would be a nice break from what she'd dubbed the legal brief from hell.

Although her workload had been significantly reduced so she could participate in the task force, she still had the cases David had requested she retain. And for some reason, the brief on the Nicholson murder case she was handling was giving her headaches.

The bigger problem, to her mind, was why.

She usually enjoyed this part of her job, organizing her thoughts on a case and then writing the encapsulation of all she'd reviewed. It not only helped her consolidate her thoughts, but inevitably in the process, she gained more clarity and refined the approach she was going to use to argue the case.

"If clarity's what you're after, maybe you need to write a legal brief on Gavin," she muttered to herself as she crossed toward the door.

Which made the fact that he stood on the opposite side an unexpected shot beneath the armor she'd vowed to put into place. "You're not Aunt Robin."

"Not last time I checked." He held up a bag that emitted the most delicious aromas. "But I do come bearing dinner."

She recognized the logo on the side of the bag. "You brought shawarma."

"It struck me as I was walking home from work that I wanted this for dinner, and then I thought, maybe Sera would like it, too."

"I love it."

"Then I chose right." He leaned forward as if checking out the inside of her apartment. "Is it okay if I come in?"

"Oh! Yes!" She quickly gestured him in, her surprise at seeing him obviously killing any semblance of manners. "I was just doing some work."

"You usually work through dinner?" The question was casual, but she caught the subtle notes of censure. Before she could call him on it, he'd already turned from where he'd set the bag down on the counter. "I'm sorry. I was thinking about you *and* the baby on that one."

"Since the baby is the one who has put me off food for the past few months, I'd say you're putting blame in the wrong place." Since he looked genuinely chagrined, she opted to cut him some slack. "But since we're both hungry this evening, I'd also say your timing is perfect. And," she added, "it's further proof I'm hungry since I'm grumping at you even as you come bearing one of my top three favorite foods."

With that particular land mine disarmed, she crossed to the cabinets to get plates. "Help yourself to anything you'd like in the fridge. I've got some beer leftover from a party last year and a few bottles of wine in addition to diet soda."

"You sure about the beer?"

"Please, help yourself."

"It won't bother you if I drink and you can't?"

The deep, genuine sincerity in his gaze caught her up as she stared at him across the small expanse of the kitchen. "No, I don't mind at all. But thank you for asking."

It was a small kindness, but a welcome one. And it was only as she sat, nestled in the small drop-leaf table for the second night in a row, that Sera saw the sheer exhaustion that rode his features.

"Is everything okay?"

"Sure. Why?"

"It looks like you might have had a tough day." She stopped, realizing going any further would add a layer of intimacy she wasn't sure they'd progressed to. "You just look a bit tired."

When he didn't immediately say anything, the conversation the day before in the precinct conference room came winging back to her.

"Today was Hell Gate. How was it?"

"Tough, as usual. That stretch always is."

She'd read up on it last night after he'd left, curious what something so darkly named might be like as an actual dive site. The confluence of waterways and the sheer history of the location had sparked her worries, and she'd quickly closed her laptop for fear of moving down a path she wasn't entitled to.

He had a job, and it wasn't her place to question his choices. Nor did she have a right to those questions—to *any* questions, really—simply because she was carrying his child. Even if the reality of what he did for a living had embedded a level of worry in her chest she'd never expected to feel.

Which was just one more layer of weirdness in all that was happening to her.

No, she corrected herself, to *them*. And to the family they'd inadvertently created.

Gavin smiled as he unwrapped his meal. "Those look like very heavy thoughts in the face of this delicious pita wrapper full of seasoned meat."

"I—" It had happened so many times in the past thirty-six hours that she should be used to it by now, but as she set down her dinner, Sera had the odd sensation of not knowing what to say. Or more, feeling she had to say something yet having no idea how to navigate the discussion.

She hadn't felt this out of her depth since she was a teenager, trying to move on after her mother's death and feeling like the person she used to be was gone. It had been true then, and Sera suspected it was true now.

Why did it feel as unsettling at thirty-two as it had almost two decades ago?

"Why don't you start wherever you want to start?" His suggestion was gentle yet seemed like the exact right choice.

"I worried about you today. Quite unexpectedly, actually. What you do for a living, it's...dangerous."

"It is."

"And then you showed up, and you look really tired, and you sort of pissed me off with the eating thing, which..." she waved a hand "...I'm over. Truly I am. But I don't know what to *do* with you."

"What to do with me?" He grinned, quite at odds with the serious expression that had ridden his face through her outburst. "I'm not a pile of laundry."

"I—" She stared back, not sure if he was laughing at her or just making a joke.

She and Gavin didn't actually *know* one another's quirks or moods or what set them off. Because that came in time. After you got to know someone. Day by day.

Not after a night of fevered passion that resulted in a degree of involvement with each other that was going to last, oh, about forever.

"I stand by the statement," she finally said, sounding rather lame even to herself.

"Then I guess it's my turn to stand by something, too."

"What's that?"

Before she knew what he was about, he'd actually stood up and moved beside the table, extending a hand.

"What are you doing?"

"Isn't it obvious? I'm standing." He reached for her hand, tugging lightly. "Now it's your turn, too."

"Okay."

It was the last thing to escape her lips and, she'd admit later, the last coherent thought she had for quite some time.

The moment she stood, steady on her feet, Gavin had an arm around her waist, pulling her close. And in less than a heartbeat later, his lips captured hers in a kiss so intense, she could only wrap her arms around his neck and hang on.

## *Chapter Five*

It might not have been one of his most inspired moves, Gavin thought as the kiss spun out, but it was hands down the best choice he'd made all day.

All month, if he were honest.

He'd wanted Sera back in his arms, and all the strange tension swirling around them since he'd arrived at her place seemed in need of taming. So he'd gambled, figuring kissing her could go one of two ways.

And he was damn glad it was this way, with her arms around his neck and her mouth open beneath his like a warm welcome home.

Because whatever else she was, Gavin thought as a hand drifted down over her spine while the other one remained firmly wrapped around her shoulders, Sera Forte felt like home.

She had from the moment they'd met.

A small sigh rose up in her throat as their tongues met, a joyful sort of remembrance that let him know whatever fantasies he'd had these past three months, nothing could compare to the real thing.

Nothing in his whole life had ever felt like Sera in his arms.

Memories of their time together blended with the reality

of holding her again and Gavin recognized the truth. Reality was so much better.

Another small sigh lingered between them as he shifted the angle of the kiss, and he couldn't help but smile at her full response. Whatever else was between them, they had this.

Even if he'd nearly bungled it beyond recognition.

He was still frustrated with himself for his behavior on their first day of the task force. Yes, he'd been shocked to see her, but he'd been even more shocked at that pure rush of emotion during their reunion.

And with all those feelings he had no business swimming in came the endless questions that had haunted him since the new year.

Why did she leave? What could he have done differently? And perhaps the scariest of all—why had it mattered so much? It was that persistent confusion—and the sheer power of whatever it was between them—that had him pulling back.

*I don't know what to do with you.*

Her words still lingered in his mind, even as he had a few ideas of exactly what they could do together. But if he were honest with himself, Gavin thought, there was also way too much unspoken between them to jump back into bed.

But oh, the temptation…

Even as he thought it, Gavin admitted temptation was too simple a word. These feelings for her? They haunted him. Made him want a future with someone who, by all accounts, hadn't wanted one with him.

His behavior was ridiculous.

All of it.

His moony attitude. His inability to shake these feelings.

Even his mental gyrations that insisted they had a connection that went deeper than a one-night stand. A feeling he'd had long before he'd known they'd created a life.

"Gavin?" Her voice was soft, a bemused expression tilting her still-wet lips.

"I interrupted our dinner. We should probably get back to it."

Bemusement shifted to subtle confusion, and Gavin recognized, once again, his behavior was so far out of the norm for him it was almost laughable.

He simply wasn't a person set with wide-sweeping emotions. He wasn't made for that; his early life as a "Park Avenue Hayes" ensured that he knew decorum and had a certain measure to his emotions at all times.

A range of emotions flitted across her face, some he could decipher and others that remained a mystery, before she finally spoke. "Why are you pulling away?"

"Is it that obvious?"

"No more obvious than my own hesitation. So why don't you grab a fresh beer, and we have the talk we really need to have?"

"About the baby?"

"No." She shook her head. "About us, Gavin. We need to talk about us."

SERA HAD ALWAYS considered her willingness to tackle conflict—especially when rooted in the vastness of what remained unspoken—as one of her greatest assets in the practice of law. She'd understood from a very early age that the things people said or didn't say often hid something far deeper going on inside.

A point that became patently obvious when those words didn't match behavior.

She used that skill—honed it, really—to a sharp point in her legal work. What were the circumstances that led up to a crime? What was the perpetrator's motives? And what made them act in that moment?

There were times, of course, when people simply acted poorly. But more often than not, asking the questions that probed deeper gave far more insight into a case than simply assuming the worst of someone. It was the lodestone she hung onto, even on some of her worst cases. Finding that humanity in others. *Believing* it existed.

It was essential to how she lived. She needed it like she needed air.

To make sense of her past.

To believe she was making a difference.

To move beyond her parents' choices.

And with that knowledge, Sera recognized something else. She hadn't been at her best these past few days, and she knew herself to be a decent person. Which only made it fair to question what was driving Gavin.

From their tense moments on the first day of the task force to his sudden reappearance two nights in a row, they needed to get underneath it all. Because however much they didn't know about each other, she *knew* he was a good man.

She took her seat and waited until he sat back down before launching in. "I know we haven't been an 'us' for all that long or with any level of permanence, but there's a lot we haven't talked about."

"Is there something specific you'd like to know?"

As questions went, Sera had to admit, it was a good one. Because the reality was, there was a rather large chasm between claiming she wanted to *talk about us* and then knowing exactly what to say on the matter.

"Are you a native New Yorker? Why police work and the dive work specifically? Why Brooklyn?" She lifted her hands and knew the smile on her face had to be distinctly rueful. "Who are you, Gavin Hayes?"

"An expectant father."

It was sweet that he started there, and Sera felt a small clutch beneath her heart. Especially because the sheer look of awe that filled his face as he spoke the words touched something she'd never thought possible.

"And as you said, I'm a cop." When she only nodded, saying nothing, he kept on. "I didn't grow up wanting to be a cop. It wasn't in my life plan, as it were. But—" He shrugged, and while the action was casual, Sera sensed a pain there she'd never have expected.

Something tugged on her to probe further, but she'd finally gotten him talking, and although she couldn't explain it, every instinct she had told her if she pushed too hard on that front, he'd shut down entirely.

So she tamped down on her own curiosity, instead following whatever he was willing to share. "But what?"

"But it's who I was meant to be."

"And the diving?"

The flash of a quick grin erased whatever lingering melancholy she saw in his face. "That's the fun part of being a cop."

"Risking your life and diving in the shockingly disgusting waters that surround our wonderful city is fun?"

"Why does everyone focus on that part?" Gavin reached for his sandwich, taking a large bite, the direction of their conversation apparently having zero impact on his willingness to finish his dinner.

"The dirty part?"

"Yeah." He waited until he was done chewing his bite. "It's getting better."

"Than what? A vat of toxic waste?" She picked at a small corner of her pita, unable to hide a smile of her own. "Or is that an insult to toxic waste?"

"It's not quite that bad. And yes, as the Harbor team we're encouraged to avoid opening our mouths or allowing any water to get past our lips. I also have a few extra shots each year to ensure my safety and physical health."

Sera shuddered at that. "And that's just the water risks. What about the other risks?" Her eyes widened as a new risk popped into her mind. "What about animals? Sharks? Eels?"

"No sharks. Eels yes. And feral goldfish, to name another."

"No way! Goldfish can be feral?"

"Absolutely. I've seen some that are as large as four pounds. Where do you think all those innocent little fish won at street fairs go?"

"I assumed the trip down the toilet and on into the sewer system was too much for them."

Gavin set down his napkin and leaned back in his chair. "Perhaps all aren't up to the trip, but a lot of people think taking their fair winnings and dropping them in a body of water themselves is a good idea. News flash. It isn't."

"I'm not sure I can keep eating."

"Which is another important fun fact. Women under fifty are encouraged to avoid any and all fish pulled out of local city waters."

Although she knew it was a reference to child-bearing

age, Sera couldn't resist teasing him. "What about women over fifty?"

"They should plan their menu at their own risk."

It was a silly, innocuous conversation, and Sera was surprised by how good it felt. Especially because when she'd started down this path, the need to question him—to *know* him—had felt weighted somehow.

"See," she said, unable to hold back the smile even as the creepy concept of a four-pound goldfish would likely haunt her for days. "That wasn't so hard. A few fun facts about Gavin."

"Which means it's my turn. Tax, title, license." He made a come-hither motion with his hand. "Come on."

She knew this moment would come. Turnabout, after all, was more than fair.

Yet now, faced with the chance to tell him something that mattered, she felt the mental noose tightening around her neck.

What should she actually tell him?

That she was a workaholic with an unquenchable need to prove herself? Or maybe that she was a semi-loner adult whose guarded attitude had resulted in minimal friendships?

Or perhaps she should just go for it and watch him walk out the door. After all, who didn't wonder about a person who'd been abandoned by their parents?

Oddly, she felt the need to tell him all those things and so much more.

It was a first for her and no matter how much she believed he'd listen, a lifetime of *not* sharing those aspects of her life held her back.

"I'm a lawyer, which you know."

"I do."

"But you may not know why I chose public defender."

"I assumed it was your unerring need for fairness and justice."

"Not too far off the mark."

"Then what is it?"

"It's people, Gavin. I have a need to believe in people. In their innate goodness. Their ability to be fair when really pressed to the wall. And that even if they make a bad decision, they don't have to be defined by it."

"And what about you, Sera?"

"What about me?"

"Do you give yourself the same credit?"

THE CONVERSATION HAD turned far deeper, far more quickly than he'd have anticipated.

And yet…

Something about the look in her gaze and the way she'd leaned forward slightly in her chair and the earnestness in her voice. Those emotions all spoke of something even more than passion.

They spoke of desperation.

And maybe, Gavin considered, he'd been a bit too focused on himself to think about what really happened on New Year's Day. He'd let his pride keep him from thinking that she'd left for any reason other than she had no interest in seeing him again. How humbling, then, to realize he'd not only missed the mark, but had lost three months out of sheer, stubborn idiocy.

As if realizing she'd stalled out their conversation, Sera finally spoke. "I don't know what you mean."

"This need to believe in other people. Do you give yourself the same credit?"

"Well, of course."

"Then why did you leave on New Year's? The real reason, not the potential for it to get awkward."

He wasn't sure why he was pressing it, but somehow, Gavin knew that he needed the truth. He needed to *know*. And he needed to hear her reasons, instead of living with the ones he'd made up in his mind. Perhaps he wouldn't like them, but at least they'd be the truth instead of something he'd managed to manufacture out of his own battered pride or bruised ego.

"It was a one-night stand." Although she didn't put nearly as much heat behind that argument as the day before, Gavin still sensed that reason was a lifeline she was hanging on to by the edges of her fingernails.

"It was."

"Most people prefer those have no strings attached."

"I'm not talking about most people. I'm talking about us. About our night together. About the connection we had that put us together in the first place."

Because whatever else he wanted to think or believe, he couldn't shake that sense of connection.

Of belonging.

It wasn't a sensation he was familiar with beyond his work with the Harbor team, and it had stuck with him for all these long months. Upended him, really, because for the first time in his life he'd felt attraction and desire in lockstep with the innate sense that he *fit* with another person.

And he'd reveled in that sensation of belonging in those hours with Sera. Of being understood.

Of fitting.

Maybe it was why her attempts at being casual—dismissive even—had him finding an odd sort of humor in their situation.

Sera blew out a breath that fluttered the hair that framed her face. "You do realize there are about a million articles in women's magazines saying not to have feelings for your one-night stand. And about ten times that of cautionary tales told on social media sites, talking about what a bad idea it is to bring emotion into casual sex."

"And there we have it."

When she only looked at him, he realized that she'd inadvertently given him the opening he needed.

"You're assuming what was between us was casual. Or scratching an itch."

"Scratching an itch?" A small bark of laughter escaped her. "How eloquent."

"Giving in to desire, then?"

"What does it matter?"

"It all matters, Sera. I was attracted to you, yes. And there was a hell of a lot of desire." He reached out and laid a hand over hers, willing her to understand what was so damned hard to put into words. "But nothing between us was casual. Nothing at all."

She sat there, her gaze focused on their hands for several long moments. Whatever progress he'd believed they had made seemed to fade, wisping away like smoke.

Until she turned her hand beneath his, their fingertips meeting the other's palm.

"It wasn't casual." She stared up at him then, those irises as blue as a spring day meeting his. "But we don't know each other. A single day, even a non-casual one, doesn't negate the fact that we don't know each other."

"So we get to know each other. Day by day."

"Fate seems to think that's a good idea. Between the baby

and the task force, we've got a lot of together time in front of us."

"Then let's take it."

She nodded and didn't remove her hand from where it linked to his.

Gavin gave himself a few more moments to revel in the simplicity of that connection before his day came rushing back to him. "Lest you think I'm just the neighborhood stud you can ogle, I did come here with information we might be able to use for our task force project."

"The neighborhood stud?" She snatched her hand back, the slight shake of her head proof she already knew him well enough to get the joke. "Smooth, Hayes."

"I am that, but tell me you're not intrigued all the same."

The raw intimacy that had arced between them since the kiss began to fade as they both shifted toward work. Whether by design or simply to find some ease after several tense moments, he wasn't sure, but the shift was welcome.

"Oh, I'm intrigued. So tell me more about how we're going to create the best plan of all the task force teams." She picked up her shawarma and took another bite, her renewed interest in dinner a good sign they were back on level ground.

"My team and I had a big day up at Hell Gate."

"You find a school of feral goldfish?"

"Not letting that one go, I see. But what we found was way better."

With the economy he'd learned in briefing his captain on case progress, he quickly caught her up to speed on the cache of weapons they'd discovered and the work underway to bring everything up to the surface.

And with her legal mind and understanding of local

crime, Sera caught on quick. "Someone had to know that was the perfect place to make an illegal drop like that. Difficult waters. Active tides."

"Without question. Add on that we haven't found a serial number on anything we've brought up, and it looks like this was deliberate."

"There are potential trafficking elements here. The Feds are going to want in."

"Which is why this is the perfect subject for our task force project. It's real work, and we can use it to map out a plan of action in real time."

"I like it for the project, but, Gavin, what about the actual implications? Something that size? And that deliberate disposal? *Especially* when it wasn't the reason you were diving that area to begin with."

He'd turned the case over in his mind, but it wasn't until she doubled down on the real-world implications that Gavin realized all he'd missed. He'd been so focused on making a success of the task force that he hadn't fully appreciated the advancement this case would provide all on its own.

"It's a lucky hit, no doubt."

"It's more than luck, Gavin." Those notes of justice— the ones she was so determined to find—lit up her gaze. "Whoever put that stash of weapons there didn't think they were going to get caught."

THE DAY'S NEWS out of the 86th was late in arriving but pertinent all the same, the Organizer thought as he considered the details.

The damned Harbor team had struck again.

The ongoing drop at Hell Gate had been an inspired approach to their problems around weapons disposal. And they'd been getting away with it for some time now.

Until the water cowboys over at the 86th nosed around.

And now that they knew, it was time to not only find a new drop but deal with the fallout of this one. He glanced at the other items spread over his desk. The ones he kept secreted away on his person, pulling them out only in his private moments.

The burner phone he changed out religiously each week.

The single sheet of paper on which he kept a list of rotating passwords, also changed out every seven days.

And the phone number he planned never to use.

Although he'd committed that number to memory, he knew well enough that should he need to use it, he'd have no time to worry if he could recall those digits in their precise order.

So yes, he held on to the number, the paper it was written on faded and thin from where it had worn, rubbing against the inside breast pocket of his suit jackets.

Even as he took great pride that he'd never had need of it.

Pushing aside thoughts of his *partner*, the Organizer tapped a finger on the burner phone, considering all the angles.

None of the weapons had serial numbers. It was a requirement of the work he'd insisted on from the first, along with a distributed work pattern so that no one person had access to all the information of the operation, and things had been progressing smoothly.

He considered himself the finest puppet master, after all.

And, as such, he understood his other options. Knew where he could push or pull, shift and maneuver the situation to his bidding.

This was a bump in the road.

Those guns were untraceable, after all.

And he'd simply find a new way to dispose of his garbage.

## Chapter Six

Gavin stood at parade rest as Captain Dwayne Reed considered all he, Wyatt and Arlo had just shared about their recovery dive up at Hell Gate.

Captain Reed had first listened to their overview, and now his deep brown gaze was engrossed on the report Gavin had come in early to write up.

The man's attention was laser-focused on the work. It was a style, Gavin knew, that showed both a measure of respect to his team as well as a razor-sharp intellect that was already processing implications with each word he digested.

He listened.

He considered.

And then the man never failed to seamlessly nail the most pertinent questions in a matter of minutes.

Kerrigan and Jayden had already gone out again this morning to direct a second team who was fresh for the work while Gavin took point on the briefing. He'd already been scheduled off the Harbor team today because of his task force work, so Wyatt had given him the opportunity to debrief their captain.

That was Wyatt's style, too. He was more than comfortable sharing the work of their team, allowing everyone to shine. He might be their de facto dive head, but he ensured the leadership at the 86th always knew harbor work was a full team effort.

"This is good work, Gavin." Captain Reed looked up from the report, deep lines grooved in his deep brown skin, framing his mouth, forehead and beneath his compassionate gaze. Although he wore the mantle of responsibility incredibly well, the pressure of the work was never-ending. "And this cache is a big deal. Based on what you've got here, you're confident this would have gone undetected for some time?"

"Yes, sir. The dive was a recovery mission, and if the waters hadn't been so churned up from the storms earlier this week, we'd likely not have moved into the quadrant where the weapons were discovered."

Gavin kept his comments brief and saw a solid gleam of approval shining from Wyatt's eyes.

"Would someone have a way of knowing what quadrants you regularly dive?" the captain asked.

The question cut straight to the heart of the matter and a theory Gavin had been playing around with on his own. "We don't publicize our dives or the patterns we follow, and the quadrant management is as much how we map out the area ahead of time that we're going to dive rather than being an actual location."

"So you'd have missed these for an indeterminate period of time?" Captain Reed persisted.

"Yes. The rocky area beneath the surface where we found the weapons isn't directly aligned or easily reached simply by tossing something off the Hell Gate Bridge. Or the RFK Bridge to its south. To position the guns in the place we uncovered, you'd need to do it deliberately and down near the water to make a drop."

"Nor is that an area we regularly check for incendiary devices," Wyatt added.

It was a sad reality that some of their team's work was aligned around regular bomb checks under bridges and city access points. Wyatt's added comment only reinforced the situation—that these guns were also in a place where they'd not be discovered on those regular dives.

Captain Reed stood and came around his desk, taking a spot perched against it. "I'd like you to work this, Gavin. I know it's a lot, and I don't want to take away from your task force work, but I'm hoping the additional days off the water will give you the time to lead this investigation."

That same shot of excitement that had filled Gavin when he'd been chosen for the task force lit him up, a deep sense of pride welling in his chest. Captain Reed was exceedingly fair in his distribution of work, and Gavin had never felt overlooked, but the task force and now this opportunity demonstrated he was getting the chance to show he was increasingly ready for the rank of detective.

"I'll give it everything I've got."

Captain Reed smiled, his first of the morning. "I believe it."

"The task force might be a good conduit for this one," Arlo offered up. "A way to talk with other teams and discuss how to approach something like this."

At the man's words, thoughts of Sera filled Gavin's mind, and the anticipation of seeing her once he wrapped up this meeting grew. Their conversation the night before had been a revelation. Part getting-to-know-you and part professional brainstorming session, it amazed him to see how easy it was with her to shift seamlessly between any number of topics.

Even that kiss—hot and needy in her kitchen—hadn't

stopped their ability to talk to each other. To listen to one another's opinions. And to willingly share thoughts with each other.

He wasn't used to that. He was raised in an environment of *children should be seen, not heard*, and after he was past the point that such a rigid structure would matter, life took a dark turn that left him far more willing to keep his own counsel than share parts of himself with others.

And wasn't that the miracle of Sera?

They didn't know each other, and there was a long road toward whatever the future held for them, but he had this clear sense that they *would* figure it out.

It was Wyatt who spoke first, clearly finding humor in Arlo's words. "This suggestion from the man who famously loves to close his cases with as little help as possible."

"I take help. I just don't need it," Arlo shot back at Wyatt, their long-standing friendship more than evident in the banter.

"I think I want to watch you say that in front of Kerrigan."

It was Captain Reed who finally broke up the byplay. "While Detective Prescott's lone-wolf status has taken a hit these past few months, I think his point's a good one. Use this time, Gavin. Talk to others and see what they think. Working through a case with someone else is never a bad idea, and getting a different perspective can open a new line of thinking."

"I will, sir. And I'll have an updated report on your desk tomorrow after seeing what the team brings up today. I'll head over to the site later this afternoon."

Their captain nodded before circling around back to his chair, signaling the close of their meeting. They all thanked him for his time before Captain Reed called out to Gavin, "A few more moments, Hayes?"

"Of course, sir."

Arlo and Wyatt kept on going, their obvious trust of their captain ensuring they didn't even look back. A sign of respect to Captain Reed and, Gavin realized, one to him, as well. He had this case, and he'd do it well. It felt good to have colleagues who believed that, too.

Captain Reed tapped on the printout of Gavin's briefing. "This is good work."

"Thank you."

"You understood the implications on this one immediately, and you've suggested some strong lines to tug quickly to see what's going on."

He nodded, curious to see where the man was going.

"Arlo's task force suggestion is a good one, as well. Use your partner there. Get their feedback."

"I will, sir. I—" He stopped, careful with his words. "I admit, I'm a bit surprised. Are you open to other jurisdictions coming in on this one?"

"*Resigned* is maybe a better word."

"Resigned how?"

Those lines that had been so obvious earlier only cut deeper in his captain's face. "These guns are concerning. They're going to draw attention. A find like this is going to get the FBI involved, and I get why. This smacks of a criminal ring with potential interstate traffic."

"Of course."

Although he avoided sharing any disappointment, Gavin knew himself and knew how much he wanted to handle this on his own. *Without* federal interference.

"If you can demonstrate from the start that you're open

to support and collaboration, it'll grease the wheels early. Show you can run an op and work well with others."

"Yes, sir."

Captain Reed's smile, normally soft and gentle in the way he spoke to his team and dispensed his leadership, turned positively wolfish. "And when you do all that great work and communicate well with others, I'll have a very clear pathway to step in and ensure that you can remain lead on the case. This is your show, Officer Hayes. You have my full endorsement on that."

SERA SHOWED HER credentials at the front desk and put her work bag and purse through the X-ray machines at the entrance to the 86th. The spring day was bright and crisp, and she'd gotten away with only her raincoat as she'd headed out that morning.

The air had a decided nip in it as she hoofed it from the subway to the precinct, but she simply couldn't wear her thick winter coat one more day if she could help it.

The bracing fresh air had an added benefit, helping the morning queasiness she hadn't fully shaken yet. Her sour stomach was slowly improving day by day, but bright sunshine and a cool breeze certainly helped.

All of which served to put her in a very good mood when she walked into that small conference room Gavin had reserved for them again.

He wasn't in the room, but had obviously beaten her to work, because his notebook and files were at the end of the conference room table, along with a scrawled note that he'd be right back addressed to her.

Sera took in the bold scrawl and nearly picked up the note to trace her fingers over the letters before she caught herself.

Tracing his handwriting? Seriously?

For someone who was doing her level best to keep her heart in check, she certainly had her moon-eyed moments. Especially after the past two evenings in his company.

Last night had been…special.

Even if at times she'd felt the intimacy clawing at her, knocking on the doors of her past.

It was a silly thought, Sera admitted, but it was a fit for how she felt. And last night's discussion—and her deep need to know more about Gavin—had left her more than aware that if she wanted answers from him, she'd need to be prepared to share some of her own.

Wasn't that the whole reason she'd avoided building deeper relationships with others, sexual or otherwise? Her friendships were surface level. Even Uncle Enzo and Aunt Robin, who knew her past, were kept at an arm's length most of the time.

They tried to get in, and Sera probably gave Aunt Robin the most leeway when it came to deeper discussions about life, especially her own, but that was the extent of it.

She'd always told herself it was a matter of privacy, but was it?

Or was it initially an armored response to life that had somehow become a prison?

"Sera!"

She glanced up to see Wyatt Trumball framed in the doorway. "Hey, Wyatt."

"I had to run up here to check in on another team and realized you were here waiting for Gavin. We just had a briefing meeting with the captain, and he needed to stay a few extra minutes to wrap up."

"Of course. I've got plenty to do while I wait."

He looked about to leave before seemingly thinking better of it. "Gavin mentioned that he told you about our discovery yesterday and that he'd like to put it up as an item for consideration on the task force you're both working."

"It seems almost purpose-built for what we're doing. How to share jurisdictions and more seamlessly communicate and hand projects back and forth."

"I was more intrigued that you pushed him to focus on working the case."

"Intrigued?"

"I get this task force is important. Everyone selected for it was handpicked by their leadership, and it's a sign you're being considered for more. To encourage Gavin to work the case before prioritizing the task force, that's a credit to you, Sera."

"Thank you. I—" She wasn't entirely sure what to say in the face of such obvious praise, so ended up simply sharing what she truly felt. "I appreciate the opportunity to grow my career and my work. But the reason we're even on a task force? It matters because we're keeping the city safe. No amount of ambition can stand in the way of that."

"Not everyone can say that. I hope you know it only reinforces why you were selected for the task force in the first place. I will make sure Captain Reed communicates the same to your DA."

"Thanks, Wyatt. I appreciate that."

Visit at an end, the man headed off almost as quickly as he'd arrived. Even so, Wyatt's support of her lingered in her mind long after he'd left.

That ready sense of encouragement was special. And while she'd never have said David Esposito didn't offer similar encouragement to his team of ADA's, she could also honestly say there was a distinct sense of competition in her team. One that came from a pace and tone David set with all of them as their district attorney.

"What's the frown for?"

She looked up from her laptop to see Gavin standing behind his seat at the table.

"Frown?"

"Yeah, you looked like a cross between angry and sad with distinct notes of annoyed." He laid a hand over his heart. "What did I do?"

She had the urge to toss her pen at him but held back. "Every thought in my head doesn't include you."

"Pity." Gavin pulled his phone and a thick leather folder that held his badge from his pockets before taking his seat. "Why'd you think I was angry?"

"I don't know, but you just looked really upset there when I walked in."

"Wyatt stopped in to tell me you were delayed by your briefing. And he said something quite nice." Without knowing why, Wyatt's words fell from her lips, and she couldn't deny how much it had meant to her that he'd acknowledged her in that way.

"And that put an angry look on your face?"

"That's just it. I realized that there's a lot of competition in my own team. I guess I always saw it as a good thing, but maybe it sort of pisses me off, now that I think about it."

"Teams are all about personalities. I see that with the Harbor team, which is a good blend of personalities. But further back, when I went through training with my academy team. We were—" he shrugged "—let's just say I've heard more than one person mention my class had a lot of high-maintenance personalities."

High-maintenance personalities.

Wasn't that the very definition of a lawyer? Yet even with the realities of living a cerebral life, constantly strategizing and building counterarguments, Sera sensed there was something more beneath the surface.

"Well, I guess I never realized our collective personality in the DA's office is a bit like a rabid wolf pack." With an odd sort of sinking in her stomach, she added, "Or how much I seemingly enjoyed running with the pack."

"I wouldn't be too hard on yourself. A little healthy competition isn't always a bad thing."

"Maybe so."

And there it was. Once again, Gavin had a way of seeing straight through to the root of her questions, nailing whatever it was she was gnawing over in her mind.

"You know, that might be an interesting angle to apply to the task force work," she said.

"Competition?"

"Oh, we've got plenty of that. But I mean more the dynamics of interdepartmental groups through the lens of team personalities."

Although they'd maintained a solid veneer of professionalism in public, Sera didn't miss the distinct heating of Gavin's dark gaze as he stared at her across the table. "Inter-departmental dynamics, you say?"

"Not *those* sorts of dynamics." Heat flooded her veins in response to his innuendo, the magnetic draw of this man something she was helpless to fully deny. A fact that felt more than clear when her voice quavered at the edges all while the space of the table felt like it was shrinking somehow, so that nothing existed in the room except her and Gavin.

It was a heady sensation, one she'd never had to juggle in a professional setting before. Heck, she admitted to herself, not really in *any* setting.

"Why, Sera Forte, whatever do you mean?" His gaze had grown even more heated, and she could swear she felt that gaze on her body like a caress.

She felt the heat, but underneath it, she also felt the subtle play of humor. And wasn't that something? Although she wouldn't have called past relationships staid, now that she'd met Gavin, she had to admit there was a deeper dimension there. One she'd never have expected.

There was fun.

Which made her next comment as easy as breathing.

"You know exactly what I mean, Gavin Hayes. The naked kind."

THE NAKED KIND.

The implications of *that* hit him with a tsunami of sexual longing that, if he wasn't sitting, likely would have had his knees buckling.

Gavin knew this way lay madness, but he was helpless to turn away from the simmering physical need that wasn't far from the surface where Sera was concerned.

It had been that way from the first.

Those initial moments in the bar, when she'd come up and asked to share his high-top table with her friends on New Year's. He'd quickly obliged, and his own group had opened the space in the crowded bar to welcome the newcomers. Their group had fallen into conversation, one of his friends recognizing one of Sera's friends as a mutual acquaintance, and talk had come easily from there.

The two of them had found a rapport instantly, one that

was as much steeped in attraction as it was in the sheer enjoyment of each other. They'd only briefly talked of their jobs, instead focusing on everything from favorite museums in the city to deep discussion on their latest binge watch on a streaming service. Whatever the topic, they'd flowed in and out of it with ease.

It had also been the first time in a long time that his social conversations didn't hinge on work or on his family. He loved his job, but a group of cops tended to talk almost obsessively about work.

And time spent with his family was…fraught.

Yet with Sera, he'd experienced neither.

And because of it, for the first time he could ever remember, he'd felt like Gavin Hayes.

Not Gavin Hayes the cop.

Or Gavin Hayes the survivor.

It was *that* reality about himself that had him stepping back from the sexy talk.

Time to get back on track.

Putting on a faux, world-weary voice—and adding a wink for good measure—he said, "Much as I'd like to interrogate that line of thinking, Ms. Forte, I'm afraid we have work to do."

"So we do."

They caught each other up on the work they'd done independently against their project. While they would come together to create the final project, they'd also decided it would be helpful to map out how each of their team's interacted with each other, pinpointing all the places where a case could be handed off from one owner to another.

"That right there." Sera pointed to one of the handoff steps Gavin mapped on the room's whiteboard as they'd talked through the various angles each had sketched out. "The chain of evidence. There's risk there."

"Risk how?"

"Your team captures it and goes through several areas of documentation within the police department. All those details are handed off to the DA's office, and we have matched handling rules on our side. But how clear is the handoff itself?"

"There's standard operating procedure. To your point, it's all noted and documented."

"But is it a gap? We're focused on city-based jurisdictions, but what about when the Feds are involved? Or what if something has to be further reviewed between two jurisdictions?"

Gavin considered what she was saying. Although evidence was taken very seriously, people were human. And those moments where evidence shifted between parties were the places where there was the most risk for a mistake.

"We could use the new case I'm working on. The captain endorsed us considering it for the task force, and I'd honestly welcome a set of eyes that aren't, first and foremost, cop."

"The weapons find?" She stepped back from the whiteboard and took the seat beside him. "It makes sense to use that. Walk me through it."

Since he'd already given her the key elements over dinner the day before, he focused instead on the evidence recovery and handoffs specifically.

"So your team brings it up, with the rules you follow when making a retrieval."

"We do. There's nearly always another handler on the police boat as well, who will take point on keeping track of everything and do a quick log as we're bringing it up."

He remembered that time well. Those early days of his training when he so desperately wanted to be under the water, but he had to pay his dues by learning the ropes and every single aspect of the Harbor team's work.

"Do you bring the evidence in or does a team come to you?"

"It depends on what we've retrieved. We went out yesterday to recover a single weapon. If that was all we'd found, we'd bring it in and hand off to the team that does intake on evidence."

"But in this case?"

"Because it's so large and the recovery area needs photographing, too? A team comes to us."

He watched, fascinated, as she considered what he'd shared. He could almost see her processing the information, working through the angles. But it was her next question that made him realize Sera wasn't one to sit and wonder.

Instead, she was a woman of action.

"Can we go out with the evidence team? See how they're handling what your team's brought up?"

He glanced at his watch, but already knew they'd be in time. Kerrigan and Jayden had gone on shift about an hour before, and they'd likely be there until early afternoon.

"You sure the water won't upset your stomach?"

"I'm sure." She glanced down where she laid a hand over her ever-so-slightly rounded belly. "I think I could ride roller coasters and be okay. It's the smell of food that seems to set me off." She glanced up. "Or should I say, sets us off?"

What had started out as a simple question quickly turned profound as he realized it was his child beneath her palm. His child they were speaking of.

His child in the small space between them.

"The good news is there's nothing in the way of food on the boats. I can't promise you there aren't any smells. It is the East River."

"I'm willing to risk it. I really want to see the whole operation."

Gavin allowed his gaze to linger another few beats on her stomach before turning to look at their work on the whiteboard. He reached for his phone to take some pictures, capturing their discussion, before erasing all they'd mapped out.

When he turned back, she'd already gathered her things, an eager look on her face.

"Let's get out of here, Hayes, and go kick some task force ass."

## Chapter Seven

Although she knew the Harbor team who worked out of Brooklyn were based out of the 86th Precinct, Sera had never realized how extensive the dock area was or appreciated their impressive setup.

She should have, she admitted to herself as Gavin led her out to the dock situated about five hundred yards from the precinct building. They'd stowed her personal items in his locker, and she felt a bit empty-handed, out on a workday with just her purse, a small notebook stowed inside.

But wow.

She *really* should have imagined this setup, she thought as she took in the array of boats and equipment, immaculately kept and all neatly ordered around the open-air structure. The Harbor team was a small unit compared to the overall size of the NYPD, but it was still a large operation, tasked with covering hundreds of miles of shoreline and waterway. Their equipment was testament to that.

"So this is where the magic happens." She turned to Gavin, surprised to find him watching her closely.

"It all starts here."

"It's quite a set up. And a much bigger operation than I'd have ever imagined."

"We have an incredible number of tools at our disposal. It's a privilege to work on a team outfitted like this."

While she'd never argue that point—and was beyond grateful there was an infrastructure in place to keep him as safe as possible—she also recognized the NYPD was exceptionally well funded for their work.

"I wonder if you realize how obvious it is on your face when your mind starts working."

His statement was voiced in low tones, with an intimacy that went straight to her very core, as she stared up at Gavin.

"I'm sorry."

"Don't be. It's fascinating." He reached out, tracing a soft line over one of her eyebrows before smoothing a flyaway piece of hair that caught in the breeze. "The way your forehead scrunches up a bit when you're considering something."

"Oh, lovely." She meant it as a bit of a joke, but her voice came out sort of like a croak and her skin was all warm and tingly where he'd touched it.

"It is lovely. And incredibly cute."

"Thank you."

Thank you? *Really, Sera? That's the best you can do when a sexy man's touching you at 10:00 a.m.?*

She wanted to play this cool. Wanted to be one of those women who came off like they ate men like this for breakfast and found a new one by dinner. Women for whom flirtation came quick and easy.

Women who didn't carry the scars of abandonment into adulthood.

But she wasn't.

Which was why she stepped back, instead focusing on the questions that had rolled through her mind as they'd come onto the harbor docks.

"Well, um. I *was* thinking, actually…"

Gavin seemed to sense her reluctance and stepped back himself. "Go on."

"What about other jurisdictions? There are endless miles of waterway in and around the country. How do other places do the same sort of work? This is an impressive outfit you've got here, and I can't imagine it's nearly this sophisticated in other places."

"Most large cities have the same. Los Angeles and San Francisco are well outfitted. Miami and DC, too." He stopped and looked around at all that lay before them, from boats to equipment to an even larger ship docked outside the shed-like overhang that protected this area of the marina. There was a crane built into the boat and an oversize deck wide enough to hold several vehicles.

"But yes, we're incredibly fortunate to have all this. And there are a heck of a lot of water-based locations that simply get by with what they have. Several have volunteer services, too. Better-than-amateur divers who choose to train for rescue certifications and offer their skills."

"I saw something about that recently," she realized. "That big news story out of Bucks County last summer, down between New Jersey and Pennsylvania. There was a whole team of volunteers who saved several people from the rushing waters of the Delaware River."

"That's exactly it. There are many municipalities who benefit from that sort of support."

"Which circles us back to the start of this. How is evidence managed in those places?"

"It's part of training."

"Sure, but I have to imagine your training and the professional expectations of you are considerably higher."

"They are. But those groups are also more search-and-rescue-based than evidence recovery. Much as we'd like to believe every criminal is caught, a lot of people get away with a lot of bad things. And capturing the evidence correctly makes it easier for you and your colleagues to do their jobs."

As if to punctuate his point, a loud shout of laughter echoed off the cavernous space as a team came walking down to the dock. Several had large bags swung over their shoulders, and despite the obvious camaraderie, there was a seriousness in their demeanor as they all headed for the boat she and Gavin stood in front of.

"We picked a good time," he said. "That's the forensics and evidence crew. We'll go out with them if you're still up for it."

"Absolutely."

After brief introductions and an explanation of what they were doing, she and Gavin boarded a large boat with the NYPD's logo printed on the side. After safety checks and a quick run-through for her on where to find life vests and where the radio system was housed, they were on their way.

Gavin moved into a discussion with the leader of the forensics team, getting an update on the day before. Sera used the time to head for the back of the boat. The slip they'd left and the overhang that protected the docks grew smaller as they pulled out of Sunset Bay and began the journey toward New York Harbor and the entrance to the East River.

The city rose majestically in the distance, the iconic New York skyline unmistakable beneath a gorgeous blue sky. That decided nip in the air she'd ignored on her morning walk was positively frigid in the breeze kicking up off the water, and she crossed her arms, unwilling to go back inside the boathouse and miss the views.

Which made the jacket that came around her shoulders, already warmed by Gavin's body heat, a welcome treat. Especially when she could inhale the soft scent of him enveloping her. It wasn't anything she could put a name to, but she was attracted enough—and pregnant enough—to know there was a sizable hit of pheromones making her own hormones work overtime.

Who knew her increased scent receptors that had made it so difficult to keep food down would augment the scent of him in such a wonderful way?

"It's cold out here."

"It's too pretty a day with too gorgeous a view to sit inside."

He pointed out a few last things around the Brooklyn shoreline before they made the turn for the East River. "It won't be too much farther, and you can see the team in action."

She glanced around once more, her gaze seeming to look everywhere all at once. The Manhattan skyscrapers to the west, the Brooklyn and Manhattan bridges rising above them as they passed beneath and the East River stretching before them as they navigated north.

"We're almost there."

"I can't believe you do this all the time." She turned to him, and once more was caught up in that warm gaze.

No, warm *hungry* gaze, she corrected herself.

Each encounter they'd had since the start of the task force only grew more intense than the last. Only made what they'd shared at New Year's feel that much more tangible.

As if a baby hadn't already done that.

Even so, she'd managed to separate her pregnancy from her feelings for Gavin in her mind. She loved this baby already and had from the very first moment she'd discovered she was pregnant. But the father...

What she felt for Gavin was complex and confusing and...well, wonderful. She kept trying to ignore that fact, yet circled back around to it, over and over again. She enjoyed his company.

So as they stood there, side by side on the back of a boat navigating the East River, Sera let down her guard and leaned into him.

And didn't try to move away when his arm came around her shoulders, pulling her close.


THE STEALTH SURVEILLANCE cameras caught the work up near Hell Gate in exquisite clarity. Proof that you could get what you paid dearly for, the Organizer thought as he watched video so clear he could make out the puffs of breath from the divers coming up out of the water in the cool morning air.

The cameras had been a risk: discovery always a possibility, but a worthwhile one. He hadn't regretted their installation for a minute.

But it was this moment that had paid off.

He'd had a clear view of the work pulling up the weapons he'd so carefully hidden. And he'd watched the crew managing the find, already thinking how he could take care of each and every one of them.

They were liabilities.

Even as the fantasy played out, one thought more gruesome than the next, he knew it was just that. A fantasy. No matter how angry, you simply didn't take out roughly a dozen NYPD officers without anyone noticing.

But someone would have to pay.

He wasn't sure who or how, but there would be some retribution demanded for this. A needful sort of accounting.

Although he kept himself separate from the operation as a whole, his inner circle still gave him a wide berth. They all realized his carefully leashed temper could turn on them, and everyone was keeping their distance, hard at work looking for a new location.

Nothing would be quite as perfect, but there would be other places. Other forgotten spots that could take the place of this one.

He just needed to do damage control in the meantime.

The activity had been robust around the dump site, and he'd cataloged what was coming up out of the water and the speed of the operation. At the rate they were going, they'd likely have every last weapon by the end of the day.

Which meant he needed to put his plans with the evidence team into motion.

He'd nearly shut down the feed of the dump site and the waters beyond—he would watch more later—when movement at the edge of the screen caught his attention. No sooner did he lean in closer to the monitor when one of the evidence boats moved into view before nearly heading out of the top of the camera's frame.

But it was the figures on the back of the boat that caught his attention.

Two people, huddled together.

He paused the video, recognition instantly flashing as he looked at the slender figure wrapped in an oversize coat, leaning into the man beside her. Zooming in on the couple, he watched Sera Forte fill his screen, the man beside her looking far more like a companion than a colleague. What the hell was a Brooklyn assistant district attorney doing on the back of the evidence boat?

And why did he have the sinking feeling that the task force he'd used to get her out of the way for a while had just reared up to bite him in the ass?

Unlike his earlier fantasy of just doing away with his enemies, this particular betrayal needed addressing. He'd think on it, but he would find the right moment. In the meantime, it might be worth tossing a diversion everyone's way.

He hated acting on impulse—it rarely paid off—but his gut told him this required swift action.

And with all those people out on the water, he was pretty sure he knew what would shake them up once they all came home.

THE DISCOVERY SITE was a hive of activity, and Gavin took it all in after helping Sera back into the large cabin set atop the recovery boat. A big part of him itched to be in the water with Kerrigan and Jayden and the rest of the team, diving down to pick up the weapons, even as a bigger part of him knew that the opportunities he was being given aboveground mattered.

Captain Reed's faith in him mattered.

And if that meant he would spend less time in the water over the next few weeks, he had to accept that.

The evidence crew that had joined his Harbor team that morning was pulling out, heading back into the precinct to continue cataloging the weapons. In its place, the boat he and Sera had ridden over on pulled up alongside the NYPD boat that was the epicenter of the Harbor team's work.

"This is quite an operation." Sera looked around, her continued questions and awe at the work evident in her voice.

"We're usually not this heavy with personnel and boats concentrated in one place. Normally, our work's spread out around the city each day, but this is priority one right now."

"Yo, Gav!"

He turned to see Kerrigan Doyle waving at him from the water. She was in full gear, and all that was visible was a bright, vivid smile beneath her heavy face mask.

"You've got the whole damn department doing your bidding, Doyle! Crews are coming and going for you."

If possible, that grin grew even wider before she gestured that she'd come up on the boat.

Gavin turned to find Sera taking it all in, her hands on her hips.

"You surprised a woman's competently doing that job, Hayes?" She'd teasingly called him Hayes before, but this time Gavin didn't miss the distinct notes of challenge in her voice.

"Never."

"Good. I don't want to be wrong about you, you know."

As he moved around to the ladder side of the boat, he had the distinct realization he didn't want Sera to be wrong about him, either. A stark reminder that for all they didn't know about each other, he couldn't stop the increasing hope that they had a way forward. One that wasn't just co-parenting, but something more.

"Kerrigan's one of the best divers on the team," Gavin said with absolute sincerity. "And she's an incredible cop. She and another detective in the department were responsible for bringing down that up-and-coming crime ring last fall."

"Incredible work that we're still processing in the DA's office. Wendy Parker managed to do a heck of a lot of damage in her quest to rise to the top of the New York crime syndicate pecking order."

"She was a determined woman. And she left a wake of destruction, a term I'm using quite literally."

They'd dived the wreck of a boat in the harbor in the midst of a nor'easter the prior October, a drug trafficking incident gone very bad. The sunken boat and the violent murders of two of the drug runners on it had opened up the case, and Kerrigan had worked it with Arlo Prescott.

"It was great work. And I shudder to think what Wendy would have done if Kerrigan and Arlo hadn't figured out she was the source of it all."

Kerrigan crossed over to them after shedding her mask and tanks. "Are you talking about my former high school classmate?"

"You went to school with Wendy Parker?" Sera asked.

Kerrigan nodded as she worked the tight confines of her wet suit down to her waist. "Sure did. And while I'd never have said we were close or even all that friendly, I can honestly say I never took her for a crime lord wannabe." Kerrigan screwed up her mouth. "Or is that a crime lady? What's the equivalent of a crime lord?"

"I'm not sure it matters." Sera laughed, extending her hand. "Sera Forte. I'm from the DA's office and am working with Gavin on an interjurisdictional task force. I'd love to find out more about what you do."

"He hasn't talked your ears off about it yet?" Although Kerrigan was friendly and warm, Gavin didn't miss the way her gaze cataloged the fact that Sera wore his jacket.

Or the fact that she was on the boat at all.

"I figured this would be a good chance for Sera to get firsthand knowledge of how we manage evidence," he quickly jumped in. "It's an angle we're playing for our task force project. Especially those instances where evidence is handed from one group to another."

Whatever speculation she might have carried vanished as Kerrigan pointed toward the front of the boat. "Let me show you how we've been doing this. I think it'll give you a sense for our steps, even though these are all still NYPD protocols, not handoffs outside the department."

Kerrigan stopped, her gaze drifting toward the water, Hell Gate Bridge rising in the distance. "You know, this is a really good case to use. It's not busywork or theoretical, but something that can help make our work better, and it's good you're here to see it in person."

"Thank you," Sera said. "That's one of the things that's been impressive about the task force so far. It's set up to be more than just theory. We're working on outcomes that can have practical application."

"I think you'd take away a lot from the Parker case, too. The volume of evidence, and bringing that boat up off the harbor floor, is a textbook case of evidence management."

"I'd love to talk to you about it."

Kerrigan and Sera exchanged a few more questions before the action commenced on their boat. Jayden and another diver, Marco Hennessy, were on point to bring up additional guns.

Gavin considered the initial find and his and Wyatt's estimates of how much was on the riverbed floor as he gave Jayden a hand up. "How much is left down there?"

"This should make thirty-five and thirty-six," Kerrigan said from where she took the evidence package from Marco, her facts on the dive well in hand. "I figure there are about fifteen more to bring up."

"And you're doing it one by one?"

"One by one?" Jayden asked as he slipped off his tank. "If she had her druthers, we'd bring up each piece in pairs."

"I'm not quite that bad." Kerrigan playfully stuck her tongue out at Jayden, the member of the team she was closest to, before updating Gavin on the past twelve hours. "We considered bringing down a container and trying to retrieve multiple pieces that way, but after talking through it, we really want to keep as much integrity as we can with each piece. So we're bagging everything down there, bringing it up one gun to one diver."

"It's tedious work."

That grin flashed once more, Kerrigan Doyle's excitement and enthusiasm for her work stamped in that wide smile.

"Oh yeah, but it'll all be worth it when we catch the bastards with airtight evidence."

AIRTIGHT EVIDENCE.

She'd overheard Kerrigan use that term earlier, and as Sera looked over the expanse of guns laid out on the floor of the evidence boat, she recognized that was clearly the goal.

Late morning had drifted well past lunch and on into the afternoon as the work went on and on around her: photographs; audio memos recorded by each diver on how they found the piece under the water; and the tapping of keys on several laptops as each evidence recovery agent managed their portion of the haul.

After making her initial observations, she'd asked where she could help and had been quickly put to work with a laptop of her own, cataloging what was on the ground and adding her impressions. After laboring over each piece and thinking about how to describe it, she added in the same impressions she would use when building a case.

And now, reading through her notes, Sera felt a distinct shot of pride at what she'd added to the process. She might not know how to scientifically and accurately assess decomposition timelines, but she knew exactly how to use decomp stats to make a case around intent, possible motive and probable guilt.

"You want some lunch?"

Sera glanced up from her screen to find Gavin standing before her, a paper plate full of a sandwich and potato chips. "What time is it?"

"Almost two thirty. I know I said there's no food on the boat, but when they traded out the last team, they brought in sandwiches, too."

"Then I'd love some lunch." Her eyes widened just as her stomach let out a low gurgling sound. "I'm not sure how, but for the first time in two months this work has made me forget about eating. It's a novel experience, let me tell you."

She gently closed the laptop lid and put it on the bench beside her, gesturing Gavin into the seat next to her. He'd built a plate for himself, and they sat in the bright sunshine with their meal, eating in companionable silence.

"You've made quite an impression on everyone," Gavin said as he picked up a chip.

"All I can say is likewise. I never doubted the work your team did was impressive, but this is something beyond my wildest imaginings. It's grueling, yet everyone seems to have an endless drive for the work."

"We're a bit of an odd lot."

"You're a family."

She saw the moment her words registered, something between a direct hit and a shot clean through the heart.

It made no sense—and she had no idea how she *knew*—but in that moment, Sera recognized the truth beneath Gavin's demeanor and those sometimes-sharp spikes she'd seen in his personality. Those moments where he fumbled to articulate what he wanted or needed. She'd sensed it from the first, but hadn't had words for it. Only now she knew.

The concept of family didn't come easily to him.

And with that understanding came one of her own. It had never come easily to her, either. Yet here they were, making a family of their own.

"We certainly have each other's backs."

Which, she almost added, was one of the definitions of family, but held herself back. There was no need to press her point, and she could circle back to it later. When he'd had time to process it, and so had she.

His team did have his back, and he had theirs. The ease between all of them—and the reality of how dependent they were on one another for each drop beneath the water—had forged serious bonds. Ones that went well beyond the professional.

Most cops had it, she admitted. She'd seen it in her work from the earliest days of her career: so much of what they did in the DA's office linked to the work of the NYPD. That sense that their professions weren't just what they got up each day and did, but were a calling that each went into, knowing full well the risks.

Being a lawyer wasn't risk free, and her office certainly got its share of threats, but they weren't out on the frontlines, either. Nor were she and her colleagues putting their lives on the line when writing a brief or arguing a case.

But what Gavin did? Not only did he face the standard risks a cop did, but he then did this incredibly difficult, physical job that carried additional danger.

Their gear alone fascinated her. Each diver that came up was outfitted in suits and air tanks and an additional, smaller tank Gavin had called a bailout bottle. And then there was all the additional equipment, from cutting tools to communications equipment to camera and video equipment when needed. All while putting the body through the physical rigors of a dive.

If that didn't make a family by choice, Sera didn't know what would.

"You do have each other's backs," she finally said in agreement. "It's impressive. But I wonder if you know how special it is."

"I work with a great group of really dedicated people."

That subtle resistance from him—the one that didn't want to fully acknowledge what she was saying—had her reaching for her sandwich. She'd been pressed in the past by well-meaning comments she wasn't ready to hear and could recognize carefully built armor shifting into place.

What was the real surprise was how her own carefully constructed armor had begun to chafe, rubbing at convictions she'd held so long she'd nearly forgotten the armor was even there in the first place. Because if she wanted to poke at Gavin, she'd have to accept the requirement to open up, too.

And, oddly, it didn't fill her with the same sense of panic it might have in the past.

There was no way she could have a child with someone who had no idea who she was or what she'd lived with. It was uncomfortable and took the concept of intimacy to a place well beyond friendship or deep conversation or even sex.

But he deserved to know.

And, if she were fair to herself and even more fair to their child, she deserved to tell him. About those experiences that had shaped her from the earliest age. The memories she fought to keep buried and hidden away from others. The ones that, on the rare occasions she took them out and examined them, left her feeling wanting and less than, even though she knew she shouldn't feel that way at all.

Which meant she needed to figure out how to tell him. And as they sat there, each of them taking a few minutes of respite with each other, she had the first inkling that it might be okay.

She could *do* this.

Because, in an odd and deeply strange parallel, it was a lot like those weapons laid out at the front of the boat.

What Gavin chose to do with the evidence was going to be up to him.

## Chapter Eight

Something had changed.

Hell, Gavin thought ruefully, a lot had changed.

But specifically today, something had decidedly and determinedly shifted course between him and Sera. Something that went well beyond what happened at New Year's or their work on the task force or even the baby.

It was the *something* between them.

He could see her now, talking to Kerrigan at the front of the boat, both of them perched over the evidence and talking about the various aspects of the weapons recovery. He'd joined them at first, but after the continued distraction of all that consumed his thoughts, he'd made an excuse to go talk to the evidence lead, leaving them to their discussion.

*You're a family.*

Her comment was made so simply—so casually, even—and it had haunted him.

For a man who considered himself fitted with rather loose familial bonds, it was jarring to realize that he had formed them anyway. He just hadn't realized it.

"Hey, Gav." The greeting was punctuated with a mild pat on the back as Jayden Houston came up beside him, his demeanor casual as he took up the spot beside him at the back railing of the boat.

Gavin wasn't fooled for a minute. Jayden was a stellar member of the Harbor team, his physical conditioning and dive skills making him excellent in the field. But it was his innate kindness and understanding of the crew he worked with that truly made him a standout.

His body language might be saying cool-as-a-cucumber, but Gavin was well aware the man missed nothing. He was also inscrutable about it.

The fact that he'd come up to Gavin in a relatively deserted area of the boat meant he likely had something on his mind. But since Jayden didn't give anything away until he wanted to, Gavin figured he'd lead the conversation and see where it went. "That was some damn fine work today. The recovery was really smooth."

"Thanks. All the credit to you and Wyatt for the first on scene. You both knew what you had."

Gavin let out a long, low sigh. "And what we have is a lot."

"A whole freaking lot. Any theories yet on who's doing it?"

"Not a one. I briefed the captain this morning. He's put me on point on the investigation since I'm already splitting some time above the water for the task force."

"That's fantastic!" Jayden's dark eyes lit up, even though exhaustion rode his features after two straight days of diving. "And don't fool yourself that this is just about being on land with the task force. Good things are happening for you, Gav, and no one deserves it more."

It was just like Jayden—a man who had confidence in himself and support for his colleagues in equal measure.

And once more, Sera's telling comment pushed through Gavin's thoughts, refusing to be silenced no matter how hard he'd tried to push it away.

*You're a family.*

"The task force is turning out to be quite an experience so far."

Jayden tilted his head in the direction of the boat. "If Sera's any indication of the caliber of people chosen for it, you're in really good company. Man, she's great. Sharp. Smart. And super interested in the work."

"She's amazing." He waited barely a breath before pressing on. "She's also Miss New Year's Eve."

Jayden turned from where his gaze had drifted to the Brooklyn Bridge overhead and simply stared at him. "She's what?"

"The woman. The one I told you and Kerrigan about. From New Year's Eve."

Gavin wasn't sure why he was sharing this or why he'd chosen this moment to do it. Maybe because Jayden would have pulled it out of him anyway. Or maybe it was because his head had been so far in the clouds the past week, he just needed to get it off his chest.

But here they were, heading out into the open waters of the harbor, and he was spilling every bit of his life's current events to one of his dive partners.

"I thought you didn't know how to find her."

"I didn't. And then I walked into the task force meeting Monday morning, and she was standing at the sideboard they had set up with breakfast pastries and coffee, talking to some guy she went to law school with."

Jayden shook his head. "Seriously small world, dude."

"Minuscule sometimes."

"And mind-numbingly vast when you're looking for someone."

Even now, Gavin had no understanding of why he'd shared the whole story of his mystery woman with Jayden and Kerrigan. He had vowed to not only keep it to himself, but he'd believed he was getting past the subtle ache that he'd carried those first few weeks of the year each time he thought of her.

Instead, he'd found himself spilling his tale of woe over a few beers after a tough shift in late January.

*Like a sap*, Gavin thought, still unsure why he was continuing to share now. Especially because he'd tried to play it off after they'd left the bar, outside in the cold hoofing it to the subway, but both had seen through it. And neither of them had been fooled by his attempts at smoothing over his confession.

They'd been equally fair in avoiding asking him the more obvious questions of why he hadn't shored up his problem to begin with and gotten his mystery woman's full name and phone number.

"Well, now that I've met her," Jayden continued, "I can see why you weren't ready to let her go. She's great, Gav."

"She's pregnant."

Although he mentally braced for something between shock and overt sympathy, the sudden whoop of laughter and grab for a tight, backslapping hug was its antithesis. "Gavin, that's amazing. Congratulations, man."

He leaned into the embrace, surprised to realize how good it felt to tell someone. And how much better it felt to hear such elation from another person at his news.

News he hadn't shared with anyone else yet.

And as Gavin pulled back, he couldn't hide the smile. "It's really good. And it's all pretty new, but it is most definitely good."

"I'm happy for you. My mother has always said it, and it's one of the truest things in the world. Babies are wonderful news."

"Since Mama Houston's never wrong about anything, I'll take that as the best validation when those moments of sheer panic rear up and grab me by the throat."

"She's going to be over the moon with this. You and Sera had better expect an invite for Sunday dinner soon."

Gavin's apprehension must have shown through because Jayden added, "My mother doesn't care about what's going on between the two of you, though she'll find a way to give you a talking-to regardless. When she brings you out to her small cookery on the back porch and waves everyone else away is usually when it happens."

Gavin could already picture the small prep area off the kitchen in the Houstons' Sunset Bay row home and braced for whatever was coming. Not only because it came from a place of love, but because he deserved it. "Forewarned is forearmed."

"Did I ever tell you the set down I got over Darius?"

"I don't think so."

Jayden smiled, warming up to his story. "We'd been dating for a few months when it went down. My family knew I was gay, but I preferred to keep my relationships away from them."

Gavin realized he hadn't heard the story before, but also realized it seemed disconnected from what he knew of Jayden's welcoming and effusive family. "Because they weren't okay with your relationship?"

"Nah, it was all me. Because I wasn't comfortable." Sadness seemed to increase the exhaustion beneath his dark brown eyes. "I almost lost Darius because of it, too. But well, with her bat ears, Mama heard through the neighborhood grapevine I was getting serious, and this wasn't something casual.

"She dragged my ass out there to her cookery the first opportunity she got and waved a wooden spoon at me. Told me she and my big beautiful Black family loved me and whoever I loved, and if I was going to hide something special from the rest of them, I didn't deserve to have it. And that I was insulting all of them, too, while I was at it."

"That sweet woman who welcomes me with kisses and hugs and sends me home with leftovers for a week?"

"Don't let it fool you. If you're acting like an ass, she'll make sure you know."

"Darius is a good man. It would have been a shame to let him get away."

"I think about it every day, man." Jayden turned to look back toward the boat. Sera was just visible through the windows where she and Kerrigan were still talking. "Every. Damn. Day."

Gavin's gaze followed Jayden's before turning back to his friend. "Is the back of this boat the equivalent of your mother's cookery?"

Jayden grinned at that, the flash of white teeth and laughter breaking through that lingering exhaustion. "She'd love the comparison, but no one dispenses the wisdom and sass in equal measure like my mother." Jayden slapped him on the back once more as they turned to look out over the water. "And besides, I don't have a wooden spoon."

Gavin laughed at the image as they made the last turn into the waterway that led to the 86th's docks.

The words that had haunted him this afternoon settled a bit, along with the lingering excitement Jayden had shared over the baby.

*You're a family.*

It was a compliment in every way.

And as he and his brother-in-arms headed for the ropes to help secure the boat to the docks, Gavin figured that was something well worth leaning into.

"CLUB SODA FOR YOU," Kerrigan said as she deposited drinks on the high-top table at Case Closed.

The bar was old, dating back a good two decades, started by a retired detective. One who knew cops liked a place to call their own. Although anyone was welcome, tables were reserved for parties of cops, and in kind, the 86th generously rewarded the owner with their business.

"News travels fast," Sera said, surprised she didn't feel more anxiety about the fact that Kerrigan knew she was pregnant.

"Good news certainly does." Kerrigan clinked the top of her beer bottle to Sera's glass. "So. You and my pal Gavin."

"So."

She'd originally thought to hide the news of her pregnancy, but Kerrigan had surprised her by leaning in and whispering that she figured it out as they all walked into Case Closed. Sera had been too shocked to deny it and too happy to have been invited out to complain.

Which now left her with the very real question of just how obvious she was. As a pregnant woman, yes, but also

as a pregnant woman who couldn't stop looking at Gavin
in a way people noticed.

"He's a good man," Kerrigan continued, ignoring the lack
of a response. "His outer shell is way too tough but not in
the grizzly bear sort of way."

Although he'd been prickly when they'd first gotten reacquainted, it was interesting to hear Kerrigan's perspective. More than interesting, Sera admitted to herself. She
was hungry for the information.

"He's definitely not grumpy or unpleasant."

"That's how you miss it!" Kerrigan snapped her fingers.
"You think he's all salt-of-the-earth, Mister Easygoing, and
then you hit a point where you open your eyes and realize
just how crafty he really is."

"How so?"

"That man's fathoms deep, and he never lets anyone
deeper than a foot."

It wasn't quite how she'd have characterized him, yet as
she turned over Kerrigan's comments, Sera had to admit they
fit. Hadn't she sensed his reluctance to discuss his family?
And even with their conversations the past two evenings,
there was a definite sense she'd been held at arm's length.
It wasn't cold or even distant, it was just…well…to adopt
Kerrigan's term, it was well crafted. As if he'd figured out
how to orchestrate the world around him to stay just outside
an invisible fence.

*Like someone else you know, Forte?*

Maybe that was their real connection—that ability to fit
in without giving much away. Giving people a foot, as Kerrigan put it, where most gave a fathom.

It was also humbling to realize how much deeper she
wanted to go.

"I didn't mean to upset you, by the way, mentioning your pregnancy. I come from a big family, and I can smell baby hormones at fifty paces. I'm not a gossip, and I promise to keep it to myself."

"No, it's fine. Really. I mean, well, I haven't told work yet, but I'm three months along, so it's only a matter of weeks before I can't hide it any longer."

"No, I get it. There's already an assumption we're delicate. Add on the worry that it'll affect how you're seen at your job, and I don't blame you for holding on to the information."

"The baby is Gavin's."

"I figured as much."

"Was it because I was wearing his coat?"

"Not a bit. Like I said, he's a good guy. If anyone was cold, he'd have given them his coat." The young woman with the sharp gaze took a sip of her beer. "It's the way he looks at you."

"Oh…oh. Well." Sera caught herself before curiosity got the better of her. "How does he look at me?"

"Like you're precious."

She'd never felt precious before. Competent, yes. Effective, that, too. But precious?

It humbled her to know that someone saw that sort of attention for her in another person. Like she mattered.

"Well, if it isn't the princess of Hell Gate." A large man with tawny blond hair and vivid blue eyes made the pronouncement just before pulling Kerrigan into his arms for a big smacking kiss.

The sassy friend Sera had made that afternoon turned into a pile of mush, staring up at the big man once the kiss ended.

He recognized they had an audience, and he naturally shifted gears, extending a hand. "I'm Arlo Prescott."

Sera introduced herself, with Kerrigan quickly adding in color commentary about their day and the fact that Sera was part of the same task force as Gavin.

Arlo was kind and attentive throughout, but as the conversation shifted around the table, Sera didn't miss how his voice lowered, all hints of earlier humor vanishing as his attention narrowed in once more on Kerrigan.

"Heard it was a hard day. How are you?"

"I'm good."

Sera looked away to give them their privacy, quickly introducing herself to the other newcomer to the table. A gorgeous Black man, still dressed head-to-toe like he was ready to take on Wall Street—or had just finished conquering it—extended a hand. "I'm Darius St. Germaine." He pressed a quick kiss to Jayden's head. "This one's husband."

"Sera Forte."

"How'd you fall in with this motley crew?"

"Luck?"

"Well, who can argue with that?" Darius took a seat next to her with his glass of whiskey over ice, that smile still in place. "Are you part of the Harbor team?"

"No, I'm an ADA with the Brooklyn DA's office. I'm working on an interdepartmental task force with Gavin, and he was kind enough to take me out on the recovery today. It's tied to the approach we're taking on the task force."

Darius nodded. "What they do is intense."

"And they're amazing in how they orchestrate it all. I was able to see a lot of the evidence recovery today. They're athletes and serious jugglers with all that equipment in addition to being cops."

"I tell Jay that all the time. I swear he's part fish." Darius shot his husband a wink across the table where Jayden had glanced over at their conversation.

It was a warm moment. Intimate, even, yet not out of place. Just like when Arlo had come up to wrap Kerrigan in a tight hug.

It made her...*want*.

There really was no other word for it. That easy intimacy at the end of a long day that wasn't overtly sexual but rather was a sort of caring awareness of each other. And the absolute delight of being together.

Since she wasn't there with Gavin in the same capacity, she willed the emotion away and turned back to her new friend, the very interesting Mr. St. Germaine.

"And what is it you do?" She tapped a finger lightly over the cufflink that winked off the edge of his shirt, visible now that he'd settled his suit jacket on the back of his bar chair. "Not diving, I presume?"

Darius let out a hard bark of laughter. "God, no. I don't even like putting my head under the water."

The two of them fell into easy conversation after that, and it was only twenty minutes later, as a second round of drinks made its way to the table, that Sera realized she'd made a fast friend.

Gavin had kept his distance throughout, obviously unwilling to overtly pair the two of them up in front of his friends. They both went out of their way to talk about their partnership on the task force and that seemed to allay any discussion of their relationship.

Or lack of one.

Realistically, she should have been grateful for that. She and Gavin didn't know each other well, and they'd both gone through a lot this week while getting reacquainted. So why was she increasingly irritated that it felt like they were the only two at the table not a couple?

They *weren't* a couple. They were two people who'd had sex and were now having a baby.

Yet because of their circumstances, all that *want* that seemed to be swirling in her gut suddenly had no place to land.

Similar to Kerrigan and Arlo's conversation when he'd first arrived, she heard Darius and Jayden shift into a discussion of the day's work and how hard the dive was. Since she recognized there was a lot to discuss and she'd monopolized Darius up to now, she gave them their privacy.

Which left Gavin on the other side of her.

The security blanket of conversation with her new friend—all while diligently avoiding too deep of a conversation with Gavin—had vanished and she had to figure out how to control the increasing irritation they weren't a couple.

Or maybe better said, why they hadn't discussed being a couple up to now.

They'd discussed the baby. And their work. And even danced around the edges of what had happened back at New Year's. But they hadn't discussed the concept of what *they* were to each other. And suddenly, without any warning at all, that seemed to matter.

More, she had to admit she didn't like the feeling of not knowing.

"I think I'm going to go," Sera said, suddenly wishing she'd have thought of it earlier when they were in the midst of rejuggling their positions at the table.

"We just got here. Why are you leaving?"

"It was a long day and—" She stopped. It was tempting to make up reasons or, worse, use her pregnancy as an excuse, and she stopped herself.

She wanted to leave.

In fact, it suddenly felt extremely important to remove herself from the social construct that was Gavin and his friends and their significant others.

"I'm going home."

"Then I'll take you."

"You don't need to take me." She gave a pointed glance around the table. "Please stay with your friends."

"You're not walking home alone."

She already knew they were being loud enough to be overheard, and the last thing she wanted to do was create a scene. So she tried once more to soften the situation, only this time without excusing herself.

"You're here with your friends. Enjoy the decompression time. I think they need it. You all do. This has been a tough week."

She believed the conversation done and, with a bright smile, made her excuses to Jayden and Darius and Kerrigan and Arlo. She even promised to follow up with Kerrigan on her big case and the evidence tour they'd discussed. It was mature, kind and congenial. A lovely way to end a long day.

Which made Gavin's determination to walk her out another frustration.

They had no claims on each other. And she knew how to come and go where she pleased. Hell, she was rather good at it, considering she'd been doing it since she was fourteen.

Sera traversed through the crowded bar, unwilling to make a scene inside.

Why was Gavin pushing this? They'd made no commitment to each other, and it was early enough. It wasn't like she was in any danger taking the subway a few stops to home. She often worked later than this and navigated her trip without incident.

Finally past the throng, Sera slammed through the door, stepping out into the street. The air was cold, a testament to the fact that winter still wasn't quite ready to relinquish its grip, especially once the sun went down.

"Sera! Would you stop?"

She came to a halt about halfway down the sidewalk, the sounds of the bar heavy and throbbing through the frosted windows. Whirling, she turned to face Gavin. "What is the matter with you? I'm going home. I told you that you don't need to follow me."

"I want to know what's wrong. One minute we're all having a good time, and the next you're running out like the hounds of hell are on you. What happened?"

"Nothing happened."

"Then why are you leaving?"

The urge to make an excuse hit her once more, but Sera ruthlessly pushed it back and went for the truth. "No, Gavin. That's my point. Nothing happened. We were in there with two couples, both of whom were supportive and loving of one another. Both of whom had quiet moments of intimacy talking about their day. And it made me realize—"

She stopped, aware this sudden burst of honesty was tied to a stressful day that capped off a stressful week. Gavin was back in her life. She was pregnant. And, based on her conversation with Kerrigan, she wasn't hiding that fact particularly well.

And then Kerrigan went and said that incredible thing

about how Gavin looked at her like she was precious, and somewhere after that she'd managed to lose her equilibrium.

Did she even want that?

A small voice whispered very loudly in the back of her mind that yes, she most certainly did. Even as another one wanted to shut it up with copious amounts of ice cream and cake.

"It made you realize what?"

"We're not a couple. We had amazing sex, and we're having a baby, and we're not a couple. And I have no idea what to do about that."

She didn't. For someone who usually had an answer for every challenge she faced, this was a new experience. She was fresh out of answers. Worse, she was so confused she didn't even make sense to herself, let alone to anyone else.

Which made her next move that much more puzzling.

Right there in the middle of the sidewalk, she moved straight into his arms and wrapped hers around his neck, dragging his mouth down to hers.

WHITE-HOT NEED ELECTRIFIED his body as Gavin quickly caught up to the woman who'd wrapped herself up in his body. He sank into the warm welcome of her and the even warmer welcome of her mouth, desperate to convey all he felt, even as he knew there were so many emotions he hadn't fully figured out yet.

The confusion that had carried him through the past few minutes—all while trying to understand her abrupt change of heart—wasn't any closer to abating, but he had to admit he definitely preferred this version of Sera to the one storming out of a bar and leaving him in her wake.

Even if the question behind all of it was *why*. A point his body was presently ignoring as the kiss spun out between them, wanting and needy and even a little bit sad.

It was the sad that had him lifting his head, his gaze never leaving hers. "It'd be my greatest pleasure to kiss you straight through to next week, but what's this about? Talk to me."

Sera slipped from his arms, and while he was loath to have her pull away, he recognized the dangerous emotional ground they were both treading. Heavy emotional territory that included a new life they still hadn't spent all that much time discussing.

Was that what had her upset?

"Oh, Sera, I'm sorry. I know we need to talk about the baby. Really talk, about their future and how we're going to parent. Maybe a night out wasn't what either of us needed."

"We do need to talk about the baby." She nodded her head, her gaze distracted as she focused on something across the street. "But that's not why I wanted to leave."

"Then what has you upset?"

"I'm not upset. I'm emotionally all over the place. And it should be about the baby, but, I don't know. We'll work it out. I want what's best for our child, and I might not know you well, but I do know you well enough to understand that you want the same. We'll figure it out together."

"Then what's wrong?"

She stared across the street once more before turning back to him, the warm woman in his arms vanishing beneath all those emotions.

"It's us, Gavin! I'm trying to figure out *us*. What we are to each other. We have attraction, that's for sure, and we have from the first. But we don't have a relationship. We're not beholden to one another. We don't *know* each other!"

That last piece seemed practically torn from her lips, almost like a plea.

But before he could respond, she pressed on, "I stood there at a table with two couples who not only know each other, but are so intimately involved with each other's lives that they read each other. Effortlessly. And I'm having a baby with a man I don't know. Not you or your moods or even what you like for breakfast."

Her gaze drifted off again at the end, and Gavin finally turned to follow her line of sight before turning back to her.

"We'll get there. This is all new, but I'm committed to getting to know you, Sera. To letting you know me."

"You mean that?"

"Of course I do."

"Then why did you clam up when I said you were part of a family with the Harbor team? And why haven't you mentioned any family member at all to me? Not once, even a casual reference?"

Her gaze drifted once more, and Gavin felt rising anger at how Sera had seemingly split her focus. "What the hell is so important over there? All while you're accusing me of not sharing things with you."

She shook her head, her attention snapping back to him. "Something over there keeps moving. And I saw something flash in the light of the streetlamp."

Her split focus kept distracting him, especially since he'd wanted to ask her the exact same questions she was pressing on him.

Where was *her* family? Beyond Enzo and Robin, she hadn't said a word. Had she told her parents she was pregnant? Had she told anyone? Because nothing they'd spoken of to date suggested she had.

Yet despite all that and what was possibly the most important conversation of his life, his cop instincts had kicked in and he couldn't let her comments go. "Flash how?"

"I don't know. It was probably somebody's bag or shoes or who knows. But something keeps catching my eye."

Gavin shifted his own attention across the street, trying to see anything that might be in the shadows, but all he could see were a row of storefronts and a small alcove to a doorway that led to the stairwell for the apartments built above the stores. Nothing flashed, nor could he even make out a shadow of anyone, even as something nagged at him to walk over and see what had her so distracted.

He wasn't armed, and he should grab Arlo if he was going to investigate anything. Gavin nearly said as much, asking Sera to follow him back inside to wait until they could take a look at whatever was over there, when Darius walked past them.

The man had his phone shoved to his ear and a steady stream of instructions crossing his lips about keeping a client happy, all while encouraging whomever he was speaking with to not get caught up in said client's problems. It was good, sound advice, delivered in a measured, confident, managerial tone that belied the man's expertise and professionalism.

If the man wasn't so focused on work he'd have asked him to stay with Sera while Gavin went to investigate. But he wasn't going to interrupt him now.

"The way something over there keeps distracting you, I need to go check it out."

"Why would you do that?"

"Because I'm a cop, and something has set your instincts off. I just need to go get Arlo to come with me."

"Look, it's fine. I'm just going to go—"

She hadn't even finished the sentence when the rapid clip of gunfire filled the air. Gavin moved on sheer instinct, throwing himself across her and tackling them both to the ground all while her screams filled the air. He cradled her against him and twisted at the last minute, cushioning the blow of hitting the sidewalk at a dead drop.

Before he could even catch a breath, everything seemed to move at once.

The few other people milling around on the sidewalk screamed and all raced toward the opposite corner, away from the gunfire. Gavin held tight to Sera, unwilling to let go for fear another round would start.

But it was the heavy shouts and familiar faces that he recognized as he looked up from where they lay on the ground that finally had him moving.

Arlo, Kerrigan and Jayden had barreled out of the bar at the distinctive sound of gunfire. All three now stood over him and Sera, yelling orders for information.

What had happened?

Gavin kept replaying it all in his mind as his three colleagues frantically looked around, assessing the situation.

But it was Jayden's scream that rent the air, agony layered in every syllable as he raced away from them.

"Darius!"

## Chapter Nine

Sera rubbed the soft material of her hospital gown and stared down at her feet. She'd been poked, prodded, given a sonogram and a physical exam and was just waiting to be cleared to go back to the waiting room and the vigil being kept by the entire Harbor team.

One of their own had been targeted. Another of their own was sitting with family and praying for the life of his husband. And no one was any closer to knowing why.

Gavin was pushed into an exam room himself, and Kerrigan had kept up a steady stream of visits to Sera when she had information to pass along, but Sera had spent much of the past hour alone. With her thoughts and a sort of liquefied, bone-deep fear that vacillated between the baby's safety and the fact that she and Gavin had been targeted and Darius had been collateral damage.

The doctor had assured her after the sonogram that the baby was fine, which was a deep relief. But it had left the other end of the fear spectrum to consume her thoughts.

Why had someone shot at them?

"Sera!" Gavin came into her hospital room, quickly rushing to her side. "I'm sorry I wasn't here. I kept at them to let me in, but no one would let me out of observation. I just kept getting the runaround."

"The baby's fine. I'm fine. It's all—" Whatever else she was about to say sort of petered out against his chest as he pulled her close.

"The baby's really okay?"

"Safe and sound." The words were garbled against his shirt, but the sheer relief she felt shimmering off his body went a long way toward calming her own tension. She clung to him, taking solace in the comfort.

He loosened his hold, but kept contact as he settled himself on the bed beside her.

"Is there any news about Darius? Kerrigan's been in to update me a few times, but all she knows is that he's in surgery."

"Nothing yet. I came straight here, but Kerr's been texting me. Jayden's family is here and with him, and they're all praying in the waiting room."

"What happened?"

"Arlo's trying to find out. He stayed on scene and has called in half the uniforms at the 86th to help him canvass the area."

"Anything yet?"

"Nothing. Not even a shell casing. It's like whoever was there was a ghost."

"Ghosts don't leave flashes in the light. I saw him, Gavin. That had to be what kept catching my attention across the street."

Even if *saw him* was a bit of a stretch. She'd seen that weird flashing and the form across the street, but she'd never seen an actual face. In fact, the more she thought about it, that had been part of what had caught her attention.

"The person was in a mask."

"You remember something?"

"That's just it. I kept seeing that flash under the lights in my mind, and I wasn't paying as much attention to the person, but there *was* someone there. I never saw a face, but I've been trying to remember. And then I thought maybe I didn't see a face because of the big hoodie they were wearing, but I realize now I never actually saw the person's face."

Gavin held tight to her hands, his thumbs stroking her flesh. It was such a simple gesture, but it brought so much comfort, and she didn't feel alone anymore.

"I should have gone after him."

"No, Gavin. No, you shouldn't have. He'd have hurt you."

"So instead, he hurt Darius? I could have disarmed him or unmasked him or stopped this from happening."

He needed to say it. For his own healing and peace of mind, he needed to get it all out. But the thought of Gavin walking across that street and confronting a masked stranger with a gun had her entire body going cold.

Especially because she was convinced they were the targets.

"That's not what I meant. He shouldn't have hurt anyone. But we were out there first. We were in his crosshairs. It's an awful, terrible mistake that he shot Darius, but we were the targets. I'm convinced of it."

"Why? What possible reason would anyone want to shoot at us?"

"That's what we need to find out. But I had to have seen the flash of his gun in the lights. And I knew whomever it was had been focused on us. That's why I kept looking over."

"So someone was just there, waiting for us to come out of the bar?"

The question stopped her, and she realized it was a valid question. Some gunman was waiting around on the off chance they might walk out?

What she'd seemed so certain of only moments before grew fuzzy at the edges.

Was tonight just some random attack? One that could have tilted in a bad direction toward anyone? And Darius had just happened to come out of the bar at the wrong time?

Or was it something more?

"Miss Forte?" The doctor tapped lightly on the door frame before walking in. "I'm Dr. Monroe. I'm the attending on call, and I've looked at all the tests my resident ran earlier."

Gavin stood, giving room for the woman to look her over. Sera answered the same questions she'd given the resident and the nurse before him, before being given the all clear.

"Um, Doctor," Sera started in, gesturing Gavin back to her side. "Our friend is here, in surgery for a gunshot wound."

The doctor nodded, her expression grave. "He's still in surgery now, but I can get you an update."

"Thank you. But, well, I want to be there. To be part of the group waiting on news." Sera glanced down and laid a hand over her belly, a gesture she'd done on repeat for the past hour. "But is it safe for the baby?"

"The baby's fine. Your fall was cushioned, and your tests all indicate there's nothing to be concerned about. I'm sorry for the stress and the trauma, but please take that particular worry out of the mix. Your baby is progressing right on schedule."

Sera nodded before glancing at Gavin. "Our baby. It's ours."

The doctor turned toward Gavin, gesturing him forward

before laying a hand on his shoulder. "Your quick thinking kept them both safe. I know there's not much to take solace in this evening, but take comfort from that."

Gavin nodded, and once again, that quivering sense of relief was nearly palpable.

Their small family was safe.

She might not know what their future held as a couple, but tonight had proven that she, Gavin and their baby *were* a family and would be for the rest of her life.

TEARS AND PRAYERS.

They would be the two things he remembered about this night, Gavin thought as he sat vigil in the emergency room waiting area. Except of everyone here, he was the only one who'd been through this before.

The only one who knew the horror.

And the only one who remembered. The fear and hope, fused so tightly together they were one emotion. One deep, throbbing need.

Jayden's family was assembled around the room, his mother, brothers and sisters and their spouses. Their faces all wore perpetually shell-shocked expressions, and their voices had descended into monotone whispers as they spoke quietly to each other.

He'd learned that Darius was an only child from Connecticut, with deceased parents. He also learned that he was a graduate of Yale, summa cum laude. And he also learned that he might have come into the Houston family by marriage, but he was as much one of them as every one of the children Mama Houston raised in that house with the cookery in the back.

Although Gavin had wanted to take Sera home and come

back, she wouldn't hear of it. So after she was formally discharged, she took the seat next to him as they waited.

Kerrigan had kept up a steady string of texts with Arlo as he worked the crime scene, sharing the minimal news as she had it. No one they'd questioned so far had seen anything suspicious around the neighborhood. Nor had they come up with any security camera footage, since all the establishments on the block were closed. They did manage to get the feed from the bar, but other than more flashes glinting off the man in the shadows, similar to what had aroused Sera's suspicions in the first place, there was nothing usable.

Like a ghost.

"Do you have a minute?" Kerrigan came over to sit beside him, her movements casual even as her eyes said anything but.

"Of course. I actually need some coffee."

Sera was lightly dozing against his shoulder, but woke instantly with Kerrigan's arrival. She seemed to innately understand the need to stay put and quietly sent them on.

Although Gavin expected they'd be waylaid by Mama Houston's all-knowing stare, she was entirely focused on Jayden, holding him close and murmuring words of encouragement to him as Gavin and Kerrigan passed out of the waiting room.

"Bastards." Kerrigan might have whispered the word, but it held a world of fierce disdain and deep, frustrated anger as they hit the privacy of the hallway.

"What's going on? Did Arlo find something?"

"Not yet, but one of his informants reached out. Said he might know something."

Although Gavin recognized Arlo's connections in Sunset Bay ran deep—and solid information was gold, after all—he couldn't help but wonder if there was a better way. A world where people didn't turn on each other, and criminals didn't exist at all.

A rather silly thought for a cop, he acknowledged, but one that seemed more fervent somehow.

Was it the fact that he was going to be a father?

"Is the informant reliable?"

"She's a working woman in the know. She's got sharp eyes and is highly selective about who she shares her information with. And she knows all there is to know about the block where the shots came from."

"Keeps her eyes peeled for customers?"

"Among other things."

Although most of the women who worked the streets in Brooklyn steered clear of cops, it didn't surprise Gavin at all that one of Arlo's trusted informants was a prostitute. The man could charm the devil to give him ice, so it made sense he'd made friends with a woman who was both in a position to know things and whose vulnerability would be something Arlo Prescott was bound and determined to protect.

The fact he'd managed to make friends with the woman who worked the block outside a cop bar was another level entirely.

"Jade's a sharp cookie. Knows how to protect herself and the girls around her. So the fact she came forward with this so quickly is indicative of how much she respects Arlo. And she likes his ass."

If Gavin had already gotten his coffee, he'd have likely choked on it. "What?"

Kerrigan shrugged. "The man does have an exceedingly nice ass. I can hardly blame her for noticing. And it's those powers of observation that got us a break so quickly."

It was an odd sort of logic, but if Kerrigan didn't mind women ogling her boyfriend, who was he to argue?

"What did she tell him?"

"There have been rumors floating around for a while. Some important people have found a way to get rid of their evidence. They pay through the nose, but after they're done, they walk away basically scot-free from a crime."

"The cache of weapons we found." Gavin exhaled. Hard. "There were so many because they've accumulated over time. They weren't dumped all at once."

"Likely part of it. And a discovery like that, when your hidey-hole for all your bad deeds is suddenly discovered? Well, that's bad for business."

He thought about Sera's upset earlier: the fear that the two of them had actually been the intended target. He'd dismissed it, but was she right? Were the two of them the end game, and Darius had simply gotten in the way?

It didn't make sense. Especially since all those guns had just been discovered. Why put any plan of attack in place so quickly?

They walked up to the coffee machines in the hallway, and Gavin dug out some cash for their coffees. Kerrigan put her order into the machine next to his while he picked his blend, the machine whirling to life in time with his thoughts.

"I'm just not getting this. Someone decides to start shooting cops over a routine evidence discovery? That's a pretty bold choice when no one's done any digging on those weapons yet."

"Preemptive strike?" Kerrigan asked, pulling her cup from the machine. "Bold assertion of dominance? Who knows why criminals do what they do? All I do know is you need to watch your back. We all do. Sera, too."

"Sera, too." Gavin turned that over, her earlier fears that she'd been the target opening up yet another avenue. "She thought she was the target earlier. That Darius was shot because of her. Wrong place, wrong time sort of thing."

"Is she working any big cases?"

"I don't think so. Her schedule was shifted, like mine, to focus on the task force."

Kerrigan took a sip of her coffee. "Let's talk to her. See if she's made any enemies recently. Arlo got the sense this was a cop problem, but when criminals start a war it's not necessarily for a predictable reason."

"But why go to war at all? Those weapons were only just discovered. I still don't get why you'd draw this sort of attention."

"I don't have the reasons, Gav. I just have a new line for us to tug."

As he followed his friend and colleague back down the hall, Gavin wondered about that. It was an awfully flimsy line, with very few facts attached to it. What if they tugged too hard and unraveled something far deeper than they ever expected?

Yet as he thought about the deadly weapons laid out on the boat deck earlier, Gavin had to admit that they'd already started to tug that line. And maybe there was more in motion than any of them realized.

SERA HAD NEVER considered herself someone comfortable with grief. She had her own, of course, but she kept it carefully buried. And she regularly came up against grieving families in her work. People decimated by the loss of their loved ones at the hands of another.

She'd found a way, through the years, to compartmentalize those tearstained, distressed faces. They were a part of her work, and that same work was what would give them some measure of closure. It didn't bring their loved one back, but she remained hopeful they found peace in the fact that justice had been done for them.

But now? Watching the entire Houston family rally around Jayden as he waited for news of his husband? Sera understood something else.

Just how clearly grief was an expression of love.

With that sudden understanding so present in her mind, when Sera saw an empty seat beside Jayden's mother, she moved over to offer whatever comfort she could.

"Mrs. Houston?"

The woman looked up, her expression still welcoming even in the midst of her sadness. "Sera, sweetie. Come take a seat."

They'd been introduced earlier after Sera had been re-leased from her hospital room, and the kind woman had peppered her with questions about how she was feeling and how the baby was.

Sera hadn't even questioned how Mrs. Houston knew. She simply accepted that she did.

Weathered hands took her own, cradling them. Sera stared down to where they held on to each other, the seamless blend of youth and age wrapped together, and she wondered what it must be like to have such warmth and encouragement. Such care and love. Even before her mother's fall into apathy and recreational drug use, she'd never been a warm woman. Her parenting style was tepid at best and flat-out cold much of the time. For as much as she hated the reason she'd been given a peek into the Houston family dynamics, clearly led by their matriarch, Sera was touched and awed by how present they were for each other.

"This is a terrible time." Mrs. Houston shook her head, her dark eyes solemn.

"I only just met Darius and Jayden today. There's such love there. Such a deep bond."

"There was from the start." Mama Houston smiled, even through her sadness. "My boy thought I didn't know. Kept him and Darius a secret when they first started going out."

Although Sera didn't want to assume, not every family welcomed gay children and their significant others. While it flew in the face of what she'd expect from this family, you never could fully know what someone went through.

Which made the continued explanation that much more special, Sera realized.

"I know my children, and I've always given them all my love and told them to share that love with others. To be careful with others' hearts and ensure others were careful with theirs. But my Jayden was scared. Of the relationship. Of his feelings. Of the fact that this might actually be real."

And as the woman wove her story, Sera was astute enough to see a reflection of her own behavior in Jayden's all those years ago.

Even more, she recognized the fear Mama Houston spoke of with bone-deep understanding.

She'd recognized it after the night she'd spent with Gavin all those months ago.

Their night had been extraordinary, their connection even more so. And instead of staying and, at minimum, seeing if he wanted to continue talking, she'd fled.

"Did you convince him?"

Mama Houston smiled at that, one that reached all the

way to her eyes and broke through that haze of sadness. "It took longer than it should have, but he got in line quick enough. Love has a way of doing that, you know." Mama patted her knee. "You'll see. And you and Gavin will figure it out, too."

"Oh, I don't—"

There was another gentle pat to her knee. "You don't have to have it all figured out tonight. Or tomorrow. Or the day after. But that baby's going to have a way of solidifying all the things you're not quite ready to talk about. And then the two of you can figure out where you go from there."

Gavin walked back into the waiting room with Kerrigan, and their eyes caught and met.

*Then the two of you can figure out where you go from there.*

It was good advice. Wise, even. But she wasn't sure she and Gavin had the same base of love and understanding as Jayden and Darius had. Or if they were destined for the same.

Oh, they had attraction. And something that could blossom into a real friendship, which would be important toward building a stable future for their child.

But love?

"Thank you for that. Especially given all that's happening."

Mama Houston reached over and squeezed her hand once more. "It'll all work out, sweet girl. It will."

Sera nearly responded when a doctor came into the waiting room, her expression grim. Her gaze was unerring as it found Jayden and was full of a compassion that left Sera with a distinct sinking in her stomach. "Mr. Houston?"

Jayden stood, his attention on the doctor as he crossed to the entrance of the waiting room.

Sera watched it all play out, even as there was an odd awareness already filling her mind.

That grim look.

The compassionate yet resigned expression in the doctor's eyes.

And the seeming lack of air in the room.

"Mr. Houston. I'm sorry to tell you that there were complications. Your husband succumbed to his injuries."

Sera felt the collective wail of grief wash over the room. And without thinking, she wrapped her arms around Mama Houston and pulled her close, the grief that was an expression of love rising up around her in an overwhelming wave of pain.

## Chapter Ten

Numb.

Gavin had felt it once before—this absolute base functioning and little else—and had believed he'd never go through it again, but he'd been wrong.

So very wrong.

Because this evening he'd gone to have drinks with his good friends, and now he was taking Sera home in the knowledge he'd never speak to one of them again, all while another would be broken beyond repair.

Sera had been more than willing to stay at the hospital as long as was needed, but it had become evident that while he, Sera, Kerrigan and the rest of the department who'd gone to sit vigil were welcome, the family needed to be alone.

Jayden would have need of them in the coming days, weeks and months, but for the moment, he needed privacy and his family. So as a unit, his brothers and sisters in arms, they'd stood before him, paying their respects before leaving him to the open maw of grief.

Sera had gently fussed when they'd first come in, asking Gavin if he needed anything, but he just shook his head, taking a seat on her couch after asking if he could stay for a few minutes. She'd been quick to let him know he could stay as long as he needed before disappearing into the kitchen and returning a bit later with a steaming mug of tea that smelled fruity for herself and a bottled water for him.

"Can I get you anything else?"

He shook his head, trying to find the words that were rolling around inside of him. The ones tied to big emotions he normally kept hidden.

Which was why what came out next was as much a surprise to him as it was to her.

"My father was murdered when I was fourteen."

He kept his expression neutral—a skill he'd honed over the years for the rare occasion this subject came up—and studied her face from where she sat on the opposite end of the couch, her knees drawn up.

Would she be shocked?

Horrified?

Angry he hadn't spoken of it before?

Only she was none of those things.

Instead, she unfolded her legs, laid her tea down on the coffee table and moved in closer, reaching for his hand. "Tell me about him."

Not *it*, Gavin thought. The murder. Or *what happened?*

But *him.*

His father.

"Robert Sinclair Hayes the Fourth. Of the Fifth Avenue Hayeses, a bastion of Manhattan society since the turn of the twentieth century."

When she only nodded, encouraging him to keep going, Gavin recognized the gift of simple understanding. And while it didn't make it easier to get through the story, it did make a difference that she was holding his hand.

He wasn't alone.

"My parents had a love match, which was a bit of a surprise for their upbringings, his especially, where duty was still somewhat expected. My mother wasn't from society, so that made waves for a while. But they got together in the '80s at college, and my grandmother ultimately stepped in with Bobby Three, as she called my grandfather. Told him to get with the times."

"Bobby Three?" Sera smiled. "As in Robert Sinclair the Third?"

"Yep."

"I like that."

"She coined it at their first meeting, and it's stuck for almost seventy years."

And it had stuck. Because while his grandparents had started out with a marriage of duty and social station, love had grown in its place through the years. Love and a heck of a lot of fondness and understanding.

Recognizing he was stalling, Gavin kept on with his story.

"My father had been through a difficult stretch at work. Late nights and, what we later found out, threatening phone calls almost daily."

"Who threatened him?"

"My father was a lawyer." He smiled as the recognition dawned, oddly, for the first time. "Like you."

Her smile was gentle, a sweet counterpoint to their dark conversation. "Clearly ensuring our child will have a balanced and measured legal mind."

"Obviously."

"Please tell me more, Gavin. I'd like to know."

Why did this never get easier?

He'd have thought, after nearly twenty years, talking about

that terrible day and all the terrible days that followed would be easier. Or, if not easier, something he could dispassionately recount, the emotion of it all shoved down so deep he could find his way through to the other side.

Only as the tears welled up, shaking his shoulders with wracking sobs, he knew an irrevocable certainty.

It would never truly be better.

And now his friend would live with the same.

SERA MOVED IN, wrapping her arms around Gavin and pulling him close. He was a large man, and the embrace should have been awkward, but somehow they found a way.

They fit.

Hard sobs echoed through him, and Sera couldn't help but wonder how a person moved on past that sort of shock and grief. And then she realized it wasn't about moving past. Perhaps it wasn't even about accepting. It was simply about getting through to the other side.

Although she wouldn't compare her own life to this sort of devastating, shocking act by another, she did know what it was like to push through. To force yourself to keep going, even when the acts were small, destructive ones that added up over time until a person was simply numb from them. Until you finally accepted that the place you had to get to in order to survive wasn't like anything you'd ever imagined.

"I'm sorry." Gavin shifted to pull away, but she held firm.

"It's a terrible experience to live with. And it made all the horrors of tonight even more present. You're entitled to your emotions, Gavin. It's right you should feel them."

"Feeling them doesn't change a damn thing about the outcome. Not for my father and certainly not for Darius."

"But it does for you."

Of course, the reality was that his father and Darius were no longer in pain. There was no suffering for wherever they'd moved on to. It was those left behind who had to deal with the unbearable grief of their loss.

He didn't answer, but she got the distinct sense that while he acknowledged what she was saying, he wasn't ready to accept it. That he'd somehow convinced himself if he didn't feel his way through the loss of his father, he could simply hold it at bay.

*Seem familiar, Forte?*

Since the internal shot of honesty hit a bit too close to home, Sera refocused on Gavin. She did owe him the same honesty about her past, but now wasn't the time.

"Are you ready to tell me the rest?"

"It's not especially surprising. A disgruntled criminal he prosecuted found a way to strike back. His record was already much too long by the time my father came into his life, but somehow my dad became the scapegoat for all his anger and discontent with life. He'd gotten it in his head that someone had to pay and was already orchestrating things from inside prison. Two weeks after he got out on parole for good behavior, he shot my father coming out of his office in Midtown."

It was a risk lawyers lived with—the justice system was nothing if not public—but the actual number of lawyers who faced threats to their lives wasn't nearly as high as TV and movies made it out to be.

But it did happen.

And it was a risk.

One Gavin's father had paid a terrible price for.

"I'm sorry."

He turned to look at her, his dark brown eyes still grief-filled, even if some of it had dimmed slightly with the telling. "Thank you, but it was a long time ago."

"I'm still sorry. For your father. And I'm also sorry about earlier. About rushing out of the bar. I wish I could change that." She pulled away from him, suddenly unable to touch him as she faced the reality of what her impulse and anger had wrought.

All that upset and anger and weird reaction she'd had to the other couples had sent her out into the street, desperate to go home and be alone. Wrapped in her cocoon of isolation where she felt safe and warm and in control.

"I brought this on. By leaving the bar. By putting us outside. By putting Darius in the crosshairs."

"You didn't do this."

"How can you say that?" And suddenly, the whole night crashed in on her, the terrible truth of it all. "And how could I have blocked it out up to now? I was the reason we were outside."

"You didn't aim the gun, Sera. Nor did you pull the trigger." He reached for her, but she'd already stood, moving away from him and whatever comfort he thought to offer.

"I let my emotions carry me outside like a child. How can you say I'm not responsible?"

"Because you didn't pull the trigger!"

The outburst was a surprise, Gavin's words sort of echoing through the sudden quiet of the room.

And in its wake, she simply crumpled. "That wonderful man is gone."

Gavin was by her side immediately, pulling her into his arms and holding her upright. His voice was soft in her ear, and any lingering harshness in his tone vanished as he crooned softly to her. "I know he is. I know."

"I—"

"Shhh. You didn't. This wasn't you, Sera. You didn't do this."

The fierce urgency in his tone and the deep conviction that she wasn't at fault echoed through her mind, a discordant counterpart to what she already thought.

Nay, what she already *knew*.

They were targeted this evening. She didn't know how or why, but she and Gavin were the target of the shooter. The way she'd seen that flash under the lights. And the fact that there was such a focus on the two of them as they stood there, having their argument.

Yet why had the shooter missed, hitting Darius instead? He wasn't all that far from them, but he wasn't so close that she believed the shooter had simply had bad aim.

Which circled her back around to the why of it all.

And how much could have been avoided if she'd just remained inside.


THE TEXT HAD come late confirming the early morning meeting at the 86th, but Gavin had expected it. He'd already spoken to Wyatt and Arlo the night before and had been anxious to get in and get going with whatever information Arlo managed to uncover on scene outside the bar.

What he didn't expect was the full turnout at the 86th.

Officers spilled out of every doorway and filled the bullpen near to bursting as everyone gathered around to hear Captain Reed speak, updating the precinct on the events at Case Closed. After he spoke, Arlo was on deck to present his findings.

"Everyone really turned out for Jayden," Kerrigan whispered where she stood beside Gavin. "He'd be so touched."

"Somehow I think he'd prefer there wasn't any reason for us all to be assembled in the first place."

Kerrigan's mouth dropped in shock as she turned to him. "Well, yes, of course."

It was all so close, and his emotions were all jumbled up, simmering at the surface and just waiting to erupt. Or find a convenient victim.

"Kerr—" He broke off, running his hand through his short-cropped hair and tugging. "I'm sorry. I know what you meant. Honest, I do know. I just— Truly." He hung his head. "I'm so, so sorry."

It was a testament to her goodness and the friendship they'd forged over long shifts together that she was quick to forgive. "I get it. I bit Arlo's head off this morning, and he basically hasn't slept in thirty-six hours." She reached for his hand, squeezing tight. "So yeah, I know."

"It sucks, Kerr. It sucks so bad." He could only nod as she laid her head on his shoulder just as Captain Reed got up to speak.

Everyone quieted, and Gavin couldn't help but think of his time with Sera the night before. He never spoke of his father's death. It was something he'd gone to grief counseling for, addressed and then moved on. It never went away, and he wasn't trying to fool himself that it would, but he deliberately kept that part of his life separate. And instead, chose to honor his father in a way that was both meaningful to him *and* filled him with purpose.

Yet he had told Sera.

Was it because they were having a baby? Or because she'd experienced the horror of Darius's death, too?

He'd considered all those reasons, but it was only as he walked into his apartment around three that morning that he'd finally accepted the truth. He had wanted Sera to know. He wanted her to understand that part of himself.

It was only after he'd told her that the real panic had set in.

Would she pity him? Or worse, would she think less of his police work, believing it was a vendetta of some sort instead of his calling in life?

Only she hadn't reacted that way at all.

She'd said please. And she'd told him she'd like to know more.

It was a level of compassion and understanding he'd never felt before. And, perhaps, he admitted to himself, he might have felt it more often if he let people into that area of his life. If he shared who he was with the people who cared about him the most.

Jayden certainly was going to need that understanding in the coming weeks and months. And Kerrigan, Wyatt and the whole rest of the Harbor team had shown themselves to be his brothers and sisters in arms from the first.

Would telling them be so bad?

He considered it as he took in those same faces he trusted implicitly, all solemn as they stood before their captain. And he vowed to think about how he could be different. How he could show up differently for all of them.

Captain Reed's assured voice complemented that thought as he began to speak.

"As you all know, one of our own lost a loved one last night to an as-yet-still unknown shooter."

Captain Reed caught everyone up on the investigation to date, and even though most everyone knew the basics of what had happened the night before, the room was eerily silent.

"The team has already put calls into every business on the

block to secure street cameras as soon as everyone opens. The bar has cooperated and already provided footage from their sidewalk cams."

"Which proved to be a dead end," Arlo said dryly from where he stood beside the captain. "The shooter stayed in the shadows, and as far as we can tell from some vague footage at a distance, they were masked to avoid easy detection."

When Captain Reed only nodded and turned the room over to Arlo, the detective shared all he'd managed to uncover.

Gavin looked at his friend—Kerrigan's comments about thirty-six hours without sleep looked pretty spot-on. Arlo's face was wan, his normal robust look drawn and pinched with fatigue. If he also knew his friend, the man wasn't going to rest until he had a suspect in custody. It was then that Gavin hatched a plan.

He and Sera had made considerable progress on their task force work. There was no reason he couldn't devote more time to the investigation, supporting Arlo and figuring out what the shooter was after.

Because he was increasingly certain Sera was right. They were the object of the shooter's attention.

He had no idea why. Nor did he have any clue why Darius ended up being the target.

He hadn't had a chance to run it past Arlo yet, but Gavin wanted to share his ideas with their smaller group and see what everyone thought. At minimum, he wanted to get these jumbled, roiling emotions out and see if anyone else could make sense of what he felt much too close to.

Because with the exception of Wyatt, they'd all been together last night.

So what was the motive for killing Darius?

AROUND 5:00 A.M., after tossing and turning all night, Sera decided to spend the day in the office. It would give Gavin some much-needed space with his fellow officers, all while burying herself in work. She was still processing what had happened the night before and knew that she'd be climbing the walls by ten if she attempted to work from home.

Which made Gavin's text message asking her to come over to the precinct and meet in "their conference room" about fifteen minutes after she got to her desk something of a surprise.

Had they had a break in the case this soon?

Anxious to know the answer and desperately hoping that they had, in fact, caught the monster who'd killed Darius, she'd quickly packed up what she'd just unpacked at her desk to head out.

And came face-to-face with David.

"Where's the fire?" Her DA smiled, his impeccable bearing practically regal even this early in the morning.

"Oh, David! Hello! I'm sorry to rush out, but I have to run to a quick meeting—" She nearly fumbled over her words, stopping herself at the last minute before giving the explanation for where she was going.

His smile was indulgent, and Sera had no idea why she'd had the weird premonition to say nothing. Yet even now, with a few beats to consider it, she still wasn't inclined to tell him where she was going.

"A meeting? Why'd you even bother coming in?"

"I thought I'd get ahead of a bit of work before going to my meeting. The task force is amazing, but I'm definitely juggling a few things."

His eyebrows slashed hard over brown eyes so dark they were nearly black. "It's not too much, is it?"

"No, no, of course not."

If she hadn't had such a strange reaction to the whole conversation, she'd have likely been a bit more eloquent, but finally she landed on something that wasn't a fabrication. "I've been a little under the weather these past few weeks, and I've fallen a bit behind on some of my case reading I typically catch up on in the evenings. I figured I'd try powering through with fresh eyes."

"If you're sure?"

"Of course." She nearly had the urge to push past him before stopping herself. A few extra minutes wasn't going to make or break her meeting with Gavin, and her boss did deserve her time.

Even if she was struggling with this antsy feeling she couldn't define.

A feeling that had come in steady waves since the night before. Gavin had stayed a bit longer after their discussion about his father and her guilt over Darius. While they had no difficulties talking with each other, they'd both acknowledged there wasn't a lot to say.

After he'd gotten a text from Arlo letting him know about the early morning meeting scheduled at the precinct, she'd encouraged him to head home and get whatever sleep he could.

It was more of those vacillating emotions that had sent her out into the street at the bar in the first place. She and Gavin had been thrust into a level of intimacy that at moments felt right and at other times…left her struggling to find her footing.

"I do apologize for rushing out on you."

"Of course," David waved her on, his smile benevolent.

"Please get to your meeting. And let's plan some time to catch up before end of week on your caseload."

"I'd like that." She smiled, trying to diffuse her impatience. "I'll bring the coffee."

"You're on."

Her impressions of the brief conversation lingered as she headed out of the office and toward the 86th. It was an odd, unsettling feeling, and she couldn't quite pinpoint the reason for it.

Yet David's attention had seemed…sharper, somehow.

Did he sense she was pregnant?

It hadn't been a secret she'd had a few difficult mornings in the bathroom throwing up. And a suspected pregnancy was the sort of news people loved to gossip about.

Whether someone had overheard her and deduced the truth or David figured it out on his own, it was the push in the direction she needed. Because what had originally felt like maintaining her privacy and taking the time she needed to ensure her pregnancy was progressing well had passed.

The time had come to share her news. With her family, as Aunt Robin and Uncle Enzo had every right to know. And once she shared the wonderful news with them, it was time to share with her boss and her office mates.

Putting the awkwardness behind her and resolving to think on how she'd give David the news as well, Sera walked into the precinct. She quickly moved through the security check-in and went on up to the conference room, where she found Gavin, Kerrigan, Arlo and Wyatt assembled inside.

"Is there news?" The question came out in a rush before she'd even said her hellos, her anxiety over discovering Darius's killer more pressing than she even realized.

"Not yet," Gavin said as he stood to give her his seat.

"But we wanted you here for Arlo's briefing. He took the department through his findings, but he's got a few more ideas for how we might crack this."

She took the seat Gavin had vacated, briefly touching his hand as he held the seat for her. It was more outwardly affectionate than she was normally comfortable with, but it felt good to offer that small shot of reassurance.

To feel the warmth of his skin beneath her fingertips.

To connect.

Arlo started in quickly, his delivery succinct and pointed. "While we haven't found any details that give us a name or a gang to follow up with, the video we have gotten so far corroborates your instincts, Sera."

"Someone set up across the street from the bar, and they were lingering there," Gavin said, before adding, "planning something."

"That's what doesn't make sense, though." Sera considered the steady stream of thoughts, memories and random theories she'd cycled through on her way to the 86th. "What I can't wrap my head around."

"Around what?" Kerrigan prompted.

"How would they know we were there? That any of us would be there? It was an impulse decision, made on the boat coming back into Sunset Bay. Targeted implies advance knowledge and planning. *We* didn't even know our plans."

Arlo took a seat next to her, his attention laser-focused. "Walk me through it."

It was the question she'd turned over and over in her mind. The one, when she got past the sharp grief over Darius and that horrific feeling of responsibility, that she couldn't stop thinking about.

"The shots felt distinctly personal. The fact that Gavin

and I were in the crosshairs from across the street. It was noticeable, for lack of a better word. The guy was there, and despite trying to hide, it was obvious he was watching us." A small shiver raced down her spine in remembrance of that flash of reflection under the lights across the street. "But then Darius's murder doesn't feel like an accident."

"The gunshots seemed to reinforce that," Kerrigan said, her expression pained. "A shooter might have one bullet that went wild. But three?"

Which was what had Sera pressing on. "Yet Gavin and I were the people being watched."

Arlo just nodded throughout her telling, taking in her impressions. "Go on."

"What I'm trying to put together is how would someone, obviously watching us and lining up a shot, shift gears and hit Darius? It wasn't like he was in the middle of my and Gavin's conversation. He was on the phone near us but having his own call."

"You think it was deliberate?" Wyatt said. "Like he was the real target?"

"No. Yes." Sera shook her head, trying to find the words to explain what she only felt. "I have nothing to go on with this. Nothing that's proof or even a solid image. All I do know is I kept being distracted by this reflection across the street. Gavin even remarked on it, that I was distracted from our conversation and kept looking away."

She heard Gavin's small laugh before he spoke. "I was sort of pissed about it, to be honest. We were having a serious conversation, and she kept looking away."

"It was distracting. But it was *us*. We were the object of this guy's attention."

"And you never saw a face?" Wyatt pressed.

"No. Nothing." She shook her head, remembering those weird moments of awareness. "Which added to my unease. But then Darius comes out, and he's the one who's deliberately shot. Why?"

"Could he have been the target?" Kerrigan turned toward Arlo, obviously testing it out. "We keep looking at this like it's a cop shooting, but Darius had an important job. He runs with some big players. Is it possible he was the target all along?"

"I've got Cormac and Sanjay looking into that angle," Arlo confirmed, naming what she assumed were two officers in the precinct. "They're heading straight to Darius's office this morning to talk to the staff as well as his boss. Anything's possible, and we're going to turn over all the stones. But based on everything Sera's describing, it still sounds a bit like wrong place, wrong time."

"Yet not," Gavin said, his voice grim.

He'd been solemn since she walked in, allowing her the space to share her impressions and thoughts. But now... Now she heard the anger and the grief, mixed together in a powder keg of emotion.

"Not how?" Arlo pressed.

"I heard those gunshots. I protected Sera myself, also convinced we were the target. But Darius was the intended victim. Three bullets, precisely delivered, with deadly intention."

"Forensics aren't back yet," Kerrigan argued. "I know I already went there, but it's still a leap, Gavin."

Despite the sound arguments from his colleagues, Sera saw clearly that Gavin wasn't buying any of it.

"Come on, Kerr. We both saw it. Forensics can have the time to do their work, but you know as well as I do. That was a sharpshooter with perfect aim. And Darius paid the price."

## Chapter Eleven

Gavin could see Kerrigan wanted to argue, if for no other reason than they were all fixed on the idea that last night was meant to be a cop shooting.

And it *felt* that way.

He kept circling around that point, over and over in his mind. But Darius was the obvious victim, too. Those gunshots were too precise, not shots that went wild, missing their intended target.

Forensics report be damned.

What was going on?

"Deliberate. That's what you mean." Sera's blue eyes were hazed with that same layer of guilt he'd seen last night, but beneath it he was pleased to see the determination shining through.

"It's exactly what he means," Arlo added, stepping in. "If that's the case, and I'll take a cop's gut instinct as a lead to tug any day, then what it also means is that there's some larger orchestration behind this."

"But no one thought we'd be there." Sera turned to Kerrigan. "I'm not wrong about that, am I? When it came up on the police boat, it had seemed like a last-minute decision."

"It was," Kerrigan agreed. "But that bar's known as a

cop hangout. And even without preplanning, it wouldn't be that hard to follow a group of us if someone was determined enough to do so."

It fit, Gavin had to admit. The bar wasn't far from the precinct. Their police boats came in and out of the dock area every day. If someone wanted to do harm, he and his fellow cops weren't too difficult to find.

So now the real question was why.

"Son of a bitch." Gavin exhaled on a hard sigh. "The guns."

Wyatt and Kerrigan caught up just behind him, their expressions grim as everyone started talking at once.

"Someone's covering it up," Kerrigan said.

"Was Darius a diversion, like the kayakers last fall?" Wyatt asked.

"What sort of diversion?" Sera interrupted them, and Gavin felt a distinct shot of pride at how easily she fit in and how quickly she was able to go toe-to-toe with the entire room.

"I went through it on a case last year." Wyatt quickly filled her in on the investigation involving the father and grandfather of his new wife, Marlowe, and the dead kayakers who were set up by a local crime group to divert the cops' attention from what they were really doing with the drug trade. "The initial approach was to keep us so busy chasing our tails that we wouldn't put as much focus on the real crime."

"Which didn't last long." Arlo grinned at his friend before he shifted the conversation. "But something about this feels different."

"Different how?"

"Yours was a diversion, Wyatt. A very deliberate one

that used Anderson's reputation at the 86th and his history with his son to keep things quiet. But this has the marks of a vendetta."

Gavin turned it over in his mind, and he had to admit, it checked a lot of boxes. That feeling that he and Sera were the targets, inducing his fear for her safety. *And* the fact that Darius was shot with evidence that pointed to him being a very deliberate target.

"So now we have a new problem," Gavin said, a level of certainty he'd rarely felt on a case slamming into him with all the force of an Atlantic hurricane. "Who's in a position to know what Harbor was doing up at Hell Gate?"

Kerrigan shook her head. "A lot of people know a lot of things, Gav. Why would this be different?"

"Yes, but how would anyone know this fast? The discovery hasn't been publicized. The local reporters haven't even caught wind, and Captain Reed's gotten agreement from the chief to hold on any press for another few days."

"So whoever's doing this figured out their hidey-hole is compromised?" Kerrigan might press him, challenging him as she always did, but he also saw her gaze light up in agreement as she processed his point.

"Exactly."

They still didn't have a lot to go on, but it was a direction. And the sooner they figured out if it was the right one, the sooner they could get justice for Darius. It mattered, Gavin realized. For Darius and Jayden. For that bone-deep, aching fear that had rushed him the moment he believed Sera was in danger.

And for their unborn child she carried.

The protection of that life mattered to him in ways so profound he hadn't even realized it until this moment. But now that he knew—now that he *felt* it clear through each and every cell of his body—he also knew what needed to be done.

They had a killer to catch. And he'd be damned if he was giving the bastard an opportunity to touch anyone else.

FOUR DAYS.

Four long, lonely days, Sera thought as she finished the last layer of noodles on the lasagna she was prepping for dinner.

Other than a few text messages each day, email exchanges on their task force work and one brief call to update her on the funeral arrangements for Darius, Sera had had minimal contact with Gavin.

She understood why. She'd even encouraged it, the clear-eyed focus Gavin and his colleagues needed to hunt down the culprit up at Hell Gate something she supported.

The time apart had given her the space to work through her own thoughts and the overwhelming grief over Darius as well. Sera knew that she wasn't at fault—Gavin, the rest of the Harbor team and pretty much the entire 86th were hunting the one responsible—but the terrible sorrow continued to batter her in waves.

And none of it, no matter how levelheaded she sought to be, changed the fact that she missed Gavin.

It was an odd sort of ache, she'd finally admitted to herself late last night as she tossed and turned. One that had actually developed after their night together and had only grown stronger with his reemergence into her life. What did it mean, to want someone this much after so short a time? And how was it possible she could feel this wide range of emotions for someone she didn't really know?

Even if she had begun to know him better, seeing various sides of him with each hour they spent together. His dedication and devotion to his work, tied so intimately with his dedication and devotion to the people he worked with. It was fascinating to watch and something she really didn't understand in her own life.

Yes, she supported her fellow ADAs, but their lives weren't intertwined in the same way.

Yet the men and women of the 86th? Their lives depended on each other. Each dive together. Each day out on patrol. It was appealing in a way she never would have expected, Sera admitted to herself as she thought about her outing on the boat up to Hell Gate. There had been collaboration and a sort of coordination that spoke of deep training and shared responsibility.

It had been obvious later, too. The way the Harbor team had rallied around Jayden. And then the next day, the way Gavin, Arlo, Kerrigan and Wyatt had shared ideas in the precinct conference room. That shared risk created a bond that was as resolute as it was absolute.

And it gave her the inward courage she needed for what lay ahead that evening.

Aunt Robin and Uncle Enzo were coming to dinner to spend some time with Gavin, whom they only knew as a tenant and to learn about the baby. Her aunt and uncle were the closest thing she had to parents, and she'd owed them an update far sooner than now.

"But you're doing it now," she whispered to herself, breathing in for a shot of courage. They were her family, but she was still entitled to manage the personal details of her life as she saw fit. And, well…today she was managing those details by sharing her good news.

And introducing her aunt and uncle to Gavin.

Which was why, she told herself later, her heart leaped in her chest when the knock came at her front door at precisely seven. And why it positively melted as she took in the sight of him, in a dress shirt and slacks, two bouquets in hand.

"Gavin. They're beautiful."

"One for you." He extended a handful of spring tulips in a riot of colors before leaning in to press a kiss on her cheek. "And one for your aunt."

"She's going to love them."

"I hope so."

Sera gestured him into her apartment, and as she did, she caught sight of the set of his lips, the tight wall of his shoulders and the way he kept clearing his throat.

He was nervous, too.

Whether it was the four days apart or her own nerves or the simple happiness at seeing him, it probably didn't matter. But she laid a hand on his arm to stop his forward motion and, with her free hand settled her fingers against his shoulder and pulled him close.

Their lips met in a rush, a mix of need for one another and the most lovely sense of comfort at the end of the day. It was heady, she realized, to be able to find both with one person.

Desire and comfort.

Security and a needy sort of heat that scorched the blood.

Gavin wrapped an arm behind her waist, pulling her so close she worried she might crush the flowers between them.

And then she didn't care as his lips ravished hers, his tongue sweeping against hers in promise.

They'd done a good job up to now of keeping a tight leash on the attraction that had driven them in their first meeting.

It was never far from her thoughts—that exquisite night they spent together—but it wasn't something she'd expected they could act on again, either.

Only now...

Now it seemed a bit inevitable, really. That there was some laughable shortsightedness she'd carried, thinking she could resist this man.

Why would she even want to?

Gavin lifted his head and stared down at her. His dark eyes held a wealth of emotions, but it was the gentle smile that struck a chord deep in her heart. "Your aunt and uncle will be here soon."

"They will."

"And we have a lot to tell them."

She nodded, the seriousness of the evening coming back to her. "We do."

"There are going to be questions about us. About what we mean to each other."

She tried to pull away, the sudden dash of cold water on an otherwise heated moment harsh. Jarring.

And it was altogether a surprise when he held firm, gently keeping her in place in his embrace.

"Beyond the baby, I don't know what our future holds, Sera."

Wasn't that part of what she struggled with, too? She cared for him, yet she didn't really know what he wanted.

Or, if she were honest, exactly what *she* wanted.

Which made his next words a wonderful balm to those roiling thoughts that never seemed to fully land.

"But the part that's just about you and me? I do know I want to find out."

"Me, too."

The knock at the door had them pulling apart, a reminder there was still a lot in their present they needed to work out.

But as she opened the door to her smiling aunt and uncle, gesturing them in and watching as Gavin exchanged respectful, warm pleasantries with them both, she had the first real assurance that things would be all right.

She'd already found that months ago for her future with the baby. From those very first moments, she'd known things would work out. She was going to be a mother, and the deepest part of her embraced that from the start.

But this time with Gavin? It had given her hope for their future, too. Hope that no matter where they ended up, they'd find a path forward.

Romance? Friendship? Co-parenting?

Who knew?

Maybe she didn't need to have all the answers right now. Maybe, Sera thought as she left Uncle Enzo and Gavin to talk in the living room and she and Aunt Robin crossed to the kitchen to check on the lasagna, it was enough for right now to simply know that he'd be there.

THE NEWS OUT of the 86th was encouraging.

Slow, like a drip feed, but encouraging all the same.

No leads. No suspects. And not one single witness. Which meant no one, not even a crew led by the biggest hotshot detective in the department, had made a dent in discovering the sniper across from the bar.

Nor had anyone actually figured out how Darius St. Germaine fit into the equation.

But it *had* given him an idea.

It was so pedestrian to target cops. Going after their families was far more effective. It did maximum destruction and damage, all while inciting panic and fear. Two traits that made even the most stalwart professional lose their ability to think clearly.

And it was a fitting punishment while he hunted for a new dumping ground for the weapons.

Which, despite the satisfaction he got from sowing these seeds of unrest, was his real problem in all this.

That dumping ground up at Hell Gate had been perfect. Easy to get to, isolated enough to be ignored during the dump itself and not on the beaten path of Harbor's normal routines. That miserable confluence of water patterns had been his saving grace. Literally, the perfect hiding place for his crimes.

Only now, all he needed was for the NYPD to put one weapon together with a former case out of his office, and they had a problem on their hands. The chances were slim, but possible all the same.

And he preferred his odds absolutely stacked in his favor.

It was why he'd put Sera on the task force, effectively removing her from an upcoming case that might require… disposal of evidence. It was also why her appearance on that harbor boat was a concern.

He kept close tabs on all his ADAs, and she'd never given a whiff of anything improper or outside of team norms. Nor would he have pegged her for fraternizing within the task force.

But she'd been on that boat.

And his sniper, Bart Alonzo, had described her to a T.

Even more interesting, he'd described her *with* one of the Harbor team members. Even after considerable probing on that front, Bart had maintained his belief they were a couple.

So he'd keep an eye out. And he'd see if there was something going on with her and one of the Harbor guys. He'd use that knowledge to probe a bit further when they were together, gently coaxing whatever he could get out of her.

In the meantime, he had a follow-up assignment to plan for Bart.

Harbor was targeted first. He'd considered going after another one of theirs—that safecracker was a hot number and had a lot of name recognition in the borough—but that was awfully high-profile, too. Maybe too high-profile. Besides, the scare tactics would likely work better across a broader swath of the department.

He considered all the work underway on the cache of weapons and knew he had his next target.

Forensics.

Give the brave and honorable science geeks something to really worry about. They weren't used to the danger on the streets or under the water. Which would only ratchet up the fear factor tenfold.

The plan had merit. A hell of a lot of it, as a matter of fact. And he had all the resources he needed, right here at his fingertips. Case notes. Discovery files with reams of data. All underpinned with the name of every man or woman who'd ever worked forensics out of the 86th.

It really was good to be king, David Esposito thought as he tapped in a few commands into his computer.

Very, very good.

THE STINK EYE he'd expected from Robin and Enzo when he and Sera shared their news was, thankfully, short-lived.

Gavin had braced for it, well aware Sera's aunt and uncle were a test run for their meeting with his own mother.

Sera's aunt and uncle had certainly sized him up, asking several pointed questions about his intentions. But it was a testament to their love for Sera that they quickly shifted gears to excitement over the baby and all the plans to welcome him or her to the family.

Of marked interest was the lack of mention of her parents.

No reference to them or the standard question of *what do they think?* Not even a subtle nod to them if they'd passed away.

Nothing at all, as if they didn't exist.

He'd thought to ask Sera about her mother and father more than a few times, but the flow of their conversation would shift, and he'd file it away and vow to ask later. And she certainly hadn't mentioned them beyond that vague dismissal during their first real conversation after getting reacquainted.

Which he supposed hadn't been all that strange, the actual number of hours they'd spent in each other's company having been somewhat limited. Their time alone even more so. It had been less than two weeks since that first day of the task force, and they had spent several days apart since that first meeting. So, really, it shouldn't be a surprise that the subject of her parents hadn't come up.

Only he was beginning to suspect that was on purpose and *that* stung a bit. Especially since he had shared the details of his father's death.

Which was dumb, Gavin thought as he picked up a small plate to select a few items from the charcuterie board Sera had laid out. This wasn't a tit-for-tat situation, and if he wanted to know something, he could damn well ask.

But it would have been nicer to learn the information voluntarily.

A fact that he'd have to ponder later as Robin came up beside him and laid a hand on his arm. "The flowers are beautiful."

"I'm glad you like them."

"It's big news," Robin said as she began fixing a plate for herself. "Happy news, but very big."

"It is. And while unexpected," he launched in, more than willing to set the stage succinctly with his intentions, "it's happy *and* welcome news."

"It most certainly is."

"Sera and I haven't known each other all that long, but—" He left the thought trail off because, really, how did you talk to a woman about how sexy and attractive you thought her niece was?

Even if Robin's knowing smile came winging back at him, whip-quick, her gaze doing a quick flight to Enzo before returning to him. "When you know, you know."

"We're still trying to figure that part out."

"Figure it out or just go with the feeling." She winked at him. "Since you started with feelings, maybe you should just stay on that path. Keep the brain out of it altogether."

"Aunt Robin!" Sera came up behind her, wrapping an arm around the woman's shoulders. "Discretion."

"I'm only speaking the truth."

Sera shot him a helpless look, and for the first time since that explosive kiss when he walked in, Gavin felt something unclench in his stomach. He wanted her, that had been clear from the first. But he'd struggled with whatever his brain kept tossing at him.

Statistics on their likely success rate as a couple.

The pressures of both their jobs.

Starting a family without that rock-solid, get-to-know-you time together before as a couple.

All fair points. And all equally relevant to living a life he took responsibility for, but maybe there was something to be said for not allowing those thoughts to take over.

Raw attraction had brought them together. It had been quick and electric, unlike anything he'd ever felt before in his life. And maybe—just maybe, Gavin admitted to himself—he wasn't giving that base connection enough credit.

Especially since there was no way he could think his way out of this one. He and Sera had shared something extraordinary, and it had momentous, life-changing results. Whoever he was last year, he'd become someone else entirely different as the page turned on a new year.

Wasn't that the real truth underneath all of this? His life had changed exceptionally quickly. The last time that happened, it had brought immeasurable grief.

But this time?

This time it brought a tremendous power for change and opportunity and *need*. Bone-deep and soul-defining.

He needed her.

Sera.

And as he kept imagining the child who would be here in a few short months, Gavin realized he needed the family they would become.

"Your aunt's right, you know," Gavin said, the words springing to his lips with ease. "Feelings and gut instinct are never to be underestimated."

"I knew I liked you." Robin patted Sera's hand where it rested on her shoulder. "Listen to the man, my dear. He's got something there."

"Are you two in cahoots?"

Although she voiced the question with serious tones, Gavin didn't miss the light in Sera's eyes or the quick wink, so like her aunt's, that she shot him before turning to Robin.

"And don't let her fool you, Gavin. This is the same woman who made Uncle Enzo propose three times before she said yes."

"Four!" Enzo hollered from his perch on the couch in front of a basketball game.

Robin shushed her husband before pursing her lips. "I needed time to figure myself out."

Unwilling to be dismissed, Enzo kept pace. "Took you long enough."

"A woman shouldn't be rushed."

"But what about all those feelings, Aunt Robin?" Sera pressed her point, and in the insistence—even one based in humor—Gavin had a sense of Sera's dogged pursuit of justice in the courtroom.

Robin simply laughed in the face of the pressure. "How do you think I got so smart about it all? I hemmed and hawed with all those ideas in my head. They were just getting in the way of what my heart already knew."

She lifted her face to press a kiss to Sera's cheek before slipping from beneath her niece's arm and crossing to Gavin. With a gentle smile, she pressed a matched kiss to his cheek.

"Don't repeat my mistakes. If it's what you both want, take the joy of the moment. Don't let all those pesky thoughts get in the way."

The kitchen timer went off, effectively snapping everyone's attention away from Robin's words. And as he watched Sera and her aunt move into the kitchen, Gavin had to admit he was deeply comforted and, oddly, more confused at what should come next.

So when Enzo waved him over to the couch after complaining about a bad ref call, Gavin went willingly. If he was going to feel his way through it all, he could at least holler some smack talk at the TV with his child's great-uncle while they waited for the lasagna to cool.

It wasn't an answer, but it sure felt like a solid start toward the future.

## Chapter Twelve

Sera had her feet up on the couch, her eyes drooping, when she heard the distinct sound of a dropped dish in her kitchen.

"Are you okay?" she hollered in the direction of the noise, well aware she should get up and help. Even if her body felt like it was weighed down with lead.

The morning sickness had continued to improve along with her energy levels, but something about the worry over the past few days, prepping for the dinner, had taken more out of her than she'd realized. But after an absolutely outstanding dinner with Gavin and her aunt and uncle—with the pressure suddenly gone—she'd crashed hard after Aunt Robin and Uncle Enzo left.

It felt a bit silly now, with things having gone so well, but she could acknowledge that she'd been anxious about the dinner.

Would they like Gavin? Would Gavin like them? How would they take the news of the baby?

She certainly had the maturity and lifestyle to handle an unplanned pregnancy, but that lingering sense of...well, not shame but *old-world values*, she finally settled on, had weighed a bit. Maybe more than she'd realized, if the exhaustion dragging at her was any indication.

"I got it!" Gavin's voice rang out from the kitchen. "Nothing broke."

She supposed she should leave him to it, and really, who even cared if he broke every dish she owned? It would be worth it not to have to scrub that lasagna pan. After Robin and Enzo headed out, Gavin had ordered her to the couch with a cup of fruity tea and said he'd handle the dishes.

She settled in for the indulgence, sipping her tea and letting the evening float through her mind on a hazy loop.

He'd been charming. In a way that had been so deeply genuine and caring. Her aunt had been enamored from the first, and in a small way, it had helped that her family already knew him as one of their tenants. Her uncle had been stern at first, but he'd warmed quickly, that preexisting knowledge of Gavin enough to smooth out a few rough moments.

After all, she was a grown woman. One who'd seen her fair share of life and was excited to bring a baby into this world in spite of that. Robin and Enzo were the only ones who truly understood that.

And it was time Gavin understood it, too.

She stood to go in and help him with drying the dishes when he walked into the room, a fresh mug of tea in his hand and a cup of coffee for himself. "The lasagna pan's soaking and also happens to be the only thing left."

The sight of him—standing there with two mugs in hand and a soft smile—nearly undid her, but she held on. She'd resolved to tell him about her past, and there was no chickening out now. "Let it soak overnight, and I can get it tomorrow."

He waved a hand. "I'm all-in. It'll be a quick cleanup before I leave. In the meantime, I'm going to enjoy my coffee and not think about having a second piece of that pie your aunt brought for dessert."

"Since Aunt Robin's apple pie is widely known throughout Brooklyn as being the best, I might join you."

"Watch out. Lucille might bar you from entering her shop if she hears you spreading that one."

He spoke of one of Sunset Bay's most well-loved proprietors, the ageless Lucille, who ran one of the shops on Main Street. Her pies were excellent, and even Robin would give the woman the edge on her peach pie and on her coconut-custard. But when it came to apple, Sera's aunt owned the ribbon.

"Then it's a good thing they're fierce friends," Sera said, unable to hold back the smile.

"Fierce?"

"They would fight to the death not to reveal their respective pie crust recipes, but trash talk either of them in earshot of the other and prepare yourself for a rant and then, as I believe it's called, 'the cut direct.'"

"So noted." He took a seat on the chair that sat beside the couch where she'd been dozing, his dark gaze appreciative as he looked at her over the top of his mug. "That went well, all things considered."

"It did. It definitely helped that they already liked you *and* have checked your credit score." At Gavin's easy laugh, she kept on with the truth. "But you're also easy to like. Charming and earnest, and your words about being all-in as a father went a long way."

"I am. All-in. And getting more and more excited every day. I'd like—" He stopped, but she was more than curious to press for more details.

"You'd like what?"

"If it's not too much to ask, I'd like to come with you to your next appointment."

Sera didn't consider herself someone easily rattled. She had to be firm and think through all the angles in her job, a trait that had carried over to the rest of life. Or perhaps she'd found a job that accommodated the traits she already had.

No matter, she mentally shook her head.

What mattered, she realized as she stared into those deep brown eyes, was that he was *in* this with her. They might not have a relationship, but they would co-parent together. It meant a lot.

It meant everything, she amended to herself. And because it mattered, she owed him all the rest.

"I'd like that. It'll be at the end of the month. I'm having an ultrasound, so you'll get to see the baby, too."

"Have you had one before?"

"Just once, at around eight weeks. Actually—" She glanced toward the small treasure box she kept on the coffee table. Opening it up, she pulled out the small stack of black-and-white images. "I have a few copies. Please take one."

Gavin set down his coffee, his gaze unmoving from the photos in her hands. Gently, almost reverently, he took the small stack and flipped through them, one by one.

The photos were mostly the same, Sera knew. The baby was so small, almost little more than a blob in the center of the picture, sort of like a bean. Even with the vague outline, there were a few telltale signs including the clear shape of his or her head.

"We should be able to see the arms and legs in the next one. And more definition of his or her head. Who knows, we may even get a little wave at the technician taking the ultrasound."

"That would be amazing." Gavin traced the outline of

the baby with the tip of his finger before lifting his head. "This is amazing."

"I'll give you all the details for the next appointment."

He nodded, his gaze returning to the photos, and in that split second of time, she felt an easing of an anxiety she hadn't even realized she'd carried. She had a partner and ally in raising a child, and until that moment, she hadn't fully comprehended just how much weight she'd carried at the idea of raising a tiny human all on her own.

"Gavin. There's something I'd like to tell you."

He set the photos on the end table, his focus fully on her.

"Actually, I don't normally talk about it, but it's something I think you should know."

"What is it?"

"My mother abandoned me when I was fourteen. She didn't love me." Sera shrugged, the truth of that still able to sting nearly two decades later. "Or maybe said another way, she didn't love me enough."

GAVIN WAS STILL reeling from staring at images of his child, so he'd later consider the fact that he might have handled Sera's words with more finesse. More understanding. But at the moment, the social subtlety his mother had drilled into him since birth was nowhere in evidence.

"That's the most ridiculous thing I've ever heard."

"Ridiculous? Excuse me?"

"You're wildly lovable and perfect. Your mother's the unlovable one."

He watched as that shot landed, her mouth briefly scrunching up in confusion before she parried back. "How would you know?"

"Because I have eyes. Because I talk to you. And because

any parent who would walk away from their child has something deeply, irretrievably wrong with them."

"Way to toss the judgment, Gavin."

Was it judgment?

In the strictest sense of the word, yes. But in a broader sense, he wasn't going to apologize for his ready defense of her. A point that was only reinforced by the fact that Sera's words didn't hold censure so much as resignation. Wasn't she entitled to anger at being left? By her mother, of all people?

"Yeah, well, I'm not apologizing for it, either."

"You don't know someone's situation."

"No, I don't. And I do recognize no one can understand every circumstance, so my attitude may seem harsh. But my first instinct will always be to defend the child. I'm certainly not apologizing for that."

It would have been his reaction before, but now? With photos of his own child sitting in his direct line of sight? He simply couldn't take back the words or feel badly about them.

People had reasons for lots of things, and he'd never understand or know the hearts that beat behind those decisions.

But he did know Sera Forte.

He knew *her* heart. And there was nothing that would convince him her mother's reasons were good enough or strong enough or reasonable enough to excuse her actions.

But that sort of dogged stubbornness wasn't what Sera needed, either. So he shifted gears and focused on what *she* needed. Because that was really all that mattered.

"Why don't you tell me about it?"

"My mother and Robin are sisters. I think Robin had a sense things weren't okay, but she was almost twelve years older than my mom and was out of the house when my mom was still pretty young."

He'd hit fairly hard with his initial comments, so Gavin only nodded, giving her the space to tell him the rest.

"My dad wasn't really in the picture. He was older than my mom. He got her pregnant a few weeks after she graduated high school, and they sort of tried to make a go of it for a while."

If the similarities to their own relationship reared up at him, Gavin fought to tamp them down. Other than the way they were starting their parenting journey together, it wasn't the same. He'd make sure of it because he absolutely intended to *be in the picture.*

Only he said none of that, opting for that continued calm, easy understanding. "Do you remember him?"

"A bit. He'd leave for a time when things got bad between them, and then he'd show up again a few years later. I don't remember the first time he came back because I was too young, but he did it again when I was five and then again when I was eight."

"Any reentry into your life would be difficult, but those are impressionable ages."

"I suppose."

Since Sera had shifted into a sort of robotic telling of her childhood, he stopped interjecting. It was time to let her get through this.

"Anyway, my mom wasn't the most attentive mother. She spent a lot of time in her head and forgot me a lot. That improved during those short bursts when my dad was around, but it got worse each time he left. I was sort of relieved when he never came back after that last time."

Once again, he fought to hold back what she'd termed judgment, but which he could only consider basic decency. To abandon your family? To go into some sort of ignorant state where your child—a small child by Sera's own admission—was left to fend for themselves?

He couldn't find a way to justify that simply to make her feel better.

But since he hadn't lived those years and she had, he also recognized pushing her on it was hardly fair. Even if a small part of him broke at the thought of her fending for herself at such a young age.

"I'm sorry for all of that. Most of all I'm sorry that the people who should have made you feel the safest in this world took no responsibility for that."

Something flashed in her eyes. Memory? Hurt? A lingering anger she was fully entitled to?

It was hard to decipher and perhaps that was the point, Gavin acknowledged to himself. Emotions were complex and rarely black-and-white. All he could do was reinforce that he was there for her. For their child.

"Where is your mother now?"

"She died about a year after she left. Robin always worried it was suicide, but I looked into it a few times with the access I have at work." She shrugged, the move anything but careless. "She was driving around late one night out in the small town she'd settled in on the end of Long Island. A drunk driver came at her the wrong way, and she was killed in the accident."

"What was she doing out?"

"That was core to Robin's concerns. That she'd gone looking for trouble. But she had nothing in her system, nor was she the one in the wrong lane. And while I'd agree she lived an aimless life, I don't believe she made a deliberate choice to end it."

Again, he recognized his job in this moment was to listen,

but Gavin would hardly agree her mother's choices weren't deliberate. *Not* engaging in her daughter's life was a choice, no matter how you cut it.

"My father was long gone by then. I don't know if he even knew. Or if he even cares."

In the end, it was those words that broke his heart. Because everything about Sera made him care.

Her heart.

Her ideas.

Her warmth.

There were so many facets to her, and he knew— positively *knew*—he'd only skimmed the surface so far.

And all he could really do, Gavin recognized, was prove to her that he wasn't walking away.

A STRONG BREEZE kicked up, the wind carrying that bite early spring was capable of. Sera marveled at the turnout all around her as various members of the NYPD and what looked like nearly all the Harbor team stood in their dress uniforms outside the church deep in the heart of Sunset Bay.

They were burying Darius today.

She'd anticipated finding a quiet spot alone in the church, but Gavin had arrived bright and early at her apartment, ready to escort her for the day's sad events. It was one more show of warmth that she was coming to learn was so like him.

They hadn't seen each other since the dinner with her aunt and uncle and all the family information she'd shared after.

The conversation had left her rattled, but also glad she'd finally gone there. Told the tale. But maybe best of all, that she'd told Gavin and he'd…understood.

Oh, he'd pressed her, too. Given her quite a few things to think about, actually, in the two days since. She *had* taken on the abandonment of her parents as something wrong with her. And while the calm, rational, adult part of her knew the responsibility didn't rest with her, the child inside struggled to find that truth.

But Gavin's ready defense had gone a long way toward opening her adult eyes and shuttering the ones of her inner child a bit.

Especially now that she was going to be a mother.

The fierce protection she already felt for the life she carried had given her an additional perspective she'd never had before. There was nothing she wouldn't do for her child. And the mere thought of abandoning him or her left her feeling bereft inside.

"Sera?"

With that lingering shot of conviction still roaring through her mind, Sera turned to find an elegant blonde woman who'd moved up next to her in the crowd. "Marlowe, right?"

"Yes. I'm married to Wyatt." Despite the somber mood, a small smile tilted the woman's lips at that statement. "I'm still getting used to saying that."

"I hear you got married recently. Congratulations."

"Thank you."

They kept their voices low as they spoke of the service and the outpouring of love to Jayden and his family.

"I can't stop thinking about Jayden. About the senseless loss. As a cop's partner, you understand the risks to them." Marlowe shook her head. "But when that risk is turned back on their partner? It's got everyone upside down."

Sera knew the description fit. Gavin's obvious frustrations with the situation since the night of the shooting had been clear. It was like the order of things was wrong. *Off.* And it had all of them on edge.

"Do they have any additional leads?"

"Nothing. Arlo has put together a small team, and they've scoured whatever they can get their hands on, from doorbell cams to a full canvass of the neighborhood in a five-block radius around the bar. Nothing's turned up. Not even a hint of the shooter."

"Which makes it feel even more ominous. And deliberate," Sera added, piecing it together.

Gavin had let her know they were still short of any real leads, but the additional information from Marlowe added an important dimension. That absolute lack of details meant they were dealing with someone more crafty and cunning than originally thought. To be that deft in avoiding detection meant someone was determined not to be identified or even seen.

Like a ghost.

"That's Wyatt's take, too. He's not sure what they're dealing with, but the entire team has ruled out anything random." Marlowe glanced around at the assembled men and women in uniform. "My grandfather is a veteran cop, and I married one. I've been around the 86th precinct my entire life. When the force turns out like this, you know it's important."

Sera had sensed the same, but hearing the words—*seeing* it for herself—made it tangible somehow.

It reinforced those same thoughts she'd had the week before about her own work. Although she considered herself part of a unit with the rest of her fellow ADAs, their work didn't carry the same camaraderie. Did that come from putting your life on the line?

Or was it something more?

Were the people determined to live with honor and sacrifice and protection more able to feel these things, so they were drawn to police work? Or did it embrace you the moment you became a member?

"That's what will get Jayden through," Sera said, conviction and certainty coursing through her. For the first time, she felt a small shot of hope that the smiling, happy man she'd met out on a sunny spring day would find a way to piece his life together. He'd never be the same, but someday he *would* feel the sun again. More important, he'd have support to keep the dark at bay.

His biological family and his work family would ensure it.

It didn't change the reality of what he faced, Sera knew, but it was assurance that he wouldn't face it alone.

The sense of motion had them both quieting, and Sera and Marlowe turned their attention to the front doors of the church. Jayden stepped through the doors, holding his mother's arm as he helped her down the marble steps.

The casket followed, carried by six officers in their finest dress. Wyatt and Gavin were at the front, with Arlo directly behind Gavin and three others she didn't recognize making up the rest of the pallbearers.

Each moved with purpose, their steps heavy with the solemn duty they carried.

And as she brushed away tears, Sera prayed for the man she barely knew. For the family who held him up. For the lovely, vibrant man who would never grow old.

## Chapter Thirteen

Gavin stared at the heaping table of food that ran along the wall of the large hall in the basement of the church where they'd honored Darius's life. The delicious fixings were designed to be comfort food on an impossibly hard day, but as he took in the tables generously laden with food, he found it anything but consoling.

Instead, his need to rant and rail—to *break* something— only increased moment by moment as they moved closer in the receiving line. Nothing could distract him for long from staring at Jayden's positively destroyed visage. From bristling at the sheer anger of an absolute waste of a life.

Or from how vividly he still remembered those days.

Although the loss of a parent was different than a spouse, the pain of such sudden and explosive loss after a murder was unfathomable. No matter how much living prepared a person for death entering their world, such a cruel, deliberate action added a layer of heartbreak that simply shattered the soul.

The soft hand that touched his shoulder pulled him back into the moment, and Gavin looked over to see Sera, her gaze gentle. "Are you okay?"

He only nodded and was grateful as she took his hand

in hers, holding tight as they waited their turn to speak to Jayden and his family.

The Houstons' church family had turned out as magnificently as the NYPD, preparing a feast in honor of the family's loss. They'd extended the food services to three other locations in the neighborhood to feed every single person who came to the funeral.

But it had been at Mrs. Houston's insistence that he and Sera had come to the church seating.

It was an honor neither of them had taken lightly. It was also one that she'd handled beautifully up to now, seeking out Jayden's brothers and sisters, sharing her condolences.

Although he wasn't surprised, he had been deeply touched to see how much warmth and kindness she'd extended to each person by name. In return, so many had asked after her own well-being since the shooting, a warm, embracing circle that could still provide care even in the midst of such grief.

It gave him hope, that circle. It was one of the few things today that managed to push its way past that need to break things. The other was Sera's unwavering support. Of him. Of his friends. And of the entire Houston family.

She might have carried her own grief over Darius, but she'd set it aside to focus on Jayden and his family. And she'd done it with an effortless grace that simply awed him.

He wanted to tell her all of that, but the line that had seemed interminable suddenly felt much too short as he and Sera stood before Jayden. His friend's dark eyes were red-rimmed, a layer of exhaustion Gavin had never seen before in their depths. Their work ensured that they regularly pushed themselves to the physical limit, but what Gavin saw now was a soul-deep exhaustion that wouldn't be erased with rest.

"Jayden. I am so very sorry." Sera leaned in and pulled Jayden close in a hug, the move so easy and natural it stunned him. That this warm, caring woman had ever had a stray thought—even once—that she wasn't lovable or deserving of her parents' warmth and affection...

Especially when her innate kindness welled up and spilled over with such care and compassion for others. She murmured something to Jayden, the words themselves far less meaningful than the warmth of her touch and the obvious outpouring of support.

And then she moved on to Mama Houston, leaving Gavin to his friend.

To the stark reality that nothing he could ever say would bring Darius back. That he and Sera had been the object of the shooter before they'd somehow shifted their attention to Darius. And that forevermore, the time in his life when he learned he'd be a father would be wrapped around his friend's dead husband.

It hit him in a wave, even as Gavin also knew he was one of the few people in this room who understood the grief and loss and sheer anger at the senseless killing of a loved one.

How did he reconcile that?

And how did they navigate through it?

The weight of it all had been far heavier than he'd realized, until Jayden reached out and pulled him close. Tears laced the man's words, the hard echo of a sob vibrating against Gavin's chest.

"Thank you for being here."

"I'm so sorry." The words were a croaked whisper, but they held all the interminable grief he couldn't wash away. "We were there. On the sidewalk. I'm so damn sor—"

Jayden's arms tightened once more before he shifted back,

his broad, capable hands never leaving Gavin's shoulders. "Be sorry he's gone, but don't, for one damn minute, think you're the reason this happened."

"But we were…"

"There. You were there, Gavin, that's all. And you stayed and cared for him and did everything you could. We're going to find the bastard who did this. I will never stop searching for answers, and there's no distance they can run I won't follow."

"You're not going to chase him alone. We'll make sure of it. None of us will rest, you have to know that."

Whatever carried him through the hug and the conviction of his words winked out, Jayden's eyes shuttering with the weight of it all. And somewhere down deep, Gavin knew, the inner vow the man had made to himself had become his north star above all else.

There was no way Jayden was going to rest until Darius's killer was found. Which meant Gavin and his fellow cops just needed to be sure they found the killer with him.

Because he had every idea what Jayden was capable of.

And he had no desire to lose the man to the darkness that waited him on the other side of it.

SERA FILLED A PLATE, the heaping platters of food ensuring no one would go hungry. It would have helped if she had an appetite, she admitted to herself as she took a napkin-rolled set of utensils. But appetite or not, she'd eat for the baby, and she'd eat in gratitude for all that had been prepared to comfort the Houston family.

Her skin still bore the imprint of Mama Houston's warm hug, her soft, whispered words a mix of grief for her family's loss and an innate well of care, asking after Sera's pregnancy and how she was feeling.

It was amazing, to have someone who should have no thought or care for anyone else's need in that moment still so firmly in control of their own ability to think of others.

*You're wildly lovable and perfect...*

*Your mother's the unlovable one...*

*And because any parent who would walk away from their child has something deeply, irretrievably wrong with them...*

Gavin's impatient arguments from the other night had rolled through her mind more than once, forcing her to question herself and her long-held assumptions.

She'd accused him of judgment, but as she'd stilled and really listened to all he said, it had ignited a change inside of her. A new way of seeing her situation and her place in the world.

But something about speaking with Mama Houston had made it real. As if Gavin had built a bonfire, but Mama Houston had tossed the match.

She wove her way to the table where Gavin, Wyatt and Marlowe had settled, making additional room for Arlo and Kerrigan and a man she remembered from the day on the boat up at Hell Gate, along with his wife.

Sera went to reintroduce herself, but the man with the kind eyes beat her to it. "You're Sera. I'm Mack, part of the forensics team." He turned to the pretty Latina woman beside him. "This is my wife, Valencia."

Although everyone carried the proper notes of somber reverence, it was good to sit with others. And over the next hour, she learned more about Jayden and Darius. How they met. Their funny quirks that somehow made it not only possible, but *right* that a cop and a businessman found each other. And then there were the silly stories that made each of them smile around the table.

It was Kerrigan who'd laughed the longest, even when a hard sob punctuated her dying laughter. Arlo pulled her close, his arm solid and reassuring around her shoulders.

All of it, Sera admitted as they began the process of saying their goodbyes and heading back for the street, mattered. And if it weren't for the task force, she'd have missed all of it. Would have missed getting to know these people.

But maybe she and Gavin wouldn't have been on that sidewalk. And Darius wouldn't have been outside. And none of these horrible events would ever have come to pass.

"Sera?" Valencia's smile was kind as she worked her purse strap up over the arm of her coat. They stood in the small lobby at the back of the church basement while everyone had gone to say their goodbyes to Jayden. "You look lost, sweetie. Are you okay?"

"I—" The pragmatism she fought to keep in check all day fell away, the harsh reality of having been so close to Darius's death taking over. "We were there. Gavin and I. On the same sidewalk where Darius was shot."

"Shhh." Valencia moved in close, her arm a solid support as Sera fought for air. "Deep breaths now."

During the course of their lunch, she'd come to learn Valencia was a nurse, and Sera did as she was told, desperately seeking some calm in the big, steady breaths.

Small hands rubbed circles over her back, and even through her coat Sera felt the firm strokes and tactile efforts to calm her down.

"If only we hadn't been there. If only…" The words died on her lips, the endless string of what-ifs and if-onlys so endless they'd become maddening.

"You can't take ownership of an evil act, Sera. You didn't do this. Your presence didn't do this."

"I know. I—" Sera took one more of those deep breaths, willing herself to not only calm, but to also breathe in the truth of what Valencia was saying. "I know this. I prosecute crime for a living, and I know to the depths of my toes the person who perpetrated the act is the guilty one. I just can't stop going over it in my mind. The senseless act. Being so close to it."

"It's a weight. I'm not suggesting it isn't, but you must separate the sadness from guilt that isn't yours to own."

Sera nodded. "Thank you."

It was all so new, so recent, and it was going to take time to get the proper perspective back. A day immersed in the loss of Darius was, by its nature, the opposite of getting perspective, and Sera knew that.

But in the coming days and months?

She had to work on this heavy weight that seemed determined to drag on her, twisting her emotions toward places she didn't own. She deserved it, but more than that, her child deserved it. Their lives had been spared at the hands of someone who could have decided differently. Negating that grace and the work of a deadly moment was not only dismissing the future for both of them, but it meant Darius had died in vain, and she refused to allow that.

Her if-onlys be damned.

Gavin, Wyatt and Marlowe, Arlo and Kerrigan and Mack had returned, everyone with coats in hand. The time had come to leave the family to their grief, and they all understood it as they ascended the basement steps to the street. The sea of uniformed officers that had filled the blocks around the church had dispersed, traffic having returned to normal.

It was still a bit lighter than Sera usually saw, the midafternoon crowds still in offices and the kids still about twenty minutes from school dismissal.

Maybe it was that lack of traffic—one she rarely saw—that heightened her awareness of the moment. Or perhaps it was just that lingering sense of sadness over being so close to a murder victim that had her on high alert. But as each couple started off in their own direction for home, she saw Mack head for the corner where someone had gestured him over to talk.

Valencia waved him on as she dug her phone out of her coat pocket, lifting it to her ear.

Kerrigan and Arlo, then Wyatt and Marlowe had already stepped onto the crosswalk when Sera heard the squeal of tires and a distinctive image visible through an open window.

She turned away from Gavin and toward the woman on her phone as a heavy scream filled her throat, leaving her lips in an agonized shout.

"Valencia! Watch out! There's a gun!"

SERA'S SCREAM STILL echoed in his ears, along with the heavy, rat-a-tat-tat sound of rapid gunfire.

Gavin didn't even think, he simply reacted, wrapping himself around her body and moving her deftly toward the ground, cushioning her every bit of the way.

Shouts filled the air even as the thick squeal of tires indicated the car was already racing away from the scene. Arlo and Wyatt ran after it, picking up a few other cops along the way, more shouts indicating the shooting was already called in.

Satisfied the immediate threat was over, Gavin shifted

off Sera, her screams gone, replaced with steady, cool-eyed anger.

"She needs help. Now."

Before he could stop her, Sera was on her way to Valencia, kneeling down on the sidewalk, on the opposite side of where Mack cradled his wife.

He wanted to stay with her, but Kerrigan was already at his side, urging him on toward the chase through downtown Sunset Bay.

Sera must have seen his indecision because she was already waving him on. "Go! Go help them. I'll stay here."

Everything in him wanted to stay by her side and keep her safe, but Gavin recognized where they were both needed, and it wasn't watching what went down together. They each needed to act, and Sera already had a towel out of her purse, pressed to Valencia's wound.

He'd ask her later where the towel had come from. Just like he'd check her out head to toe for himself to ensure she was okay. But right now, he was a cop, and every officer was needed on the chase.

He and Kerrigan ran in the same direction as Arlo and Wyatt.

But it was Kerrigan's shout that had them switching course. "Gav! There!"

Their late start gave them a different perspective on the fast-moving getaway car, and even at this distance he could see far down the block that there was enough of a police presence that the driver had abandoned ship and was trying to flee on foot.

Random, wild shots flew into the air as the driver fired off a gun, and the already-considerable risk to civilians suddenly ratcheted up.

"You wearing your ballistics armor?" Kerrigan said, even as she kept rushing toward the shooter.

"Yeah. You?"

"Yep."

The confirmation they were both armed with some measure of protection pushed them both harder, racing toward the fleeing perp.

He'd briefly considered the armor to be overkill as he'd dressed that morning, but now, with a threat still lingering, Gavin recognized it would have been the height of stupidity to have gone without. They still didn't know who shot Darius, and now, he'd bet every dollar he'd ever earn the shots directed at Mack's wife were done by the same perpetrator.

Or group of perpetrators.

What the ever-loving hell was going on?

Resolved to worry about it later, he put on another burst of speed, narrowing the gap with the fleeing gunman. The man had picked up his pace since he'd stopped the random shooting, likely needing to reload. But as they got that small reprieve, Gavin and Kerrigan let out twin curses when his next move became evident.

"Damn it! He's headed into that shop." Kerrigan dragged her phone out, hitting the face of the screen.

Arlo's voice, winded from running, flowed out of Kerrigan's speaker, barking out whatever he could remember from chasing the perp from the opposite direction. "One gun we can account for, no idea how well armed he is beyond that."

"We're assuming to the teeth," Kerrigan said as the two of them came to a halt about twenty yards from the shop, out of immediate view from the inside.

"Perp entered the sub shop on Ninth," Gavin reported as he scanned the area around them.

"Do you have a visual?"

"Not yet," Kerrigan said as the two of them crept closer to the shop.

"Civilian risk?"

"School's not out yet, and we're past the lunch rush." Gavin quickly listed out risks as they moved closer to the storefront. "No visual through the front windows yet."

Sirens filled the air, their whiny shrieks indicating they were getting closer as Arlo and Wyatt rounded the corner. Both slowed, careful not to move within viewing range of the window. They stood on the opposite end of the store from Gavin and Kerrigan, Arlo remaining on the phone to avoid shouting and possibly being overheard from inside.

They continued an assessment of the location and possible risks to rushing the building when the door opened, and a petite older woman was pushed out. She stumbled before catching herself, her eyes flashing with terror as she ran from the building.

"Ma'am!" Gavin intercepted her, gently moving her out of the sight line of the sub shop windows. "I'm an officer. What happened in there?"

"A man! He has a gun! He ran in and started screaming at us."

"How many people are inside?"

"Three now."

"Patrons?"

"No, four total including me. I worked a few extra hours on my shift and stopped in to grab a late lunch. Two workers behind the counter and one other person inside besides me."

Gavin had to give her credit—she was shaken, but she was sharp.

"The man with the gun sent me out. Said I was to tell all the cops outside the other three are hostages because he 'don't kill old ladies.'" She sneered at that, her fear over the situation not enough to remain unaffected by the insult. "Those other people don't deserve this."

No one deserved it, but Gavin directed her toward the pair of uniforms who'd arrived on scene as he discussed the details with Kerrigan. Arlo had heard most of what was shared on the connection and confirmed that SWAT was on its way.

With the instruction everyone needed to remain in place, Gavin could only wonder about Mack's wife, Valencia, and how she was doing. Had the ambulance arrived? Was she alive? Or would they repeat today's tragic sadness in a matter of days?

The rush of activity had slowed to a crawl as they waited for SWAT's arrival, and that sudden hush gave him far too much time to consider what was really going on here.

Civilian targets both married to cops.

High-profile shootings in public places full of NYPD personnel. First at a known cop bar and now at a funeral riddled with cops paying their respects.

It wasn't coincidence. Just like he'd have bet everything on the two incidents being related, Gavin sensed the targeting of loved ones was by design.

What would instill maximum fear in a group who already willingly put their lives on the line for their work? Go after their families.

It played. Way too well, it played.

SWAT arrived on scene, and a perimeter was quickly set up, keeping direct view from the restaurant to a minimum. Their training collectively kicked in, and Gavin and Kerrigan outlined what they knew as they helped with the setup: blocked perimeter; shields to minimize onlooker views while also limiting the view from inside the sub shop; and a relay of the woman who'd been taken hostage and her step-by-step recounting of what had happened.

Gavin stepped back, giving them the room to work as he marked steps around the building, stopping every ten feet to turn in a full circle and consider his surroundings. Unlike the incident in front of Case Closed when Darius had been shot, the street opposite carried no hiding places. Instead, a large storefront took up the majority of the block. Other than heading inside a store, which their perp had done, there was nowhere to hide.

Which meant they were now dealing with a cornered predator.

He continued his mapping of the street, taking in the small, aged smoke shop beside the sandwich shop that was the center of their focus. The few people lingering inside had already come out based on the commotion on the street and had been quickly herded away from the storefront.

Beside that was a small alley. It was small, barely wide enough to fit the width of a truck. It was one of those weird quirks of the way the street had built up that the squat structure housing the smoke shop didn't fully touch its neighbor, a six-story building with a dance studio on the first floor.

Gavin cataloged it all, waving Kerrigan over. "We need to get down that alley."

"SWAT has part of the team on the street a block over, coming in from behind. They'll cover it."

"Do they know about—"

The words vanished as he caught sight of a body running

through the alley behind, the form visible through the tunnel made between the buildings.

He took off and paid no heed to Kerrigan's shouts behind him telling him to stop.

There was no way the runner wasn't related to this.

Was it the shooter?

His limited visuals earlier suggested that man was tall and slim, and this figure was smaller but more solid.

Accomplice?

A partn—

The thought died in his mind as his entire world tilted on its axis. Heat like the opening of an oven consumed him in a huge roar before everything went silent. Just before he was bodily lifted by the swirling inferno of violent power and sheer force.

He slammed into something hard, his head hitting the ground the last thing he felt before the world went black.

## Chapter Fourteen

Sera paced the hospital waiting room, the four walls fading around her as her mind still only processed an open street in Brooklyn, full of madness and terror and someone determined to mete out death.

The ambulance had arrived shortly after Gavin and Kerrigan took off to chase the shooter, and she'd stood with Mack, his arms empty and his bearing bereft as the EMTs worked over his wife as a team before rushing her away. She'd been in the midst of trying to figure out what to do for someone she'd only just met when one of Jayden's brothers, Tariq, came to them, his voice warm, caring and his touch easy as he showed them toward his car parked across the street.

*I'll take you to her.*

Over and over, those words had thrummed through her mind as Tariq drove them to the hospital.

Would Valencia meet the same end as Darius?

Would there be another funeral?

Would she—

"Sera?"

Kerrigan stood on the opposite side of the waiting room, Arlo and Wyatt flanking either side of her. All three still wore their dress uniforms, but each was covered in a fine white dust, and Kerrigan even had a cut along the side of her cheek.

"Kerrigan!" She rushed toward her. "What happened?"

"Sera, I'm sorry. I have to tell you—"

Sera heard the words, but they sounded like they were coming from very far away. It was only Wyatt stepping forward and taking her elbow, leading her toward an empty row of seats that kept her grounded.

Kept her somehow in her body.

In the moment.

"What's wrong?" She stared up at Wyatt, his eyes bleak with whatever news they'd come to share.

But it was Arlo who finally spoke. "It's Gavin, Sera. There was an explosion. The ambulance brought him in, and he's in with the emergency team right now."

"An explosion?"

How had she missed it? Yes, she'd been focused on Valencia and then on Mack, but how could she have missed an explosion?

"Where?"

Arlo quickly gave her the updates of what had happened since she and Gavin had separated at the church. How they'd given chase to the gunman who'd fired on Valencia. The way Gavin and Kerrigan had gone one way and Arlo and Wyatt had closed in from the other side. Then the stakeout while they all waited for instructions from the cornered gunman.

And then the blast.

"Gavin saw something, Sera," Kerrigan added. "And he took off after the person."

Questions bubbled up in her mind, a witch's cauldron of dark thoughts and even darker images, but she put none of them to words. Instead, she let it all flow over her.

She'd watched death come for Darius. She stood vigil even now to know if it waited for Valencia. And now Gavin faced the same. The need to run—to move and rant and rail to *someone* on Gavin's behalf—filled her, but Sera stayed in place.

What right did she have?

She wasn't his wife. They barely knew each other. She could hardly go chasing everyone at the nurse's station for updates.

And yet, they had a connection. Something so deep and intimate between them her life had irrevocably changed. They had a child together.

"We need to let his family know," was all she finally said. All she could say when faced with the very real truth that she had no claims on Gavin Hayes. Certainly none the hospital would or could acknowledge.

"They're getting that information from the office. I'm sorry to say none of us know how to reach his mom," Kerrigan said, her mouth thinning with obvious chagrin at the fact that, even as Gavin's friends, they didn't have that knowledge.

Sera let that sink in, the truth that Gavin kept his personal life so private even his friends had been kept at a distance. It didn't comfort her, exactly, but it did galvanize her in ways her and Gavin's conversations up to now hadn't been able to.

Hadn't she been living the same way? If something happened to her at work, would anyone know how to help her? How to reach Aunt Robin and Uncle Enzo for her? How to find her family? That number might be counted on one hand, but they were her family. And she'd held them and everyone else in her life at arm's length.

That had to stop.

For herself, yes. But for the child she carried? She had to break the pattern of choosing a life kept separate from the people around her.

Her child deserved more.

Just like her child deserved to grow up with a father. It was that need—one so deeply felt—that had her pushing all the rest away. She'd focus on it later and she *would* make changes. Starting with introducing herself to Gavin's mother when the woman arrived and letting her know she wanted her to have a place in her grandchild's life.

But for now, they had to get through whatever was going on around them.

Whatever had decided to make the 86th a target.

"Mrs. Hayes?"

A doctor came into the waiting room, pulling their collective attention toward the door. It was Arlo who spoke first, wrapping an arm around Sera's shoulders. "She's here."

*Mrs. Hayes?*

Sera shot Arlo a side-eye, but he didn't say a word, just kept his attention focused forward.

"What can you tell us, sir?"

"He's going to be okay. Took a solid hit to the body when the blast knocked him down, but his ballistics armor did its job. It's not going to feel like it when he's sore for the next few days, but nothing's broken. His exceptional conditioning is going to go a long way toward a quick recovery, as well."

The doctor eyed Arlo, Wyatt and Kerrigan. "I understand you all were at the site with Officer Hayes. I'd like each of you to get checked out, too."

"Why don't we get Sera back to Gavin first?" Arlo slid in smoothly, pulling her forward across the waiting room lobby. "She's been beside herself waiting for news."

The doctor looked unconvinced, but he did extend a hand, gesturing Sera from the room. "Please come with me, Mrs. Hayes."

Sera's head was spinning, the adrenaline rush from hearing that Gavin had been hurt to the second spike when the doctor had asked for her as *Mrs. Hayes.*

Where did he get that idea?

It was only as she passed Kerrigan, the woman's strong arms coming around her in a hug, that Sera got her first clue. "I wanted to make sure you could see Gav as soon as possible. Don't be mad."

Sera hugged back. Hard. "Thank you."

How could she fault the woman for giving her exactly what she wanted and what she feared she could never have?

GAVIN LISTENED TO the steady hum of machines and the air conditioning system and the comings and goings in the hallway and tried to remain steady. Calm. And with his mind *off* the thrumming pain in his body, rippling out in great waves each time he so much as lifted a hand.

God, he felt like he'd been run over.

In a way, he supposed it was an apt description since whatever had detonated at the sub shop had an effect equivalent to an oncoming truck.

He'd been disoriented when he came to in the ambulance, drifting in and out of sleep, but the EMTs had been determined to keep him awake. The fact they kept the back of the emergency vehicle meat-locker-cold had likely helped, as well.

They'd talked him through the ride to the hospital, asking questions and keeping him talking on any number of subjects including the Mets' chances that season. The doctor who took over when he came in had continued the idle chatter, checking him out and peppering medical requests with odd questions obviously designed to make him think.

"Mr. Hayes? I have someone here who'd like to see you." The nurse who stood in the doorway had a smile on her face. "Your wife's been so worried."

Wife?

How hard *had* he hit his head?

And then Sera peeked around the corner, a wry smile on her face that suggested she was in on the joke, even if the nurse was completely serious.

"Hi." He waved her forward, and Sera came straight to him, leaning down and wrapping her arms around him.

If this was a dream, he wasn't going to argue, but when he saw the nurse's indulgent smile from the doorway, he figured he'd better play along and worry about the truth later.

Or just keep flowing with a dream that had suddenly gotten way better than his aches and pains. He had Sera in his arms and all that pain seemed to fade away.

When the nurse was gone, Sera pulled back from the hug. His reflexes weren't at maximum capacity, and he nearly let her before thinking better of it. Lifting a hand to the back of her neck, he tugged her back down for a real kiss.

If she was surprised by the move, she didn't show it. Nor did she even offer a token protest, instead sinking in and kissing him back with a fervor and urgency that matched his own.

He reveled in the moment, unable to believe she was here. He wasn't going to question his good fortune. Instead, he drank her in, savoring everything about her and desperately trying to forget how close he had come to never touching her again.

She finally lifted her head, resettling herself beside him. "Those very hot lips aside, how are you feeling?"

He grinned at that, even as the movement had him wincing slightly at the pain that insisted on going head-to-head with his hormones. "Mrs. Hayes, huh?"

"Kerrigan's doing."

"I'll make sure to thank her later."

"What if we get caught?"

Pain aside, he couldn't stop the bark of laughter at that one.

"What's so funny?"

If he didn't have Sera's hands held tight in his, Gavin suspected she'd have crossed her arms over her chest. "Do you think they ask for marriage licenses at check-in?"

"It was a lie."

"One delivered by a cop. I think you can put your worries aside. Besides—" he lifted a hand out, tracing the curve of her cheek "—I want you here. The patient's always right, you know."

"The patient took a hit to the head if those bruises are any indication." The vivid blue of her eyes clouded over. "What happened to you? Kerrigan said there was an explosion."

"We chased the perp into Archer's sub shop off Bay Street. He took hostages."

"Oh, Gavin. No."

"We got lucky timing-wise. School wasn't out and the big lunch rush was over." He pictured the older woman who'd been pushed out of the restaurant. "But there were still innocent people inside."

"You went into the restaurant?"

He recounted the wait for SWAT and his review of the building and his surroundings.

"Was it like last time?" she asked. "At the bar?"

"No, and that was what got me. The bastard who shot Darius was able to hide in darkness and the various doorways on the opposite side of the street. He also had some sort of exit strategy that got him out of the way quickly. But this time?" Hazy images refilled his mind, and Gavin realized he'd forgotten those last few seconds before the blast.

"What is it?"

"An alleyway. Between the buildings. I had my attention there and told Kerrigan we needed to make sure no one could escape that way. But she said we needed to wait for SWAT."

"She was right." He must have looked ready to argue because Sera barreled right on, cutting him off. "You're lucky you had armor on, but you weren't in full gear. How would you have gone up against someone back there determined to do harm?"

"Which I did have the sense to listen to when Kerrigan made the same basic argument. And I would have stayed put."

"Would have?"

"The moment I saw someone running back there, someone who didn't look like the perp? All bets were off."

"This is your life, Gavin."

"And it was Darius's life. It might be Valencia's life. You think I could let the person responsible get away?"

"No." Sera shook her head. "I know you couldn't."

"Whoever it was, they had other ideas."

"You think there are two killers?"

"It plays. I didn't have a close look at the gunman, but he had a long leanness about him. Whoever ran down the alley was shorter. More solid. And the guy in the alley wasn't dressed like the perp we chased."

"He could have changed inside. Maybe taken clothes from someone there?"

"Sure." Gavin considered it but dismissed it. "Lead the witness all you want, Counselor, but even with my head addled, I'd swear they were two different people."

The small tease was enough to draw a smile out of her, and Gavin had the overwhelming desire to kiss her again. But he held back, also fascinated to see how she worked the puzzle with him. Because while he might prefer kissing her, the increasing sense they had a ticking clock over their heads had become evident with the panicked gunman abandoning his car and making a run through the streets of Brooklyn.

"So you think they're partners, then?" Sera finally said, aligning to his belief there were two perps.

"'Partner' suggests some sort of collaboration. Not one leaving the other for dead."

"It's an oldie but goodie for a reason. There's minimal, if any, honor among thieves."

"Maybe, but—"

He broke off at the high-pitched wail echoing from the hallway, before a very recognizable figure burst into his room.

"Gavin! My baby!" She kept moving, heading straight for the bed where Sera sat beside him, her hands still firmly in his.

He could already feel Sera trying to pull away and off the bed, but he hung on tight. There was no way he was facing this new threat alone.

"The nurse said your wife was with you! Wife! What wife, I said!"

Gavin knew his head wasn't functioning at optimal capacity, and the headache he'd diligently ignored was equally unprepared for the shrieks that hit his skull like the repeated stab of an ice pick.

But pushing it all aside, Gavin still recognized he had a duty. And if he ever hoped to have sex with Sera Forte again, he'd best get to it.

"Mother. Let me introduce you to Sera."

SERA HAD ALWAYS recognized that if she were lucky enough to find someone to be in a long-term relationship with, they were going to come with parents. Her personal circumstance—basically orphaned by her early teens—wasn't the norm, and most individuals in the dating pool still had at minimum one parent. It was the reality of modern life, and she was happy for it. She'd even dated a guy a few years back who had both parents, two stepparents and three other former stepparents, all of whom had remained in his life.

That one had been…a lot. A sweet sort of *a lot*, but somewhat overwhelming all the same.

But even that expansive set of parental figures hadn't prepared her for Evelyn Hayes.

Gavin had determinedly hung on to her hands, but the moment his grip loosened as his mother crossed the room, Sera took her shot and slipped away, getting off the bed. How awkward would it be to meet his mother practically draped over her son?

It was awkward enough the rumor of his "marriage"

had reached her before anyone had the chance to do damage control.

Although Sera stepped away from the bed, she didn't go far. It was time to see this through *and* explain how the hospital staff had come to call her Gavin's wife. Wasn't that what she'd vowed to herself a short while ago, awaiting details in the waiting room with the others? That she wanted her child to know their grandmother? To have a family to lean on and depend on?

"Mrs. Hayes?" Sera addressed the woman, oddly aware she'd been addressed similarly not that long ago.

Evelyn Hayes turned from her son, her face settled in soft, albeit confused, lines.

"I'm Sera."

"Mom, I'm sorry that the two of you are meeting under these circumstances, but Sera's someone very special to me."

"Your wife?"

Although she couldn't be entirely sure, the question sounded more intrigued and excited than angry or upset, and Sera wasn't quite sure what to make of it.

Gavin, however, seemed far less confused. "No." Gavin smiled as Sera fought the grimace. "There was, ah, some miscommunication with the nurse's station about that."

"I see."

Again, Sera searched for something dismissive in the woman, but she was fast catching on that Evelyn Hayes had a bit more fortitude than her initial shrieks entering Gavin's room might suggest. A point she proved as she turned toward Sera and extended her arms for a hug. "I'm Gavin's mom, Evelyn. It's lovely to meet you, dear."

Sera went into those open arms, shocked to realize just

how badly she needed the hug. And how worried she'd been about this meeting. "It's so nice to meet you, too."

Evelyn squeezed her once more before pulling back. "Now. Why don't you two tell me what's going on here? Because you might not be married, but I'm a woman of a certain age who has had plenty of years to read any number of signs as well as social cues."

"Mom—"

Evelyn waved a hand at Gavin, ignoring the urgency in his tone. "Hush. It's not every day a woman's son is nearly blown to bits by a bomb, *and* she finds out she's going to be a grandmother. I'd much rather focus on the latter so I don't fall to pieces over the former."

"How'd... I mean, how do you know I'm pregnant?"

"A mother knows, dear. And since this will be my first grandchild, I can't say I'm sorry about it in the least."

"But we're not—" Sera stopped abruptly, suddenly uncomfortable painting a picture for Gavin's mother of exactly what she and the woman's son were to each other.

It had been convenient to categorize them as a *one-night-stand with consequences*, but that no longer seemed to fit very well. Neither did *two people in a steady relationship*, though, so she was sort of at a loss for how to categorize them.

Evelyn reached out and grabbed her hand. "You don't need to define anything for me. That's for the two of you to decide." With the matter seemingly all figured out, she turned back to Gavin. "How are you feeling?"

"Good."

Sera was close enough to see the exasperation on Evelyn's face before she spoke. "Want to try that again?"

"I am good, all things considered. I thought I'd cracked

a few ribs, but the body armor did its job, and they're just bruised. I did hit my head, but the doctor said it's a mild concussion."

"It's a wonder you escaped something far worse."

"Yeah, well, it's a good thing I have a hard head."

Evelyn leaned in, maneuvering through the wires and the tubes to wrap him in a hug. Although her words were whispered, Sera managed to catch most of them. "It's an even better thing you had on protection."

Sera stepped back, giving the woman a few moments to talk to her son. If it also gave her a few minutes to collect herself, well then, she'd take it. It wasn't every day you met the future grandmother of your child, after all. Nor was it every day you got a hug that felt a lot like welcome, not a whiff of censure anywhere to be found.

She was still reeling and not quite sure what to do about it all.

"It's okay, Mom. Really. I'm fine. I promise."

"What exactly happened?" Evelyn's gaze skipped to the machines, IVs and the two large bandages visible, one on his shoulder, the edges clear beneath his gown, and the other along his jaw.

"We were chasing a suspect, and someone rigged the sandwich shop he ducked into."

"Rigged? What does that mean?" his mother asked.

"Someone blew it up. With a bomb."

"With people inside?"

"I'm afraid so. I've been waiting for updates, but they just released me to have visitors and haven't talked to anyone yet."

She'd watched the tennis match of a conversation between Gavin and his mother and finally realized she had something to contribute. "Kerrigan, Arlo and Wyatt didn't have any details before I came in here, either."

"How did you get here?"

"Darius's brother, Tariq, drove Mack and me over."

"Valencia!" Gavin's eyes widened. "How is she?"

"Unfortunately, there hasn't been any news there, either. She was still in surgery, and none of us had any more details down in the waiting room."

Sera quickly got Evelyn up to speed on what had happened to Valencia outside the church.

"Two shootings? Of family members?" Evelyn shuddered. "Just like your father."

She murmured the words, and Sera saw the way Gavin's expression went cold and bleak. A match for his mother's.

"It's been a long time since Gavin's father died, and that horror is still something I live with every day. This feels similar. Deliberate, even."

"But why?" Gavin asked. "Why would anyone even know who Darius and Valencia were? Or care that one was married to a member of the Harbor team and another on forensics?"

"Fear doesn't need a reason, Gavin. It just needs a target."

DAVID ESPOSITO WALKED into his office and closed the door. He had a slim briefcase with him, but it was big enough to hold a spare change of clothes. He'd changed into that extra suit after leaving the back of Archer's sub shop.

The store had been a good front for him for a long time, Dex Archer more than willing to share the secrets of the neighborhood in exchange for payments and protection.

David had always delivered both. He'd made it his business early on to understand who he could use in each of

Brooklyn's neighborhoods and who had the loyalty to remain silent.

Only now Dex was dead, along with his son, another patron in the shop and the shooter who couldn't handle a damn assignment.

An assignment, David considered as he pulled his soiled clothing out of his briefcase, that he'd planned down to the most minute detail. He'd set it all up perfectly. He'd given the shooter a target, the exact timing to take her out and the perfect place to create maximum chaos with others so he could avoid detection and get away.

And instead, the ass had screwed around, been late to the funeral, hadn't set up well with his long-range scope and had been scattered with his overall focus on the job.

So what had he done?

Instead of ending the job and picking another time to make the hit, he'd rushed it, then proceeded to race through the streets of Sunset Bay waving a gun and shooting into the air.

*Come the hell on.*

David caught himself just before he rested his clothing on the top of his desk, the distinct odors of bomb materials and the dust of the building emanating from the material.

Damn it. Now he was the one who was scattered, making idiot, amateur mistakes.

He'd brought the clothing here to hide it in a legal box on his shelf. No one touched his files, and he'd leave it here, disposing of it at a later time. It always amazed him how little people paid attention to the files at work and how easy it was to use innocuous cardboard boxes people ignored every day as a parking lot for things he wanted to go unnoticed. He'd collect the soiled clothes in a few weeks and dump them, no one the wiser.

Right now, he had a bigger problem.

Because his shooter had botched the job, there was no way of knowing if the lovely wife he'd targeted was dead or not. And he needed her dead for this all to work.

Mack Phillips was leading the Hell Gate forensics work and had been lead on several other cases David's team had prosecuted. The man was thorough and often caught things others missed.

It was why he required this distraction from the Hell Gate work. And it was why David had required the man's wife pay the price for that dedication.

With the clothes safely stowed at the bottom of a brown file box, David finagled a few folders on top of it, then closed the lid. With a deep breath, he considered his next moves and then repeated them in his mind.

He was in control, and he would see this through, exactly as he'd planned. No case was perfect. No trial flawless. Realistically, he knew that. Hell, he'd made a damn career out of it. And always—*always*—he managed to come out on top. Just like he'd do here.

He'd deal with the clothes later.

Pending the wife's surgery outcome, he'd figure out how he wanted to handle Mack Phillips.

And he'd line up the next target.

Because David had learned the most important lesson early in his career as a young lawyer: when the momentum was building, you didn't let up off the gas.

You pushed and pushed until you got the verdict you were aiming for.

## Chapter Fifteen

Gavin would have preferred to be in the emergency waiting room with the rest of the team, supporting Mack however he could, but the doctors refused to let him go without overnight observation.

They had moved him out of the emergency ward into a regular room, and it had become something of a war room for the team, people coming in groups, two by two, as they got information throughout the evening.

Gavin had caught the frustration of one of the nurses after Arlo had brought burgers in, but the head nurse on duty had addressed the situation with him.

"Give the cops the space to do their work," she'd admonished before giving Arlo a wink.

That was all it had taken. She'd even given the man he was sharing a room with his own private one down the hall to allow for more space to work. And Arlo had called out and ordered up more burgers for the nurse's station to smooth over any ruffled feathers.

It wasn't a conference room at the 86th, but it would have to do.

Which made the quiet moment, with no one in the room except for Sera, a reprieve he hadn't known he needed.

"How are you holding up?"

She glanced up from writing in a small notebook, a gentle smile on her face. "I could ask the same of you."

"I'm…" He stopped, realizing he could only give her honesty. "I'm tired."

"Would I be a traitor to the cause to say same?"

They'd reduced the number of attachments running in and out of his body down to a lone IV, and he used the additional freedom to extend a hand. "Come sit with me."

She nodded and tucked the notebook in her bag. When she made to sit on the edge of the mattress, he shifted, pulling her closer. "I'd really like to hold you."

It was a bold ask, one that he wasn't necessarily entitled to, but when her blue eyes went hazy and slightly unfocused, he realized he'd asked just right.

"I'd really like that, too."

She slipped out of her shoes—heels he had no idea how she'd managed in all day—before climbing in next to him and stretching out.

"Are you o—"

He had his lips on hers before she could finish the sentence, sheer relief washing through him at having her close. The soft sigh that escaped the back of her throat made him wish for different circumstances. For a different place to see this through to completion.

Because whatever else had happened over the past few weeks, the two of them drawing closer to one another had been the most important.

The heat and desire and overwhelming *need* he'd felt at the New Year had only grown stronger, with the added dimensions of their journey to parenthood as well as the opportunity to see her passion for her work.

Her deep commitment and belief in what she was doing.

Her determination to seek justice.

And her deep, deep feelings and care for others.

All had touched him, reinforcing that initial attraction with the realities of what made a life with someone.

Of what made two people fall in love.

She was so responsive to him, her kiss as warm and welcoming as the rest of her. And as Gavin lifted his head, laying his forehead against hers, the things he'd only been able to *feel* up to now suddenly had words.

He loved her.

He loved Sera.

And he wanted to make a life with her.

He was as sure of those things as his next breath, but he wasn't as positive she felt the same. So he'd give her a bit of space. Give them a few days to get to the other side of this latest eruption of violence and hate, and then he'd tell her. They had her appointment with the ultrasound coming up, and he could already picture drawing her close after and telling her how he felt.

In the meantime, he was going to revel in the moment. And he was going to take these few minutes of peace.

Which made the stirring in his arms and whispered "I'm sorry" a jarring counterpoint to the quiet he floated on.

"Sera?"

"I'm sorry. Really, Gavin, I am. I just…" She disengaged from his arms and ran back to her purse, grabbing the notebook she'd stuffed in the side. "It's just that I think I put something together."

Sera had contributed throughout the evening, just like she had a few days before back at the precinct, so it was no surprise she was set on something. Her lack of police procedural knowledge was offset by one of the keenest minds he'd ever seen, and she caught on quickly when there was a topic she wasn't fully versed on. She also wasn't afraid to ask questions, no matter how small or specific.

In fact, Gavin had to admit it was that focus on the specifics that had led to a few key discussion points, namely how the shooter had gotten so close to the funeral and why Mack's wife, Valencia, was targeted.

"What are you thinking?"

"It's what your mom said. Before. About fear not needing a reason. Just a target."

"You think someone's trying to incite fear."

"Yes, but for a very specific reason. Darius. Valencia. They were specifically chosen targets."

"Targeted why?" Gavin watched as the connections lit up inside of her, the past few weeks seeming to coalesce in a flash.

"It's the guns, Gavin. Up at Hell Gate." She paced back toward him, rattling the hints off as she saw them. "That's the start. Of all of this."

"Which is why they should be coming after cops. Instead, Darius and Valencia are collateral damage?"

The words practically burned his lips, the raw anger something he hadn't felt in a long time.

Not since his father…

But it was Sera who had the calm logic to see past it all. "Darius is married to one of the divers who worked the guns. Valencia is married to one of the forensics team members who handled them. It's fear by association."

Gavin felt the way the room seemed to electrify, her idea taking root and bringing him to a sitting position. He winced at the movement, but there was no way he could lie down for this.

"Here." She was by his side in an instant, fiddling with the electric riser function. "This will be easier."

With his bed set into a sitting position, Gavin pieced it together along with her, poking and prodding, adding and subtracting along the way.

"Okay, but let's pressure test this. I get the connection you're making, but Darius was murdered the day the team brought up the rest of the guns. That's awfully fast between Jayden working the dump site and his husband being shot."

Sera stilled, turning it over. "You've all said it, but in different ways. The guns were a sophisticated operation, not some random find. The dump location. The missing serial numbers. Someone planning like that would have to have an exit strategy."

"Okay, then next point. Why Darius specifically? Why Valencia? There are other divers. Other forensics team members." He knew he was playing devil's advocate, but they needed to ask the questions.

If the Hell Gate guns were the root of all this, then they'd been looking in the wrong place, just trying to find a shooter. It was a necessity, but if the gunman was nothing more than a tool, catching him stopped the violence, but it didn't stop the underlying problem.

And like a hydra, it would only regrow a head somewhere else.

"Jayden brought the guns up. Mack was on the team processing the evidence." Sera's mouth fell as that last piece clicked. "Spouses. Partners for life. Maybe there was some selection process, but it has to be tied to the NYPD members who worked the site."

"You go after the cop, you get a lot of cops riled. Go after their loved ones, get them scared," Arlo said, stepping into the room. "Kerrigan's been saying that all along. And sorry if I'm interrupting, but I couldn't miss overhearing it all outside the door."

"It's a horrible strategy," Gavin considered. "But it's effective."

"It's also a perfect way to hide." Arlo took a seat in one of the small folding chairs the nurse had brought in for him and the others earlier. "And it gives even more credence to the angle I've been running down on a well-run, organized offering to those who can pay for it to dispose of their guns, essentially making their crimes go away."

"Your informant," Gavin remembered. "Kerrigan mentioned her."

"Jade's rock-solid with the intel, and I think she's onto something. Unfortunately, I haven't been able to find a single line to tug on that one. Whispers and rumors aren't evidence, no matter how telling they really are."

Sera had remained quiet in Arlo's overview, but finally spoke, adding one more dimension to the problem. "The chain of evidence. Remove the gun, and it's awfully hard for someone like me to prosecute you."

Arlo nodded. "Damn hard."

It made sense. And more than that, it gave support to why someone would create a fear campaign to protect their interests.

*Fear doesn't need a reason. It just needs a target.*

"The loved ones *are* the target," Gavin said, seeing it all in his mind's eye. Remembering those tense moments out in front of the bar and that feeling of being watched. Because they had been. But they weren't the end game. "We thought it was us, but we were the diversion. It was Darius all along."

Even as the reality of it all hit him, Gavin felt that anger and fury riling him up, just like Arlo said.

And as fast as it came on, it quickly shifted in a new direction.

Because if the loved ones of cops were now the target, he'd just put a bull's-eye on Sera.

And he was wholly, desperately, irrevocably in love with the mother of his child.

WYATT AND KERRIGAN rejoined them, fresh bottles of water in hand for her and Gavin, coffees for the rest of them as they swept through the door of Gavin's room.

And they brought good news. The best news, Sera thought, as Kerrigan recounted all she'd learned in the past half hour.

"Valencia came through surgery. She's got a long recovery ahead of her, but the doctors have every confidence she's going to be fine. She'll spend the night in intensive care, but they're already talking about possibly moving her tomorrow."

"That's amazing." Sera swallowed hard around the distinct tightening of her throat, the prick of tears behind her eyes hot as they spilled over.

Kerrigan came to stand with her, her support absolute as she wrapped an arm around her shoulders. "Now fill me in on what I missed."

Gavin caught everyone up on all they'd discussed.

"Weaponizing our fear," Wyatt practically spit out the words.

"And preying on cops' families," Arlo added.

Although the tears still threatened, the renewed round of anger as Wyatt, Arlo and Kerrigan got on the same page as she and Gavin went a long way toward reigniting her own fury. And with it, Sera considered all she knew from her job. All the cases she'd prosecuted and all that she understood about the inner workings of the city she'd served for nearly a decade.

At the heart of it all was data.

Human beings were the victims, but they were targeted via databases. And someone with access and motive.

"Everything since Darius was shot has been focused on the gunman. We need to look at the data. The forensics on the guns. Who would have access to HR data. And how to trace any comings and goings at Hell Gate."

Gavin added, "It's like the work for the task force. What are the systems in place? Where are the gaps? And if you can find those, you can find the points of risk."

"I can clearly see all you've laid out," Kerrigan started in, "But I'm not making the connection with the gun recovery. Where's anyone getting the details on our work? It's not like they can get up there and see what we're doing."

"Cameras?" Arlo asked.

Kerrigan shook her head. "That bridge isn't easily navigated. It's not a pedestrian bridge. It just carries the Amtrak trains."

"Via electrified train lines," Wyatt added. "You'd have to be a fool to try to walk up there. Even if you knew how to skip the lines, trains run through there all day."

"You can bike and run the Hell Gate Pathway to Randall's Island," Kerrigan said, considering. "If someone found a way there, they could try watching what's going on. It's been a while since I've been up there, but I don't remember a lot of easy water access, though, to get a good lookout."

"The guns weren't directly under the bridge, though." Sera brought up a clear picture in her mind of the area where the Harbor team had brought up the cache. "It was a bit of a ways down the shoreline, on the Manhattan side just below Randall's Island. Maybe they're not watching from the bridge at all."

"All true." Kerrigan nodded.

"Very true, Kerr," Wyatt said. "Remember how bad the water was? We'd scoped several quadrants north and south from the dump point off the RFK. It was sheer dumb luck we found that cache. And we only found it because the water was running so hard, we had to expand our search."

"I'm not sure your work was dumb luck, Wyatt." Gavin was quick to support his friend and dive partner.

"But it sort of was," Wyatt pressed. "We'd never have been that close to the shoreline if we'd found what we were diving for. Those guns could have stayed there for who knows how much longer, and we'd never have been the wiser."

"But you did find it. And someone's awfully upset their dumping ground is gone." Arlo three-pointed his empty coffee cup into a nearby trash can. "So now we need to figure out who."

Sera might not have a physical component to her job, nor was she trained in cop work, but she did know research. Forward, backward and upside down if needed. She knew how to dig into the most obscure points until she had an answer. She'd done it in law school and had spent the better part of her professional life doing the same.

"Those guns are evidence, Arlo. If you can get me

descriptions, I can look at recent cases. See if anything pops there."

It felt ridiculous to be talking about teeing up her work databases in the middle of a hospital room, but she needed to do *something*. And this was something she was very, very good at.

Through a cop's eyes, the goal was to find physical evidence. But for her? The evidence was just the place to start. She was on the hunt for motive.

One strong enough and desperate enough to kill without compunction.

A WEEK.

It had been a damn week, and she had nearly made her eyes bleed she'd hunted through so many files. Haunted every database she could find to search for details. She'd even gone to the file storage facility they housed in Red Hook to get her hands on a few old files that had seemed promising.

And still, nothing.

Not one damn thing.

Sera threw her pencil on top of her desk, about ready to call it a day. She still had a brief to write, and she wanted to get to Gavin's for dinner.

And to surreptitiously see how he was doing.

She hadn't made a big deal of it, but she suspected he had downplayed the pain from his injuries. That, along with the worry for his concussion, had her working hard to avoid the mother hen routine. She hadn't fully succeeded, but had usually been able to subdue his suspicions with a well-placed kiss.

Since they turned heated quickly, it was enough to distract him.

Even if she was paying for it with a raging case of hormones—amplified even further by her pregnancy—and a healing man who wasn't fit yet for sex. No matter how much he tried to convince her otherwise.

Even with her hormones on overdrive, she refused to be swayed. The doctor had discharged Gavin the day after the explosion, but he'd been put on medical leave from active duty for a week, with a required appointment to be cleared to return.

His checkup was tomorrow, so there was that, at least, Sera admitted to herself. It would hopefully confirm he'd healed, it would get him back to work and, if she were lucky, distracted enough for her to figure out what she was going to do.

Because with every day she spent with him, she was forgetting all the reasons she'd believed she needed to hold her heart separate. In fact, each day had brought them closer, the kissing only a portion of the growing intimacy between them. They spoke of everything, from the case to their task force to their overarching career ambitions. Places they liked in Brooklyn, favorite restaurants and a rather heated debate over the best slice of pizza.

He also wasn't afraid to keep pushing on her lingering feelings over her parents, gently drawing her down the path of accepting their responsibilities and shortcomings in raising children by contrasting it to how the two of them wanted to raise their own child. And in return, she ensured they invited his mother to dinner one night and gave her one of those ultrasound photos, too.

But it had been the day he'd brought up names for their

child when Sera finally admitted that the careful wall she'd built to keep her heart intact was crumbling, brick by brick.

Which only further reinforced why she had to focus on the work and off Gavin's body. Or the way she felt when they were together. And definitely off parts farther south.

*It's not like you can get more pregnant...*

That little voice had grown stronger, popping up with that argument at inopportune times.

Like when she was kissing him.

Or brushing her teeth.

Or pouring a cup of coffee.

Pretty much every hour no matter what task she was engaged in.

It was why she'd started a nightly visit with his team to keep them all mentally engaged.

Each night Gavin, Kerrigan, Arlo and Wyatt would regroup. Arlo outlined whatever he'd discovered in the course of the investigation while Kerrigan and Wyatt provided updates on the harbor work and feedback from the forensics team on the guns. Sera and Marlowe would then apply their non-cop brains to alternative theories. So far, they'd run the gamut from another crime leader trying for the top spot in town to a new drug node making a go of it to a murder-for-hire group.

Even as each one netted out as a dead end.

Through it all, Sera couldn't stop thinking there was something they were missing. Something that would explain the erased serial numbers of the guns. No matter how many times she considered the woefully small set of details they knew, that was the one she kept circling back to.

Even the cleanup from the burned-out sub shop hadn't given them a lot to go on, although they did find out the name of the gunman. He'd been a careful criminal who tended to operate alone, with a relatively short rap sheet after a lifetime of crime. He hadn't been high on Arlo's list of local suspects to investigate, but when a search of his home produced ballistics evidence that matched the shots that killed Darius and also shot Valencia, it had given them some measure of reassurance they'd caught the right guy.

It wasn't much, but it was the one bright spot they'd had in the case, and she knew they were all clinging to it.

"Sera, do you have a minute?"

The interruption was welcome from the endless maze of her thoughts, and she jumped at the opportunity for a diversion. "David! Of course."

They hadn't seen much of each other with her task force work keeping her out of the office, and she was surprised, as he took a seat on the other side of her desk, to see that he was looking tired. Even more, he looked *worn*. While she fully recognized everyone went through periods of difficulty, she had to admit it was a shock to see him looking less than the dapper figure he cut in the courtroom and around town.

It was hardly a fair assessment. The pressure on him was immense, the responsibility for ensuring justice for a borough filled with more than two million people unrelenting.

With her smile firmly intact, she wondered how she could provide support. "Is there anything I can help you with?"

"I came to ask you the same. The news of what's been happening out of the 86th is concerning. Especially when it came to my attention that you were involved."

"Oh, well, I—" She wasn't sure what to say. His tone was conciliatory, with a clear layer of concern. But it was overlaid with...well, *censure*, Sera admitted to herself. "I wouldn't say I was involved."

"You weren't there?"

"Yes, I was. But thankfully, I wasn't the target. I was able to help."

"These are terrible risks, Sera. I put you up for the task force because I wanted to see you advance. But I can't afford to lose you."

"I hardly think—" She'd barely worked up a head of steam when she stopped at the strange twist of his lips.

What was going on with him?

David Esposito hadn't become one of the city's top legal minds—*or* the district attorney of New York's largest borough—because he was easily swayed. But she also wasn't comfortable sitting by letting him think she was going to kowtow to some ridiculous order to stand down when someone needed help.

Or was this simply a different side of him?

She'd worked for him for years and had believed she knew him, but it was entirely possible she'd only seen a side of him that he wanted her to see. And since she'd cultivated a reputation of quiet acceptance of the endless workload all while driving impeccable results, he'd had no reason to show her displeasure.

But now?

*I put you up for the task force because I wanted to see you advance. But I can't afford to lose you.*

Lose her?

Well, he'd shown his true colors that every action—every opportunity given—was only to advance his own standing. It was sad, but really, why should her boss be any different from anyone else?

"You hardly think what, Sera? That you're not at physical risk from the madman prowling the streets? You're fraternizing with the same people who are being targeted. How does that make you safe?"

Whatever else she might have said, it all died away. David actually thought she might be at risk of being killed?

"David, it was two incredibly unfortunate incidents. The gunman for both crimes has been caught, and the case has been closed. I'm fine."

"Until you become a target."

Something distinctly cold uncoiled in her gut at his insistence.

"It's a risk we all carry working in this office," he pressed on. "One that you're now flaunting by traipsing around town with a killer on the loose."

What was wrong with him? And using words like *flaunt* and *traipse*? As if she were flouncing around town in a ball gown and heels, taunting a killer?

One who'd been caught in a trap of his own making.

None of it made sense, coming from someone she respected.

And it was only because of those long years of working together, on top of that worn-out look that stretched his normally smooth veneer, that Sera tried to find some sort of common ground in the midst of his put-downs.

"David, if you're concerned about my work, please tell me. Otherwise, I'm afraid I need to stress that I'm hardly flaunting anything. I may be a public defender, but I'm also free to live my life as I see fit."

"I care about you, Sera. About your well-being."

"I care about my well-being, too. In fact—" She hesitated briefly, almost thinking better of saying anything during this odd and inappropriate debate between the two of them. But her body was changing by the day, and she wasn't interested in hiding the truth any longer, either. "I have some happy news."

"Oh?"

"I'm pregnant."

"You're—" It was his turn to catch himself, more of those strange emotions crossing his face. "That's wonderful news, Sera. Babies are a celebration. A wonderful affirmation of life."

"I think so."

She got the distinct sense he was about to ask her about her personal life, especially since he knew she wasn't married or in a relationship, when he seemed to think better of it.

In fact...

If she wasn't sitting right opposite him, watching for his reaction, she had no doubt she'd have missed it. But with a brief flash of awareness, she saw it.

A sort of knowing in his dark brown eyes.

And quite without knowing why, Sera fought off the wash of cold that gripped her bones with fierce fingers and refused to let go.

ALTHOUGH HE TECHNICALLY wouldn't be cleared for work until tomorrow, Gavin had refused to sit home when he'd heard that Captain Reed was going to honor Mack and Valencia with a small reception at the hospital.

Valencia had made incredible progress, her own determination to leave the hospital matched with the incredible good fortune that the gunman had missed several major organs when he'd shot her. And this evening she was going home.

It was just like Captain Reed, his focus and care for his people the endless proof of how strong a leader he was and why they all had such unswerving loyalty for the man. And because of it, Gavin had headed out to the hospital, pleased to be there for something hopeful instead of the reasons for the past few weeks' visits.

He'd also gone to visit Jayden on his way over. He was finishing up his bereavement leave and would be back on Harbor the following week. Gavin had extended an invite to join him for the small party, but Jayden had declined, using a dinner at his mother's house as his excuse for missing it.

Gavin gave him the space, well aware the man could have done both, but recognized why this was too big a leap right now. And why, no matter how positively Jayden felt that Valencia was heading home, it couldn't erase the fact that his husband would never do the same.

But his parting words still stuck in Gavin's chest.

*Thanks for being there for me, man. At the hospital and in all the time since. And thanks for inviting me tonight. Keep asking. One of these days I'll be ready.*

He'd lived years with that lack of readiness. Probably too long, if he were honest with himself. And it made the reality of the changes Sera had brought to his life deeply affirming.

It was also proof that people could not only heal, but they could find their way back to something good.

Oh, how he wanted that someday for Jayden.

His text notification went off, and he pulled his phone out as he walked the last block to the hospital.

Almost there. You won't believe the day I had.

He stopped to text her back, stalling on the sidewalk so he could greet her and walk in with her.

Can't wait to see you. You can tell me all about it.

As he hit Send, Gavin couldn't hold back the smile. The fact they could share things at the end of the day had very quickly become one of the best parts of his evening, and he couldn't wait to put an arm around her and pull her close.

It was that steadily growing need to be with her, to talk to her, to *touch* her that drove him. Where before he had found that solace in a job well done and in pushing himself to be the best physically and mentally, all that energy had shifted.

Not that the work was less important or that he wanted to cut back on his conditioning, but it...consumed less. And instead, he was consumed with Sera. With their talk of the baby that would be here in a few short months. With the future he envisioned for the three of them.

What had begun as intense sexual desire had combined with the deepest sort of intimacy and interest in another person. And the more time he spent with her, the less he could see his life without her in it.

It had his heart catching in his throat as he saw her walking toward him from the opposite direction. And even though she was so close, he couldn't stand still, waiting for her. He caught her up halfway down the block, pulling her close and nearly off her feet.

"Gavin!" The breeze caught strands of her dark red hair whipping around her face, carrying her laughter up on the air.

"I missed you."

She stilled, her smile dimming as it moved to her eyes while her arms lifted to wrap around his neck. "I missed you, too."

Their mouths met, an affirmation of all he'd anticipated while waiting for her. And as he sank into her, taking her lips with his own and spinning them on a wild ride of yearning and fulfillment, he knew it was time to tell her how he felt.

Later. When they were alone and could talk. It was time to tell her how he felt. How much he wanted her and a future with her. And how determined he was to show her every day what she meant to him.

"Well, I think I know why all my days used to drag." Her arm was still around his neck, her smile flashing in the dying light of the day.

"Drag how?"

"They didn't include welcome kisses at the end of the day like that. I like it."

He nipped her lips for one more quick kiss. "Me, too."

They turned to head into the hospital complex hand in hand when he heard his name from across the street. Captain Reed's wife, Miranda, and their youngest daughter, Zuri, waved at him from the crosswalk, and he waved back, indicating they'd wait for them.

The early evening was quiet, the steady hum of traffic moving through the light at a sedate pace. It was only as it turned yellow, the various cars slowing, that Gavin heard it. The crazy, out-of-control swerving that indicated someone wasn't stopping.

He shouted to Miranda and Zuri, who were already stepping off the sidewalk. And then he took off at a run, determined to reach them before whoever was bearing down could get to them first.

Determined that one more loved one of a cop wasn't going to end up in the building behind him.

## Chapter Sixteen

Sera distributed the small pieces of cake even though she had no interest in eating. Gavin was still outside with Captain Reed, Arlo, Wyatt and Kerrigan as well as several other uniforms on patrol in the neighborhood, viewing the crime scene and taking pictures.

Captain Reed hadn't been able to stop touching his wife and child as they'd stood out on the street corner, recovering from the shock of the oncoming car and Gavin's race across the street that had tackled them both to the ground.

She'd wanted to do the same for Gavin, but had given him the space to focus on what happened, relaying each detail to the captain including what little he'd seen of the driver.

When the initial shock faded, Captain Reed had finally brought Miranda and Zuri into the hospital cafeteria where they'd set up the cake for Valencia and asked them stay there.

"I still don't know what to say." Miranda had moved up beside her to cut the cake after Valencia had done the honors on the first piece. Sera suspected the busy movements were keeping the woman from mentally reviewing each and every moment of the attack, and she'd avoided suggesting she sit down.

Sometimes action was the best medicine, and right now

she could console herself that she was taking care of her husband's team.

"You're sure you're okay?"

"We are because of Gavin." Miranda's hand shook as she picked up a few more plates to move them to the end of a long table where people were helping themselves to the cut squares. Her gaze unerringly found her daughter, where Zuri played with Mack and Valencia's daughter, Gia, across the room. "I can't stop going over it in my mind."

"It's so fresh it's hard to digest. But it will fade in time." Sera tried to offer as much consolation as she could. "Become less urgent."

"I know." Miranda nodded, grief filling her deep brown eyes. "And I know there will come a day I don't want to latch myself onto my child and never let her go. Which I promise I won't do." The woman smiled. "Or won't after I give myself a solid week of overcompensating."

Miranda took a deep breath. "But we will get through this. Because I'm a cop's wife, and I know the risks. What I won't get over is why some monster has decided my family and Mack's family and Jayden's family are disposable targets, used to meet some sick end."

Miranda's use of the word *target* had Sera's mind shifting back to that odd conversation with David earlier.

*David, it was two incredibly unfortunate incidents. The gunman of both crimes has been caught and the case has been closed. I'm fine.*

*Until you become a target.*

He'd used that word, too. Target.

And now there was a third incident, in such a short period of time. The risks had expanded, the inclusion of a child in this attack a dark sign of escalation. How did they fight this? Because if random street-level attacks were suddenly the norm, no one was safe.

Which made the large hand that covered her shaking one as she picked up a few more small plates of cake a welcome relief.

"Hey there."

She looked up to find Gavin, his expression soft as he gently took the plates from her, setting them back on the table before pulling her close.

There wasn't even a heartbeat of hesitation as she went into his arms.

And as that same heartbeat thrummed against his, she tried to calm her racing thoughts. Who was doing this? And if they'd escalated their fear-based targeting to children, how much more appealing would it be to go after a pregnant woman?

IN HIS NEARLY ten years at the 86th, Gavin had seen their captain mad—even furious on occasion—but nothing had prepared him for the blind rage that had cloaked the man this evening.

Someone had come after his family.

That reality would always have been upsetting, but now that he was facing fatherhood, Gavin understood the rage in a whole new dimension. All-consuming, with a desperate need to protect that refused to be sated.

He still struggled with it as he took Sera home, hypervigilant to any possible threat. It was only when they finally reached her door, both of them safely inside the apartment, that he let out his first easy breath.

"Why don't you come in and sit down for a bit?" Her voice was gentle as she gestured him toward the couch. "I know you keep telling me you're fine, but you're still re-covering from bruised ribs and a mild concussion. Today was another difficult day."

He tried to process Sera's words, but all he heard—all he really understood—was that his family was in danger. He'd lived with that outcome once, and there was no way he could go back there. No way he'd survive it again.

"I can't lose you."

"Gavin, I—"

Her words vanished as his arms came around her, burying his head in her neck. Breathing her in. Wanting desperately to build a life with this woman and the child they'd created.

"You're not going to lose me," she whispered against the side of his head. "We're here, and we're not going anywhere."

He wanted to believe it. Even now, with all the strife and uncertainty, he could see that future he wanted. Could see the life he wanted to create for his child.

"But, Gavin. Right here. Right now. It's just us."

He felt her meaning before it registered, the kiss she pressed to the side of his head followed by featherlight kisses over his forehead, his eyebrows, his cheekbone. She con-tinued that miraculous exploration, on down over the day's worth of stubble on his cheeks to his lips.

Only then did she take his mouth fully with her own, the warmest welcome he'd ever known.

"Come all the way inside with me."

She took his hand and without waiting for him to say anything, drew him into her apartment and back toward the bedroom.

The work bag she'd carried home fell somewhere along the way, as did the raincoat she'd worn.

He vaguely felt her stop their movement to discard her shoes and insist he do the same.

Halfway down the hall to her bedroom, she slipped off the blazer she wore. His shirt ended up floating to the floor beside it.

And by the time they stepped into her bedroom, he had her slim figure in his arms, clad in nothing but a thin blouse and skirt, pressed to his bare chest. With her hands on him and his deftly removing what little remained, in a matter of moments Gavin was laying her down on the bed, naked and gorgeous beneath him.

"You're even more beautiful than I remembered." He ran a trail of kisses over her throat. "And I remember really—" he pressed a kiss "—really—" and then another "—really well."

She sighed under his mouth, and he continued his exploration, on over her pretty expanse of cleavage before trailing his tongue over her breast. Soft moans filled the air, her body growing more restless beneath him as he took a nipple between his teeth. Her throaty response grew deeper, huskier, and he was gratified to know he gave her pleasure.

The signs of her pregnancy were everywhere, and as Gavin sat back and looked his fill, he had to admit the changes were gorgeous on her. Her breasts had an additional roundness that wasn't there before, her hips, too. But it was the light swell of her stomach that captivated him.

Their child was there, nestled safe inside of her.

Sheer awe coursed through him as he bent and pressed his lips to that slight mound, imagining the small, perfect little form growing just beyond. Once again, that fierce need to protect rose up and swamped him, practically stealing his breath with its intensity.

*His.* They were his, and he'd give his life for them. Without thinking. Without hesitation.

Even with those feral thoughts raging through him, he felt the gentleness surround them. But it was the soft light in Sera's eyes, as he lifted his gaze to hers, that nearly did him in. Whatever had brought them to this moment—whatever trials they'd faced so far and whatever they'd face in future—he knew he wanted to face them with her.

As partners.

As protectors.

And, with the miracle growing between them, as parents.

"Gavin."

Her voice was whisper-soft, even as he heard the distinct notes of a demand beneath the quiet. Had his name ever sounded so sweet? So perfect?

And had he ever been more ready for a woman than he was at this moment? That insistent hum in the blood that could only be sated by making her his had ratcheted up so that he could hear nothing else. So that he could only *feel*.

He removed his slacks and underwear, the last barrier between them, and gave himself up to her.

It had been more than three months since they'd been together, but the pleasure arcing between them felt as familiar as breathing. And as new as a sunrise.

He positioned himself at the entrance to her body and stared down into her eyes. The woman he'd believed he would never see again—never touch again—had somehow found her way back to him.

It was a miracle mixed with a beautiful twist of fate.

And he would never take any of it for granted. Would never take what they had between them for granted.

There was still so much to figure out, but what had

seemed unconquerable only a few weeks ago now seemed like an open road ahead. One they'd navigate together.

And as he felt her deft touch take him in hand, teasing his flesh as she guided him to her core, Gavin knew another truth. There was no other woman in the world for him. No other woman who could be so utterly perfect for him. No other woman who felt like home.

*Home*, he thought as their bodies joined, quickly finding a rhythm that worked for them both.

Whatever life had thrown at them both up to now, none of it mattered. Instead, the winding path to each other had provided perspective, wisdom and an understanding of why no one else had been right before. Why this time and this place was finally, perfectly, right.

When he felt the tell-tale signs of her release, his quickly followed.

And he let her welcome him home.

WAS IT POSSIBLE to live on sex alone?

Sera knew the realities of her body suggested she'd have to move sooner or later for food and water, but in that instant, wrapped up in Gavin, she'd be content to stay here forever.

"Are you awake?" She whispered the words into the air, unable to move for the heavy sprawl of man who lay over her. It was a magical sensation, even if it limited mobility. Or, she hated to admit, a bit of her breath.

She didn't have to wait long for an answer, his smile wide when he lifted himself up onto his elbows to look down on her. "Sorry. You made me forget my own name there for a while."

Sheer delight coursed through her at his compliment. "Aren't you sweet?"

"Actually, I'm a bit brain-dead, but who really needs the ability to balance a checkbook?"

"Those are the brain cells you gave up?"

"I wasn't all that good at it anyway, so you've given me an outstanding excuse."

She laughed at the silliness of it all, even as she had to admit his thoughts weren't too far off the mark. "I was trying to calculate how long a person could stay in bed having sex without needing food or water."

"And miss out on the decadence of having food in bed after sex?"

"You're hungry?"

"For you, always." He bent down and pressed a kiss to her shoulder. "For pizza?" A wry smile lit his face. "Always."

Sera laughed again, pure, simple joy roaring through her in a flood. For the magic of being together again. And the warm, wonderful reassurance of his body covering hers.

"Now that you mention pizza, I am a bit hungry." She tickled his side, the motion enough to have him moving slightly, giving her the opportunity to slide out from beneath him and neatly flip their position.

And while she was hungry for pizza—and would dial up her favorite neighborhood delivery in a bit—she was more interested in exploring the man in her bed a bit longer.

*Or forever.*

The thought whispered through her, beating in time with the heavy pumping of her blood.

Where that would have scared her even a week before, now…it didn't. And wasn't that a miracle in and of itself? The belief she wasn't worthy of something good and lasting—or worse, that she was incapable of it—had faded. What was actually fear, way down deep, that she'd held to so tightly for so long had been upended by this man.

By his patience. His insistence. And by the amazing fact that he showed up, fully present. Hadn't that been something of a revelation? From the first moments of knowing about the pregnancy, he'd made it clear he wasn't going anywhere. He was a part of his child's life, and nothing about that had wavered, not for one single instant.

And maybe, if she took the leap and voiced what she wanted, he'd stay for her, too.

It was a risk, Sera knew. But the reward was so very great.

Bending down from where she straddled his hips, she kissed him. And in the sweetness of meeting lips and the responsive male beneath her, Sera finally knew what she needed.

To be happy.

To feel safe.

To find her future.

All of it was more important—even more than sex or food or the safe cocoon she locked herself in—if she wanted to find the pathway to a future for her and her child.

And it all rested with Gavin.

"I love you."

The words she'd never spoken as an adult felt right. *Perfect*, actually.

His dark eyes never wavered from hers, but the hands that had settled on her lower back while they'd kissed moved to gently cup her cheeks.

"I love you, Sera. I want to build a future with you. For

our child, yes, but with you. Somehow, someway, I sensed that from the very first moments."

"Me, too." She closed her eyes before allowing them to pop back open. Here. With him. There was nothing to hide from. "I ran out on New Year's Day because I didn't believe this could be real. That you couldn't actually feel this way about someone so quickly. But I was wrong."

He lifted to meet her halfway for a kiss, their love for each other wrapping around them. And as she sank into him, the two of them falling back to the bed, it was a long while later before either of them thought about anything but each other.

"I HAVE TO hand it to you, Gavin Hayes. Sex pizza is pretty great."

"Sex pizza?" Gavin asked, still floating on a satisfied mix of outrageously good sex, perfect pizza dough and the woman beside him in bed.

The woman he loved.

"I can't say I've had all that much sex pizza." She eyed him as she took a small bite of her cheese slice. "Or any sex pizza since I assume it requires sticking around and sharing a meal. But I have to say, it's an inspired choice."

If he were honest, he couldn't say he'd had all that much "sex pizza," either. He'd had pizza after sex, standing alone in his kitchen, and he'd had it before, grabbing a slice somewhere before going out. But never in his life could he remember eating it naked in bed with a woman. "Me, either."

"I wonder why that is. It's pretty great."

He leaned in and licked a small drop of sauce at the corner of her mouth she hadn't yet gotten with her napkin. "It's awesome with the right person. Which you most definitely are." He reached for another slice from the heavy cardboard box they'd laid out in the middle of the bed. "But I'm not sure I've ever wanted this sort of intimacy with another person."

"Sex is intimacy."

"So's eating food. And sharing stories. And talking. I never had that before you, Sera."

"I've never had that, either." The smile that filled her face dimmed, the carefree light seeming to fade from her eyes.

"What's wrong?"

"I can't help but think of Jayden. Of all he's lost. I found you over these past few weeks, and he's lost the same beautiful life."

"I know."

And he did know. The loss his friend was facing was the pain none of them could forget. The stark counterpoint to the sheer joy he felt in finding Sera again and preparing for their baby's arrival.

Sera set down her pizza and turned, laying a hand on his arm. "He's not alone. You, Kerrigan, all of you, really. You'll see to that. But for him now? The future must feel like an endless stretch in front of him. Something to be dreaded instead of embraced."

"It's the senselessness of it I still can't get my head around. And you see a lot of senseless waste as a cop. But to target loved ones to hide your crimes? To scare cops and divert them from the work?"

The hand on his forearm tightened, Sera's gaze going wide. "Gavin!"

"What's wr—"

"Me! How did I miss this? Arlo said he's not been able to

find any leads on that crime ring. That he can't get a handle on what amounts to rumor on disposing of weapons."

"What does that have to do with you?"

"I have access to the files. I've spent all week looking at prosecuted cases, but I can also see what's been thrown out. What never made it to trial. What has gaps in evidence." She scrambled out of bed, clearly unaware of her nakedness, as she raced to her dresser for one of her ever-present notepads. "All we need is to get the dates forensics has estimated on the guns. I can use that to set my date criteria in the databases and work backward from there."

It couldn't be that easy. There was no way it was that easy, Gavin thought.

But even as he tried to keep his excitement in check, he knew she was right.

"Cross-jurisdictional work at its finest."

She looked up from where she was making notes to grin before crossing over to him and laying a big smacking kiss on him. "And score for the local team. You and I, Mr. Hayes. We're going to kick task force ass!"

## Chapter Seventeen

Sera wasn't quite sure how she'd gone from the glories of an evening in Gavin's arms and the joys of sex pizza to an all-nighter at work, but she couldn't deny how right this felt.

*Finally.*

They had a lead. It was slim, and it was going to take a lot of digging, but it was something they could actually work with. He'd dropped her off at the DA's office before heading to the precinct to run down whatever he could on the forensics work, with Arlo, Kerrigan and Wyatt heading in to meet him.

They all exchanged texts throughout the night, with a steady drip feed of dates as they got the information off the guns, which she'd cross-reference with as many files as she could find in the same time frame.

She hunted through it all. The discovery process. Briefs. And then actual trial notes and transcripts. All of it filled page after page of her legal pad, but as of yet, she couldn't find a connection.

But she did find threads.

Sera sat back and stared at all she'd written down. There wasn't an exact pattern, but there was a consistency. Somewhere in the discovery process, she could see references to gun activity and crimes. But by the time she got to the actual trial notes, evidence wasn't available.

It was frustrating and slow and she'd nearly given up, vowing to come back at it tomorrow, when she saw movement outside her office door.

"Sera!" David's smile was broad as he peeked his head in the door. "You're here late."

"You, too. I didn't see you when I came in."

"I just got here."

At three in the morning? "Your work ethic's impressive, David, but that's an early start for anyone."

"The work's been on overdrive lately. I couldn't sleep and had some ideas on a few cases I wanted to get down. Figured I'd get ahead of my day."

"Of course. Justice might be blind, but she doesn't sleep." She made the joke, smooth and easy, just some of the simple banter she and David had shared for years.

*Years.*

It was the camaraderie of colleagues. Laced with the respect she'd always had for her boss.

Her boss whose name she'd seen at the bottom of each of the files she'd looked through. His bold, scrawling signature dismissing each case she'd flagged with a suspicious lack of evidence.

But it all hit her now, a vicious gut punch as dot after dot connected in her mind.

Seemingly oblivious, David waved at her from the door. "I'll leave you to it, then."

As he moved out of her line of sight, her phone rang, Gavin's name filling the screen. The ringer was on silent, and she opened the line, about to tap the speaker button, when David stepped back into view.

"What are you working on this late, Sera? I reduced your casework so you could take full advantage of the task force."

"I know, David, and I appreciate the consideration." Her heart throbbed in her throat in a heavy pounding sensation and she forced herself to remain calm. To speak in as normal a voice as possible as she made a point to use his name. "I'm actually here because of the task force."

"Oh?"

"The work my partner and I have been doing. We're focused on the chain of evidence. How much it matters and how much can go wrong if any team mishandles a single bit of it."

"It's a good angle."

"It certainly is." She prayed Gavin got her message, well aware she was about to take the biggest gamble of her life. "And it's amazing to realize just how many facets of the police touch evidence. The cops first. Then the forensics team takes over. All under the captain's leadership."

She avoided even looking at her phone, afraid to tip David off to their audience, but she had her messaging app also open on her computer screen and saw Gavin's text come through.

I've got you.

He did have her. And it was that rock-solid knowledge that had her making the final leap. "But you already know this, David. Don't you?"

"You couldn't just stay out of it." David took a few steps into her office. "I put you on the task force to give you advancement. To give you opportunity."

"And I appreciate it."

"I had some selfish reasons for it, too. Namely to get you out of my hair. You've always been way too attentive, working long hours to make sure you're number one."

Before she even had time to be insulted, he had a gun out of his pocket, directed at her. It was an odd-looking piece, like something a person could assemble on their own.

And not for one minute did she believe it any less deadly.

"How'd you get a gun inside the building?"

"You'd be amazed what you can get in and out of here. Especially when you're the most favored man of the people."

And as he cocked the trigger, gesturing her up and out of her seat, Sera gave one last glance to her phone and prayed Gavin would get here soon. Because the man she'd respected—the one all of Brooklyn had voted to represent them—had betrayed them all.

EVERYTHING IN HIM was cold.

Not like huddling in a jacket on a winter's day or trying to find warmth on a January dive, but bone-deep cold.

Soul-deep cold, actually.

It was all Gavin could think as he briefed Arlo, Wyatt and Kerrigan before Wyatt rushed out to call Captain Reed.

All he could feel as they strapped on Kevlar and collected their weapons to head to the DA's office.

All he knew as they drove the nearly deserted streets at 4:00 a.m.

David Esposito had proven he would kill for no more reason than to instill fear. With all her knowledge, did Sera have any hope of surviving his wrath?

Gavin willed those thoughts away, even as he went through each required step. He called in backup for a probable hostage situation while Kerrigan called in the orders to get SWAT in place.

Each step felt like a century, but they had everyone mobilized and heading toward the building that housed the DA in under five minutes. Along the way, they briefed the security team in the DA's office.

That team was instructed to quietly assess what they could and they quickly affirmed that all office cameras were off on the DA's floor. Add to that the tinted exterior windows, and they were effectively blind to the situation.

All they had to go on was the intel Sera had gleaned by keeping him on her phone line and the understanding of what risks David posed to his own discovery. Intel that had vanished when the DA had ordered Sera out of her office.

That was the lone thought that kept Gavin going as they raced through the night. If David hurt Sera in the building, he had no hope of ever covering up his crimes. The man still didn't know she'd had him on speaker, which meant he might still be under the illusion he could get away with it.

And if he thought that, he'd have to get Sera outside the building.

"We're going to get her, Gav." Arlo had said the same thing over and over as they navigated the neighborhood.

"He's a good guy, Arlo. Sera has talked several times about his leadership and how much she liked working for him."

Gavin tried to map that description—one from someone he respected—with the realities of what they were racing toward. "And now he's a messed-up human being in over his head. Which makes him dangerous and unpredictable."

The worst combination they faced as cops.

And as they got out of the car a block away from the DA's

office, Gavin realized he felt dangerous and unpredictable, too. He had to get a handle on it. Had to push it away and remain focused only on getting Sera safely out of the clutches of a madman.

It was the only way to save her and the baby.

THE BABY.

Sera couldn't stop thinking about the life growing inside of her. Couldn't stop thinking about the ultrasound photos nestled in the treasure box on her coffee table and the excitement she and Gavin both carried about the new images they'd get at her upcoming appointment.

They might even find out the baby's gender.

They'd talked of both wanting to know, excitement humming between them as they talked about names.

The baby was their future. One they were building a foundation for now.

And if all she knew of her boss was true, all of that was now at risk.

David hadn't tied her up, but he kept the gun trained on her, forcing her to stay seated in one of his plush office chairs while he sat in the one beside her.

"Why are you doing this?"

"Why?" He looked up from where he flipped through something on his phone. "Isn't it obvious?"

"Actually, it's not."

"Money, Sera. Please don't tell me you're also a naive workaholic who doesn't actually understand it makes the world go round."

Once again, she opted to ignore the insult. Was she really going to get upset over the opinion of someone who was so broken? So utterly, absolutely bereft of a soul?

With that firmly in her mind, she peppered him with questions instead.

"Then why go into law for the city? If you only cared about money, there are enough corporate legal jobs to have kept you in designer suits for ten lifetimes."

"And then you're stuck with partner politics and all the ridiculous BS that comes with getting along well with others."

Since the common wisdom at the big firms was "eat what you kill," Sera wasn't ready to give him the point on that one, but really, what did it matter? He'd created some story for himself that separated him from what he was doing. What she had to do was create enough of her own story to get her and the baby out and away.

Memories of that text message filled her thoughts, pushing her on.

I've got you.

Gavin would have put everything into motion by now, so her focus had to be on getting *out*. Because staying in was the worst thing she could do.

No one could help her inside.

And David had likely rigged everything to his benefit in here.

She needed out.

"I always respected your leadership. It's why I've stayed here. Why I choose to work for the city, each and every day."

He looked up from where he tapped on his phone, an overbright grin marring his features. "Glad to know the ol' act worked."

"If you won't consider letting me go for me, at least consider it for my child."

The grin fell, and in its place was a rapid set of calculations. "The cop. It's his baby. The one you were cozying up to on the police boat."

The police boat? "What—" The question was nearly out before she realized what he meant. "You have a watchman up at Hell Gate?"

"People get in the way, Sera. Modern tech is so much better. Removes too many sets of eyes and gives me all I need."

Somewhere down deep, Sera realized that was the final piece of the puzzle. A part of her—bigger than she'd realized—had kept hoping he had been dragged into this somehow. Influenced by darker forces who seduced him with money and promises of even more power.

But there was no one else.

"It really is you. Behind all of this."

"You seem surprised by that." The statement was said so clearly as to be almost academic. It nearly tripped her up, because it felt like so many other conversations they'd had through the years. Debating a legal point. Discussing motives. Reviewing various legal theory.

But it wasn't any of those things. It was just the horrible, terrible truth that one more person she trusted had betrayed her.

"It's time to go now."

"What?"

He'd already stood, the gun in hand unwavering as he pointed toward the door with his phone. "It's time to go."

"Go where?"

"Where I can get rid of you and still have a shot at keeping my little enterprise going."

THEY WANTED DAVID ESPOSITO ALIVE.

Arlo had run him through it. Captain Reed had added his requirements via a call before confirming he was on his way. SWAT had been given the same set of instructions.

Unless the risks were too great, the man was to be kept alive at all costs.

The fallout would be enormous, a betrayal on this scale from an elected official in the largest city in America. And the very highest echelons of the department wanted it all on record so they could make an example out of him.

Gavin understood the orders. He even had every intention of following them.

Unless there was a whisper of risk to Sera. Then all bets were off.

He and Arlo had set up with the SWAT team in front of the DA's office. The fact that Esposito had bombed the sub shop was enough to get the bomb squad in as well, and they were on point should anything suggest David had rigged the government building.

"Heat signature!"

Gavin moved closer to the SWAT team manning the equipment. "Two bodies, on the move."

He watched the movement on screen. Saw the awkward way the two people walked, like one was restraining the other in some way.

They moved through the third floor, from the back of the building toward its center to a stairwell. Step by step, he could see them walk, before they arrived on the second floor. He'd only been in the building once, but could still picture the large stairwell that ran up the middle of the structure. It had reminded him of high school, those stairs a sort of common meeting ground on the lobby and each ascend-

ing floor. Stairs that, once descended, would bring someone to the lobby where you could go out the front door to
the main thoroughfare or out the back door to an alley and
a small parking lot beyond.

"He's moving her. Getting her out of the building," Gavin
said, certain they'd exit in the back. Even more certain no
one on point in the back would take the needed shot.

With absolute conviction, he recognized the truth. David
Esposito was too important. And that made Sera expend-
able.

He took a few steps back from the assembled SWAT
team and the expert manning the heat signatures. He was
the only one who had her best interests at heart.

One deep breath.

He stilled himself for one deep breath, but in the end that
was all he needed.

His took in the screen SWAT had set up, his gaze never
leaving the moving forms visible as heat signatures.

He watched as those two figures rounded the stairwell,
just about to head down to the lobby.

Watched when one pushed the other.

And watched as a body fell down the stairs, the other
one taking off at a run.

"COULD YOU SLOW DOWN? I am pregnant."

David kept a tight grip on her with one hand, the gun
never wavering in the other. "You barely look any different."

"Yeah, well, I've been sitting for a few hours, and my
ankles are swollen."

As lies went, it tripped off the tongue, and she gave mental thanks for the *What to Expect* book she'd been reading
each night for the inspiration.

But she did feel him slow, whatever lingering chivalry the man possessed coming to the fore. It was what she'd banked on, and it gave her the slight advantage in position she needed.

Slow step. Down.

Slow step. Down.

Slow step...

Sera took a deep breath and pushed David as hard as she could.

Whether it was the years of trust they had built between them or his sheer underestimation of her, she didn't know, nor did she care. All she did know was she had the small space to get out.

*Away.*

And if she could get out, she'd find Gavin. She knew it.

Ignoring the shouts behind her, she ran as hard as she could down the rest of the stairs, zigzagging her way toward the front exit as soon as she hit the main level. She briefly debated the back alley and parking lot, but the front would give her access to the street and, if the cops were there, ready and waiting protection.

David continued to shout behind her, firing off a shot just as she got the heavy front doors open. They led into the main lobby and screening area, and she pushed through there, desperate for fresh air.

For the street.

For Gavin.

Shouts went up as she slammed through the main entrance door, lights so bright she thought it was daytime.

And still, she ran.

Away from the building.

Away from the oncoming threat.

# COMING SOON!

We really hope you enjoyed reading this book.
If you're looking for more romance
be sure to head to the shops when
new books are available on

## Thursday 15th August

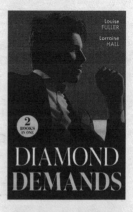
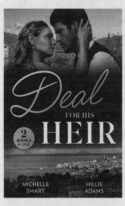
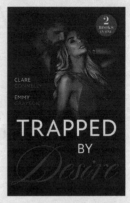

# LET'S TALK

# Romance

For exclusive extracts, competitions and special offers, find us online:

f MillsandBoon

𝕏 @MillsandBoon

⊙ @MillsandBoonUK

♪ @MillsandBoonUK

Get in touch on 01413 063 232

And straight into Gavin's arms.

"Sera!"

He wrapped her up, turning so that his back was to the building and the threats that lay beyond.

"You're here." She clung to him, the shouts behind her fading away at the protection and warmth and safety that enveloped her.

"I'm here."

They stayed like that for long minutes, arms wrapped tight around each other, whatever tableau playing out behind them someone else's worry.

Someone else's problem.

"I can't believe it was David all along."

"I'm so sorry." He kept her tight against his chest, his words a thick murmur in her ear. "One more betrayal you don't deserve."

His concern was so caring—so deeply felt—and it caught her in the moment that she hadn't given that aspect of David's actions a single thought.

His betrayal of the people and the office he held? Absolutely?

But of her?

Not once.

She lifted her head from his chest, gazing deep into his eyes and willing him to understanad. "You came for me and our baby, Gavin. You. That's all I need."

The old part of her would have wanted to be in the thick of it all. Part of the action and excitement to hide all she was missing in the rest of her life.

But she didn't need that any longer. She no longer needed work or cases or the perception she was number one from an external source. She still intended to strive for it, but she no longer *needed* it. And as she held Gavin close, murmuring over and over how much she loved him, Sera realized that made all the difference.

The things that had made up her days were important. Justice for the people of the city she loved would always matter.

But the life she and Gavin would make for themselves and their child?

Well, that was everything.

\* \* \* \* \*